DA

D0486279

HIGHSMITH #45114

Also by Lindsay Townsend

A KNIGHT'S VOW

Published by Kensington Publishing Corp.

A
KNIGHT'S
CAPTIVE

LINDSAY TOWNSEND

ZEBRA BOOKS
Kensington Publishing Corp.
http://www.kensingtonbooks.com

ZEBRA BOOKS are published by

Kensington Publishing Corp.
850 Third Avenue
New York, NY 10022

All Kensington titles, imprints and distributed lines are available at special quantity discounts for bulk purchases for sales promotion, premiums, fund-raising, educational or institutional use.

Special book excerpts or customized printings can also be created to fit specific needs. For details, write or phone the office of the Kensington Special Sales Manager: Attn. Special Sales Department. Kensington Publishing Corp., 850 Third Avenue, New York, NY 10022. Phone: 1-800-221-2647.

Zebra and the Z logo Reg. U.S. Pat. & TM Off.

ISBN-13: 978-1-4201-0362-5
ISBN-10: 1-4201-0362-8

First Printing: April 2009
10 9 8 7 6 5 4 3 2 1

Printed in the United States of America

With love to my family and friends

Chapter One

"Uncle Marc! Is she not as beautiful as the sun? That is what her name means. She is Sunniva, Sun-Gift. Do you not think she is like the sun?"

"Steady, little one. You will wake your sisters. But yes, you are right. She is most comely."

Ignoring the powerful temptation to look where Alde was pointing, Marc tucked the ends of his big traveling cloak around his excited niece and encouraged the child to lie down again by doing so himself. A swift, anxious glance confirmed that Judith and Isabella were sleeping, sprawled under his cloak, their small faces sunburned with weeks of travel. Isabella was sucking her thumb. The day had been long, the riding hard and tiring. He prayed she would sleep through, free of nightmares.

Just one night, Lord Christ. As a mercy to her, and to her sisters.

"Uncle Marc?" Alde whispered, tugging on her lower lip, the pupil of her left eye sliding toward her small, faintly hooked nose as she fought her body's weariness,

"Can I have—" A tiny snore escaped her pouting mouth.

Marc waited a moment, watching his charges. His brother had spoken of the "fierce love" a parent feels for a child: in these past months he had come to understand what Roland meant. He would kill for these three.

Beside him a female peddler, as gnarled as the sticks she carried for sale on her back, snorted and shifted closer to the central fire. Turning carefully so as not to disturb Isabella, Marc lounged on his side, one hand absently rubbing his aching spine as he scanned the company.

Two-and-twenty figures, hunched in various attitudes of slumber, some snoring, most silent, were ranged about the fire, their dun and dust-stained clothes orange in its fading glow. Outside the ruined, roofless square fort—an old Roman castle, according to their escorts—he could hear the night guards walking and talking softly. So far, the pilgrim party he was part of had journeyed in safety, although he slept with his sword close to hand. Even main roadways such as the one they traveled on were haunted by footpads, ever ready to prey upon the unwary or unprotected. There were rumored to be horse thieves hereabouts in these rough lands of the north and worse still, slavers.

He knew of one who would be a great prize to such creatures. Blonde—such fair eyebrows and skin must betoken blonde hair, although he had never seen so much as a strand of it: Sunniva was a modest girl who hid her tresses under a plain russet headsquare. Lithe, with a tumbler's body: that much he could guess from her graceful walk, though her robe hung on her as if made for a larger woman. And her face . . . Marc smiled in the semidarkness. Even at a distance, she was more than comely, she was spectacular, a prize—

"Sunniva! Damn you, wench!"

The carping voice broke into Marc's guilty daydream, causing him to stare where he had sworn he would not. Straight across the fire from where he and his three darlings were snuggled into a corner, their backs safe against the fireproof stone walls, a hulking scarecrow of a man sat bolt upright. Cloaks and scraps of precious cloth and even tapestry rolled off him, scattering like chaff as he whirled his beefy arms. "Here, girl, attend me! Look at me, girl! You should not be sleeping!"

"Not when my leg troubles me!" Marc finished for Cena under his breath, clenching both hands into fists as he fought his own temper. Since he and his girls had joined the pilgrim party five days ago he had grown weary of this graybeard's mewling complaints— the Englishman moaned more readily than six-year-old Isabella.

"Is it your knee, Father, or your arm?" his daughter whispered, rising to her knees, her hands outstretched. Her face and form were in shadow, but even so she made a sinuous, lissome shape that instantly made Marc's body stiffen, his heart quickening further at the sound of her warm, soft voice.

"Shall I rub the joints for you? I still have some of the comfrey compress I made—"

"Bring wine," was Cena's graceless interruption, "and do not dally."

He gave her a spiteful shove that had Sunniva rocking on her heels but she did not complain—the wonder was, she never did.

"Of course, Father. Is there anything else you desire?"

"Why are you wearing old clothes? You look like the lowest pot-scourer, not a lady of means!"

"But Father, as you have often told me, I have no means and it is my duty to serve you."

"Aye, and your brothers, remember that!"

"How could I forget, Father?"

"My God, when you smile that way you look as sinful as your mother . . . Why that rag of a headrail, girl? Do you mean to shame me? I want you to look good to men; you're no use to me ugly. Your blue headsquare is better."

"It must be washed, Father. Is there anything else?"

"More wine!" Cena's broken teeth were visible as black patches in his mouth as, grimacing, he raised a scarred hand. "Now!"

"I am going." Seemingly unafraid of her father's threat, Sunniva bent close to him. "The dressing on your knee, is it comfortable?"

"No thanks to you. I said you had bound it too tight. And your brother's teeth are aching again."

"I have looked to Edgar's hurt, father, and to his horse's."

"Wine! Where is my wine? Must I tell you again, idle slut?"

"Of course." Sunniva drew back, deftly avoiding Cena's flailing fist. "Wine will lift your spirits and if you are a little 'hazy' mounting your horse tomorrow, I am sure the saints will protect you. St. Cuthbert will surely reach down from heaven to save you from falling on your rump." She raised two elegant, ghostly hands, paler than moonbeams in the guttering firelight, and made the sign of the cross. "I will bring the comfrey, too."

"Get on, chatterer!"

Cena subsided under his mound of makeshift bedding and Marc quickly closed his eyes, in case she noticed him watching. As with many of these father-daughter exchanges he found himself grinning and wondering: she had bested Cena in words yet again, but did that old misery realize she teased him?

I would do much more than teasing, Marc vowed, his mood darkening as he listened to her lightly stepping amidst the sleeping pilgrims toward the baggage heaped in the doorway. Only the girl's own unfailing good humor stopped him intervening: he longed to take on Cena and Cena's three useless sons, who, as usual, slept on through these nightly conflicts.

What did Cena mean, "I want you to look good to men"? Surely such a beauty as Sunniva would be betrothed—

A tiny snuffle close to Marc had him raking his head round swiftly, but Isabella was all right, peaceful and tranquil, still fast asleep. Kneading his wry neck, Marc settled onto his side, his eyes drawn inevitably to the other, golden girl.

I do not spy, he told himself. I look out for Sunniva because her father and brothers do not.

She was at the saddles and packs now, a small shimmer of movement against sooty stones, carefully easing her eldest brother off one of the trunks, gently ruffling his dirty-blond hair to calm his muttering slumber. To his chagrin—he was no longer a gangling youth—Marc found himself blushing, envying the brother her touch. In his own mind, he instantly imagined those slim fingers stroking him—a pleasantly distracting thought. Suddenly, he saw her direct a single, piercing glance to Cena. The fellow was snoring again.

Sunniva acted fast. Her hands burrowing nimbly inside the trunk, she retrieved a wine flask and salve and then she was off.

She was going outside!

Even as Marc marveled at such folly, he was straightening, seizing his sword. Striding over the peddler woman, a scrawny monk and a serving-lad with bare, wind-chapped legs, he reached the other side of the fire before realizing he had misjudged the moment: Sunniva was standing by the threshold, breathing in the sweet night breeze.

She was merely snatching an instant for herself, Marc guessed, feeling foolish at his overreaction. Reluctant to intrude further on her, he turned to go back.

A slight shift in the air was his only guide that anything was amiss. With a warrior's quickness, Marc whirled about, freeing his sword, feinting a stumble, lunging his counterattack. His blade slashed through shadows and there were only the grunting sleepers round his feet. Beyond the hot-iron glow of the banked-down fire was an utter darkness, where any creature, thief or troll, might linger. He squinted into it, looking for anything stirring, listening intently for the rasp of metal, his head full of old Breton stories of deadly night elves, lethal elf-shot and the evil of the devil.

Isabella and the others, were they still asleep? Safe? Was he failing them again?

"God help me!" The whisper burst from his clenched lips and was answered at once by a flash of gold, bright as lightning, and a choked cry.

His purse, its long strings newly sawn through, was fixed to one of the few remaining crossbeams, scarcely two spears' lengths from his own head. Outside there was a rush of fading footsteps, quickly lost in the still night as the thwarted cutpurse ran off the road into cover.

Marc was still staring at what had nailed his purse to

the beam. Slowly, as in a dream, he sheathed his sword and freed the long dagger, catching the purse as it fell.

"He will have escaped over what is left of the roof by now," Sunniva observed softly. "I spotted him scrambling in by the same way, just before you sensed him and reacted, but could not warn you in time to be on your guard. Our night watchers missed him, or never expected a thief to come in that way. I am sorry."

"I heard him leaving." Amazed that she was talking to him—to him!—Marc stretched out the arm that was clutching the dagger. As she stepped closer to take it back, he wanted to snatch it away, snatch her away.

Rapidly, he schooled his expression into what he hoped was a polite smile and said, "Thank you. That was . . ." He hesitated as a thousand questions flooded through his mind. How had she done that? How had she learned such throwing skill? How had she seen anything? "That was unexpected," he finished lamely.

"I see right well in the dark," she said, taking the knife back most carefully, as if she had guessed part of his thoughts.

"Better than most. Far better than me."

She smiled at him for the first time then, another lightning flash in the darkness of their makeshift sleeping quarters, and he felt a bolt of pleasure strike deep in his loins.

"You need apologize to me for nothing," he grunted, retying his purse to his belt for something to do. She could have ridden over him on a war horse and if she smiled that way he would have been smitten afresh. "Nothing."

She looked troubled, but did not answer.

Marc knew he should say something: about his nieces, perhaps, or the changeable English weather, or the pilgrimage they were both on for their different reasons. What were hers? He almost asked her, but then the moon broke through the gray ramp of clouds and lit her fully.

He almost gasped—it was the first time he had been this close to her and, even as Alde had said, her sheer beauty was unearthly. He had seen no one to compare with her except for the glittering icons of Constantinople, city of wonders. Like an empress in those sacred pictures, Sunniva glowed.

Like the icons, she drew him first with her eyes. Large and bright, they were the color of the Breton seas of his childhood, a brilliant blue-green, flecked with gray. Mermaid's eyes, he thought, glimpsing the pensive dreamer beneath the clear, direct gaze. The skin around them was as flawless as a pearl but briefly, as she blushed and gave him a swift warm smile, he saw her eye corners crinkle and knew how she would look when old: a laughing Madonna, with a long, straight nose, limpid eyes and a bountiful mouth, red and sweet as a pomegranate.

Her lashes were long, slightly darker at the tips—as her hair would be, he guessed. When she smiled—and Sunniva, it seemed, would often smile—she had a slight gap between her front teeth. It made her endearing, more approachable.

So why was he not approaching?

"Are you bound for the shrine of St. Cuthbert?" he asked, an obvious question, but anything more seemed beyond him right now. Like strong sunshine, she mazed his wits. "Have you been traveling long?"

"Ten days. And you, sir?"

"Five by road. We were at sea from London before then." Marc did not elaborate: he was reluctant to draw attention to the fact he was a foreigner. After a year in this country he thought his accent passable. His clothes were English and even his hair, once cropped Norman-fashion, was now almost as long as Cena's.

"Do you go to the shrine for your father?" he asked.

Sunniva nodded, glancing Cena's way. "We hope the saint may cure his knee," she said. "And my brother Edgar's toothache. What is London like?" she added, breaking off as her father loudly belched in his sleep.

Marc wanted to laugh, but quelled the impulse. Another long, deepening silence wound between them, as the rest of the ruined fort rustled with dreaming sleepers and foraging mice. The fire crackled and spat, the night guards outside stamped their feet, stared at the northern hills and blew on their hands, a man with a filthy bandage on his elbow flopped onto his back and ground his teeth but here, now, he and Sunniva were silent.

"Only we two in here are awake," he said at last. "Or this is a dream?" He leaned forward and kissed her lightly on the cheek.

"My thanks to you," he said, and tore himself away, returning to his nieces without looking back.

Chapter Two

Next day, Sunniva was eager to see Marc again, but also wary. From her father and brothers she knew men were changeable, keen to chase women, just as they might hunt down a hare, but then losing interest the instant their quarry was captured. Marc might have kissed her on a whim.

She had been kissed before, not willingly. Her face burned with bitter memories as she toiled to load her baggage onto her packhorse—her father always wanted to be first away every morning and she had told her maid to help him instead. Her brothers left her to her struggle and for that she was glad.

Too much she remembered the friends of her brothers, grabbing her in the yard or the kitchen corridor at home, pressing their sweating bodies and greedy, groping hands against her as Ketil and Told, her twin older brothers, guffawed and bragged about poking a peephole in the wattle wall of her tiny bedchamber, the better to spy on her. It was her eldest brother Edgar, dour yet strong, whose relentlessly sour mood was not improved by persistent toothache, who inevitably dragged such youths off her. Inevitably, too, he would scold her for being too forward, for smiling too much, but then Edgar did not care for women.

Forget them, Sunniva told herself, resting her forehead against her packhorse's flank to catch her breath. This pilgrimage was a chance for her, a chance to escape. She had her plans and they involved no men.

And yet . . . Sunniva's mouth twisted into a bleak half smile. She longed for children, for a home of her own. She coveted Marc his three little girls. Watched them as often as she could. They seemed happy children during the day, quick and curious as kittens, and Marc was patient with them. She would have liked to make friends with the girls, but that might have alerted her father to Marc.

So far, thankfully, Cena had dismissed his fellow pilgrim. Marc was not showy in his green cloak, mud-stained leggings and green tunic, patched at the elbows. He rode an excellent horse, a glossy chestnut, but had no baggage except a small saddlebag. She knew how her family thought. Cena had assumed Marc was not rich and so he had felt free to ignore him. Marc, too, was big and broad, a bearded, hairy bear of a man, an obvious warrior, and her father, like most bullies, preferred his victims to be smaller and weaker than himself.

Sunniva shivered, fingering her dagger. She had learned to match her actions to her name, to be fiercely cheerful and to smile—smile as her mother Ethelinda had been too fearful to do. *Never let them know they hurt you*, her mother's voice whimpered in her head, and Sunniva answered aloud, "I never will."

As ever, the vow gave her renewed heart. She patted the packhorse and lifted her head, wondering what new people and places she would see today. The day was bright and mild—too clear for thieves, she decided, fixing her eyes forward, toward the north, while part of her remembered, with a swift burst of joy, that Marc's eyes were a rich, deep amber. She spent the first hour of traveling daydreaming of her own child with amber-colored eyes, mentally pointing out cloud shapes and wind-bent trees to her imagined companion, the loose stones of the old Roman road ringing beneath her horse's hooves like bells.

The gladness did not last. The pilgrim party, blowing horns to announce their coming so that suspicious farmers and haughty northern lords would not attack them as possible brigands, came to a crossroads. There they stopped and soon Sunniva heard her father's voice raised in furious complaint.

Cena often argued, especially with those he considered of lower rank. The crossroads was in a narrow gully, where the road sank between high banks to meet a second, sunken road. On this road was a shepherd with his flock, who wished to cross first. Cena was objecting.

"We are on the bigger road! We are the larger party! Your sheep must wait and so must you!"

The shepherd answered in an incomprehensible local dialect; he and one of the pilgrim escorts talked together, beards wagging, while Cena fumed. Finally, the shepherd stood back, his crook barring his black and white sheep, while the pilgrims moved on. Cena flicked his whip at one of the shepherd's dogs while Sunniva prayed the man would not notice the insult. He was staring at her, instead—that flat, greedy, calculating look that she had learned to fear since she was twelve years old. Meeting her eyes, he leered, openly scratching his groin. She felt him watching as

she desperately ignored him, cantering so close to
Edgar, riding alongside, that her brother cursed and
raised his fist to her.

They passed through, the shepherd whistling piercingly as he waited, some strange, repeated jingle that
seemed to echo over the moorland and sparse woods
of this northern land. She was relieved when the road
emerged from its tunnel and she could see distance
again: the hills to east and west, the odd farmstead,
woodland, no towns or villages and much pasture.

She glanced back. The tall, lanky shepherd had vanished and Marc was riding as he always did, close to the
wagon. If he knew she was studying him, imagining—
as she did—what tapestry threads and colors matched
his thick, wavy brown hair and lightly tanned skin, he
did not show it. Last night, she had been fascinated by
his big, square hands and powerful arms, such a contrast beside the fluffy tufts of hair sticking from his
ears. He was indeed a very hairy man! If his jaw had a
cleft, if his stark, strong face showed dimples as he
smiled she had no way of knowing, for his beard was
combed and neat but worthy of Samson.

Was he hairy all over?

Sunniva felt herself growing pink as she contem-
plated that question and swung round swiftly to face forward again, leaning over her horse's neck and making
great play of checking her shoe fastenings. Marc—*What
was his full name? Where was he from? Why was he on this
pilgrimage, and with such young children?*—did not look
any different from their encounter of last night. Did she
really think he would? She wanted to stare at him again,
make him look at her, but was nervous of what she
might read in his face.

It was safer to lavish attention on his girls. Today, his

three little ones were riding on the wagon, their sturdy ponies tied on leading reins to his glossy chestnut horse. He was passing something—a toy, a scrap of food—to the youngest child. The elder girl saw her watching and waved and Sunniva smiled and waved in return.

"Do not waste your time on such brats!" Edgar drew rein beside her, rubbing his jaw. His horse, a gray gelding, already looked lathered, and was limping again although it was still early, the sunlight a glowing red mantle over the hills.

Sunniva thought of her brother's miserable tooth-ache and answered amiably, "They are as merry as star-lings. I like to see them on our journey; their play makes the miles melt away."

"The man was a fool to bring them—or is it him you want to impress? Another oaf to moon over your footprints! Do not imagine father will want such a luckless fellow kept dangling on a string: he is but a bow and scrape from a serf; I have known peasants with less hair and more wit."

"Hush, Edgar!" Sunniva replied, indignant on Marc's behalf and keen that her twin brothers did not hear. They would torment her if they suspected she was paying any man any attention, however small. "There is a priest ahead," she added, glad of the dis-traction. "I think he is waiting for us. His cloak is very rich and his horse very fine." Nearly as fine as Marc's, she almost said, but stopped herself in time.

At the word "rich," Edgar lashed his horse forward, leaving Sunniva in a cloud of dust. Behind her, she heard the twins chortling at her discomfort and sensed Marc glowering at her eldest brother's stiff, straight back. Tempted to turn to meet his strange, compelling eyes, she too spurred on her restive bay palfrey. Where there was a priest, there might also be a church and she was keen to pray.

As the priest welcomed the pilgrims and his servants wound among them, offering cups of ale, Sunniva left them. While the rest of the party remained on horseback or stayed on the main baggage wagon, drinking and discussing the wonders to come at St. Cuthbert's shrine, she slipped off her bay horse and made for the simple barn of the church set back from the road.

She sped quickly through the mass of horses and riders, hearing snatches of conversation.

"St. Cuthbert blessed a loaf of bread and cured a man with it . . ."

"The Northerners are a lewd and wicked race . . ."

"Everyone north of the great river is uncouth. Even the Normans are not as devious."

"Have you not heard? The Normans are gathering in force across the narrow sea; a great company of men. William the Bastard wants the English crown."

"They will never set foot on our soil."

"Truly, I think it is the end of the world. Do you remember the great trailing star, a few months back? It is a sign . . ."

Her father and brothers were in the thick of such talk. Her maid, Bertana, who was often a bearer of tales to her father, shamelessly spying on her, one woman against another, had drained two cups of ale already and was holding up her wooden vessel for a third. Reveling in her moment of freedom, Sunniva picked up her long loose skirts and ran, her feet pounding along the daisy-strewn green track to the church. There was a small wood beside the church and she slowed a little, glancing between the holly and oak trees to make certain no thief lurked. All was peaceful, though, and the blackbird's alarm call was against only her.

She reached the sanctuary of the church and grinned, swinging on the door a little in play as she went inside.

She touched the holy water in its simple wall nook and signed the cross, kneeling on the beaten earth floor beside a rough painting of St. Cuthbert with a Bible, being guided into heaven by an angel with vast golden wings. Briefly, lowering her head, her thoughts flashed to the embroidered kneelers and wall hangings she longed to make for convents and churches and then she focused on Cena and Edgar, begging the saint to pity them, to heal their hurts and injuries.

Was that whistling she could hear?

She tensed, thinking of the shepherd, the fingers of her left hand closing tight around her dagger, but the pilgrims outside were laughing, their amusement muffled by the thick stone walls of the church. Shamed by her own fear, Sunniva prostrated herself as a penance. The dry packed earth scratched her face as she swore to abjure dancing, music and stargazing for a month, to cook and clean and toil for her men folk as cheerfully as she knew how, to live on bread and water, if the holy saint would but graciously grant her wish.

What was her wish?

Warmth flooded up her feet and calves. For an instant, Sunniva wondered if she was blushing, or more shamefully, bleeding, but then she understood what the warmth signified—the church door was open—and she writhed about, lashing with her feet, scrabbling for her knife.

Her scream was stopped by a heavy elbow brutally

jammed into her throat as her back and breasts were bruised by the massive weight of a hooded man. Another man, also dressed in black and green and hooded, leaned against the open door, seemingly enjoying both the sunshine and her soundless struggles.

"Wi' ye take a gander at the teats on that!" he growled, in thickly accented English, laughing as Sunniva tried to roll sideways. "Fetch us a guid price, she will!"

Sunniva struggled and tried to cry out.

"Quiet, bitch!" The man pinning her down dragged at her mouth with his thumbs, shoving a hot, greasy hank of wool between her lips. She spat it out and bit him and he cursed and struck her, ramming his fist into her stomach. As she retched, he grabbed her hair through her headsquare and smashed her head on the floor.

A wave of sick darkness overtook her and she blacked out. Her last conscious feeling was of thick, clublike fingers gouging at her breasts and other sweaty, rough hands ripping and parting her skirts.

Frowning, Marc dismounted, instructing Alde and her sisters to stay on the wagon. If Sunniva wished to pray, Godspeed to her, but she should not be left so long unattended. Her slatternly maid was still drinking and as for her brothers and father—had they even noticed she was gone?

He had spied her stealing away, divined her wish for peace and let her go but now too much time was passing. The pilgrims were becoming restive and ready to move on: Sunniva needed to be warned.

"My Lord Cena!" he called out, "Your daughter—"

Cena waved aside his complaint, saying something Marc did not catch. Neither he nor his sons stirred from their places beside the priest and escorts.

"You should look to your daughter!" Marc tried again, only to be met by a bellow of laughter from the older man.

"Or you shall, eh?" Cena roared back, at which Marc pushed his way through the pilgrim crowd and stalked off toward the church, moving faster with each long stride. If he was being foolish, overprotective, so be it.

It will give me a chance to speak to her again, he thought, and quickened his steps even more.

The church door was closed, the building silent. A long, trailing streamer of raw wool hung from the door handle.

The shepherd, Marc thought, recalling the man's piercing, repeating whistle. A signal to others? Muscles tightening with anger and anxiety, he leaned against the shadowed stone, closing his eyes, listening, as he drew his sword and flung the door back to its hinges, charging inside.

With his vision already adjusted to the gloom of the church, he spotted Sunniva at once, lying just within the threshold, pale, still, and prone upon her back, two men groping her, tearing at her gown.

"*Non!*" Marc roared, his sword ripping through the leather of the smaller man's hood as he drove for the felon's skull. Yelling, the man scrambled behind a stone pillar, but Marc was already after the second, rangier figure who was lunging at the deathly silent Sunniva, trying to drag her away. Marc kicked him in the groin and stabbed with his sword, hacking a great gobbet of sheepskin from the man's long cloak. Behind his loose woolen hood, the coward's eyes flared with terror.

"Rot in hell and back!" Marc bawled, bringing his sword round in a close, lethal arc that raised sparks on the bastard's belt buckle and rent a bloody welt across his chest. "No sanctuary here—you are dead!"

He stamped on the jerking creature and raised his sword, aiming for the heart, when a low moan beside him had him tumbling to his knees to guard her. At the same instant, her two attackers crawled away, stumbling through the door and out.

Marc let them go. Dropping his sword, he gathered Sunniva into his arms, whispering over and over in Breton, "You are alive. Safe. Safe, my angel. Safe."

He had been so afraid she was harmed that having her trembling but whole beneath his hands was overwhelming. Tears stormed into his eyes, swiftly followed by rage.

Where was her father? Her brothers? Where were the useless escorts, meant to protect?

"Hush, hush," he crooned, rocking her back and forth as he struggled to keep his own grief and anger in check.

He dared not look at her too closely while he had tears in his eyes and looked so unmanly, but the warrior's sense in him told him she was not fatally hurt in the flesh. He could smell no blood or sickness on her and though she shook, she did not grimace or writhe in pain.

The injury to *herself*, however: her integrity, trust, humor, spirit—Marc furiously blinked away the moisture in his eyes as he prayed that Sunniva would soon recover and forget.

"King Christ, ruler of heaven, let her not be afflicted by night terrors, as my poor Isabella is. Let her know peace."

He should be raising the alarm, since none of the other fools of the pilgrim party seemed to have realized yet that anything was amiss. He should be returning to his own three. In a breath, his memory went back to the fire that had carried off his elder brother Roland and his wife: on that dreadful night he had cradled his niece Alde in his arms, even as he was now clutching Sunniva; he remembered how his and Alde's tears had mingled as they clung to each other.

Sunniva did not cling. She was still too stunned to do anything save take great gasping breaths and shiver. There was a dark, welling bruise on the left side of her cheek and her eye was puckering, threatening to close altogether. Tears had streamed down her face; he saw them glistening near her nose and quivering lips. Such a red, soft mouth—

"Do you hurt anywhere else?" he asked softly, relieved when she shook her head. Longing to wipe away her tears he held her close.

Outside, he heard no hue and cry, no galloping horses, only birdsong and laughter. Incredibly, appallingly, had he not come in time, she could have been raped and carried off and neither Cena nor her brothers would have known anything.

"Idiots!" he growled, his body burning with barely suppressed fury. "Stupid! Are they blind? What kind of men are they? Where are they?"

A small, narrow hand touched his arm, returning him to himself. Slowly, Marc realized that only a few moments had passed and he also began to understand that Sunniva was trying to speak.

"What is it?" He unclipped the water flask off his belt and offered it to her. She drank deeply and he was glad to see her swallow without pain.

"Rescue," she croaked. "You rescued me." She flopped

her hand against her breast, flinching a little. She closed her eyes. "They were trying to . . . you came . . ."

"You did well," he said. "Two against one." Now was not the time to speak of the need for a chaperone: that should have been her father's concern.

She swallowed again. "Daytime. Never expected it . . . in church. Foolish."

"No." Marc chafed her cold fingers in his, unbuckling his cloak and netting it about her, sinking her battered body into its fleecy warmth. "They had planned something. Those bast—those *things* were doubtless slavers. Such creatures haunt the roads, waiting their chance." They were cowards, too, who might not have stalked the pilgrims had Cena not angered the shepherd.

But who was he trying to convince? One glance at Sunniva would have been enough of a draw, especially as she was now, soft, vulnerable, with her face uncovered and her headrail torn from her hair.

Her hair. How had he not seen it at once? Even as Marc was ashamed of his raw, brutish feelings—not so far from the slavers'—he was lost in the glory of Sunniva's hair.

A bright red-gold, a mass of waves and curls, it swept over her wiry little form in a brilliant froth. She had tried to bind it into a plait, but there was so much, such abundance, that tendrils exploded from the simple coil of cloth to sheath her slender arms and surprisingly opulent breasts.

Mermaid's hair, Marc thought, quickly averting his eyes from her body. He wanted to smother his eyes and ears with her hair, to kiss and stroke and wind great handfuls round his wrists.

With her still snug in the crook of his shoulder he drew his head away, as far as he could, until his back

cracked. He had already failed one woman, failed her
fatally: he would be finished forever if he did the same
with Sunniva.

"Can you stand?" he said, ears pricked for the sound
of approaching footsteps. Surely they would not have
much longer together.

She tried to smile. Her valiant struggle wrenched at
him, an actual physical pain in his chest. He was so astonished by it, he almost missed her answer.

"In another moment, my lord."

"I am no lord." *Yours least of all.* "Are you betrothed?"

Fool! Marc berated himself. He had meant to say *Are
you dizzy.* What in God's name was wrong with him?

She stared at him, and no wonder. "Yes," she said,
flatly, all attempts at humor gone. "He is a good man.
Truthful. Brave. Very strong. Very kind."

"Ah." Instantly Marc hated him. He drew her so
that she was sitting up, braced against his knee. "We
should move. Those bas—the slavers might be returning with friends."

She closed her eyes, briefly. Still very pale, she grew
paler but then she looked at him directly.

"Thank you for saving me," she said, and, leaning
sideways, she kissed him on the cheek before he realized what she was about. "May I ask you something?"

The sheer unexpectedness of her action—and the
courage it must have taken her to do it—stopped his
breath. His face felt to be burning yet cool where her
lips had brushed, every bristle standing erect. His
hand patted where her mouth had been.

"What?" he demanded, feeling as dazed as he had
been after the first time he had lain with a woman,
with saucy Caterina the fisher-girl. Sixteen years old,
he had been, and utterly besotted. He had asked her

to marry him, knelt on the Breton beach and begged her to be his. She had been very kind in saying no, and let him take a lock of her billowing brown hair, as a keepsake.

If only his dealings with women had always been as sweetly harmless.

"What?" he asked again, staring at Sunniva's exuberant golden tresses.

"Why are you on this pilgrimage?" she asked. "For your nieces?"

"Yes, yes," he said distractedly, before his mind caught up with her question. He did not want her probing too far with this. "What is his name?"

"My betrothed?" Sunniva said in a low voice. "Caedmon of Whitby. What is your name, sir?"

Since she was still in his arms, he was amused by her formality. "Marc de Sens," he replied, interested to see how she reacted.

"A Norman? From across the sea?" She seemed intrigued.

"A Breton, but close enough." Pleased she was not shocked, Marc grinned.

Her answering smile was fleeting but real, revealing a tiny, charming gap between her front teeth, and suddenly he could no longer help himself. Breathing her in, inhaling her clean linen scent and warm, glorious hair, he lowered his head and kissed her.

Her lips were chapped, he noted with pity, but as soft as Byzantine silk. She tasted of salt and sunlight, her mouth innocent of experience, tensing under his, wary but not afraid. For a moment he yearned to go further, tease his tongue against her teeth, yield in return and have her tongue flicker delightfully against his mouth. The very thought stirred him and he forced himself to stop, lifting her so that she would not realize his arousal.

"You are a brave lady." With her still in his arms he rose to his feet. She was as light and fine-boned as Alde, but far more disturbing. The feel of her made his blood sing. "You can stand now?"

"I can." She smiled, her smile faltering as she glanced at his mouth, then, gratifyingly, blazing out again. "Yes, I can stand, Marc de Sens."

"Good for you." He swung her down, sad to let her go.

"Good-day, my lady sunlight." He released her, took a step back and bowed, just as finally—finally!—Cena and an escort blundered into the church.

Chapter Three

"Sunniva, get on, will you? Idle girl!" hollered her father, standing with his round-shouldered back to the main altar, legs astride and hands on hips. "Everyone is waiting! What have you been doing? Why are you wearing that fellow's cloak?"

She could not tell him. It was years since her father had sensibly talked with her; now he barked orders and complaints. Shriveling inside at the notion of trying to explain, Sunniva gave Marc back his green cloak. She missed its weight and warmth at once and, worse, the sense of protection it had bestowed.

"Thank you," Marc said softly. His thumb brushed hers, a gesture of comfort, and he smiled at her as she had seen him smile at his nieces.

"Your youngsters," she began, but Marc shook his head.

"The carter is looking after them," he said, motioning with his hand where she had missed tucking away a lock of hair; a small, ordinary thing that again put distance between her and the horror she had so recently endured. Silently, Sunniva finished retying her headsquare.

Feeling less vulnerable once her hair was covered, she turned to her father. "I am ready."

Cena instantly picked up her lifeless tone. "Stop sulking!" he snapped. He made to grab her arm and drag her outside. Sunniva flinched: she could not help it.

Cena reddened, his broad nose screwing up as if her very smell offended him. "Do not make a worse show of yourself!"

"Forgive me, Father." Her nerveless fingers tried to grip her dagger, slipping on the handle. She wanted only to be away, before the walls of the church closed in on her or, worse, began to spin.

"What is wrong with you, anyway? You are getting to be as witless as your mother ever—"

"King Christ in heaven, are you blind as well as deaf?" Marc strode in between her and her father, causing the slighter, bandy-legged escort-rider who had entered with Cena to step back. "This child was set upon by rogues of the worst sort and still she tries to placate you! Where were you to protect her?"

Her father's deep-set eyes narrowed into slits of rage. "The girl is twenty!" he spat back, ignoring the escort-rider's rapid, "What men? How many? What kind?"

"She should have more wit!" Cena raged on. "Look to your own brats, pilgrim, and leave me to deal with mine!"

"As you say." Towering over her father, Marc seemed to grow larger as he squared his shoulders. The escort-rider hastily backed away farther as Marc took another step toward Cena. "Your daughter, Englishman, something you and your wastrel sons seem to have forgotten. Had I not come in here when I did, Sunniva would have been violated."

"Sunniva? Very cozy . . ." Cena's complaint faded

suddenly into the dust. Marc had his back to her, so she could not see his expression, but her father's jaw dropped and he began to bluster excuses. "This is a church! She should have brought her maid—"

"Then the maid would also have been raped," Marc answered relentlessly. "These were brutal men, Cena, armed and hooded."

"Leather hoods?" The escort-rider demanded, his sallow complexion graying further as Marc swung round and glowered at him. "Master Marc, there is a slaver and whoremaster in these parts who wears a leather hood. I heard he was raiding across the border, in Scotland."

"Then you heard wrong, man." Learning this, Marc glanced at her to ensure she was all right. "Does *it* have a name?"

For an instant, Sunniva thought the escort-rider would ring his hands; he looked so embarrassed. "It is said his name is Magnus Long-Nose."

"That will be shorter now," growled Marc, while Cena was strangely silent.

"Has this Long-Nose friends?" Marc continued. "Allies to draw on? Should we not be going?"

"To be sure," the escort-rider said quickly, hurrying from the church so fast that he collided with the priest coming in through the doorway.

"Cena." Marc did not bow to him. Instead, turning on his heel, he offered Sunniva his arm. "May I be your escort, my lady?"

His mouth was solemn, even grim, but his eyes were warm. Sunniva knew she would leave with him—she was keen to leave with him, for her father would be in a foul mood.

"My thanks, Marc de Sens." It gave her pleasure to say his name.

Side by side they walked from the church, Marc exchanging a pleasantry with the hovering priest exactly as if they were lord and lady here. The foolish, happy thought buoyed Sunniva's humor until Marc had seen her safely mounted on her horse.

Once the party was traveling again, however, she found her spirits darkening. Reaction overcame her as she tried and failed to forget her attackers. She recalled the hooded Magnus' crow of delight, "Fetch us a guid price, she will!" and wanted to be sick—so close she had come to being ravished, kidnapped and enslaved.

And Marc de Sens, her rescuer? What did he think of her now? Why did I kiss him? Sunniva thought, staring blankly between her horse's pricked ears, seeing nothing of the road. Hers had been the act of a camp follower—a slave, her father would have said.

Yet Marc had kissed her, too, and she had known such a sense of peace, of gentle rapture, as if for that moment the two of them had been sped away to paradise. For that blessed time, she had felt not only desired but valued, as if her feelings and thoughts mattered.

Still, she wished he had not seen her hair. So many men assumed things by it. When she was one-and-ten years old, a chapman coming to the homestead had called her "witch" because of her hair. Others had termed her man-eater, man-eager, man-hater—all this before her breasts had budded.

Did Marc like her hair?

"Look at me, girl." Cena prodded her roughly between her shoulders—his usual way of demanding attention. Conscious of her sore back and bosom, Sunniva braced herself.

"Yes, sir?" she regarded him steadily, unwilling to smile.

"Do not play the martyr with me." He reached across her horse to jab at her left temple. "Can you not disguise that bruise? You are no use to me ugly. You will not capture men's attention if you are ugly. Get Bertana to cover it. Bertana!"

He raised himself in the saddle to shout again for the maid when Edgar, who ever hung about their father, said quickly, "I will bring her." He savagely dragged on his gray gelding's bit, dropping back into the main pilgrim group, and Sunniva was left alone again with her father.

He wasted no time on asking how she was.

"That bearded oaf from church, Marc de Sens, what is he to you? Edgar said you were gawking at him."

"His children interest me," Sunniva replied, alarmed at the smarting resentment she felt against her brother. Edgar's malice was old, so why should she be so disconcerted? "They remind me of my childhood, and my mother."

Cena cleared his throat, a rare sign of embarrassment, but soon returned to the attack. "Does that fortune hunter know you have no dowry?"

"We had no chance to speak of it." Sunniva absently touched her mouth, remembering the gleam in Marc de Sens' eyes as he lowered his head to kiss her. "Not all men are interested in money."

"Pah! You are more witless than I guessed if you believe that. Bed sport fades and I must tell you frankly, you are no bonnier than many serf wenches."

"So you have told me. Often and at length." His spite twisted an ancient, invisible blade in her heart but Sunniva kept her countenance. "What do you want of me, sir? Your usual game?"

"What mean you by that? You will attend to what I tell you, girl!"

Sunniva waited and after a moment, when he had hawked and spat, Cena continued.

"The lands we are passing through now belong to one of Earl Tostig's followers, Orm Largebelly. We stay at Orm's homestead tonight and you will wear your best clothes. You will be pleasant to him, understand?"

"As you say." Borrowing one of Marc's phrases gave Sunniva some comfort, but did nothing to assuage her sense of guilt. It was, in the end, the usual game: Cena wanting her to charm and beguile. Always powerful men, rich landowners, whose favor and influence might prove useful. Often and most shamefully, he would even go so far as to suggest an alliance with such men, with herself as bait. Betrothal bait. She had been "almost" betrothed to seven different men in as many years. As a result of men desperate to pay her court and to win her hand, Cena had gained treasure, hawks and hunting dogs, passages of safe conduct, introductions to other wealthy men, promises of help with his harvests. He had done well from his exploitation of her beauty with men.

"I dislike it," she said aloud. She had already had enough of this behavior, had her own plans to thwart it, but now, perhaps because of what had happened to her in the church, perhaps because of Marc's gentle, genuine interest, she resolved to speak out. Her father knew she disapproved but for once he would know by how much. "I am no prize to be dangled before any suitor who takes your fancy. It is not honorable—"

"Stop your mewling!" Cena reached across and

grabbed her thigh. To onlookers it might seem an affectionate act, but Sunniva bit her lip strongly to prevent herself from crying out as he pinched her. Fingers digging into her flesh, he brought his bearded, rank-breath face close to hers and hissed, "You will do as I say, or be left naked on the roadside! Your coy tricks are no use to me! This is for the family!"

He released her with a final painful, twisting pinch, warning, "Your mother's dead, but I can still flay you. And I might let Ketil and Told have a turn with you, one night, to teach you about defiance! Half sister's not the same as full and when all is said and done you are nothing but a slave's whelp. Remember that!"

He cantered off, leaving her in a shock beyond tears and to the clumsy, grudging ministrations of Bertana, who now appeared with a stinging salve to fuss at the bruises on her face.

Orm Largebelly matched his name, Sunniva thought, hiding her face as she sipped a cup of warm mead. He was stocky, russet-haired and with a wind-reddened nose and chin. He was closer to forty than thirty, a widower who stared frankly at her breasts and hips. When she smiled at him as her father hurried to introduce her, he winked at his widowed mother and smacked his lips.

I am but another kind of food to him, Sunniva thought in rising despair, wishing she could escape this evening of feasting. Usually she loved entertainments: the music, the bright hall, people laughing, strangers telling of wonderful distant lands. Tonight would be an ordeal: her father expected her to sparkle, to blind Orm into doing whatever he wanted.

Or he would allow Ketil and Told to—

I must escape, and soon, she told herself. The feast would give her no chance to do so, she would be constantly watched by both her father and her brothers. Half brothers. But here before the feast was something: Orm's mother Hilde had invited her and her maid into her own room to change and prepare themselves. Sitting by the central brazier, eyes closed in sensual enjoyment, sunburnt, birch-thin Bertana was having her feet washed by one of Hilde's maids. Sunniva smiled to see her so relaxed: her maid might be a tale-bearer, but she had little joy in her service of Cena.

A light touch on her hand caused Sunniva to raise her head.

Hilde stood before her, stocky as her son but with more life and intelligence in her lined, homely face. "You are the seamstress, I think," she said, running a fingernail over the faint callus on Sunniva's index finger. "'Ware!" she warned, her quick brown eyes flashing to the stolid Bertana, sitting beside Sunniva on the great day-bed. "Come. I have something to show you."

"This is my sewing room."

Transferring with surprising agility, Hilde stepped from the simple wooden ladder to the upper chamber and pushed open the door. Following on, Sunniva saw the shuttered windows and many expensive candles and gasped.

"But it is above the barn!" she exclaimed, astonished at the contrast. Beneath her feet, she could hear the stamp of their own horses and smell the rich scents of hay, feed and manure. Here in this room, though, was a different world, a world she knew and longed to join.

Swiftly, after receiving a nod of permission from

Hilde, she passed along the embroidery frames, some at standing height, some where the seamstress worked sitting on a stool. Beside each was a box containing needles and thread. She touched a skein of brown wool, looked at the embroidery being worked on—a scene of Beowulf and the dragon, where the dragon's jaw and flames glowed a vivid orange and red—and sighed.

"My ladies and I work here whenever Orm and his drinking companions grow tiresome in the main hall," Hilde remarked.

How wonderful, Sunniva thought, but said nothing.

Hilde sat on a stool before an embroidery of Jonah being swallowed by a whale and hooked another stool with her foot for Sunniva to sit. From a hidden pocket, she produced a narrow piece of intricate, delicate work—a child's belt—that Sunniva knew at once.

"The Prioress of St. Oswald's received this from the messenger your father sent to Lord Morcar. There was a spoken message, too, where the seamstress told of her profound desire to work great altar cloths and stoles and robes, for convents and churches throughout the north. A noble, if naïve aim."

Sunniva blushed and said nothing. She had sent out many such "messages": pieces of her own embroidery and a verbal wish. Each time Cena had sent a herald, Sunniva had begged the herald to include her own small packet. She had hoped, rather foolishly perhaps, that it would reach someone who would take notice.

"Your work is exquisite," Hilde said softly. "You must know this."

"Thank you, my lady," Sunniva murmured, wondering what Hilde would say next. If the prioress had passed the belt onto Hilde, did that mean St. Oswald's convent was interested? Were they perhaps going to offer her some kind of place? Her heart beat fast at the thought, while her mind sang, *escape, escape . . .*

"I do not see you with a vocation for holy orders," the older woman went on. "What did you hope for? A position as a lay-woman, perhaps? A place at a noble-woman's court?"

"Yes." Sunniva saw no reason to deny it.

"And you seized the moment of pilgrimage to make your play." Hilde smiled, taking a needle and marking a place on her own embroidery. "Clever, my lady Sunniva, and I note you are also polite." She tilted her head to one side, her smile gently mocking in her round moon face. "Or did you consider it politic not to point out the mistake in my work that you noticed?"

"I—" Sunniva bit her lower lip. She did not realize she had revealed anything. "I am sorry."

"Do not let it trouble you." Hilde drew back and plucked one of the lit candles from another nearby stool. She lifted it, studying Sunniva as if she were another form of tapestry.

"Any lady would be mad to have you in her household. No, Sunniva, please do not take my words amiss. I mean no disrespect. You are modest and able and if you could be as veiled as a woman of Byzantium, I would offer you my protection at once. But, as you are, you are the flame that draws all men as moths. You cannot help it."

Sunniva tasted the bile of defeat. She wanted to scream in frustration: instead, she scraped her foot under her stool, not caring that a splinter drove into her heel, welcoming the bodily pain as a distraction. "I am grateful that you should have thought of me within your home," she said. Hope flared again in her. "Perhaps you know of a convent nearby?"

Hilde pushed Sunniva's headsquare back from her hair and nodded, as if to confirm what she had expected. "None that could withstand the rage of your father and brothers once they learned—as they surely would—that you had passed within its walls."

I must not cry, Sunniva thought. I could be a knife-thrower, she mused, her ideas growing wilder as her sense of being trapped increased. I have the skill. I know the tricks.

"You cannot consider making your way alone in the world," Hilde added as if she guessed part of Sunniva's mind. "The world now is full of troubles and angry men. To them you would be a bauble."

"I am already that," Sunniva answered, recalling the rough handling she had endured earlier that day. She raised her chin. "I shall live alone, in the forests."

Hilde clapped her hands together. "For summer, yes, I think you could. But winters?"

"Times change," Sunniva said.

The older woman laughed. "I see you are as optimistic as your bright hair. That is good, for I vow you have much to be glad of. Not with my elderly son," she went on, careless of Sunniva's muttered denial that he was old, "but with another. You are meant to have children, I vow, and a home of your own and a good husband."

Sunniva bent her head, her eyes pooling. She hated her own weakness. At that instant, she hated being a woman. Why did men have so many choices in life, and women so few?

"I will pray for you."

She opened her lips, tempted to ask why, but another sound, in the stable below them, had her rising to her feet.

"Listen," Hilde pleaded. "It is not your kindred. The man is singing." She snapped her fingers in time with the jaunty tune. "Good voice. Marc de Sens, is it not?"

Could this woman read her thoughts? Sunniva said "Yes," faintly and had to sit down on the stool again as Hilde smoothed down her skirts and announced she was leaving.

"I must look to our supper table," she said. "Stay as long as you wish. Oh, and please blow out the candles."

She was gone before Sunniva could protest, slipping down the ladder as nimbly as she had mounted it, bidding Marc de Sens good evening, complimenting him on his well-groomed horse. Although she could not see him, Sunniva sensed Marc raising his head, looking with curiosity at the room above the barn.

What if he came up the ladder?

Testing each footstep, she crept to the doorway, knelt and looked out, drawing her sleeve across her face so her pale features would not catch the light. Marc was in profile to her, standing in the middle of the barn and stretching, arms above his head, a brush in one hand and a cloth in the other. He had stripped to his leggings, his tunic draped over the back of his snorting chestnut horse.

"Careful with the comb, Alde," he was saying. "You do not wish to lose it in Theo's mane. Isabella! Judith! Wash your hands in the trough before supper! If I must tell you again, it shall be tickles before you eat!"

Tickles? Sunniva was suddenly light-headed at the idea. She swung round and crouched on her heels, trying to forget the sight of Marc naked to the waist. She had never seen so many muscles, or such swirls of body hair. She thought of teasing her hands across his chest and the flat plane of his stomach and buried her head in her arms, convinced she was losing her wits altogether. Perhaps she was truly man-mad, perhaps the legacy of her coloring was finally coming out.

I was attacked by two men this morning, how can I be thinking of stroking any part of a man this evening? St. Cuthbert, have mercy on me!

"What am I to do?" she whispered. How long would Marc and his nieces remain in the barn? How long before she herself was missed?

What should she do next?

Chapter Four

"Hey, ho, sweet holly!" Marc caroled the refrain of the lilting song, turning in the stable and reaching down, lifting one of Theo's great legs to clean out his horse's hoof. Theo whinnied at him and Marc settled his shoulder against the chestnut's flank, muttering, "I know, she disturbs me, too, but what would you have me do?"

He knew who was up there, in that mysterious chamber above the barn. Orm Largebelly's widowed mother had confirmed it when she wheezed her way down the ladder, granting him the kind of knowing look that all mothers seem to have perfected and saying under her breath as she passed, "Luck to you, sir. You may do well there, if you are patient and true."

"Alde?" he called out again, patting Theo's shin bone and releasing his hoof. "Shall I tend your pony?"

He wanted to ask the nervous girl above if he should look to her mount but decided if he asked she might never venture down.

"Judith, are those hands clean yet?" He turned his head away from the ladder and busied himself with pretending to check Theo's feed bucket, making great play of stirring the contents with a stick as if seeking a lost jewel. *Come along, sunlight. Steal down the ladder.*

She glided as silently as shadow, scarcely breathing, but he sensed her flitting past because of his own rapid heartbeat. As blood roared in his ears he backed out of the byre and stretched out an arm to block her way to the door.

"And your hands?" he asked.

She came to a stop, skirts swirling as she glanced about. "I thought your nieces were here with you, not that you spoke to empty air. You tricked me, Marc de Sens," she said, in a voice so low he was not sure if she was angry or afraid.

His heart, which had felt to be jammed into his throat, now plummeted into his guts. "Forgive me, I meant no disrespect or harm," he said hastily, before realizing that she was chuckling.

"You tricked me!" he exclaimed.

"Then we are quit, are we not? Where are your youngsters, really?"

"Still with the carter and his wife," Marc admitted, knowing he should not leave them too long, especially now darkness was drawing in. Isabella liked him to be with her while she went to sleep and Judith probably would need to scrub her hands before turning in: she picked up anything she found on their travels, from daisies and old coins to rusting iron nails.

"Do you really tickle them?" Sunniva surprised him afresh with her next question, so much so he answered automatically, "Only when they drive me to distraction with their bickering. They try to tickle me, too, without success." He grinned. "I am bigger than them."

"Hairier, too." Sunniva looked startled by her own

response and then she was blushing, pinker than a sunset. "Sorry—"

"No need. I am as you say." He tugged on his shirt, covering the offending hair, and reached for the door-jamb again, barring her way in case she bolted. "Better?" he asked.

She would not look at him, but stared intently at his horse.

"His name is Theo," Marc said. "Short for Theodore, the soldier-saint. Both have often saved my life while on campaign."

"Where have you fought?" she asked, still without looking at him and without moving to the great war charger.

"Outside the walls of Constantinople."

That swung her eyes round to him. "You served the Emperor? As a warrior?"

Her knowledge of such distant eastern lands surprised him but he merely nodded, glad to be talking to her so naturally.

"My grandfather, Ragnar the Strong-Minded, served an Emperor once," she said. "I had a doll he had brought back from Constantinople. A pretty toy in a white and gold gown."

"What happened to it?" he asked, suspecting more to the story.

"Nothing, nothing. My brothers broke it; an accident, I am sure." She waved the memory aside and wrinkled her nose at him, nerves all gone.

"Why?" he found himself asking. "Above in the sewing room you were as taut as a harp string, I sensed it. So why are you now so at ease?"

"I do not know." She shrugged. "Perhaps because you said you were sorry. Because, too"—she ducked her head, pushing an escaping coil of hair back under the scrap of blue cloth—"you did not lunge at me."

In those simple statements he heard much of the brutality of her life.

"I will never do that," he promised. He lifted his arm from the doorjamb, heartened when she did not go. "I have a boon to ask of you."

"Are my hands clean?" She held them up, palms uppermost. "See for yourself."

Naughty imp, he thought, longing to snake an arm about her slender middle and kiss her again. Instead he solemnly studied her fingers and nodded. "Clean enough," he said. "But that was not my boon."

He sensed her confusion and beneath that an older fear, showing in the way she stiffened, the sinews in her neck tightening as she waited, poised on the brink of flight. A strange mixture she was, of fear, confidence and—dare he admit this?—interest. For all that she was a woman of twenty she acted more like a maid of fourteen. But then, given her father and brothers, what experience could she have had in the gentle sport of courtship?

Her betrothed, that Caedmon of Whitby, must also be a brute.

The thought made him angry. He wanted to take her in his arms and embrace her—really kiss her. Show her what a kiss could be—

"Yes?" she asked. "I must go, soon."

A door opening in the hall alongside the barn and raised voices warned Marc to be quick. "Will you meet my nieces tomorrow?"

She nodded and was gone, calling out, "I am here," as Edgar stamped past the barn, complaining, "Where is the brat now?"

Chapter Five

It was late and her bruised ribs hurt but her father should be satisfied.

Kneeling beside the banked-down fire, Sunniva stretched out to turn the spitted lamb she was roasting for Orm Largebelly with her "special" seasoning of plum verjuice.

She usually enjoyed cooking and the heavy, sweet savor of the meal would have made her mouth water, had she felt less sickened. By a strong effort of will, she fixed her eyes on the sizzling lamb. Sprawled beside her, lounging on a cushion and sheepskin rugs, Orm followed her every move with avid attention, a thin stream of drool falling from his mouth onto his cloak. Sometimes he pressed his foot against her leg, a caress she could not avoid without moving and colliding with her father, who sat with his legs almost in the fire.

Cena was watching Orm and rubbing his knees. Old habits of caring almost prompted her to ask him if she should fetch her comfrey salve, but that would mean leaving the fireplace and her father would not want that. Not after Orm had already picked her out for attention earlier that long night.

As the supper tables were being cleaned and taken down after the feast, Orm had given her a scarlet head-square. Cena had insisted she try it on then and there.

"Come, show Largebelly!" he bellowed, his gruff humor filling the farthest reaches of the hall. "We are among friends here, Sunniva." He only called her by name when he was talking to her in company. "Do you wish to belittle his gift? Bertana, help her—"

She had shed her headrail as rapidly as she knew how. She was no child now and a modest woman was meant to cover her hair, not display it. Smiling so she would not break down in shame, she donned the new head-square, thanking Orm Largebelly as graciously as she could.

Off in the quietest corner of the hall, where the torches were already doused and the poorer and less fleet-footed pilgrims were settling to sleep, she had sensed Marc and his nieces. She glanced their way, seeing the smallest child—Isabella?—standing facing the distant fire, sucking her thumb. Her wide eyes were curiously blank and Sunniva dared not nod to her, lest the little one reacted badly. On the first night that Marc and his charges had joined the pilgrimage, this solemn infant—with her incongruous bright brown eyes and headful of big brown curls that would seem to be the mark of the merriest child in Christendom—had woken screaming. Marc had taken her in his arms and crooned to her until she slept but the other pilgrims were now wary, calling the child touched or even mad.

Sunniva glanced into the darkness again, seeing men and women rolled into their cloaks and a man piling more rugs and rushes onto his own sleeping place. A pair of amber eyes looked back at her, coolly assessing.

Swiftly she turned the braising meat, wishing she was

with the servants and lower-ranking pilgrims instead of the "high-table" guests, settled on their rugs and cushions round the fire. The others were bedding down, not expecting more food and drink. Perhaps Orm's high-table guests would not have done so, had her father not bragged loudly of her "clever ways" with meat and demanded a demonstration.

Hilde said something she did not catch. Smiling politely in return, Sunniva handed her the first of the spitted lamb.

"Do you mean to vex me?" Cena muttered under cover of Hilde calling for more ale for those still awake. "Serve the head of house first, always!"

"Orm would agree with both of us, Father," Sunniva returned, nodding to the beaming Largebelly, who again scraped her leg with his foot. "He approves."

"I will have ale," called a pilgrim sitting with his back to one of the hall's great wooden beams. "And I!" called a few others.

Shadowy servants were dispatched to serve them, Sunniva noting that the young pages passed Marc de Sens' sleeping corner without stopping. Obscurely she was disappointed: was Marc already asleep?

"Look to your task, girl!" Cena spat on the fire, his scowl deepening as he plucked a small wriggling worm from his ear. Sunniva tried not to shudder as he flung the worm over his shoulder. Her father would not purge himself of parasites by eating a fern frond, and he and Edgar both filched half-cooked meats from her spits—as indeed Edgar did now, plucking a spit from the fire and trailing it ostentatiously in front of Ketil and Told. The twins were drinking deeply, spilling ale over their long moustaches. Told stared at her breasts, then said something to Ketil.

"Your gown is loosening." Cena had spotted Told's stare, but as usual he chose to put his own interpretation on it. "You should have Bertana tighten the strings."

"She already has, Father." Sunniva handed Orm a spit of lamb smothered in sauce, resisting the impulse to add, "Bertana has trussed me into my gown so firmly that I can hardly breathe."

"My thanks, sweet lady." Orm swallowed most of the meat in one mouthful. Resigned, Sunniva held out another spit. As she checked the pail of water she kept behind herself to soak the spits, Cena shook her arm.

"Smile, damn you!" he hissed against her ear. "I will not tell you again!"

"Of course, Father," said Sunniva, smiling. "Ever you have my interests at heart."

She sank back on her heels, her heart stampeding. Every day that she became older, growing in resemblance to her dead mother, Cena's scant indulgence toward her lessened. His grumbles she could manage, but his latest threat, to pass her to the twins, was new and had truly frightened her.

Mother of heaven, help me! she prayed in her mind, begging for an end, at least to this night.

An end came, but not one she wanted. The middle of the fire, all glowing logs and twigs, suddenly fell in on itself in a loud, crackling heap, sending a rush of sparks spiraling upwards into the rafters and out of the central smoke hole.

Sunniva flinched, although the sound was nothing much, a common-place. She was scolding herself for her own nervous state when a high-pitched, wailing scream ripped through the hall.

"Arms, to me!" yelled Orm, leaping up, dragging his mother behind him. Beside him, Cena had made a grab for his battle-axe and knocked Edgar's goblet of mead flying. The twins and other men had whipped out their daggers and lumbered to their feet, stamping up great clouds of fire ash.

"Bring torches!" Sunniva called, trying for reason in this sooty mêlée, while about her the shouting and stumbling, kicking and half-panicked scuffling continued, and that eerie high-pitched screaming in the dark went on and on.

"Quiet there!" howled Cena, face purpling in disgust. His complaint was echoed by many but then another voice, one well-known to Sunniva, began to chant the Lord's Prayer in careful, measured English.

"Our father in heaven . . ."

Sunniva added her voice to his. ". . . Hallowed be thy name . . ." she recited, straining to hear, amidst the cursing and grunts of half-drunken men, the scrape of swords carelessly handled, a lessening of the screams.

"Thy kingdom come . . ." Marc again, kind as one of the saints of heaven, steady as a tumbler on a tightrope, his voice giving no sign of the grief he must be feeling.

"Thy will be done . . ." Sunniva answered, trying to weave this calm between them, so that the overwrought Isabella would feel safe.

"On earth as it is in heaven . . ." One of the other pilgrims now joined in and abruptly, as suddenly and terribly as it had begun, the screaming stopped.

Marc emerged from the shadows, a tiny, still figure clutched in his arms. "Thank you for your patience," he said, looking directly at Sunniva. "She is sleeping now. A good sleep." *Thanks to you*, he mouthed, so swiftly that Sunniva wondered if she had imagined it.

"Is that it?" demanded Cena with hands on hips, his favorite brawling pose. "Your mad bratling drives us half into insanity by her unearthly din and all you can say is thanks?"

"It is enough, Master Cena." Hilde spoke out decisively before any other, jabbing her large son in his large belly.

Clearly accustomed to such rough prompts, Orm blinked and added, "We should all really be asleep. It is late. Let us bed down."

"Sunniva, you shall lie beside me." Hilde beckoned to her and she gladly complied, stepping away from her indignant father and an embarrassed-looking Largebelly.

"He is a soft man, my lady." Unbidden, unwanted, Bertana wormed her narrow body between Sunniva and one of Hilde's maids, her tongue busy with poison.

"Look how he deals with those children," Bertana went on, whispering as she wadded a cloak into a ball to use as a pillow. "He is too easy with them. That little girl needs a good smack."

Sunniva, who had endured plenty of Bertana's smacks over the years, said nothing.

"Big as he is, he would run away if it came to a fight."

"As much use as my father and brothers, then." Sunniva rolled away and drew her cloak tightly about her ears but Bertana was not to be put off.

"You should not speak so. Your father is ever concerned for your good future."

"And my marriage, Bertana? When will that be, do you think? Do you not wonder if I am becoming notorious: the girl offered to first one nobleman, then another? I imagine my father's name in the ranks of northern landowners is Cena the whoremonger."

"My lady! That is a wicked, evil thing to say! You should pray to the Virgin to forgive you—go on, quickly!"

Sunniva felt the older woman's fingers slap against her shoulder, twice, to reinforce her point. As Bertana drew back to deliver a third blow, she twisted round, sitting up and seizing Bertana's hand. Her father's endless proddings she had to endure, but her maid's was another matter. "Marc de Sens is a good man," she remarked, squeezing Bertana's fingers in hers. "A kind man, is he not?"

"If you say," Bertana tried to free her hand but could not: Sunniva's fingers, strengthened by years of work and exacting needlecraft, gripped hers easily.

"I do say." Sunniva looked into Bertana's mud-brown eyes, seeing her maid's plain, weasel face lit by a mingled pain, fear and malice. "And I also say that Marc may not be handsome to you, but I feel for him."

Bertana stopped struggling, her thin mouth locked into a sneer. "Him!"

"Why not?" Sunniva thought of Marc in the stable, the starlight glowing on his firm, strong body. "I wish I were only braver, then I would ask him to run off with me." *Yet would he come? Would he do right by me? Would he be honorable? I feel that he would be all of these things, but what if I am wrong? What then?*

Bertana's mouth was now an "O" of shock. "You cannot mean that!"

"But I do." Cautiously, Sunniva reached out and stroked her maid's thin cheek. "Can we not be friends, Bertana?" she whispered. She had asked and been rebuffed before, but perhaps this time— "Can you not see the rightness of it? Two women as we are, in a household of men?"

"No!" Bertana began to scratch at Sunniva's fingers with her free hand. "No! Let me go!"

"So you can rush to tell my father?" Utter frustration at her own plight made Sunniva reckless. "While you are doing so, Bertana, you may say to him that such an elopement would be very much to my liking. Now, go! I hope my father pays you well for this evening's work."

She released her maid, watched her backing rapidly into the shadows and then turned away, appalled at her own behavior. *I am as great a bully as Edgar,* she thought, and lay awake the rest of that night, ashamed.

Chapter Six

The next day dawned wet and foggy. "Too damp for you to travel in safety," Orm Largebelly declared, sucking in his gut as he waded through the stirring sleepers to ask Sunniva if she had spent the night in comfort. "You would certainly be swept away at the river crossing and the fords will be flooded and overflowing by now." he went on. "Stay another day! There is good hunting in these parts. I know many trails."

"Local knowledge always tells," said Cena, his appetite wetted by the mention of game. "We should vote on this, brother pilgrims."

"But not so much of a brother last night, eh, Father, when you threatened to break the peddler's pack over his shoulders for treading your cap into the rushes?" Sunniva remarked under her breath. She watched the vote go Orm's and her father's way with bitter resignation, angry that only the men were expected or allowed to vote. Even the thought of spending more time with Hilde in her unique sewing room brought small comfort.

Worse yet, she could kindle only a small enthusiasm at the idea of meeting Marc's three girls.

What is amiss with me? she thought as she and the other women, Hilde included, cleared the hall with stiff brooms and pails of water while the men wandered in and out from stable to kitchen, bringing their dogs and hunting hawks with them. She skirted round men shouting stories of wolves killed, boars brought down and stags run onto spears, but in all this busy to-ing and fro-ing she did not see Marc. Depressed anew, she became convinced he had forgotten his invitation, perhaps even regretted it. She moved with less speed than usual, tottering to the midden with an overfull pail of greasy, muddy refuse.

It was there, in the streaming rain, that Ketil and Told caught her.

"See, it is Tangletop!" Ketil dashed the pail from her chilled fingers, tutting as the contents spilled over the path to the midden, his clear, even features warped into an expression of disgust. "Quite pretty, if you like your maids messy and slatternly, but then, given her mother, that is no surprise." He smiled, his teeth very white, wholesome-looking in his tanned, handsome face, his eyes blue and cold.

"Tangletop doing fit work," remarked Told, ever more laconic than his twin as he checked that no one else was nearby.

"What mean you?" Sunniva already had her dagger out, backing up into the steaming midden slops to watch the hulking pair. "What?" she demanded. She refused to respond to the hated nickname, coined after many occasions when the twins had dragged off her headrail and mussed her hair.

"It is as we suspected." Ketil slid closer on her left side, cracking his knuckles in preparation. "And now our father sees it, too. Look at us, Tangletop, and look at

you. We are all tall, except you. We are all well made—
except you. We all have our father's hair and coloring
and eyes—except you."

Told tugged at his own brown-and-blond locks to em-
phasize the point and sidled nearer on her right. The
constant drizzle ran over his bushy eyebrows into his
eyes, making him squint, and Sunniva was reminded
that Told did not see objects close to him so well. It
would be perhaps a small advantage.

"I am no cuckoo." She plucked at her waistband:
the smaller, older dagger that she drew out was not so
sharp as her first but it would have to do. She hefted
it, relieved to be armed in both hands.

"I say that you are, Tangletop." Ketil took out his
own dagger and began to pare his fingernails, enjoying her frigid silence. "We all know your mother was
nothing but a slave. You know what is said of lusty
slave girls, who will go with—"

"Free or unfree, my mother was as married to our
father as yours." Sunniva had guessed where this was
going and she did not like it. "We are brothers and
sister."

Told scowled: he did not like his twin to be interrupted.

"Do you go hunting?" she asked, lifting the daggers
in her fists so her brothers—half brothers—could see
the rain bouncing and flaring off the blades. She flung
their own words back at them. "You know our father"—
and here, although her nerves were stretched so tightly
she felt her spine might snap, she forced herself to
smile—"does not like to be kept waiting."

"We are hunting," Ketil replied, "and our father is
not yours." He held up a hand, although Sunniva had
said nothing. "Father Martin told us; before we came

away on pilgrimage. He said it had preyed too long upon his conscience."

Sunniva gripped her knives more tightly, feeling the rainwater drip down her back in icy fingers of creeping cold. "Yes?" she asked.

She was looking at Ketil but it was Told who answered. "Your mother had a paramour. Our priest saw them in the arms of each other." Told frowned, knotting his eyebrows together. "The lover had red hair."

"Like yours," Ketil added, and leaped forward.

Sunniva had not anticipated his attack. She was too shocked, her mind busy with a hundred questions, her thoughts darting everywhere, like bees in a fallen hive. "How is that possible?" she was asking, numbly, when Ketil's arm came flashing down and he struck her right hand with his pilgrim staff.

She screamed at the splintering pain, but did not let go of her blade, slashing out instead with her other dagger, snagging Told's jerkin as he came in to grab her.

"Drop them, you sniveling bitch!" Ketil beat her again, the heavy knotted staff cudgeling her shoulder and back as she jerked sideways, trying to shield her head and breasts. For a second, Ketil's throat was exposed to her but she could not do it—she could not cut him.

"We are kindred!" she screamed, despair almost overwhelming her as she realized sour Father Martin's no doubt garbled "confession" had given the twins the flimsy justification they had always sought to come after her. "We were brought up together!"

"That counts for nothing with this kind of breed," came a new voice, along with the unmistakable sound of a long sword being drawn from a scabbard. "These bucks need an urgent lesson in morality."

Ketil and Told looked at each other and at Sunniva, still armed, and grinned boyishly, as if they had done no more harm than lads caught pinching apples in an orchard. "We were fooling," Ketil began.

"So am I," said Marc de Sens, punching Ketil straight in the face.

Her half brother sat down heavily on the spilled pail, rainwater mingling with blood as he brought both hands up to his pulped nose. "Yoo hi' me!" he protested, his voice blurred.

Told snatched his cloak and dragged him away, the twins lurching off into the curtains of rain.

"Are you all right?" asked Marc, kneeling before her in the mud. "May I escort you to the sewing room?"

She tried to answer but found no breath to speak. Instead, with a great shudder, her nerve gave way. She dropped her knives and began to cry.

Chapter Seven

Marc sat by the midden and drew Sunniva onto his lap. He cuddled her lightly but close, letting her know she was safe. Mistress Hilde would take care of his other girls: he had left them with her in her sewing room, exclaiming over tapestries of saints and dragons.

Other girls? Sunniva was not his, however much he wanted her to be. True, he had come looking for her as soon as he could, hoping she would remember his promise that she should meet his nieces, but he had never expected to find her in such a horrifying state.

To have to fight off her own siblings! The inhuman betrayal of Cena's younger sons disgusted him. Over and over, that terrible moment when he had first found them all ran round his mind like a whipped spinning top. In a scene like a wood carving on a church roodscreen he had witnessed a clash of demons and angels—only it was worse, because these were folk he knew and one he cared for very much.

For an instant, finding Sunniva driven back against a mound of fetid, steaming, stinking ordure and bones, her lovely face stripped down to a death mask by terror, her supple, lithe form frozen into a stiffened, defensive arc by stress, he could not believe it. She was so small against those who snatched at her, who should protect her, head and shoulders smaller, tiny and fragile where they were brute. They had been mocking her, calling her slave-born, weaving about her in a deadly dance of feint and attack. He had not dared to shout in case he sparked them into something worse, or more dreadful still, shocked Sunniva into dropping her weapons.

And then Ketil had hit her. Twice. With his pilgrim staff!

"How could he do such a thing?" Marc whispered.

Reliving it in his mind, he was again appalled, while the fighter within him was intrigued. Yet again her skill with knives had amazed him. Where had she learned that?

More importantly, where was the wretch Caedmon of Whitby? Why was he not here?

"Our father in heaven," Marc whispered, something he did for Isabella when she was at her most need of calming. Isabella loved to hear the Lord's Prayer in English: at present it was her most favorite thing. But he could not pray for himself. Each time Sunniva fought down a sob he wanted to grab Cena and hack his filthy head off his body.

"How can I help?" he murmured.

"Cannot!" She burrowed against his shoulder, adding gruffly. "Sorry."

"No need." He offered her his hand and she took it, her fingers whitening as she gripped him like a sailor washed overboard. She was drowning in fear and sorrow and he could do nothing except be there with her.

Feeling useless, helpless, he shook his head and looked up into the sullen gray sky, letting the rain beat onto his face. It cooled his temper but not enough. Already he was holding Sunniva carefully against his anger, as if she was the most delicate of flowers— a wood anemone, he thought. Her face was surely white enough.

"Rot and blast them!" he muttered in Breton. Inhaling deeply to rein in his rage, he gagged on the midden stench. At least he should bear Sunniva away from here, before the miasma overcame her or a servant came prying. If he ran again into any of her benighted "kin"—and he used that word of them most loosely— he would be paying wergild for their slaying. And if Orm Fatbelly, or whatever his name was, made him a Wolfs-head outlaw, so be it.

"Come, young one." He spoke in Breton before he realized what he was saying and by then he was carrying her off the muck and slime of the midden, picking up her knives on his way and dropping them carefully into her lap, because they were hers.

He was not sure she had noticed, but a steady "Thank you" startled him into looking down.

A slim, grave face, pensive as a Madonna, looked back.

"You should set me down, sir."

So they were back to "sir" again. "You would go sprawling in the mud if I did. You have had a great shock, so rest." While you have the chance, was his added, unspoken instruction.

Almost as if she had heard it, she sighed and closed her eyes. He relished the lacewing pattern of her eyelashes, long and blonde, flecked with gold. The tip of her nose was slightly sunburnt, making it teasingly kissable.

But there was more. She was warming quickly

against his arms and flanks, reminding Marc of more intimate embraces. Shamed—was he no better than the brothers?—he tried to wrench his mind onto other things, mentally naming each war horse he had bred and trained.

He had reached Jonah when her eyes flashed open and she squirmed in his grip. "Please set me down, sir. As a true knight would," she hesitated and swallowed, "would a lady."

She blushed deeply—the color she would go when making love, he thought, feeling heat rush to his own face and loins. But this was ridiculous, he thought. She was a mere girl, and another man's betrothed. This was not the way he should be.

"We have a problem here, for I am no true knight." Marc rubbed his nose, realizing he was feeling both nervous and playful. He realized, too, that when he scratched his nose with Sunniva in his arms her breasts squashed delectably together, stretching and pressing against the fabric of her plain gown, vividly outlining their shape, the sharply risen nipples.

Lust rammed through him; he wanted to pitch her into the stable hay and have her, make her cry out in ecstasy and weep with pleasure.

But Sunniva had already wept and her tears were ones of grief and pain. He would not add to those.

"Just a few more steps," he said, as much to himself as to her.

She stared at him, then a pink tongue clicked between perfect rose-petal lips and stayed there, defiant. *The little imp!* "I am sure Mistress Hilde does that every day," he remarked, casually lifting her higher to clear a broken broomstick, left out in the rain.

He had reached the point where the midden track

divided. Which way should he go? Stable and sewing room, or feast hall to confront her father?

No contest.

"No, please! Not there!" She was plucking at his arm and he stopped, not wanting her to be alarmed again and, selfishly, not wanting her to use those wickedly sharp knives of hers on him.

"You do not think your father should know of this assault?"

"He would deny it!"

Marc guessed that to be more than likely. "Show your bruises, in the feast hall, before others. He cannot ignore their censure, nor the evidence of his own sight."

She stiffened again, as if he had slapped her. "You do not understand!" she spat. "He would say I had provoked them! That is what he always says!"

"They have done this before?" Marc was horrified afresh, the muscles in his gut and across his spine chilling and contracting as he absorbed the punch of her words. "When? How often?"

"No! Not what you are thinking! Only slaps, before today. It was never as bad as this, before . . ." She began to kick. "Let me go! All men want to do is paw me! Let go! Now!"

Stung by the accusation, he dropped one arm, releasing her legs and feet. Though he would not have her flying from him yet. Allowing her to swing against him, he clamped his arm around her middle.

"I can be a good friend, Sunniva. I can help. Let me."

Her hanging feet glanced against his shins as she tried to kick him.

"Listen!" he said urgently. "Let me get a message to Caedmon, have him join you on pilgrimage."

"Who? Why should he? Once he suspects, once any

man suspects—" She stopped speaking by a deliberate effort, gnawing her lower lip.

Marc brushed a piece of dirt from her sleeve, heartened when she did not shrink from him. "Tell me of your mother," he said gently.

The question quietened her, as he suspected it would. For an instant she stared at him, her mouth trembling with feeling and answers, then she began to struggle again, still more violently.

"Stop that!" He wound his leg about hers, imprisoning her further. "You have nothing to be ashamed of, do you hear? I love my mother well and respect her most highly and *my* mother is a farrier's daughter!"

"So was William the Bastard's." In another quicksilver change of mood Sunniva was still and even-tempered again. "And your father?"

"My father loved and respected my mother till the day he died. No, please, do not cry. I did not tell you to make you cry."

"I know." She gave him a wobbly smile that seemed to turn his heart right over in his chest. "These are happy tears, see?"

"Yes." Marc was not convinced but time was passing. Much as he would have liked to, he could not stay here with Sunniva. There were his girls. "The sewing room, then? To meet my three whirlpools?"

"Whirlpools?" The image had caught her as he had known it would.

"All deep-minded, prone to temper outbursts, often in tears and ready to suck you into their games in a moment."

"That is surely unfair!" she laughed, settling against his encircling leg as she relaxed, her thigh and flank resting by his in a most distracting manner. "I think you do them wrong."

She went quiet. Marc reassured himself that her knives were now safely tucked back in her belt and waited.

"They are young," she said at last. "Impressionable. Do you truly wish that I meet them?"

"Why not?" He cupped her face with his hand and raised her chin. "You are not your father or brothers."

"If they are such," she muttered, blushing an even deeper red than before. "I know you must have heard that. You need not deny it."

"I do not—but you are not responsible for your parents, whoever they may be. You are yourself, and that is enough."

Marc lowered her to her feet and drew back, wondering if even now she might bolt from him, like a nervous horse. He longed to embrace her, drink in her fragrance, soothe and caress her.

All men want to do is paw me.

He stepped away and held out his arm. She took it. Together they walked toward the stable block.

Chapter Eight

Climbing the ladder to the sewing room behind Marc de Sens, Sunniva scolded herself. Why had she done what she had? Why had she lain so long in his arms, *welcoming* his embrace? He said she was in shock, but that was no excuse. She should not have thrust out her tongue at him. He would see her as frivolous, unseemly, as well as the spawn of who-knew-what.

"Mother, what did you do?" she whispered. The foundations of her world were slipping; she was no longer sure of anything. Was cantankerous, woman-hating Father Martin right?

Tell me of your mother, Marc had said, but she had not done so. Was she ashamed to do so?

She was ashamed of herself. And of Ketil and Told. Truth be told, both had struck and beaten her with lethal regularity, their violence increasing once she was past twelve years old. She had learned to keep out of their way, especially when they had been drinking.

This new accusation against her was the most dangerous yet: it stripped her of any rights in the eyes of her family.

Family? Can I even call them that now?

As soon as I reach the city of Durham I will flee, she thought. A city has need of many trades: I will find work there as a seamstress or a cook. I will survive.

And perhaps Marc—

No. There is no "perhaps Marc," she told herself, as he entered the sewing room ahead of her and excited squeals greeted his appearance.

Later that day, back from a good day's hunting, Cena was in a loud, jubilant mood. That evening as the stag *he* had brought down was roasted over the central fire pit, he knew that he was master of the feast. Even Orm Largebelly deferred to him, granting him the single great chair in the hall, where he sat with his sons at high table and Orm's mother and the other women served them.

"More ale!" He banged on the trestle with his fist, satisfied when Sunniva hurried from the shadows to serve him. She was a useful wench, though not as biddable as she should be. Look at her now, shepherding those three yowling girls, the pilgrim-chits who made decent people's sleep almost impossible. Like the most foolish of ducklings, they were following her everywhere, copying almost her every gesture and expression. She would soon tire of them and their pathetic worship.

Coolly—he fancied he was a connoisseur of female beauty—he assessed the three against their model. The eldest carried her jug of ale like Sunniva, riding it against her hip, but there the resemblance ended. She was a tall, thin girl, with thin straight hair and a strongly defined nose and chin—mannish, to Cena's way of thinking. The middle sister, attempting to balance her jug on her head, had a glint in her bright blue eyes and a pouting, sulky mouth that shouted mischief—a trait that he would have thrashed out of her years ago. She was already as tall as her older sibling, solid where the elder was wiry, and with thick brown hair. He thought of his hellions, Ketil and Told, yanking on ten-year-old Sunniva's plaits until she shrieked, and he grinned, sinking the rest of his beer in celebration of the memory. It was, in truth, poor, watery stuff, not as good as the ale made in his household, but it would do.

Cena frowned as he studied the last of the trio. The youngest pilgrim—the midnight screamer—was a pretty thing if you liked rag-doll limbs and wild curly hair. Had Sunniva looked like her at the same age? He could not remember and was not really interested. What did anger him was the fact that this brat, who spoke a mangled English and who would cry at anything, from flea bites to strong sunlight, was drinking from her jug of ale and offering it to no one.

"Stop that!" He banged down his empty cup as the little girl passed, satisfied when she jumped and slopped ale down her robe. He laughed as she sat down in the middle of the hall, still gripping her jug, and began to wail.

"You made her cry!" It was the middle, awkward one, slamming her jug down onto the trestle with such force that Cena heard it crack.

"That is not yours to break!" he grumbled.

"It is not yours, either!" she answered back, flouncing down beside her sister, pulling the ends of her sleeves back from her wrists; a new trick and one she had certainly learned from his brat.

"Father, please, where is your wit? Isabella is little more than an infant and unused to being spoken to so harshly." Sunniva crouched and swept the sniveling child into her arms, calling her ridiculous names: sweetheart, baby, curly. Then the mettlesome, middle one hurled herself against Sunniva, dragging on her headrail—the only useful thing that had happened, since Orm Largebelly and the rest of the men in the hall strained forward on their benches to stare. Twenty years old or not, his daughter was still a prick-teaser.

If she was his daughter.

Was Father Martin right? Cena knuckled his fingers into his eyes as he tried to consider the question that had been plaguing him since halfway through this pilgrimage, when Edgar finally admitted what the fool of a priest had said. He had been disbelieving, then furious, and he was still angry.

By God, if her mother had played him for a fool, then Sunniva would pay. By God she would!

"Get me more beer!" Disgusted by his thoughts, Cena stuck to what he knew, old habits. He leaned over the table and lashed out, striking Sunniva in the middle of her back. "Serve me, damn you, girl! It is the custom here, obey it!"

He wrenched back his arm again, but his second blow was blocked by a hand as large and thick as a trencher. Hard as oak wood, too: Cena flinched and sucked his knuckles, glowering indignantly into the unyielding face and narrowed eyes of his assailant, Marc de Sens.

"Look to your own, man, and let me deal with mine!" Cena bellowed, heartened to see, farther along the main table, that his three sons were standing up, fingering their sword hilts. Only Ketil looked less than eager, but then, according to Told, he had taken a tumble in the hunt and smashed his nose.

Thoughts of the hunt prompted Cena to goad some more, especially when the fellow picked up his nieces, one in each arm, and began to walk away. "Where were you, this day, de Sens? Skulking with the women folk? Afraid to get your clothes muddy?"

The man's broad shoulders tensed: otherwise he gave no sign of having heard. He stalked through the quietening hall and out into the gathering darkness, the two younger girls wrapped about him like creepers and the third trotting rapidly behind.

Sunniva watched Marc go, longing to go with him. Or was her father right? Was Marc "soft?" It was true he had not gone hunting: he had spent the day between sewing room and stable, his girls clustering with him.

"Does it matter what Cena thinks?" Hilde asked softly beside her, gathering up the cracked and discarded vessels. When Sunniva turned wondering eyes on her, she smiled.

"I could see that it bothered you, my dear," she said.

"Marc is his own master," Sunniva muttered.

"That is so." Hilde passed the cracked pitcher to a serving maid and observed in a low voice. "Have you heard the news? The beacons on dragon hill have been lit. It is a call to arms for the men folk here."

Sunniva's mind flashed to her own desperate struggles with Magnus Long-Nose, the whoremaster who had attacked her in church. And Marc had saved her: he had not been soft then.

"All men of age who can bear arms," Hilde went on, implacably clear. "My son does not wish to announce it yet and break up the feast but soon he must. The beacons are for our king. He will be marching north."

King Harold in new danger, thought Sunniva. It was well known that the king had mustered most of his fighting force in the south of England, waiting to repel the greedy forces of William of Normandy. So what had happened here, so far in the north, that he must come?

In a flash, she understood. It was an old, feared enemy. "Vikings!" she gasped.

Hilde nodded, warning her with a finger to her own lips to keep her voice down. "Where will Marc be in such a fight?" she asked. "Which side? I do not think he is English. And I know he would not desert his young ones."

"No." Sunniva was proud in her denial, proud of him for that, although Hilde's words brought no other comfort. Which lord would Marc de Sens choose to follow if William of Normandy did cross the narrow sea and land in England?

"And what will you do, my dear, if your men folk leave to join the king's army?"

She would be stranded, friendless. Sunniva's heart beat hard at such a prospect but she rallied quickly. "I will find a place," she said, hoping that perhaps Hilde would offer one. "My maid and I have skills."

"Think you of your maid?" Hilde gave her a very old, knowing look. "I do not feel she is so interested in your well-being." She nodded her head slightly along the dais and the high table to where Bertana was standing, her empty pitcher by her feet as she gnawed on a slice of roast venison handed to her by Edgar.

"But I see you already know this," Hilde went on. "Let me add something you do not know. I will be happy to have you—"

Whatever she was going to say was lost in a new bellow from Cena.

"We must travel on! A pilgrimage is a sacred trust." He was up and swaying on his feet, his face red and sweating as he appealed to the lower-ranking pilgrims gathered on the benches farthest from the fire. "Each of us swore to undertake and complete it. We cannot stop now, so close to our goal. Think of the saint's anger! Think of St. Cuthbert!"

A few pilgrims, mainly the halt and infirm, murmured their agreement.

"I believe your father has just heard about the beacons," remarked Hilde, throwing a large deer bone to the two hunting dogs lately fawning round her feet.

"So I see," said Sunniva, glancing swiftly at Edgar and the twins. At home the three of them had been loud in their praise of war and fighting, now they were strangely silent. She touched the daggers at her belt, wishing that she could answer the summons instead, defend her land and king.

On the dais, Orm Largebelly shrugged, his eyes not quite meeting Cena's. "If that is truly your choice," he said, "I suggest you prepare to leave as soon as possible on the morrow. My men and I must ride to battle."

The feast broke up quickly then. Sunniva was glad: though she did not want to admit it, she was ashamed of Cena and the others. Slipping away from the hall, she made for the stable. Only to check on their horses, she justified to herself, her spirits lifting nonetheless at the prospect of seeing Marc again, of perhaps speaking to him. She could be a messenger: he might not know of the lit beacons, and he would need to know.

"Wait, girl." An unwelcome voice from the darkness behind her. Sunniva whirled about, suddenly tired of all kinds of things.

"My name is Sunniva, Edgar. Henceforth, I will not heed you unless you address me by my name."

"Pah!" Edgar said, sounding exactly like his father, "Very high and noble, I am sure! He hawked and spat, scowling and rubbing his lower jaw. "Can you get me some salve for my teeth?"

"Ask Bertana, she should know where I packed it. What else?" There was always something else with Edgar.

"That man you fancy. Do you realize he is Norman?"

"He is Breton. And he told me."

"Breton, Norman, they are close enough to make no difference. They are both *French*." He made it sound like a disease. Edgar tugged on his long fair moustache, a further sign of his displeasure. "You have spoken to him! When did you sneak off to do that?"

Sunniva said nothing. Edgar enjoyed being the bearer of disturbing news: she sensed there was more to come.

Sure enough, when his question failed to provoke her, Edgar added, "Did he tell you why he is on pilgrimage?"

"Of course."

Edgar, who could have been a good-looking, even-featured man if he would refrain from either sneering or scowling, now gave her his third most common expression: a self-satisfied smirk.

"You really do not know!" he crowed. "My stupid *Sunniva*, your girlish daydream of Marc de Sens will have to end. The man is a murderer. What is more, he killed a woman. He is here in England because the shrines of his land cannot bring him absolution or peace. He is not for you, or any one."

He laughed at her stricken expression. "Now I must take my leave of you, stupid *Sunniva*. Next time you meet your murderer, do not send him my good wishes, for he deserves none. Farewell."

He turned his back on her without a bow and strode off, still laughing.

Chapter Nine

Stunned, she tottered to the barn with none of her usual grace, retreating swiftly when she realized Marc's nieces were also there, and awake. The questions pressing down so hard on her tongue, making her feel as if she had a dozen rocks piled onto her chest, would have to wait. She had to talk to Marc—but not in front of his children.

Ketil and later Told prowled past, the rising stars behind and above them making them look incongruously heroic, like Orion the hunter. She kept to the place she had found: a narrow nook between stable and kitchen where the roofs overlapped and dipped low, creating a curtain of thatch she could hide behind. Standing and then crouching in her den, thirst and hunger making her feel light-headed, she waited for the yard and stable to grow quiet.

Finally the pilgrims and men-at-arms crossing to the stable, checking on their horses, rechecking their weapons, dribbled to a slow halt. Bertana came calling for her but Sunniva let her go, dipping her head so her face would not catch the glimmers of starlight. Holding her breath, she listened as her maid returned, grumbling, to the hall. Torchlight spilled into the yard as Bertana pushed open the side door, throwing a beam of light into the stable where Sunniva waited. The beam illuminated a large moving shadow, then a figure, draping a cloak over an arm and hanging a flask around his neck.

It was Marc. Sunniva found herself trembling, could feel her eyes widening to take all of him in. She was alone out here and he was so big, so very tall and strong. His wrists were thicker than her forearms. He could pin her down with one leg, let alone any other limb.

He was a possible killer and he was making straight for her hiding place.

He is Orion, she thought wildly, her shivering growing worse as she shrank back, feeling no comfort when her rump hit the wattle wall of the stable. She knew she should reach for her knives but her arms were frozen, her legs threatening to give way beneath her as he stopped, lowered his head and asked, "Do I join you in your den or will you come out to me?"

She ran out, not away but straight at him, hurling her questions. "Did you kill a woman? Is that why you are on this pilgrimage? Why did you kill her? Was she your wife?"

"Hardly!" He grinned, as if the idea was the height of folly. "I have no wife, nor betrothed. Unlike you."

"What mean you by that?"

"Your elusive betrothed. And I am surprised Large-belly is not looking for you. He has stared enough and stripped you with his eyes."

"What are you talking about?"

"You must know this: a lass as comely as you always knows." He grinned again, adding, "Shall we both keep our hands where we can see them?"

"Never mind our host." From being afraid, Sunniva felt close to boxing Marc de Sens' ears: the man was deliberately trying to divert her! "What of these rumors I have heard of you?"

Marc folded his arms across his chest. "You should not believe everything you hear."

"So you did not kill a woman?"

He shook his head. "Next time you wish to hide, tuck those knives of yours well away. They catch the light. Where did you learn the skill with them?"

"From a tumbler and knife-thrower who stayed a summer at Cena's house when I was twelve. What was the woman's name?"

"A summer? That is a long time for a traveler to stick in one place."

Sunniva smiled. "He loved my cooking," she admitted, "and I did save him from a mob."

Marc's clear, deep eyes widened. "How was this?"

She shrugged, relishing her moment. "Tell me of this woman first."

"Little tease." He gave her a slow, strangely sweet smile and unfolded his arms, touching her cheek lightly with his fingers. "Come, let me take you back to the hall. It is late for you to be out alone."

Sunniva felt close to bursting with frustration. "But you have told me nothing!"

"And I intend to keep it that way. Shall we go, before Ketil looks for you again?"

"That is unfair," she rejoined, wondering as she fell into step with him. "I do not understand." She tried again. "How is it I can feel safe with you, if you did this thing?"

He stopped on the track and looked at her, his features as rigid as stone. "You should keep asking yourself that question," he said. "And ask, too, how much your betrothed means to you when you also seek me out."

He pointed ahead. "The way is clear for you, and I must return to my three before Judith and Alde quarrel, or Isabella has another nightmare. Go."

Angered and ashamed by what he had just said, Sunniva left.

Chapter Ten

The rain continued, gray rain falling from gray clouds on gray hills and drab, still trees. The old Roman road scored through this desolate landscape like a running cross-stitch, Sunniva thought, pulling her hood tighter about her numbed ears. Her ungloved fingers were wet with the rain, her feet cold and damp.

"Hey, girl, pass me a flask!" Cena ordered, the rain plastering his beard to his scowl so he looked like an angry troll. Wordlessly, Sunniva did so, aware that Cena—she could no longer think of him as her father—was angry. Although she rode beside him, she was wrapped in a voluminous cloak that hid her. While they were on the road, with the possibility of meeting other travelers who might be rich or useful to him, Cena wanted her displayed. He would have ripped the cloak off her back, had he been able to do so without questions from the pilgrims.

Sunniva glanced behind, spotting Marc riding next to the carter and his wife and their load of earthenware pots. His nieces were nowhere to be seen, which must mean they were in the covered wagon. Or had Marc left them behind, or worse?

"No!" Sunniva breathed, refusing to believe that. Only last night, Alde and Judith had thrashed themselves awake, writhing in sleep from some dream or memory too dreadful to contemplate. Marc had talked to them for a long time, crouched by their rough pallets in the corner of the hall. Then Isabella stirred, dissolving instantly into noisy weeping, but Marc was so patient with her. He taught the child a game with string, saying he had learned it from an old friend called Karl. Sunniva herself had fallen asleep beside Bertana, feeling secure not because of the presence of her maid but because of Marc's deep, sympathetic voice.

"He cares for them," she said aloud. "As deeply as a father for a daughter."

"Cease your prattle!" Cena was rubbing his knee again, wincing at the smooth paces of his horse.

Sunniva said nothing, aware of but refusing to look at Cena's sons, who were cantering alongside and listening. She tried to think of some childhood song to lift her mood, waved at the carter's wife, who stolidly remained fixed and still on her seat, tried to remember her mother's smile. In all these things, she failed. The sound of rain, the smell of rain, the scent of chilled horses and cold men, the smell of sickness that always hung about the straggling party, the groans of the limping, bandaged penitents, seeking a cure at the shrine ahead, filled her world.

I will not look at Marc again, she promised herself. *He may care for his own, but for the rest he is merely a fellow traveler under the shadow of God, a bearded brute, a woman-killer, not handsome, not worth looking at.* Desperately seeking something to study during these dreary miles, Sunniva stared off into the east, away from the chain of northern hills.

There were the tall pennants, flopping in the rain, the sign of an approaching war party carrying their standards before them.

She pointed and shouted a warning, and the escorts blew their horns, masking the sounds of the closing, galloping horses. Since none of the mercenaries paid to protect the pilgrim party had drawn their swords, Sunniva hoped the mounted warriors were allies. She heard yells of greeting and could scarcely understand what was being said, the local speech was so different from her own.

Cena prodded her back with his whip. "Smile!"

"At whom?" Sunniva indicated the shrouds of rain through which the riders emerged as flashes of color and movement. She saw a round shield with the sign of a charging boar painted upon it; a raised mailed fist; a battle-axe whirled above bearded heads. Closer now the dark, shadowy war band came: Sunniva could see a scarlet flapping cloak, more round shields with their belligerent painted boars, a man shouting, his words lost in the weather. As Cena shoved her again and repeated his instruction, she deflected him by the remark, "Be glad, sir, that we have not to fight these strangers."

"You? Fight?" Cena's scorn was total, swiftly transforming to insincere approval as the smallest, stockiest member of the two-score-and-three mounted men pushed his piebald stallion through the pilgrim escorts.

"Cena, my dear friend!" the rider bawled, "What are you about, crawling along with this band of holy cripples? King Harold marches for York against Hardrada and we must join him!"

He pulled off his helm and thrust a gloved hand at the bemused Cena. "You are a sight for these old eyes of mine! Do you not recognize me yet? Alric of Thornwyke. We and your brother rode together in Earl Morcar's war band against the Scots nine years ago. We rode out many times against them."

Sunniva kept a steady countenance, though her memories of Cena's absence from their homestead were not happy ones. It had been the year her mother Ethelinda had died, fading away, pale and coughing, shriveled and in pain. She had stopped doing anything—cooking, ordering the household, even the sewing that she had loved so much. And what had happened to her embroidery? Sunniva strained to remember but had to accept that Cena had probably given away her mother's sewing—or thrown it away. He had been in a rage all that year, while her mother was sick, as if Ethelinda had chosen to be ill on purpose. Her brothers had been no better. Edgar had gone raiding with his father and uncle but bullied her mercilessly whenever he returned home, and the twins—

Touching the knives at her belt, she decided not to think of the twins. By a deliberate effort of will, she listened to the bald, sunburnt Alric of Thornwyke, who was now praising Cena's older brother Bertolf, a tall, taciturn man she could scarcely bring to mind.

"The way he could use a battle mace was a wonder! Do you see him much, these days?"

"Bertolf often follows the court," Cena responded, tight-lipped. "Our paths rarely cross."

Behind Cena, Sunniva heard Ketil mutter to Edgar, "That perfumed, slinking old fool went raiding with you?"

"Against a few mangy shepherds and cow herders Bertolf was brave enough. He had his own filthy followers with him, too: those marsh men that seem to be made out of mud," Edgar replied. He sounded smug and Sunniva knew he would be wearing that self-satisfied smirk. Dismissing him and Ketil, she refocused on Alric.

"Pity that," the warrior was saying, unstrapping a boot and pouring water out of it. "He was ever a one for finding treasure. I've heard Hardrada's camp is very rich."

Sunniva sensed Cena and the three brothers tensing with interest.

"There will be spoils for everyone, once we win the battle."

"If we win," Cena qualified.

Alric clapped him on the shoulder so hard that Cena swayed in the saddle and Sunniva was hard pressed not to laugh out loud. Suppressing giggles, she waited for the warrior to offer Cena and his sons the inevitable invitation to war.

It came with Alric's next sentence. "You should ride with us! Look at you, with your three great sons! We ride for glory, for England, to defeat that Viking wretch Hardrada—you must be part of it."

"But my pilgrimage," Cena protested, to be quickly overridden.

"The saint will understand. These are Vikings, Cena!" Abruptly, Alric drew back and resettled in his saddle, giving the older man a hard, assessing glare. "Should Earl Morcar come to hear that you denied this call to arms, I know he will be disappointed."

Sunniva blushed: the threat was barbed.

"I am an old man now. My knees," Cena wavered, making her feel more humiliated. Please let me fight in his place, she prayed to St. Cuthbert, recalling that the saint's own holy, uncorrupted body had been taken from its resting place on Lindisfarne because that holy island had been ransacked by Vikings. True, that was many years past now, almost three hundred years, but Cuthbert would want revenge against the Vikings, would he not? "Please let me fight," she pleaded, not realizing, until Alric stared at her, that she had spoken aloud.

His face took on that slack-jawed look she was familiar with, but warrior that he was, he was on to her words in a moment, turning them to his advantage.

"See, Cena? Even your girl here wants to join in the fray!"

"Yes, yes, she is my daughter, gently bred," Cena stammered. "I must see her home safely first. My sons and I will do that directly."

"Nonsense! Let her return home with two of your serving lads; she will be safe enough." Alric gave her a huge grin. "Is that not right, pretty one?"

Sunniva said nothing. There was nothing to be said.

Farewells with Cena and the others were swift. Sunniva raised her hand but did not wave as they cantered off into the rain with the rest of the war party, reluctant conscripts to the last. She stared at what was left of Cena's original party: one limping mule loaded with bedding and cooking gear, two scrawny lads who would not look at her directly, one very sulky maid and the horses they were riding.

The rest of the pilgrims were already moving off, their escorts constantly scanning the skyline for more war bands. Sunniva heard the carter's wagon creak past, earthen pots rattling with every slow turn of the wheels.

"Sunniva!" cried Marc's eldest niece Alde from within the wagon. Sunniva pretended not to have heard, though she felt ashamed of doing so. She wanted to talk to Alde, a clever, resourceful child, very serious yet also plucky. She wanted to play "tag" with Judith, who could run like a hound and was as brave as a lion. She wanted to cuddle Isabella, so small and troubled. But Marc did not want her to "seek him out," or have her spending time with his youngsters. And she certainly did not want to encounter Marc, not when he had made his feelings so horribly plain.

Hurting inside, she tried to feel something for her departing "family," but the wound they had inflicted upon her by their leaving was mingled with a numb despair and, strangely, a relief. No more would she sleep in dread of Ketil and Told. No more would she be pestered by Cena, berated by Edgar.

Finally, she could be her own mistress.

She clicked her tongue and nudged her horse forward, saying to the startled Bertana and the two, greasy-haired serving lads, "Come along, or we shall lose our places in the column."

"But, Master Edgar said you should return home," Bertana protested.

"And we will, Bertana." Sunniva smiled. "After I have prayed at the shrine of St. Cuthbert in Durham. We shall complete the pilgrimage in my father's place and I will go there as his proxy."

And once in Durham I shall find work as a seamstress. I have samples in my pack, and I can do more. Bertana and the boys will find new places and I will be free.

Escape . . .

She touched her heels into her horse's bay flanks and coaxed the beast into a steady trot, facing forward and never looking at Marc as she cantered past him and the carter's wagon.

* * *

That night, the diminished pilgrim party bedded down in a wayside church. Haunted by flashbacks to the last time she had spent time in a church and been attacked, Sunniva could not relax. Bertana grudgingly found her a sleeping-tincture in their luggage but still it was almost dawn before she drifted into a heavy, troubled sleep.

She woke late, her arms and legs tingling painfully from lying on the church's tile-and-stone floor. Rolling onto her stomach, Sunniva tried to rub at her legs through her cloak, stopping abruptly as she realized that Bertana and the boys were no longer resting beside her.

"They ran off in the night," remarked a voice, a too-well-known male voice. "The other pilgrims have moved on now, too. The carter's wife tried to rouse you, but could not—"

The sleeping potion, thought Sunniva. *I asked Bertana to mix it with water. I saw her do it. Unless she poured the water down the outside of the cup.*

"—and when Judith's stamping and shrieking beside your ear failed to stir you, I knew we must wait."

Marc cleared his throat. "I have stayed until you woke naturally: I did not think you would appreciate being shaken by me."

Sunniva sat up so quickly, the whole nave seemed to turn upside down.

"Gone?" She swung her head about and saw the priest of the church praying at the high altar, with three small kneeling figures beside him, and a taller, much more powerfully built figure leaning against the stone font. There was no one else. Sunniva swallowed, her mind racing ahead. Had the boys run off with everything? The horses? The mule? "Has Bertana gone, too?"

He nodded. "I warned you of your maid, did I not? Though how she will fare in a battlefield unless she has your skill with knives, I do not like to foretell."

"What mean you?" Sunniva knew she should be acting, rushing outside to check if the pilgrims were already miles away, but she seemed paralyzed. How could her fortune have changed so quickly? "I would have paid them all, an honest price. Why should they leave me? Why should they creep away?"

"The lure of honor in battle for the lads, I wager. The draw of treasure and spoil plundered from the field of battle for the maid. Against that, madam, your wages are too small."

He held out his hand to raise her to her feet.

Sunniva held her ground, did not shrink back. "Why are you here?" she flung at him.

"I promised Hilde I would see you safe. There is a convent some few miles from here; one of the escorts vouched for its purity and safety and has given me most precise directions." He grinned. "The pilgrims were keen to go: they wish the walls of Durham snug about them sooner rather than later, although I do not think it will do them much good."

Still she did not move. "Why should I believe you?"

Marc leaned toward her, still smiling. "What part? That your own people have deserted you? That the pilgrims and escorts were happy to leave you in my charge?"

"Happy!" Sunniva was scandalized. "Happy, and you a man with blood on your hands!"

"Show me any man these days who does not. As for

the pilgrims, do not judge them too harshly. Believe
me, I can be most persuasive . . . a little gold here,
words there, a whisper of a threat of violence."

"You are enjoying this!"

"No." Suddenly he was solemn. "Believe me, lady,
this is not my first choice. Yet what choice do either of
us have on this green earth? Do you wish to stay with
the priest? Would that not be another scandal? With
me you travel with my nieces: even your betrothed
should find no reason to object."

Sunniva struck the tiles with her fist. "I am bound
for Durham!"

Marc de Sens shook his head. "Not anymore," he said.

Why had he lied to her? Marc considered this as he
left a "gift" with the priest for their unusual lodgings
last night and their bread and cheese breakfast. He
had given Hilde no promise and he owed Sunniva
nothing. The pilgrims had been content to leave her
in his charge, especially when she proved so impossible to wake.

There was another darker reason why the pilgrims
had been glad to have her off their hands, and it had
nothing to do with the "gifts" he had given to sweeten
his argument that they should go. Once the loath-
some Cena and his shambling, cowardly sons had finally done their duty and left for the battle, Sunniva
had become a problem. Her ambiguous position—
was she lady or not?—her lack of powerful friends or
family and most of all her outstanding beauty made
her, in bitter truth, a liability. She might be brave, she
might be handy with knives but against a marauding
band of men she was vulnerable. As before, with the

whoremaster and slaver, her youth and looks made
her an obvious prize and target. The pilgrims had
been right to leave her.

So what was he doing, rushing in as her defender?
She thought him a killer. No doubt she sought him
out because she was watching for proof of his murder-
ous nature. Or was it more than that? Did she actually
like him?

So? Marc asked himself savagely, as he saddled and
checked their horses and the girls' ponies while Sunniva and his three waited out of the rain in church.
What did her reasons matter? She was already betrothed.

*Be glad she has not asked you why you are still so keen to
have her in your company, for you would not want to answer,
even if you could.* Shaking his head free of that discom-
forting thought, Marc ducked his head under the
door lintel and reentered the church.

She came to him at once, hurrying ahead of his
nieces, wearing a glad, bright look that reminded him
achingly of Roland, his dead, burned brother. He
growled at her, to cover his hurt. "Ready?"

"We are," she said, adding in that direct way of hers.
"What did Bertana leave me?"

"Both horse and mule and I would say half the luggage." Marc smoothed out a coil in his beard, wondering even as he acted why he bothered: Sunniva would
not care how he looked. "The guards on watch last
night probably asked too large a bribe for Bertana
and the serving lads to take everything."

He had "paid" the guards that morning, when,
under his questions they had admitted as much and
clearly expected a reward for doing no more than their

job. But Sunniva did not need to know that, especially when her narrow shoulders dropped with relief.

"Thank God," she murmured, before turning her sea-green eyes on him again and asking with a perspicacity that both amused and alarmed him, "Or should I thank you, sir?"

"Marc." He wanted to hear her say his name. He ruffled Isabella's hair as she scampered to stand by him and motioned to the hovering Alde and Judith that their ponies were ready and waiting for them.

As the three hared off outside, he looked again at his latest charge. "We should go: the rain has stopped for now." He wanted to see her in her right element, in the sunlight. And they really should move.

"Why have you turned away from the pilgrimage, Marc?" The instant they were on their way, she asked the most difficult question, the one for which he had no clear answers, only instinct.

"It felt wrong," he said, surprised to be admitting even that.

She said nothing, did not even raise her eyebrows, and he found himself admitting more.

"Whatever Alfric said—"

"Alric?" she softly suggested.

He was tempted to say "Alfric" again, just to have her correct him, but said, more seriously, "The roads here in the north will be filled with men. Armed men, hungry for loot and trouble. Durham is another four, five days' travel. The convent of the holy sisters is six miles away." He scratched his beard, embarrassed to be explaining. "Those are better odds."

She did raise her eyebrows now.

"When I was in Constantinople, I often knew when the enemy would attack," Marc labored on. "The lord I served thought me blessed by God—or the devil; he did not care which. I saved him twice from assassins."

"As you saved me," Sunniva remarked, her voice very low. "For which I will be ever grateful."

Warmed by her gratitude, he told her what he had told no one else. "I do not know how I knew, but I did. I often did. A sense of impending darkness . . . It is as if you can hear a shadow: that is how it feels to me."

She regarded him steadily, without mockery or fear. "The tumbler who taught me to throw knives said to me once that our senses can be trained so that reactions can seem beyond natural. Perhaps that is what has happened to you; with your skill in warfare you can anticipate war."

"Perhaps. Mother says I am fey, like her." *Enough, Marc.* He warned himself. *You do not want to be straying any further into this, into dreams and signs. You dreamed last night, too, and there was a very clear sign—*

"And the pilgrims?"

"If they ride swiftly they should be safe. But Durham—" Marc frowned. "I feel a dark shadow in my heart about the city. I may be wrong—I have been very badly wrong before—but still I dare not ignore it. That is why I left the group. I want my girls safe. They have suffered enough."

Sunniva leaned closer. Under cover of brushing a fly from the flank of his horse, she whispered, "Their parents?"

Marc felt the breath in his chest tighten. "My elder brother Roland and his wife Joanna died when their town house in Dinan burnt down. Alde and her sisters are orphans."

He watched Sunniva blush, turning her head away from him, though not before he saw the gleam of tears in her eyes.

"They were staying in the town house, were they not?" she asked softly. "They were in the fire, too."

Marc nodded, the tight heaviness in his body persisting, like a boulder in his chest. Grief and a terrible, deserved sense of failure swept through him. For all his foresight, he had not foreseen this. "Our mother, too. She was able to escape into the street before the staircase burst into flames. I got Judith and Alde out, went back for Isabella."

Suddenly he was there again in the sooty, orange, pulsing glare, fire licking everywhere, Joanna screaming for her children, Roland coughing and retching, trying to beat out flames with his bedding.

"I had just reached Isabella when there was a huge roar from the fire, like a maddened beast. Then the roof and ceiling caved in. I saw Roland and Joanna between puddles of fire, and then nothing, only a wall of flame. They were terrified and I lost them. They were right before me, only an arm-stretch away, and then, with that roar and the ceiling going, they vanished."

Marc spurred his horse, urging it to a gallop. He wanted no more talk.

Chapter Eleven

For the first hour all was well. Sunniva felt her heart rising like the skylarks in the fields and scrubland about them and her hands stopped flitting back and forth from her reins to her knives. She was still not entirely convinced of Marc's honesty where the convent was concerned, but she trusted him enough to go with him without protest, until events showed otherwise. She was inclined to believe him about the pilgrimage and Durham, if only because the practical side of her recalled the many, many times Durham had been attacked, even in her lifetime.

And he had not been lying about his nieces or his brother.

Sunniva listened as Alde told her the end of a joke she had heard many times before and laughed as if it was new to her, her eyes skipping ahead to where Marc rode, his back very straight, flicking the ends of his reins against his long, powerful thighs. His hair was growing longer now, so much so that its ends curled against his neck and dangled over his collar. He suited longer hair, she thought. It made him look less Breton-Norman.

She wished he had not lost his family like that, so

cruelly. How can I comfort him? she thought, wishing she had been able to take him into her arms when he told her of his loss. But then, he would doubtless be stiff-necked with her, remind her, yet again, that she was betrothed.

Perhaps I should have trusted him with the truth.

As if he knew her thought, Marc twisted round in the saddle. Sunniva's stomach tingled as he smiled at Alde, Judith and Isabella, his smile including her, too.

"You do well?" he called out.

"Judith has picked up another iron nail, Uncle Marc!" Isabella shrieked, her voice bubbling with excitement. "That is her seventh this week!"

"I do not know how you find them, Judith," Marc said, scanning the road behind them for possible soldiers. "What will you make with them?"

Judith threw her older sister a knowing look. "A scold's bridle?" she suggested.

"I think you would need more metal for that," Sunniva dropped in as Alde's brown eyes darkened and narrowed into tight black slits. "But you would have enough for a cross," she added, while Judith recounted her roadside treasures.

"You are such a baby, Judy," Alde said.

Judith's head jerked up, her face flaming. "I am not."

"Are," said Alde, glancing at Sunniva and mirroring how she rode.

"Are, are!" yelled Isabella.

"Hush, little one," said Marc easily, reining in his horse. "I think I can hear another skylark."

They had made a game of counting how many larks were singing near the road, but a tension in his voice prompted Sunniva to drop back slightly, so she and not Judith was at the end of their tiny "column." Sure enough, after a few more jangling paces, Marc looked round again and said, "These woods are a good place to stop to eat whatever the priest's woman has packed for us."

"For sure," Sunniva said quickly, using a roadside boulder to dismount.

As she expected, Alde copied her, then Judith and Isabella, and soon they were leading their mounts into a copse of hazel and ash, putting a shield of greenery between themselves and the road.

"Here." Sunniva sat down in a natural basin, calculating it would be impossible for anyone to see them from the road. Spotting a fairy ring of mushrooms circling a grassy birch stump, she thought of another way of keeping the children quiet.

"If you are very still, you can hear the wood elves talking to each other," she whispered to the girls. "The fairy ring marks their meeting place. Wood elves are invisible to us, but we may listen for their voices. The closer to the ground you are, the more you should hear."

Alde and Judith looked skeptical at this, but Isabella flattened herself onto the leaves and bracken. Moments later, Judith and then Alde followed, leaving their ponies peacefully cropping the turf.

"My thanks," Marc mouthed as he passed, winding swiftly back through the trees in a half crouch to watch the road.

Sunniva nodded and began to unwrap the meat, cheese and bread from the rough cloth the priest's woman had put together for them.

"Where is Uncle Marc?" piped Isabella.

"Gone to make water," Sunniva lied, her ears straining as she felt a new spot of rain trickle down her hand. Glancing up, she saw the sky had gone gray again.

It cannot be helped, she told herself, and at least if it pours then the men-at-arms will be riding as quickly as possible to escape it. For she could hear it now: the telltale rumble of galloping hooves. How many horses? Ten? A score? How many men? A dozen?

"Eat some cheese." She handed Alde and Judith some, not reproving Isabella when the child stuffed a huge lump into her mouth. It was raining steadily now, hopefully a further shield for them. "Quiet now. We do not want these men to see us."

Even at six years old, Isabella knew better than to ask why, though she did crawl into Sunniva's lap. Her two sisters huddled close and Sunniva put her arms round both, saying in a light voice, "The fairy ring will keep us safe, we need only be still."

"Uncle Marc?" whimpered Judith, fraying a chunk of bread anxiously with her hands.

"Uncle Marc, too." It was hard for Sunniva not to check for her knives. Smiling at the three, upturned faces, she said, "I will pray for us."

In her heart she was already praying. Please let Marc be safe. Please do not let him be spotted. Please do not take him away.

A shadow crawled from a patch of brambles close to them. Even as she stiffened, her hands flying off Alde's and Judith's shoulders toward her waist, she recognized the figure on hands and knees.

His face dripping rain, Marc slithered into the hollow beside her and clasped her and his nieces. For a moment, he hugged her so tightly, Sunniva thought her back might break, then he released her, placing a finger on Alde's opening mouth.

"There are fifteen armed men riding on the road, Alde: too many even for me."

"Not pilgrims?" Alde whispered.

"Not pilgrims," Marc replied, his eyes dark. "Listen! You will hear them pass."

They all listened. The mounted band of men seemed to take a long time to ride by, rain bouncing sharply off shields and helmets, the horses clattering and slithering on the churned-up road.

"'Tis well for this rain," Sunniva found herself breathing, "for our tracks will be submerged."

He threw her a half-exasperated, half-indulgent look. "Ever you match your name. I do not know how."

"What would you have me do?" The question burst from her, startling Sunniva herself and worse, even as the band of men cantered on so close that she could feel the ground shaking, another urgent demand sprang from her lips. "Who are you to reprove me? You finish nothing you begin! Breaking your pilgrimage vow, dragging these children—"

She almost yelled as a brawny arm yanked round her middle, but that would have alerted the armed mob passing. Struggling, kicking, she tried to free herself but was dragged out of the hollow and smacked onto the springy grass like a landed fish. A hand, heavy it seemed as an anvil, pinned her shoulder.

Marc loomed above her, sitting astride her now so she could not escape. "No, you don't." He had both hands on her shoulders and she could not reach her knives.

"Let me up!" she hissed.

"In a moment, madam, but first you will attend me."

They were both whispering while the final group of riders passed by and the three little girls calmly and silently ate the rest of the cheese.

"I am listening," Sunniva goaded. Her teeth ached and her spine ached, her whole body felt jolted. She wanted to slap him but was afraid the other warriors might hear. He had not actually sat *on* her, and for that small mercy Sunniva was grateful—though she would never tell him.

Marc took a deep breath, resentment seething in his face. "'These children,' as you call them, are my responsibility."

"So why not take better care of them? Why bring them on pilgrimage?" Sunniva retorted. "A holy journey and no easy one."

"My mother is old. There is no one else for them, understand? They must be with me!" He looked as if he wanted to shake her, his fingers tightening until he realized what he was doing.

"But such a journey! When it is your own conscience you should look to!"

"By all the saints! There is no arguing with you!"

Taking her wrists in one hand he lunged. Sunniva flinched, expecting a blow, opening her eyes as she felt his body against hers, his mouth on hers.

"They are kissing," Judith cried, and Alde said something Sunniva missed. From being cold and wet and dripping with rain she felt to be bathed in sunlight, warmth coursing through her. His kiss was not rending or greedy but gentle and searching, its heat sweeping down from their lips over her breasts and belly, tingling in her loins. As he rolled off her, taking her with him so she lay on top of him, she closed her eyes and let herself go deeper into their kiss, not sure where she ended and Marc began.

"We are mad," Marc whispered, breaking from her. "In possible view of armed men and in rain, we sport like maid and lad in a woodland glade."

Sunniva licked her lips, tasting him. "We are in a wood," she began.

"But not alone, and not even, by God, safe." Marc cupped her face, his fingers trembling slightly against her cheek. "We should not do this—I should not—"

As if drawn by invisible strings he bent his head and kissed her again, then abruptly released her.

"The warriors—I must make sure they are gone," he said and scrambled away, leaving her caught between confusion and delight.

Chapter Twelve

"What now?" Alde demanded, her strong jaw setting as he had seen Roland's do so often when they were children, usually before he pitched himself into a fight.

"Your uncle will think of something," Sunniva stepped between them, gently jogging Judith's thin little arm. "May I see your nails? They could be useful. Yes. Yes!" she exclaimed, as if the seven rusting pieces were relics of the holy cross. "Keep them safe, Judith. These will be our saviors."

Alde and then Isabella bustled forward, neither sister wanting to miss anything, and three heads with drenched rattails of hair hung over a bursting-with-pride Judith and her outstretched palm. Marc met Sunniva's eyes. "What now?" he mouthed.

"Now it has stopped raining, I must look at my packs," she said, and turned away from the swollen river that faced them, walking to her mule.

"Keep away from the water, girls," Marc warned, keen to follow. As always, he was glad of the excuse to snatch a moment alone with Sunniva, though he did not want to examine his reasons why. She is betrothed, he reminded himself, while another part questioned, why then did she receive and return his kiss so ardently? Why did she have no ring, no token from the blessed Caedmon of Whitby?

"Your betrothed. What manner of man is he?" he growled, satisfied when she looked startled, then ashamed.

"Much like most farmers. Stocky. Red-cheeked. Speaking ever of the weather." She opened the first pannier on the back of the mule and began parting the cloths inside, glancing at the sky. "I know the rain has eased, but I would not have these wet," she explained, stopping a moment to examine something within the pannier he could not see. "Do you think the soldiers destroyed the bridge after they crossed?"

Marc studied the broken struts by the edge of the swirling brown river and shook his head. "The weight of water itself did this, smashed the bridge," he replied, "and you have not answered my question."

She frowned, staring at the river, then the cloud-filled sky. "Will Bertana be safe?" she asked abruptly.

"Her kind, the selfish ones, tend to prosper," Marc replied, holding up a hand to Sunniva's protest. "I do not mean all women, nor all maids. But tell me, what does your betrothed like?"

As he spoke, he realized what was wrong: Sunniva never talked of Caedmon. Most girls took every chance to mention their betrothed, so why not her?

"Is he a brute?" he asked softly.

"No!" Her face blazed as the sun missing from this bleak, lowering landscape seemed to rise in her cheeks. "Not at all! Singing," she gasped, lowering her head to rummage some more in her pack. "Caedmon loves to sing."

I can sing, Marc almost said, before sense crushed

his tongue. He watched her bring out a heavy cloth and he pointed at it, his eyebrows raised in a question.

"I thought." She drummed her fingers on the edge of the pannier. "I wondered if we might make a raft: lash cloth and timber together and float over the river."

Marc had a vision of her in the water, soaked to the skin, her gown clinging. He closed his eyes but that made it worse. Thinking he would soon need to race into the river to disguise his present state, he strove to think.

Out of a spin of ideas and feelings he snatched two. "The girls cannot swim," he said, "and the current looks strong. Even the horses could be swept away."

"Yes, you are right." She bit her lip. "I am sorry."

He wanted to take her hand, tell her never to be sorry. "It was a good idea," he said, hating the way he sounded, so stiff. "We can follow the river, find another place to cross."

"Of course." Tentatively, she asked, "But then, do you think we shall reach the convent before nightfall?"

"Better after nightfall than not at all."

The river meandered and so did they, curving this way and that through tall grasses and giant reed mace on the riverbank while the rain fell steadily on them. Sunniva played counting games with the children and took Isabella on her horse with her; then Judith must have a turn, and Alde, and still the river snaked through the valley and the rain half-blinded and chilled them.

Bringing up the rear, Marc was amazed afresh by her cheerful resilience. For himself, he was relieved when the river finally widened onto a sandy bed where it seemed they could cross in relative safety.

"There was a ford here, once," Sunniva remarked. She touched the shedding bark of an alder tree with her foot, pointing to the perfect circular mark. "See? Rope chafing."

"A guide rope across," Marc agreed. "Well spotted."

She flushed at the compliment. "I have rope," she ventured. "If you have a bow, perhaps we can shoot a line across?"

"Nothing easier," he said, and smiled as she smiled.

Why not? he decided, as he removed his great bow from its hide cover. She was betrothed and another's but that did not mean they could not speak, could not be pleasant. If she smiled at him, why not smile back?

"I'm not in Byzantium now," he said aloud.

She looked puzzled, and he could not resist adding, "In the city of Constantinople, also known as Byzantium, I learned not to smile at any pretty woman, in case her husband challenged me."

He expected her to be confounded, but instead she grinned and asked, "Really? Did you win?"

He shrugged, not wanting to admit that he had—it was a memory he was less easy with, these days. To his relief, Sunniva said nothing more but busied herself with keeping the girls' ponies and the mule well back as he notched an arrow.

He was a good shot and the distance was no more than the height of a battlement. Even with a rope attached, he could fire the arrow and hit the opposite alder tree, the iron point driving straight through the trunk. Marc gave the rope a few tugs, to be sure, then tied off the nearest end.

"I shall go first to test the way," he said, feeling the space between his shoulders prickle as he spoke. It was not exactly a foreshadowing, but he would be glad when this part of their journey was over. "Do not be troubled," he told a worried-looking Alde, "I have done this before, many times."

Never in a northern river such as this, though, where he could not see the bottom.

"Luck to you, Marc de Sens," Sunniva murmured, as he rode past her. "I know all will be well for you."

Her well-wish was like a talisman in his heart. He rode slowly into the chill water, allowing Theo to pick his own way. The river bottom was smooth and firm, with few large stones, and he was heartened when the water came no higher than the chestnut's hocks. Turning to look back, he waved to the four figures on the bank and tied the line securely around the alder. Again, he felt the space between his shoulders itch, but told himself he was merely anxious about the girls' riding abilities in the river. And Sunniva's, too.

In the event, all went sweetly. The rest of his crossing was as easy as the first part and he returned to guide Alde and Judith over without incident. Judith squeaked when the water washed over her shoes and she grabbed at the rope, but soon began to move along the line as Sunniva called out encouragement: "You are doing really well, Judith, a true credit to your noble name! That is right, keep going, hand over hand and guide your pony with your knees. That's right!"

A few more rapid steps by the shaggy ponies and his two elder nieces had reached the far bank. He hugged both, proud of their courage.

"Wait here while I fetch Isabella and Sunniva," he told them.

"No need, Uncle Marc," Alde replied, smirking at his confusion. Judith also giggled and pointed.

Following her wavering finger Marc felt himself start, his guts tensing. Sunniva, with Isabella sitting before her, was at the midway point of the river. She was riding one-handed, the other touching the rope he had strung as a guideline across the river. Recklessly to his mind, the leading reins of Isabella's pony were tied to her own horse's saddle, a trick he used himself but did not expect copied by a woman.

He could tell Sunniva was calm, in control, safe, but still it was hard to wait. Reluctant to move or even breathe, oblivious to Alde's excited chatter, he flinched each time her bay horse took a step.

Another ragged breath from him, more "Look at her ride! Look how she goes!" from the heroine-worshipping Alde, and Sunniva drew beside him, river water streaming from the hem of her gown in a lithe, sinuous shape, like the tail of a mermaid. She smiled and offered him the leading rein.

"If you will take Isabella and her pony, I can fetch my mule," she said, deftly threading her horse closer to make the transfer of the giggling six-year-old easier. "The line you set across has made it so simple and secure, easy to follow and grasp if the horse misses its footing—"

"I shall get the mule," Marc interrupted, indignant that she should think he needed such lavish praise for a straightforward task, or worse, that he would let her wade the river a second time. "You wait here."

"Yes, Uncle," she mouthed, a retort that made him choke on laughter.

"I shall know how to deal with you if you stir," he warned.

"As you say," she answered mildly.

He almost laughed out loud then, except the sky suddenly darkened above them and thunder rumbled overhead.

"No! It is not overhead!" he exclaimed, understanding

his own senses at last and plunging back into the river, urging the great chestnut to a splashing canter. "Stay back!" he yelled, as the rain streamed down again and, across the river, a group of men broke cover.

"Go, great heart!" Marc shouted, flicking his heels against the steaming sides of Theo, giving the stallion his head. On the far bank, the mule cropped peacefully round its picket, unconcerned by the appalling weather and the five lightly armed men stumbling toward it.

On foot. No bows. Spears, but no swords. Straggling foot soldiers. The calculations ran through Marc's head swifter than the falling rain as he hurled his challenge.

"Away, or you die! Away!"

He burst out of the swirl of rain, a grim-featured man on a tall brute of a horse. Yelling, he unsheathed his sword and the five scattered, two blundering into the river in their panic and screaming in English to be saved by their fellows. Leaving them to it, Marc hacked through the rope tethering the mule and prodded the reluctant, braying beast into the water. As soon as it was heading for the far bank, he severed the rope line he had set across the two banks. He and Theo knew the way across by now.

"This way, Marc!" Sunniva was calling from the distant bank. "Almost there!"

Something in her voice made him look round. More men had arrived at the river and one had a bow. Hanging low over his horse's neck, Marc urged the stallion to more speed in the churning waters.

"No!" he heard Sunniva scream, as the cold, hard prickling between his shoulders became more intense. Behind he heard the paff! paff! of arrows hitting the water and then, astonishingly, saw Sunniva standing with his bow, her face rigid with concentration and scarlet with effort as she pulled back the taut, unyielding bowstring.

"Take cover!" he shouted, but she took no notice, her whole body shaking as she struggled to draw his bow.

She managed halfway and then the string slipped from her hand, the arrow loosened too low and flat, disappearing into the river less than a spear's-length behind him.

Sunniva screamed and tried to notch another arrow but Theo was moving more swiftly now, his feet sure as they reached the shallows. He and Marc burst from the water and Marc hauled his would-be-savior across his saddle. To his surprise she was burning, her face brilliant with anger.

"Let me down!" she yowled, kicking against him, slapping his bow against him. "I can fight! I can help! I saved you!"

"So you did! No, I mean it." He was tempted to laugh, she was so prettily indignant, but he recognized the hurt behind her protest and the justice of her complaint. It was true, anyway: she had helped him.

"Easy there." He landed her lightly on the grass and slid swiftly off the saddle. His instinct warned that the soldiers had not finished their pursuit. "Where are the girls?"

Silently, almost scornfully, she jerked a hand farther along the bank and he saw them, hidden behind a stand of alders, their faces pinched and blank in shock.

"Come then." Ashamed that his three had been subjected to this latest alarm, Marc hurried them all away, closing his ears on the shouts, threats and curses issuing from the other side of the river.

Chapter Thirteen

The convent was very small and very old and they had reached it only after a long, increasingly dry, increasingly hot journey, arriving hours after twilight, but now Alde, Judith and Isabella were sleeping, bundled all together in one bed, in the novices' cell. They were the only girls there, except for Sunniva, who watched them from the threshold while she spoke softly with Marc.

Or rather, Marc spoke to her. Since he had beckoned her out of the cell he had done all the talking.

"I am glad they sleep," he was saying. "Even my haunted Isabella has slept soundly for many nights, ever since"—he stopped, words seeming to hover on his lips, then abruptly changed whatever he was about to add—"ever since the night of Largebelly's feast."

A demon goaded Sunniva to contradict him. "Isabella is not haunted."

"Not with you, for sure," Marc agreed and he smiled. "I did not think a straw pallet could survive such a pounding as she gave this one here. She has not romped in this way before sleep for months."

His voice faded and Sunniva knew he was thinking

of his dead kindred. Quickly, to divert him, she asked, "What think you of this place?"

His bushy eyebrows drew together as he scratched his beard. "I have not seen so many old women before this evening. Or is it the nuns' habits that makes them seem so gray and sparse? When I speak to them, I feel as if I talk to flitting shadows: they scurry off, squeaking, and I am no wiser."

"They liked your gold," Sunniva reminded him.

"That they did." Marc leaned past her to replace a piece of hanging wattle plaster with a dab of spit and his thumb. "I wonder if I should offer to replace the crossbeam over their refectory doorway? It is riddled with woodworm."

"A knight of Constantinople, working wood?" Sunniva teased, wondering, even as she spoke, why she did so. He had made his lack of interest in her plain, but then there were those barbed comments about her betrothed, and Marc's kiss. He had kissed her, more than once . . .

"As a boy, I made ships," he answered.

"I see," Sunniva said, intrigued by the thought but wary of pursuing it. Any conversation with this man was unwise. He might ask her more about Caedmon.

I wish I had never told him I was betrothed.

But then, what difference would that first lie make? Perhaps even if he knew she was in truth free, Marc would still deal with her as a nothing, sometimes useful as a child-keeper, sometimes pretty enough to embrace, but no more than that.

What am I but the daughter of a slave? What is he, but a woman-killer? Yet how can he be such? My every instinct tells me he is not!

"What will you do now?" she asked, speaking as much to herself as to Marc.

Again he scratched his beard, a nervous gesture.

"I spoke with the abbess before the nuns retired tonight—I think she was the abbess—she was the youngest and least timid of the seven old women here—and she has agreed to shelter you and my three . . ."

He had done that for her, Sunniva thought, her mood lifting.

". . . While I must be away for a day or so. I must find out what is happening with the Viking invasion. Though I think I was right not to continue the pilgrimage to Durham, and the signs are such that I am confident my choice has been vindicated, I dare not move the girls any great distance until I know the roads will be safe."

He straightened, dusting more loose wattle plaster off his leggings and spoke now without looking at her directly. "I mean to offer my sword to the English king, unless I am already too late."

What signs? Sunniva wondered, while her mind also explored his last statement. Had she heard right? "You mean to—"

"I have no lands in this country." He spoke as if to Isabella, very slowly, explaining as he continued, "I came to teach the old king's warriors how to fight on horseback, but now old King Edward is dead and new King Harold does not know me. I must win his trust if I am to have a choice whether to stay in England. What better way than to fight for him?"

Sunniva felt a sudden chill at the idea of Marc in battle. For an instant, she pitied his enemies, then thought of another aspect. "What of William of Normandy? Surely if he comes and you have fought for King Harold, William will be angry?"

She thought her questions reasonable, but Marc merely snorted. "He is becalmed, the winds of the narrow sea are against him. He will not come this summer. King Harold will hold England." He drummed his fingers on his sword belt, muttering, "He will if I have anything to do with it."

Suddenly, he looked at her. "Where is Whitby? When I return from the battle to collect my brood, I can take you to your betrothed."

"I, I"—for an instant, Sunniva floundered. Where was Whitby? "That is generous of you, but there is no need." Inspiration struck. "I will send for my betrothed."

"For sure." He gave her a considering look from those dark, wine-colored eyes of his, but to her relief he did not pursue the matter. "I must be away to look to our horses: I think the nuns here know little enough of sheep, much less ponies."

"And the mule," Sunniva prompted. "Do not forget him."

He smiled at her then. "How could I do that, seeing how much work the beast cost the both of us?"

He touched her cheek with his fingers and stalked away, whistling.

Chapter Fourteen

Marc hated to leave the next day. It was the first time he had left Alde and her sisters since the night of the fire and he was anxious they might slip back into grief and nightmares. Sunniva was with them, though, dry-eyed and smiling, radiating confidence as she wished him Godspeed and a safe return. He knew she disapproved of his action but for the sake of his children she restricted her comments to a few pointed words: "I trust your instincts are as sound on this as they were at the river. Luck to you, Marc de Sens."

"And to you, Lady Sunniva." He wanted to kiss her, but not while the nuns were watching. As he swung himself into the saddle she hugged Isabella, Judith and Alde, then hurried across the tiny, muddy convent yard to his horse.

"If you encounter Cena and his sons," she said, in a low, tense voice, "Give them my greetings."

"I will. I promise." He clasped her cold hand in his, felt it tremble and realized how hard his departure was for her. In a flash of understanding, he realized the courage involved in waiting—he would find it difficult, much tougher than riding to war. The not knowing, the terrible uncertainty—it needed bravery of a more resolute, subtle kind than the animal cut-and-thrust of battle, where thought was replaced by raw passion for survival.

Shamed, he rode off quickly without further speech, without looking back. As the miles sped under Theo's plunging hooves he pictured Alde, Judith and Isabella tight about Sunniva, her arms spread over them like protective angel's wings. They would be safe with her: he trusted her care of them without question.

Gratitude for Sunniva warmed him and he spurred Theo on, glad to be alive in the same world as such a woman.

She may be betrothed, he told himself, but in these warlike times, who knows what can happen? Caedmon of Whitby could die in battle. The grim thought pleased him as, whistling, he turned south, toward York, and prepared to find King Harold's war-host.

He rode hard all day and through the night, stopping only when his horse began to falter. A few midnight hours sheltering under a holly tree, with only Theo and two stray sheep for company failed to quash his spirits, although he missed his lady sunshine. He slept and dreamed of Sunniva: her smile, her walk, the way her voice lifted at the ends of words, and how she swayed in time to the beat whenever any music was made.

He stirred early, jolted awake by a sheep nibbling his cloak, and found the heavens washed and pale, the sun a silver-and-gold disc sliding free of the distant hills. Stretching, Marc whistled for the sheer pleasure of being alive, and for the lack of rain for a second day. It seemed a good omen to him, a sign that Sunniva and his three girls were still safe.

Was he right to leave them? Yet if he were to stay in England, make a new life here for him and his nieces, he had to find out what was happening. As he had learned from serving in Constantinople as part of the Imperial guard, to influence events you had to be part of them. If a battle was to be fought here in the north, he had to be in it.

And on the winning side, the cynic in him whispered, while he fell into a glorious daydream. King Harold, victorious, honoring him, granting him whatever he desired. He would ask for Sunniva: lands, treasure and Sunniva.

He smiled and rode faster, hastening to meet his new fortune.

Farther south he ran into a group of men loyal to Lord Morcar of the North. They were weary and battle-worn, having fought with the Vikings several days earlier, at a place south of York, called Fulford. Both sides had sustained losses but these men of Lord Morcar had endured enough: they were going home. Marc's questions about King Harold's force were met with blank looks and the shaking of heads. The men were friendly enough, glad he was no Viking, but they knew nothing more. Marc deemed it prudent to bid them farewell and move on.

He came to a stream and followed its winding track, knowing that York was sited on a great river and that there would be settlements somewhere close to a source of fresh water. The day grew brighter, then as the sun dipped in the west, he found the stream broadening to a ford.

By the ford he saw his first dying Englishman.

It was almost a family deathbed: Marc was reminded

of when his father had died and all his kindred and servants had filed past the foot of his great bed to bid him farewell. The Englishman was clearly a noble with a retinue of followers, all guarding him as he lay, swathed in cloaks and furs, on the damp grass and earth, and gasped his life away.

Marc felt like an intruder. Without asking the questions that had hurled themselves at his lips—Where was the battle? How was it going? Who was winning?— he raised his hand in a salute and sped off, riding across the ford and straight off the track. He made for the crown of a low hill, hoping to find a place where he could look out.

Galloping hard through grass and gorse for another half mile, he knew he had chosen the right way. There were few places in this broad vale where the ground rose enough to see far into the distance but this small ridge was enough. As he cantered to its low "peak," he saw another river spreading before him, and a wooden bridge on the floodplain of that river. Close to the bridge was the battlefield.

Marc drew rein, not caring that he was sky-lined, for there was no living warriors left to see. He had come too late to the battle: all who were left here were the scavengers and the dead.

Now he could see the corpses, black with crows, and snapped spears. A glint of a broken battle-axe, arrows stuck into a hawthorn bush and a body draped over the lower branches of the bush like a bloody cloak. He was glad the wind was blowing on his back: the stench in the vale would be terrible.

He edged Theo forward, sensing the stallion's reluctance and hardly eager to approach himself. Once, the horse's hoof kicked against a helmet without a head, causing Theo to skitter sideways and a flock of crows to streak skyward, breaking the heavy silence with their cawing. Feeling his mount shudder, Marc stroked Theo's long, glossy neck and murmured a few reassurances in Breton. After a few more paces, he dismounted and led the horse on foot.

Not a moment too soon, for here were sights to chill the bravest war charger. A head without a helmet. A severed hand. Another broken axe head. A body hacked and gouged by many spears. Flinching, Marc spotted a human scavenger: woman or man, he could not tell from the slight, ragged figure as it bent over a corpse, doing something with a knife. Feeling the bile rise in his throat he passed on.

Who had won here? The Norse King Hardrada? Or King Harold? Where were the survivors of the armies now?

"Water! Please, water . . ."

Marc stared at the whispering, creeping corpse-come-to-life at his feet then reacted. Pushing away another body, he knelt and turned the bloody wreck over, spraying the man's face with his water as he tried to find the fellow's mouth. It was hard to tell: his nose had been sliced off.

Holding the man's shoulders, Marc supported him as he drank. He had been in battles many times but never the aftermath, never lingered amongst the dead and broken. It horrified him and he wondered how many others lay injured on this field of slaughter.

"Water, please, for my father. He is close . . . somewhere. I cannot see . . ."

"Do not trouble, man," said a new voice somewhere above him.

Still on his knees, Marc twisted round and met the

eyes of a Englishman, small, wiry and sunburnt, who had approached on foot.

"What do you mean?" he demanded.

"He will be dead within the hour. I have seen it many times already." The little Englishman indicated the blood-soaked field. "Heat and weariness: it has felled both sides, especially the enemy. We have been picking up Viking mail shirts all day."

It was hot riding yesterday, Marc recalled. "What is this place?"

"The bridge by Stamford." A nod to the river and its bridge, both choked with blood and bodies.

"Who won?" he asked the stranger, who grinned.

"We did, of course," he said. "We caught the Norse napping, waiting to exchange hostages. It was hot and dry, so they must have seen our dust rising as we came, but still we beat them."

Marc scowled. "I have arrived too late. My horse went lame," he added, in case an explanation was deemed necessary.

"Do not let it trouble you." The wiry Englishman clapped him hard on the shoulder. "We will bury our own and leave the Vikings to rot and then get back south, fend off William the Bastard. Kill a few Normans, that should ease the bloodthirst of your blade."

"Water!" A straining whisper broke through this curious exchange.

The stranger shrugged. "For me, I would save my water, but you must do as you think." He nodded and passed on, exactly as if they were townsmen chatting in a street. A few moments later, Marc heard him hailing another Englishman.

Shaking his head at the strangeness of war, Marc mopped the dying man's forehead and tried to find

his mouth again to give him more drink. As he heard
the frenzied gulping, he was glad he was dressed in
the English fashion, with beard and hair to match.
The stranger had thought him a thegn, one of the
English fighters. It saved many questions.

"Better?" he asked the ruin lying on his knees.

"I know you." The man clawed at his arm. "You will
see my father and brothers and me well buried, at a
church. Promise me!"

Father and brothers . . . Marc realized who it was.
"Edgar Cena-son," he said flatly, marveling at how fate
had brought them together. Sunniva had asked him
to give her kin her greeting and here they were.

"Your promise!" Edgar gargled, coughing in his indignation.

"I promise," Marc repeated. How he would do so
with only one horse and where he would find a church
he had as yet little idea, but these were small matters.
He touched the neck of the body sprawled closest and
found no beat of life. Rolling over a second corpse he
saw Cena, mouth frozen in a shout. The third body,
with its guts spilling onto the turf, must be one or other
of the twins.

Numbly, he tried to think of a prayer for the dead,
but failed. While Edgar lived, though, he could do
one last service for Sunniva.

He gave Edgar another drink, glancing down the
man's upper torso. Edgar had a knife wound in his
belly, low down, one of the worst kinds. Marc sagged.
The English stranger was right: by the end of today,
if not sooner, Sunniva's brother would be dead.

Fighting down a wave of revulsion at dealing with a
man with less than half a face, Marc lowered his head.

"Edgar, where is Caedmon? Is he here on this field of battle?"

"Who?"

"Caedmon. Caedmon of Whitby. The betrothed of your sister."

"No sister," Edgar mumbled, spraying drool onto Marc's tunic.

Fighting a terrible pity, which urged him to let the poor man die in peace, Marc persisted. "You and she lived in the same house. She cared for you all as a sister does her brothers. She waited on her father, your father. She is your last remaining close kin."

"Not ours!"

More spit landed on Marc's tunic.

"Where is Caedmon of Whitby, her betrothed!" Marc hauled Edgar into a sitting position, wincing as Edgar grimaced. "Can you see him here?"

He knew he was being ruthless but he had to know.

"Where, Edgar? Then you can rest."

Propped by Marc, holding his injured belly, Edgar began to shake, making a curious whooping noise that Marc finally realized was laughter.

"Caedmon of Whitby?" Edgar gargled. "The man who sang for Abbess Hilda of Whitby?"

And on this battlefield, above the scrabbling of crows and the urgent, deadly work of those who despoiled the dead, Marc heard Sunniva's voice, clear as in a dream: *"Caedmon loves to sing."*

"That is the one," he said.

Edgar's small, deep-set eyes were suddenly bright with malice. "Then he is four hundred years old! Caedmon was a shepherd at Whitby who could not sing a note until God touched his tongue. The story is famous. And Sunniva told you he was her intended!"

Shocked, Marc lowered Edgar back onto the flattened grass. "You lie!"

"I speak true and you know it! She does this. Toys with men. Leads them on. Pretends she is bound. It is a game."

Marc recoiled, sickened by Edgar's malice, but still the wet, gasping voice went on.

"She likes men yearning after her. Why else is she still unwed, at twenty? My father tried to make a marriage: twice she has given betrothal vows. Both times the men paid to be released from her: they were weary of being made fools of by her, by her flirting and eyeing other men."

"Lies!"

Marc punched the grass beside Edgar, who did not flinch. He was dead, staring into the sunlight, his mouth twisted in another bout of laughter.

It took Marc the rest of the day to fulfill his now-bitter promise to Edgar. The church he found was dedicated to St. Jude, which made him smile. Jude is not so far a name from Judas.

He did not believe Edgar, he told himself, as he paid the priest for the burials. The man had been as spiteful in death as in life: he would be a fool to heed anything he said.

But Sunniva . . . Why had she not told him she was free? To preserve her chastity? Did she trust him so little, and after he had saved her from the slavers? Caught between rage and hurt he boiled. She had betrayed him. She had lied to him. Over and over, she had lied . . .

Somewhere on the road back to the convent, Marc made himself a new promise. He would have her, one way or the other.

Chapter Fifteen

"He is here! He is here!"

Wild with joy, Alde pelted out of the convent orchard where Sunniva was working, sawing out the dead wood and picking the few apples. As Judith and Isabella too scrambled down the ladder to greet the lone warrior on the chestnut horse, Sunniva remained where she was, sitting in the apple tree, trapped by her own feelings, caught between shock and a dazed happiness. Marc was alive. He had come back to her.

Picturing his homely face, she kissed her fingers, hardly aware of what she did. She wanted to skid down the tree and race through the orchard to meet him. She wanted to hold him tightly, pluck him right off his feet, big as he was, touch him to make certain he was whole and real, not simply a fragment of a dream. She wanted to wait, anticipating the moment, savoring her relief, as he sought her out. Surely he would do so?

What news did he bring? Had he seen Cena? Bertana? Edgar? Were they safe? Would she see the twins sauntering in behind Marc, secure in his protection? What was happening in the wilder world?

She could see him now, the three girls riding pillion

on his horse as he led Theo on foot. Marc was passing through the orchard gate, speaking a word or two of greeting to the gathering nuns. If he had hastened on his return journey there were few signs: he strode tall and straight, jangling slightly with each step. She saw the flash of sun on his dagger and sword belt. His chestnut looked fresh and newly groomed.

As for Marc himself . . .

Sunniva inhaled sharply, her fingers tightening on the pruning knife. Marc was Marc, yet not. His clothes were different, more colorful, and he had shaved off his beard and trimmed his hair. Even the hair in his ears, she noted inconsequentially, as he released Theo, allowing the stallion to graze where he would, and approached her tree alone.

She drew back into the shielding branches, thoroughly disconcerted. Gone was the bear-man Marc she had talked to. This smooth-faced, trim gallant was unknown. He made her conscious of her plain, apple-bark-stained gown and reminded her that her blue headsquare had a tear in it. She wished he had found her in a more elegant setting: at her embroidery, perhaps. With the pruning knife in her fist and a heap of rotten branches round the base of the tree, a basket of small wizened apples hanging from her shoulder, she felt like a kitchen maid.

"Good-day to you," said the stranger, using Marc's voice.

Even when he raised his head and looked straight at her she did not recognize him. Never before had she realized how lean his jaw was, how strong and mobile his lips. His nose was long and straight, his cheekbones clearly defined, his skin taut and toned, lighter than it would have been when he served in the east but still flawless. In profile his features had the clarity, the unblemished strength, of a blade. He was handsome, not homely, she realized with a shock, with bright, knowing amber eyes. The ends of his freshly trimmed hair curled darkly against his collar, dark-brown hair but no longer bear-brown; full rather of interesting lights: flecks of black, of red, even of silver.

Sunniva hung from the tree, closing her mouth with a snap until she remembered that she had not answered. "Good morrow," she said hastily, although it was afternoon.

"I met a barber on the road," he said, rubbing a thumb along his freshly shaven chin. "It is cleaner for the summer."

"That is a good thought," Sunniva agreed, astonished by their frivolous conversation while at the same moment wishing, for the second time, that she had met him dressed in a better gown.

He raised a hand toward her and his sleeve slipped down, revealing a tattoo of a dark blue cross emblazoned on his sword arm. He saw her staring and grinned.

"A memory from Constantinople," he said. "My friend Karl did it for me. He is a Viking, but a good one and a good guardsman." His smile faded. "I hope he was not with Hardrada's force, for they lost, and badly."

"My father? My brothers?" Sunniva stammered.

Marc stretched out both hands. "I think it best if you come down," he said quietly.

She knew then, before he told her.

Her eyes had widened when she first saw him but now she was silent as he explained how he found her father and brothers on the battlefield. When he said he had taken their bodies for burial, a spasm of sadness crossed her flawless features but all she said was, "Thank you for that."

"No more than they would have done for me," Marc answered.

Sunniva looked as if she doubted that but said nothing. She glanced at the pruning knife in her hand and drove it, with more force than needed, into another rotten branch. For a second the scent of apples swirled between them as she lowered the basket off her back to her feet.

"You will be wanting to see your youngsters," she said at last.

"The nuns have them busy with something," Marc replied, gazing at her dry eyes. He had expected a few tears, not many, for Cena was scarcely a loveable man, and he and his brutish sons had lately denied Sunniva as one of their kin, but this cool, withdrawn silence confounded him. Did the years she had lived with Cena as a daughter—harried and bullied, yes, but still a daughter—mean nothing to her?

He cleared his throat. He and Sunniva were standing next to each other: should he embrace her for comfort?

Unbidden, Edgar's words returned to goad him. He thought of how Sunniva had teased him, how she had responded to his kisses. Was she truly as Edgar claimed, a shallow, manipulative woman? Was she perhaps incapable of deep feeling?

Did he want such a woman in his bed?

She lied to me, he thought, and the idea of revenge, of punishment in intimacy, through touch and savoring and slow, searching caresses, became mightily appealing.

He smiled, glad he had taken the trouble to change

his clothes and get his beard shaved off: her stare had been intensely gratifying. Now, beginning his plan of seduction at once, he said, "You will need to go home, to your people; they are now your responsibility. I shall escort you."

"You?" He thought she paled a little. "But what of your girls?"

"They go with us," he replied blandly. "Alde has told me they have all been well in the time I was away, eating well and sleeping well. No night terrors. Our departure from the pilgrimage has done them no harm and they enjoy travel."

She did pale now, visibly, at his mention of the pilgrimage, no doubt recalling words like "woman-killer" and "murderer." Enjoying her discomfort, he added, "We shall set out today."

"When you have only just arrived? Your horse—"

He waved aside her objections. "You should make ready. I intend to leave in one hour. The sooner you are returned home, the swifter you may send word to your betrothed."

He waited, wondering if she would take the bait. Even now, if she said something, confessed she was free, he would forgive her, dismiss Edgar's dying words as the ravings of a sad, embittered man.

"It has been a while since I communicated with Caedmon," she whispered at last, examining her fingernails.

"Then he will be anxious." Infuriated afresh by her lies, Marc suddenly longed to sit down under this unruly apple tree, drag her over his lap and spank her until she begged to tell him the truth. Instead, reluctantly, he forced himself to take a step back. "I will say our farewells to the abbess and then we go."

"I cannot."

He waited again, the temper-blood singing in his ears, fully expecting her to pretend that she must pray for her dead family, but it seemed that even for her, that lie was too much.

"I have promised the abbess I will help her."

"With the rest of the apple harvest, and to repair the altar cloths and such?" Marc guessed aloud, feeling as brazen as Sunniva must feel as he now lied, "I have spoken to the abbess. She understands your first duty is at home." He smiled. "Should you not be packing your things?"

He is said to be a murderer. A woman-killer, no less. He has never denied it. Why am I traveling with him for a second time?

The question haunted Sunniva throughout the day and she had no answer, except the brutal, *I have no choice.* Marc was right, her duty was to her people at home and the black reality was that it was safer journeying with a man, even a man said to be a woman-killer, than to risk traveling alone.

That harsh truth was brought home to her just after midday when, close to the grass trackway they were riding on, a tangle of youths broke cover from a spinney of thin oaks and threatened to surround her horse. Without a word, Marc drew his sword and galloped across, putting himself between her, his nieces and the boys. The five youths immediately fled into the undergrowth, though not before Sunniva noticed their rag-covered faces and antique knives. She could probably—possibly—have seen them off, but five brawny lads, all armed, were not to be trifled with.

"My thanks," she told Marc when they and the girls

were cantering south again, this time leaving the grassy road and cutting across country to avoid a sprawling camp of shepherds and their flocks.

He nodded, a strange smile lurking on his chapped yet handsome lips. "My pleasure," he replied. "You are in mourning, and so no doubt less agile in your knife-work."

He spurred his mount on, calling to Isabella—who was sucking her thumb as she rode—to be careful. Checking the gait of her own horse, Sunniva was left feeling on edge as a result of their exchange.

What did she feel for Cena and the others? Nothing. That was the dreadful thing. She could claim shock, disbelief, but she would be a liar. She knew she would never see them again, yet that dull certainty woke no grief.

Desperate, she tried to think of some moment when she and Cena had been close, when she had felt like his daughter, but her memory failed her. Perhaps she was ungrateful, unnatural. Maybe that was why Marc seemed to look at her sidelong, as if she had suddenly grown a snake from her forehead. Or was his own dark nature finally emerging?

Keep close to Isabella, she told herself, praying that even a woman-killer would have some scruple about slaying her in front of his own niece. She would never use Bella as a shield, never put her or Alde or Judith in harm's way, but if their presence checked Marc, stopped him from some act of violence against her, then so be it.

On edge, she could not join in the childhood games of the three girls. Alde tried to teach her some French and Sunniva found she could remember nothing. Judith tried to show her a wren's nest and they all laughed, Marc included, when she asked if it was a buzzard's nest. Even Isabella failed to teach her the game of string she had learned from her uncle, cantering off a few moments later with the words, "I think she is sunstruck, Uncle Marc."

"Is that so?" With ghastly speed, "Uncle Marc" was onto that chance in an instant, turning round in his saddle and saying with seeming reasonableness, "Then we shall make camp now. A good night's sleep will see our lady right, do you not think?"

"Yes!" shrieked his three, already hooking their skinny legs off their ponies.

No! thought Sunniva, but she knew she must make the best of it.

At least the place where they had stopped was good. It was on the summit of a small hill, within sight of the track. While Sunniva dug out a small fire pit and made a fire, Marc lashed together a lean-to of whippy hazel branches, leaves and moss and a similar raised platform within the lean-to that the girls covered with dried grasses. Then Marc produced mead and dried meat, soft cheese and fresh apples from his pack.

"Bought or bartered from more men you met on the road?" Sunniva asked, under cover of the girls' cries of delight.

"Exactly." Marc met her eyes and shook the flask of mead. "We can eat and drink well tonight."

Sunniva glanced at the westering sun and vowed to drink as slowly as possible.

Alde, Judith and Isabella, excited by the novelty of sleeping out of doors on a sleeping platform, were keen to bed down as soon as they had eaten. Marc heard their prayers and Sunniva tried to delay matters a little by suggesting she also hear their prayers but far too quickly the three girls were snuggled together, sleeping softly.

"We should do the same," Marc said, dropping another dried pine cone on their fire and stretching his arms above his head. He yawned and patted the remaining space on the platform. "We must bundle together."

Not in the slightest convinced by his play of sleepiness, Sunniva rolled off the heap of baggage she had been sitting on at the opposite side of the fire and rose to her feet. "I shall take the first watch."

"No need. The horses will alert us if any strangers approach." Marc had also risen and was crossing to her place.

"Have you ever done this with your betrothed?" he asked softly. "Watched the evening star rise? Taken mead together?" He held out the flagon, sloshing it gently in his hand. "There is plenty left, Sunniva."

Somehow, he made her name beautiful. Before she realized what she was about, she had taken the drink from him and raised it to her lips.

The sweet taste was beguiling, as were his eyes, smiling into hers. She took another taste, deciding in a rush that if Marc were a killer she would do well not to provoke him. She should please him instead, throw him off guard . . .

She did him a curtsey and returned the flagon. "Now you drink."

He bowed from the waist. "As you wish, my lady."

"More," she prompted, marveling at the strong cords of tendons in his neck, revealed as he drank. "You cannot sip at mead."

He gave her a quizzical glance. "The gospel according to St. Caedmon?"

"No, mine," she retorted, irked by these references. She did not want to think of her mythical betrothed tonight. She sat down again, heartened to hear him drinking again.

"You will not make me sleepy, you know," he said, and smiled. "I once downed a whole barrel of wine, without ill-effects."

"No doubt as a bet between you and Karl," Sunniva replied, smoothing out a crease in her skirt. She did not raise her head, reluctant to see Marc's knowing face hovering above hers. She thought quickly of another strategy.

"Tell me more about your mother, Marc. Is she like you?"

"What? Large and needing to shave daily?"

Sunniva shook her head, not caring what nonsense he said: it was a safe way of passing time. "I mean, does she have the foresight?"

"At times." With a sigh, Marc settled on the ground beside her, stretching his long legs in front of him and leaning back on his elbows. "Hers comes at full moon. Then, she can look in a bowl of water—the water must be fresh, mind and the bowl of silver—and see shadows of the future. She thought my sister would inherit her gift. Instead I did."

"Do you regret it?" The question was uttered before she had thought how it would sound. She began to apologize, but Marc merely grunted, "No matter, I regret naught," and rolled onto his stomach.

"There is a treasure down here," he said, after a moment.

Sunniva raised her eyebrows. "I shall leave you to explore it," she said, refusing to be drawn. She wanted to step over him to feed the fire but his legs, now spread-eagled, were in the way. "I must go."

She waited and when he still did not stir, prodded him lightly with her foot. "Excuse—"

A large hand gripped her ankle and tugged. Losing her footing, Sunniva tried to twist away but found herself landing on top of a warm, living log: Marc.

A little winded and mightily irritated, she tried to push away, but his arms were about her, not tight, but she could not break free. "You are lucky I did not scream and wake the girls!" she muttered.

"I knew you would not because of the girls," came back the infuriatingly calm response. Marc ran a finger up her spine and across to her face, tilting up her chin so he could look into her eyes. "Will you forgive me, Lady Sun-Light? I could not resist: I knew you would fall on me as lightly as an angel."

"Hold me much longer and you will find me far lower than an angel!" Sunniva spat back, her breath stopping as he smiled again. How could the lack of beard make such a difference? How had she never noticed before how brutally handsome he was?

"You will be a little she-devil, eh?" Again he twisted her words and part of her wanted to protest, part of her wanted to goad further. But this had to stop.

Not caring for his comfort, Sunniva used her elbows on his chest to prize her upper body away from his. "You will unhand me, sir." She hoped she sounded sufficiently remote: her back tingled where his hand had touched her and she was vividly aware of lying against him, of the long hard length of him. "Would you have me think you less a gentle knight?"

He smiled, as if the question concerned him not at

all. "Have you done this with your betrothed? This kind of teasing? Or is he a solemn fellow, more suited to church than a lady's bed?"

Sunniva blushed, disconcerted by the way her own mind and imagination betrayed her; supplying a giddy rush of pictures of herself and Marc in bed together. Naked, in bed together . . .

"He is not so rough," she choked out, sagging briefly back onto his chest as he brushed her cheek with his free hand. Why, when they were thus, should his touch make her feel so thoroughly unstrung? "You should not," she gasped, "We should not—"

"You would have me gentle?"

"I would have you let me sleep unmolested!" she exclaimed, through clenched teeth. The truth was she had never known such play between herself and a man, but he must not know that: she would be even more undone. Not brave enough to kick him, she kicked at the ground. "Where is this treasure, then?"

"Here, this good, soft earth, and tickly moss." He wafted a small clump in her line of sight. "Tickling," he mused.

"You must not!" Sunniva protested, but although she stiffened and tried to break free she was lifted as if she weighed no more than the clump of moss and lain on the ground and now he was straddling her and his long fingers were tickling her, under her arms and beneath her ribs, under her arms again.

She giggled and thrashed, torn between indignation and a fear he would stop. "No!" she cried, even as her body arched for more.

"Has your betrothed ever tickled you like this?" Marc asked, pausing for an instant and in that moment, swooping lower to snatch a kiss from her unguarded mouth. "Has he?" Another kiss. "Has he?"

Abruptly, he rolled her over and swatted her backside lightly.

"That's enough for tonight," he said, and stalked off into the twilight, to the horses, leaving Sunniva trembling, her body and lips burning where his lips and hands had been.

Chapter Sixteen

That evening set a pattern. Ever after, Marc was courteous through the day as they traveled but determined to make camp at sunset. He would race with his girls and they would fall asleep quickly and easily, often before twilight. They slept soundly. Sunniva was in no haste to wake them, rather she longed to lie down with them.

Marc thwarted such plans. Shamelessly, he shifted her bedding away from that of the girls. More brazen still, he would pluck her from his nieces' sleepy embraces, unwind their slim arms from her neck, lift their soft limbs from hers and bear her off to his side of the fire.

She appealed to his honor. He smiled and did as he pleased. She threatened him with the wrath of St. Cuthbert: he remarked they were now a long way from the saint's shrine. She asked him why and he replied, "I have you close to me for your safety, and because I am curious," nothing more. No other explanation.

She tried struggling but it was like resisting a flood. Always, there seemed to be an arm blocking hers, a leg barring hers, and when she opened her mouth to scold she was tickled—not kissed, roughly, or handled roughly but brought to the brink of submission by laughter.

And his questions!

Had she and her betrothed done this, or this, or the other? Had her betrothed kissed her on the mouth like this? Or on her hands and up her arms like this? Or across the bridge of her nose?

"You have no right to ask!" she protested, when she could speak. "I do not interrogate you on your lovers!"

He had broken from her early that evening, as if her words shamed him, but the following night he kept beside her, one arm and leg draped over her in lazy possession, until well past moonrise. He had talked to her of Constantinople: the palaces of white and rose marble, the churches filled with gold and incense, the dark-browed, swift, argumentative people, where a cobbler would dispute with you over the nature of God. She had rested against his firm shoulder and flank and listened as he unveiled the city for her. That night she had fallen asleep in his arms before he moved away.

Did she fight him hard enough? She did not bite him, nor scratch him. He seemed impervious to kicks and punches. She did not use his nieces against him: she had not told Alde of his behavior, nor enlisted her help. Most treacherously, her mind sometimes rebelled against her, observing in Marc's own deep, warm voice, that he did indeed gather her to him "for her own safety." Am I weak, or wise, she puzzled, stretching out when Marc left her each night, desperately feigning sleep when he returned from tending the horses.

That was the rub: he might torment her but he did not abuse her. Each evening she could sleep in peace.

Even when he tickled her mercilessly under her ribs, his fingers never strayed to her breasts.

Does he not want me? she caught herself thinking, even as she resented the carelessness with which he could toy with her. She was wary of provoking him and told herself she did not bite for that reason.

Remember he is said to be a woman-killer, she reminded herself: too often, these days, she was in danger of forgetting.

The days were simpler in that both of them were busy marshaling the girls and horses and the mule, and in keeping a look out for strangers. Days were for riding and for thinking of Cena, Edgar and the twins. Already her memory of them was fading, like the bruises they had been so apt in giving. She tried to miss them, and she did pray for them, but could do no more. In the end, whatever they had been, they had rejected her. She was Cena's heir but no longer his daughter.

"Will you live at your home or in Whitby?" Marc asked, during one hot, airless noonday when they had stopped by a stream to water and rest the horses. "Will your people want you to live amongst them, or will you go to your betrothed's?"

"Ah." Sunniva was already leaping ahead in thought, one stage further than Marc's question. Her people would want her to marry—but not to a woman-killing Breton adventurer, who had no lands to speak of in England.

"I will leave that to my future husband," she said quickly.

"Good," said Marc. "I like a girl who is biddable."

His eyebrows jerked up and down, as if he was trying

to suppress laughter, but Sunniva was not interested in his jest.

Tell him you are free, her emotions clamored, while her conscience chanted, He is a stranger, he is a killer, he is not English. Cena's people would never follow him.

"Look at her!" shouted Alde, "Sunniva is blushing!"

Worse, Sunniva thought, turning away to the stream. *I care for a man who does not care for me. If Marc cared, he would not trouble me so.*

Or would he?

She is incorrigible, Marc decided, watching Sunniva from the corner of his eye as she plunged her arms into the stream up to her elbows, no longer taking a drink but briskly washing her hands and forearms. Always ready to copy, Alde had already done the same and now Judith was flicking Alde and Isabella with water: in a moment there would be a quarrel.

There was, between Isabella and Alde, which he broke up by suggesting to Alde that she look for dried pine cones in his pack. The cones were useful as firewood.

Hearing him, Sunniva whirled round from the water's edge so quickly that the end of her head-square streaked away and became tangled in a low-growing alder branch. "You mean to stop?" she asked, as she strove to detach her headrail from the branch. "Should we not move on while the roads are clear?"

"They will remain so, in the north. The forces are moving south," Marc answered automatically.

A pause greeted his statement. He and Sunniva stared at each other, Sunniva's hands frozen in her task.

"Watch me, Uncle Marc!" Judith shouted. "I am swinging on this branch!"

"Careful, Judy," Marc said, while Sunniva whispered, "He has crossed the narrow sea. William of Normandy. That is why these lands are empty."

Marc realized he had scarcely noticed, being so preoccupied with Sunniva and anticipating their evenings, but he knew at once she was right. He nodded.

"Can you see?" she asked, glancing to check Judith had not pitched herself into the stream by her branch-swinging antics. "Can you sense who will win?"

Marc met her sea-green eyes and let himself be lost in them. He sought darkness, foreshadow, but all he could see was light. "No," he said. He crossed to her and gently untied her headsquare, aware, with a pang of something like pity, of how threadbare it was. "Forgive me. I cannot always see," he growled. "It comes and goes."

Her bright interest melted into a mellow sympathy. He could revel in her eyes all day, like a wasp in honey. What was he doing? Why, in good conscience, were they stopping? It was not evening.

And you should not be treating her badly, his mother nagged in his mind. *Since when did no mean yes to you?* He could picture his mother saying this, her wavy thin brown hair falling over her high forehead into her piercingly direct eyes. Sometimes his mother behaved as if she knew everything, that she could order him about as if he were still six years old. The worst of it was that quite often she did exactly that, and her advice was useful, if incredibly annoying.

Sunniva does not fight me. I do not hurt her, Marc thought.

She is half your size, Marc de Sens. You are no better than every other man she has known.

If she would tell me the truth of her maiden state.

You know it already. You should not be doing this: trying to make her fall in love with you. You have changed your appearance for the sake of seduction: since when did you shave every day and travel in your best clothes? And if you succeed in your dubious quest, what then? Will you take her or reject her?

It is not all one way. She kisses me back. Yesterday evening, she ran her fingers over my arms and shoulders. She admires my best clothes.

These are excuses, Marc.

"May I ask something else?" Sunniva, breaking through his mess of thoughts, was welcome, and he smiled. It was easy to smile at her, especially as she was, standing by the water in a blue gown, the sun streaming through her thin russet headrail, igniting the glory of her hair. Tonight, he would have that hair undone.

You do wrong by her, said his mother in his head, relentless and exasperating here as she was in life. *Hot and cold. She will not know where she is with you.*

She has not stuck one of her knives in me yet, he thought, and now he spread his hands. "Ask it, Sunniva."

"If we are truly stopping now . . . Can I wash our clothes?"

Chapter Seventeen

That evening, before they made camp, the weather changed. It began to rain, very hard, and within moments they were soaked. They found shelter under an arch, part of some vanished, larger structure that Marc said was an old aqueduct, designed to bring water to a city. Sunniva wished the aqueduct could take water away, especially as she could not light a fire. It took the spark from both of her knives to coax even an ember into a bundle of thistledown and then she had to work hard to tease it into a flame. Her hands were filthy and aching before she had finished and could raise her head.

Marc had unpacked a cooking pot, tended the horses, slung two windbreaks at either end of the archway and made up their beds. The girls were already under their blankets, each one shivering and abnormally quiet. His face, when she called softly to him that she was going out for water, was bleached and drawn with worry.

"I will go," he said, rising at once from Isabella's side. "I would not have you stricken, too."

Her heart went out to him. "Children are resilient, Marc. Come the morning, they will be merry again."

"Pray King Christ you are right." He crossed himself and snatched up the cooking pot, stamping past her with a muttered, "I cannot stand to see them brought down. What kind of guardian am I, if this happens to them?"

He vanished into the swirling murk before she could answer and was quiet for the rest of the evening.

The children were also silent and ate little of the vegetable pottage she made, although Marc hovered about them with a bowl of it and spoons, declaring it "delicious." He kept close to them throughout the night, often touching their foreheads and hands. Sunniva tore up an old headsquare to use as rags and damped them to use as soothing compresses. She prayed to Christ, Mary, St. Cuthbert and Freya, explaining to Marc that Freya was a saint her mother Ethelinda had evoked whenever she was ill as a little girl. She searched through her things for a lovage potion for fever and told Marc what it was and how often his girls could have a dose. She mopped Alde's face and behind her ears and neck and Marc did the same for Judith and Isabella. Once their hands touched when they both stretched for the pail of water, but that was the only contact between them.

Sometime around midnight, Sunniva fell into an uneasy doze, with a red-cheeked, sweating Alde tossing fretfully beside her.

In the morning, Marc shook her awake. "They are worse," was all he said.

Sunniva smelt their fetid breath and noted their shuddering limbs and swollen throats and could only agree. "We need to get them under cover."

"A proper home, I know, you need not preach on it!" Marc snapped, and then he grimaced and dragged both hands through his damp hair. "I am sorry. This is not your fault."

"No matter," Sunniva replied, forgiving him at once when she saw his swollen, sleepless eyes. "We shall find a house and they will take us in."

"God willing," Marc murmured.

"My people are a hospitable race," Sunniva retorted, for she could see no benefit in assuming the worse. "By noon today we shall have found a place, you will see."

He gave her a strained, fleeting smile as he stripped down their rough hangings and gathered together their things. "It seems I am not the only one who can predict the future."

"No, you are not," said Sunniva, tying Isabella's rag doll to the little girl's stomach with a shawl. "I can take Alde upon my horse," she went on, with a briskness she did not quite feel. "Can you manage Judith and Isabella?"

"I can," he said, "and thank you."

Sunniva smiled in return although, looking at the three girls still lying on their rough pallets, she prayed they would reach a homestead soon.

After less than half a day's travel, with rain beating upon their heads and bowed shoulders, they came to a farm. No dogs skidded out of the windowless long house or the two hogback barns to yowl at them, no spit-boys or stable-lads poked their faces out of doors as Marc and Sunniva wearily prodded their horses across the crumbling boards laid over a shallow, rubbish-filled defensive ditch.

"Is any one alive here?" Marc asked aloud, feeling as if a slab of ice had been thrust down his throat while Judith and Isabella, lolling in front of him and half-dangled across Theo's broad neck, sweated and burned with fever.

"Hello, at the house!" Sunniva called out, shrugging as Marc narrowed his eyes at her. "They will know now we are no threat." She slithered off her horse, lifted Alde into her arms and set off across a wide turf and stone path shaded by an old rowan tree.

"King Christ in heaven, are you mad?" Marc gathered up his two remaining nieces and lunged after her, reaching her as she put her shoulder to the main door. "Stop there!"

The exasperating baggage ignored him and kept pushing and he could only curse as they crossed the threshold together, him conscious of attack yet carrying two ill children, her as blithe as a week-old pup.

"Do not trouble yourself, Marc de Sens," she remarked, moving swiftly to the bare, cold fireplace. "I knew this farmstead was deserted. We may rest here and take stock."

For once, Marc found himself speechless.

When Marc had fed and watered their animals in one of the deserted stable-cum-milking barns, he returned to the dwelling. He stood for a moment on the threshold of the main house, his weariness dropping away as Sunniva approached and drew off his cloak for him. Already, working some of kind magic with few resources and little time, she had made this place a home again.

The earth floor was freshly swept. She had set a bench and trestle by the fireplace, where a bright, sweet-smelling blaze warmed a cauldron of water and a griddle was being heated, ready to cook a batch of oatcakes. Sheepskin rugs were pinned around the thatched walls, adding to a feeling of comfort and safety. An earthen jug stood by the fire, filled with some newly opened roses Sunniva had gathered from the kitchen garden to the south of the long house.

The children's pallets lay beside the fire, heaped with more sheepskin rugs. More blankets, taken perhaps from the series of chests ranged against the far long wall, were draped over a wicker hurdle to air. Stripped and covered with fresh linen cloths, Alde, Isabella and Judith were resting on their low beds, a wooden cup of weak ale beside each of their pillows. Their shoes were hung drying over the fire on a spit, their damp gowns bundled at the end of the trestle.

"I have found eggs and cheese in the keep-chest," Sunniva was saying. "I can make us something with that."

She smiled at his astonishment. "I was brought up on a farm like this," she said. "I could guess where everything would be."

Marc finally found his voice. "You have done well." He opened his arms widely, feeling as if he was embracing the transformation, and glad to do so. "More than well, Sunniva."

She ducked her head, as if unused to such praise, saying quickly, "I do not think the folk who lived here will begrudge us a few comforts: I can leave them the linen as payment. Or some of my embroidery."

She had bedded his girls in her cloth, Marc realized, growing hot along the back of his neck and in the pit of his stomach when he considered such generosity. Were these the actions of a shallow, heartless woman?

"Your youngsters are sleeping peacefully now. I have given them more potion and mopped them down and combed their hair," Sunniva went on, as if she felt it necessary to give him an account of what she had been doing. "I pray they shall do better soon. Where do you think they are?"

"The farmer and his people?" Marc answered, buying a little time as he reacted to her swift change of subject. "How did you know they were not here?" he countered.

"No fire smoke, and no coming and going from the water well," came the glib answer. "But where can they be?"

Marc considered the stable, sweet with hay and with tubs filled with feed. "They succumbed to some kind of pestilence, perhaps, and wandered off in dying?"

But Sunniva was already shaking her head at this less than serious suggestion. "The place is too well ordered. The eggs and cheese are fresh, and look up." She pointed to the rafters, where joints of meat had been hung to smoke. "And there are no rat nests, no refuse. There are crocks of urine outside, kept by the back of the house. For use in washing," she added, when Marc said nothing.

"I know that." Marc unbuckled his sword belt and laid it and his sword on the trestle. "What else, Mistress Nosy?"

"The pigs must have been driven out to the woods for the acorns in the past few days. Their tracks are old, but not yet faded." She pointed to a series of rutted marks on the floor, then planted her hands on her hips, "This was done recently, yes?"

Marc nodded.

"So where are the people, Master Wit?"

She was so challenging he wanted to kiss her but decided it was less complicated to answer instead. "It must be they have marched south, to join King Harold against William."

She looked puzzled, allowing her hands to fall to her sides. "All of them? And where are the sheep? The horses? The oxen?"

"The dogs and hawks?" Marc added, walking to Alde and touching her forehead. It was cool. Hope flared like a beacon in his chest but he kept his voice steady, as he went to Judith and Isabella and asked, "What do you think, then, Mistress Nosy?"

"A wedding?" Sunniva ventured. "The whole household as guests? Their animals rented out to another farm for gold, or to settle a debt, perhaps? I have known it before." She watched him offering a drowsy Judith a cup of ale and when he had laid the child down again and Judith had settled on her side, Sunniva added, almost defiantly, "That is possible."

Marc said nothing. He was tiring of this discussion. The folk were absent, well and good, they could rest here and the children recover and that was an end of it.

Sunniva turned away, murmuring, "I have yet to find the salt."

Marc sat on the bench, savoring the thought of his first truly hot meal in days.

Sunniva washed the children's gowns, rinsed them and put them to dry on a hurdle, which she suspected was usually used as part of a screen. She coaxed Alde and Judith to open their mouths to allow her to peer down their throats and was relieved to see that in both girls the swelling had gone down. Isabella was already dressed in a fresh gown, sitting up and chattering to Uncle Marc, explaining to him how to make a daisy chain from the few flowers he had found still blooming in the yard. Seeing the two shining brown heads bent together, Sunniva smiled, a great contentment blossoming in her breast. This might be her own small hall, her own children, her own husband.

Marc threw his daisy chain over Isabella's curls and, catching Sunniva watching, winked at her. An instant later, he frowned and marched from the house, hitting his forehead on the low lintel in his haste.

Again he withdraws from me, Sunniva thought, not inclined to see the humor in the moment, as she would have done with Cena. I work for him and wash his clothes and never complain and still he looks at me sometimes as if I am the worst of memories.

She imagined adding pepper to the egg and cheese dish she was planning to cook, pictured Marc redfaced and rushing to find some ale to wash out his fiery mouth. The childish thought pleased and saddened her in equal measure.

He likes me, he wants me, yet he does not trust me.

Are you any better? Sunniva asked herself, beginning a new culinary search, this time for pepper. You still have not told him that you have no betrothed, that you are free.

Daughter of a slave, yet free.

What would Marc make of that?

Chapter Eighteen

Sunniva pinned back her trailing sleeves again, ready to cook. She enjoyed cooking and she knew she was good at it. If she could make Marc remember her kindly for any thing, even if it were only her roasts, stews and possets, that would be something.

And the girls were mending: becoming thirsty, becoming hungry, becoming bored. It was with a glad, clear head that she could approach their meal today. She wanted, in truth, to show off to Marc. If she thought she could have given him a display of knife throwing, without making him trust her even less than he did already, she would have done that, too.

Who am I to think of him trusting me? she mused, setting the newly washed-and-dressed Alde and Judith to stirring her mixture for oatcakes and giving Isabella a spoon to pretend-feed her rag doll. Why am I trusting him? Because she did. She could not believe he was a murderer, much less a woman-killer.

Whatever he was, she was determined to create a feast for him. The housewife of this farm would understand—for her man loved her enough to have bartered her some good cooking pots—and the woman in turn would be pleased with her gift of linen. The cloth in this house was serviceable, but not as fine as she could make it. She would add three strong, richly patterned belts to the linen and gather berries, nuts, mushrooms and greens for the farmer's wife, too. All would else go to rot, but she could dry these and save them. If she could find more honey in any of the nearby woodland, that would be a crowning touch—the mystery mistress of this place would be well pleased.

A fair exchange, Sunniva comforted herself, as the rich smells of roasting meats and baking vegetables filled the long house. She heard Marc whistling as he went out to the horses and later for water and wished again they could stay here forever.

Marc drew a trestle and benches beside the fire, close to the griddle and the cooking cauldron so that he or Sunniva could reach across from their bench without stirring from their places. After a swift, Breton prayer of thanks from Marc, he and his squirming, hungry girls started with fresh, crisp oatcakes, lightly baked, washed down with warmed ale.

Sunniva was glad to see them eat.

"Please forgive the informality," she told Marc, as they moved without ceremony to the next course. "Unless you prefer to carve?" she went on, offering Marc a freshly sharpened knife across the table, her heart drumming in her chest as she did so. What if her instincts were wrong? What if the rumors were true?

As if guessing her thoughts, he lounged back on the bench. "Nay, your talent is greater than mine."

She could sense him staring as she handled two

blades at once, slicing through the roast in long, sure strokes, and was not at all surprised when he remarked, "You never did tell me how you saved that juggler from the mob."

"Sunniva!" Alde sat up with a sudden clatter of her stool. "You fought off a mob?" she demanded breathlessly. "Even our uncle has not done that!"

"It was not so dramatic," Sunniva said, with an ease she did not feel. "The man had asked for my protection. I gave it, that is all."

Marc cleared his throat, silently warning Isabella to wait as Sunniva dished out the food into the finely carved wooden bowls she had found in the small back room of the hall. "The mob?" he prompted.

"It was just a mob of villagers, a few youths and the daughter of the farrier, who has the mind of a child. They knew me, knew me to be the daughter of their lord. The juggler had fled into our barn. I merely barred the way to those trailing him."

Hunting poor Osric Red-Beard would be more accurate, but Sunniva did not forget the prick-eared Alde. She did not want the child to think her people were narrow-minded, suspicious of strangers. She remembered them, fifteen angry young men, a disappointed shepherd-boy and one middle-aged, pox-scarred, simple woman wielding a hammer, each one shouting that they had paid for a show and that Osric had shortchanged them. Cena saw their approach and disappeared into his hall. She snatched up a broom to fend them off and shouted more loudly than she knew she could and all the time her eyes saw the villagers with massive clarity and swiftness, while her throat was bone dry. When they had finally slunk away, she tended Osric's scrapes and bruises very poorly, her fingers were shaking so much.

"They would not push past me," she went on. "Not even Arni No-Hair."

"No, I warrant they would not," Marc observed dryly, his amber eyes warm with something. Approval? Sunniva dared to speculate. Please Freya it was so.

"What talent?" Alde demanded, sucking noisily on her ale, while farther down the bench Judith reached over and snatched the last of the oatcakes from the griddle.

"Judy, remember your manners. You are at table," Marc warned.

"Who is Arni No-Hair?" Alde asked.

"I want to eat now!" Isabella whined, kicking her heels against the table leg.

Sunniva hastily set out the bowls, reflecting that trying to impress a man with three hungry youngsters was not so easy. To her relief, Isabella and Judith fell upon the succulent pork and braised vegetables at once and nothing was heard from them save chewing. Alde, however, was like her uncle—she would not be put off. She had forgotten the mysterious Arni No-Hair, but as soon as she had finished eating she returned to another question.

"What talent does Uncle Marc mean, Sunniva?"

"Why not show us after dinner?" Marc asked, his stark, handsome face glowing with innocence.

"As you wish." Sunniva smiled, though inside she was seething. To be invited to perform—did Marc think she was a juggler? A mountebank?

It is what you want to do, so why complain? her conscience pricked. She glanced again at Marc, seated across from her, the dark of the hall outlining him.

His dark green tunic and leggings were new to her: was he trying to impress? She could only hope so. Now he smiled back at her.

"This pork is delicious," he said, stabbing another piece with his eating dagger. "How is it so sweet?"

Did he truly want to know? "I rinsed it to take out the excess salt and braised it in mead. The onions and leeks add sweetness, too."

"As does the cook." He reached across and brushed her shoulder. "You had a spider about to spin a web on you."

"My thanks." His touch was gentle, soothing, and suddenly, she was pleased, simply pleased that she would be giving—no, granting—Marc a show. No one else, except Osric, had ever seen what she could do. In a way, she would be giving herself to him, her secret self.

Will he like what he sees?

She gave the three girls their sweets—a mix of eggs and soft cheese, sweetened with honey and sprinkled with pine nuts—and left Marc's on the griddle for him to help himself. Without a further bite of pork or sweet herself, she rose. "If you will excuse me," she muttered and sped away, taking the things she needed into the small private room at the back of the hall, where the farmer and his lady had their own bed. There, with many small, nervous fumblings, she changed, the high, rasping voice of Osric running in her head, reminding, prompting, soothing.

"You will own any audience, child. Shake free your hair and they are yours to start: the women will ache to be you and the men will ache to be with you.

"Prepare with care. A trick is like a flower: what

blossoms at the front is what you want your paying customers to see, not the dark, tangled roots.

"Smile! Always smile. Never mind if your heart is smitten and you think of your beloved and you feel as if a great invisible hand has wrenched inside you and grabbed and shaken your guts. Smile and someone will always smile back. Grin if they spit and avoid being hit. Duck if they pelt you with bones and never, never, mark you, toss them back! Keep yourself trim and clean. Bright and clean wins the crowd. Move fast but clear. Be graceful. A juggler is always a dancer.

"Go out there, Sunniva and win them. Dance for them. Dance for *him*."

Wish me luck, Osric, she thought, patting her final pin and tuck in place.

"You will never need it, girl," came back the wry reply, rich with memory, as she took several large breaths and opened the door to the hall.

Chapter Nineteen

She glided out into the hall, blue and gold, her hair uncovered, unbound and falling halfway down her back, as soft and wild as a mermaid's tresses. Marc put down his plate and cup to stare, lust hardening his loins in an instant.

She was Sunniva, yet not. Instead of her usual loose, long-sleeved gown she now wore a robe with sleeves that came only to her elbows, revealing her slim shapely arms. Such skin she had, smooth and flawless, pale and glimmering in the firelight. He thought of bracelets to place on her narrow wrists, rings to adorn her graceful fingers, and yet in truth she needed none: she was a jewel in herself.

"Her feet are bare!" Alde hissed, kicking off her own shoes, while Marc could only nod, his eyes busy. The light blue robe Sunniva had changed into skimmed her lithe figure, fitting snugly about her breasts and narrow waist, then gently flaring at her hips, its skirt made in two colors, blue and red, that flickered and tumbled together as she walked.

With a tense, painful pleasure he reveled in her approach, in the lush, spectacular beauty that was enhanced by movement. He thought of moving with her, the ancient dance of woman and man, and only the presence of the three girls stopped him from taking her now! On the table. Over the table. By the table. His body and head ablaze, he joined in Alde's furious applause.

Cool and gold as a mermaid, her sea-green eyes flicked over him and then she smiled, bowed from the waist like some saucy page and came up grinning.

It was impossible not to smile back, not to gasp, like Alde and Isabella, as she rippled her empty fingers through the waves of her red-gold hair, clapped her hands twice and held them up, showing the five glinting daggers that had not been there before.

Thrice, she whirled them about her head and around her body, so close that Marc found himself clenching his teeth lest she cut herself. Up her arms flew and the daggers flew higher, spinning, flashing in the firelight, coming down, point-first—

She caught them point-first, flipped them again, high and this time they soared in a curving arch, dropping like tired birds, bouncing handle-first on her wrists, then her elbows, then her wrists, then swooping off and aloft again.

"How does she do it?" howled Judith, her square jaw working in frustration as her eyes widened and narrowed.

Laughing, Sunniva threw what seemed to be a tiny bolt of lightning, and now Judith was giggling as she found her headsquare pinned to the beam at her back and before she could free it, another bolt issued from Sunniva's nimble fingers and the small dagger was knocked from the beam by a second, heavier blade and Judith's headrail was free again and she had a small dagger lying, flat and harmless, in her lap.

"I want," Isabella began, and then she and Alde were both bemused, touching shiny blades that had just appeared and fallen safely onto their knees, a dagger for each girl.

From the very edge of his sight, Marc glimpsed a falling gleam of light, like a shooting star, and jerked backward. The small dagger bounced flatly off his knee to land under the table, and by the time he had retrieved it, Sunniva was moving again.

Smiling still, Sunniva raced forward, running, juggling three more blades, turning a cartwheel that flashed her skirts suddenly from blue to red and back again. Bouncing lightly on her bare feet, her ankles kicked up slight puffs of dust and ash from the fire as she made a handstand—on top of two stout knives.

"King Christ!" Marc was hollering and on his feet but the slippery mermaid was already down again and demure, showing no sign of pink toes or shapely calves as her skirt swished into quietness down her thighs. Smiling, she hefted the two daggers again, high over the central crossbeam, caught them and then showed her bloodless palms.

Before he could draw breath to praise or reprove her she sank into another low bow, tucked her knives somewhere into her gown and said breathlessly. "Now, who will fetch me a drink, pray?"

As one, all three girls rose from their bench and scampered off.

A moment later she was sitting across from Marc, pouring herself another ale, while Isabella nagged to see the daggers again. Prudently, Sunniva had retrieved all of them while the girls were distracted finding her a cup.

"They are gone, child, that is part of the magic," Sunniva replied, as Marc scowled at his youngest. "Is that not so, Marc?"

Feeling himself relax at her careless use of his name, he answered at once, "For sure it is and I for one am dazzled by it. Well done!" He applauded her again, clapping harder as her flush of pretty color deepened.

"Will you show me how to do it?" Alde asked, tugging nervously on the sleeves of her own gown.

"For sure when you are older."

"And you will show me, too?" demanded Judith.

"None of you will grow to be older unless you get to bed," Marc broke in, pointing to the three pallets ranged at the other side of the fire. He was eager to have Sunniva to himself.

Replete, full and happy, the girls fell asleep quickly and soon their soft, even, beautifully healthy breathing filled the air. Marc put more logs on the central fire to ensure they were warm and placed two hurdles as screens at either side of their beds.

"I know they are well now, and fully recovered, but this will cut down drafts," he told Sunniva, who was looking skeptical.

"Surely it will cut down what they can see as well," she remarked, rising to clear the table.

"Leave it," Marc said quickly. "I will clear our crocks in the morning." Taking advantage of moving, he prowled round to Sunniva's side of the table.

"May I?" He jerked his eyebrows at the bench.

She nodded and he slipped in beside her, refilling his own and her cup without asking.

"How long did it take you to learn?" he asked, nodding to her wide, innocent-looking skirts.

Sunniva smiled and withdrew the sharp, narrow blades from their hiding place, setting them down on the freshly scrubbed board. "A few weeks. I cannot really remember. The time when Osric stayed with us seemed to pass so quickly."

"He must have been pleased with your progress. You seem a natural."

Her eyes, already bright with exercise, lightened further. "You have seen such acts before?"

Marc nodded, happy to share good memories, telling her of the knife-balancers he had witnessed in Constantinople. "They were every one a spectacle and most wonderful to see, though none were as skilled as you.

"I think they used heavier blades than these," he went on, plucking a knife from the table and testing its sharpness with his thumb.

"If they were men they would need to, perhaps. The knife has to be strong enough to support weight."

As she answered, Sunniva's eyes were following his hands and Marc sighed. He was suddenly tired of her suspicions, weary of his own doubts. Did she really believe, after all their time together, that he would ever harm her? Why should she believe the worst of him, or he of her?

"I am not your enemy, girl," he said roughly, leaning away from her.

"I know." To his amazement she followed his withdrawal, edging after him and reaching out to clasp his hand. "I know you are not, Marc."

He stared at her tiny hand in his massive paw,

winded with astonishment. "What?" he said. Whatever happened next would be up to her, he realized. It was one thing to tease, to tickle, even to kiss, but he wanted more. "King Christ, do you care for me at all?" he burst out, appalled the instant the question left his lips. It was what he had been thinking, obsessing on for days, but to spew it out like that—

Braced for her laughter or, worse, pitying scorn, he actually closed his eyes for a second, and felt instead a splash of water on his hand, then a soft pair of trembling lips brush his fingers.

"Why else would I be here?" she whispered. "Right here, before you."

He opened his eyes and she was still there, golden, unusually solemn, a trace of a tear glistening on her cheek. He wiped it away with his hand. "How can you love me?" he asked, longing to hear her say it.

She smiled then. "How can I not?"

He gathered her close, lifting her so she fit on his lap. He put his lips to her ear, lost again for an instant in the wonderful scent of her hair.

"I love you, little English," he said, realizing at once by her stillness that he had spoken his heart in his first language, Breton. He repeated it in hers. "I love you." He could not think further than that, nor beyond this night. "I love you, Sunniva," he said again. "My Lady Sun-Light."

She buried her face against his shoulder and then they were kissing.

Chapter Twenty

Marc said he loved her! She was uplifted, grateful, afraid, triumphant, enchanted and, most of all, alive. She felt young again, full of hope and dreams. This was better, far better, than being desired. She was cherished.

"I love you," he whispered a third time, dropping a rain of kisses, like a string of pearls, across her throat. "Little mermaid. I have caught you now."

He smelt of love, not rank, but clean and fresh, his breath wholesome as his lips softly brushed hers in a request without words. She bumped her mouth playfully against his and his embrace tightened.

"Do not think you can slip away from me," he murmured into her mouth. He began to kiss her again, slowly and deeply.

She closed her eyes, adrift in new, glittering sensations where every feeling and touch were heightened. She could taste him, sweet as pine seeds yet with a musky undertone she was keen to explore. His tongue flicked against hers, coiled about hers and a great blaze of color exploded behind her eyelids as they breathed each other in. His mouth guided hers, teasingly, into different shapes: a pout, then a little wider to allow a tiny, tingling nip of teeth on her lower lip, then more open. She flicked her tongue along his upper lip and felt him shiver strongly.

"Little tease," he grunted, but there was no reproof in his words, or in his fingers. He began to stroke her, running his thumbs along her bare arms and down each finger. Her chin tingled as he traced the line of her jaw with his lips and her breath stopped as his hand fleetingly cupped her breast.

"Steady, sweetheart," he said, smiling down into her eyes. "We shall go at your pace, to your direction. We have all night."

"What if this household returns?" Sunniva puffed out, her wits feeling scattered to the four winds. His fingers gently circled her nipple and even through the cloth she felt undone by a fiery sweetness. "What if the children wake?"

"The youngsters sleep. The whole world sleeps," Marc whispered against her throat, transferring his hand and his attentions to her other breast. "No one will come tonight. We are alone. At peace. Listen, Sunniva. Listen to the soft summer rain."

She heard it, throbbing against the roof thatch, dripping from the eaves, swishing against the door behind which she and Marc were snug together.

"I like to listen to the rain at night," Marc went on, lifting her hips to smooth out her skirts, make her more comfortable on his lap. "I like the scents rain brings in the morning. And you, Sunniva? What do you like?"

His words were precious to her because no other man had ever asked her that question. She leaned back in his arms, relaxed, knowing she was trusting him, and glad to do so.

"Stargazing on clear nights," she said, after a

moment. "Cooking. Dancing whenever there is music. Making a great tapestry."

"Practicing your knife throwing," put in Marc, nibbling her ear in a way that made her toes curl with pleasure.

"Tickles, please no," she gasped, disappointed when he stopped, then tensing as his fingers went exploring again, shimmering down her back and flanks. She had endured rough handling, groping hands, knees jammed between her thighs, but had never known caresses like these.

Wanting to give Marc pleasure in return, she raised her hand to his chest, floating her fingers across his tunic, feeling the hard, smooth sinews and flesh beneath the cloth. From the tension in his body, the way his breath surged like a tide with each sweep of her hand, she knew she pleased him.

There was a curl of hair poking through the drawstrings of his tunic. She kissed it, then, thinking of sewing, plaited it between her fingers.

"Should you not be doing that with your hair, Mistress?" Marc drawled, lifting her hand away from the solid shield of muscle beneath his ribs and sucking on her fingers, one by one.

"Why, when I can do this with yours?" she answered, emboldened, plunging her tongue between the threads of drawstring, tugging lightly on his chest hairs, tasting the salt and savor of him. "This is very poor work," she remarked, tonguing a small darn in the shoulder of his tunic. "Your own, Master?"

"And if I say it is, what will you do? Sew it for me, on me?" Marc retorted, paddling his fingers along her thighs. "I think, in truth, this claim of yours demands satisfaction: I would see your own mending."

"There is none, save on my undertunic," Sunniva replied, in a happy state of bemusement. Her tongue and fingers ceased their sensual exploration of Marc's magnificent frame as she realized just what she had admitted. "Nay!—"

Her protest was smothered then transformed into another aching blast of joy as his mouth kidnapped hers. Diving into a well of sweetness, Sunniva opened her eyes to find herself high in Marc's arms, lifted from bench, table and hall. Another heart-stopping instant and in a rush of speed that was almost like swooning she was down on a bed: Marc's pallet, piled high with furs. The furs tickled the backs of her legs while he kissed her afresh, his hands swirling under her skirts.

"I would see this mending," was all he said, kissing her hands as she tried to pull down her gown. "But I would not have you at a disadvantage—"

He pulled back and stripped out of his tunic, dragging it unceremoniously over his head and tossing it into the darkness. Clothed now only in linen leggings, he caught her again as she tried to squirm away.

"There it is." He touched a tiny darn mark on her undershift, rubbing his finger over it, then lowering his head and kissing the spot. "I agree. It is far more skilled work than mine. You should have a reward."

He raised his head. "You are beautiful, Sunniva."

His look of wonder drew tears to her eyes. From being exasperated and a little afraid she found a new, daring confidence.

"You are beautiful, too," she said, drawing herself against him. He was so hot, so hard and, gilded by the firelight, so powerfully handsome. "I claim my reward," she said. "A kiss, Marc. I want you to kiss me."

"Have I not been doing that already, you intoxicating baggage?"

Sunniva blushed but kept her nerve. "I want you to kiss me," she intoned clearly, "where I have never been kissed before."

"Ah," Marc lowered his head again. "The kind of gift I like. A mutual reward."

Slowly, giving her time to stop him if she wanted to, he untied the strings of her gown. As her breasts became free, her nipples crinkling in the warm air of Marc's soft breath, she moaned and closed her eyes, then, wanting to miss nothing of him, opened them at once.

"I am still here," he whispered, touching her nose lightly with his thumb, winding a long streamer of heavy gold hair about his hand and kissing that. He cupped her breasts, murmuring praise in Breton she could not understand in words yet grasped in sense. Warm, half-shattered with pleasure, she lay against the furs and touched him in return, stroking his flanks, back, stomach.

Her hands fell away as he rolled on his side, so as not to crush her, and suckled her breasts, kissing and flicking one nipple with his tongue and gently squeezing and caressing her other breast.

"So pink and white and pretty," he said, his voice deepening before he tongued his way down her breastbone and stomach. "King Christ!" he groaned, "you are enough to make any man come before his time."

Abruptly he caught her against him, his hands loosening more of her gown. Kissing her hard on the mouth, he took her head between his hands. "I love you, girl," he said. "I would have you mine."

The moment had come. Too shy to speak, Sunniva

nodded, tears of pure joy spilling from her eyes as Marc yanked off his leggings and then lay on her a moment, allowing her to feel all of him. He turned her, speaking against her back, "Give me some respite, little mermaid, or I shall be in too great haste: no, I know you do not understand me, not yet, but I beg you not to touch me."

He drew off her gown, kissing down the length of her spine, while Sunniva, hanging between pleasure and a need to embrace and caress in return said in a muffled voice, "But I want to!"

"Later, sweeting. Later you may. Hush now. Enjoy."

She squirmed under his hands, raising her hips to him as he fondled her buttocks, her fingers digging into the furs when he teased a hand between her legs to pleasure her in a way no other man had done before. She was wet, wonderfully juicy, helplessly yielding, whimpering and alive with sensations that were palpably new to her.

Her need acted as a brake on his own throbbing, urgent appetite. He still wanted her—God how he wanted her!—but he wanted to please her more.

She was naked now. He had deftly gossamered away her underthings, and the sight of her was an immense, glorious joy to him. Struggling still to hold himself back, his own member painfully erect, he glided her onto his thigh, to luxuriate in the feel of her and madly, perhaps, to torment himself more. Her skin felt finer than Byzantine silk and yet the curve of her, the bow of her lissome shape, hinted at her wiry strength. An erotic combination, charging him further.

In a futile attempt to distract himself a little, he blew

on her hair, fascinated by the way it flexed and coiled on itself. Unbound, it cascaded to her waist, shimmering against the pale hollow of her back, setting off, as the mane of a horse sets off a mare's head, the greater beauty of her nicely swelling hips and thighs. Her intimate hair was gold, too: he had caught a glimpse as she had arched her bottom into his hands.

Such a round, spry, saucy bottom. A bottom to kiss and play-bite and caress and smack and finger and wallow in and *enjoy.* He wrapped an arm about her delightfully narrow middle, allowing her to be supported and free as he handled her twin globes with his other hand. Taking his time to explore their proportions, he delighted in the way her breath stuttered and gushed, how she pushed herself up to his fingers.

"Ohhh," she hissed, reflexly clenching her hands, "please, please—"

Still smoothing and petting her behind, he began tickling her between her legs with his other hand.

"Marc!" she gasped, blushing down to her breasts, her bottom warming swiftly under his sweeping hand, her sex unfurling between his gently probing fingers like the petals of an opening lily. He moved his circling hand and his thrusting, tickling hand more quickly, picking up a rhythm as she writhed and begged.

"Please, Marc, let me touch you, pl–e–ase!"

"In a moment, little English." He tightened his arm about her, keeping her in place, his fingers slick with her as he quickened more, one hand now mirroring the act of lovemaking itself. "Let yourself go," he nuzzled against her neck. "There . . ."

She stiffened in that unmistakable spasm of rapture, moaning out his name. He stroked and fondled her quivering loins as she shivered and stiffened again, and then he rolled her over, cuddling her.

"Oh!" Her eyes were damp and her hair tangled but then she blinked and sighed, nestling against him. "I never knew—"

"It could be like that?" Marc smiled, touched and flattered by her unabashed response. "And there is more."

"Will you show me?" she asked, half-bold, half-timid, and now Marc felt his smile turn into a grin.

"My pleasure," he said.

First, Marc brought her a cup of ale. He seemed to know she was thirsty, but then tonight he seemed to know all of her better than she knew herself.

Such moments. She had not known such pleasure was possible. Recalling the touch of Marc's sweetly delving fingers she bit her lips to prevent herself from begging him to do that again. She wanted more of those feelings. She wanted Marc to have them, too, with her. She wanted to touch him intimately, as he had done with her, and give him ease and joy and release. Now, tingling all over, she watched him through half-closed eyes as he took a rough swig of ale, from the jug.

He looked straight at her and she opened her arms. "Come here." He yanked her against him, holding her so tightly she could feel his manhood twitching against her stomach while his chest hairs tickled her breasts. As he clutched her she clamped her arms even more closely about him, her hands kneading the muscles of his shoulders and back. When her questing, interested fingers reached his powerful haunches he groaned aloud almost as she had done, his face contorting.

Unsure if his grimace was one of pain, she stopped. "What do I do now?" she asked.

"Anything you like," Marc answered, flopping down on the pallet alongside her, allowing her to feast her eyes on him.

A feast it was. She had seen men uncovered before but never one as well made. He was tall—often his height surprised her, for he was so sinewy she missed his size until she saw him alongside other men. Now she could see the long, lean muscles of his thighs, the hard, flat stomach, the strong, tanned arms. Better yet, she could touch. She kissed the blue cross tattoo on his arm and then a forking scar on his left knee.

"Where a horse shied and kicked me," he said, in answer to her questioning look. "Do you not wish to check my belly for scars?"

"For fleas, perhaps," Sunniva teased, giggling as he made a grab for her, then falling across him in sheer surprise as he snaked a hand between her thighs and the melting pleasure she experienced at his caress buckled her legs.

"I know how to tame you now," he crowed, whirling the fingers of his other hand around her breasts.

"So do I—with you!" Sunniva responded, and she took him, that most male part of him, between her palms.

The heat and firmness startled her but she loved the feeling as she stroked and gripped, enjoying, too, her own sense of womanliness as he stiffened further, his whole body tautening as his face blazed with color.

"King Christ!" he burst out, "I can wait no longer!"

He turned, bearing her with him and then she was beneath him and he was drawing her left leg away with his, his fingers easing into her and then, finally, himself. He lay still a moment, taking his weight on his arms, lifting himself so she could still see his blazing face.

"Mermaid," he murmured, and began to move.

She felt him now within her, caressing her from within so that she no longer knew for sure which was his flesh and which hers—truly one flesh, as it was told from the Bible. She moved with him, darts of pleasure jangling her hips, seeming to spark directly from her loins to her breasts and then to her lips as he lowered himself, stroking longer, and began to kiss her.

One dart misfired: she shivered as a bolt of pain rippled through her and then it was gone and Marc was still kissing her, his hands now in her hair, his body embracing and penetrating hers. He was quickening in his thrusting and she was quickening, too. A spiral of tickling, exploding, melting: that new rapture she had experienced for the first time tonight with Marc, but now was far richer and deeper, because he was also feeling it.

Somewhere in the haze of pleasure she heard him cry her name and then all was golden: their bodies, her bedazzled mind and the sleep that claimed her, carrying her softly down into Marc's arms.

Chapter Twenty-One

Marc stirred early. Sunniva and the children were still asleep. Sunniva was curled against him, her hand in his. He kissed her palm and she sighed and rolled over, sleepily thrusting out her behind for him to cuddle up to.

Already, even in sleep, they fitted. Jubilant, complete in a way he had never known, Marc settled back, idly running a lock of her hair through his fingers. He was aroused again, but that did not matter. They had months, years to make love. He anticipated their unions with a grin.

He would tell her everything now. The real reason why he and his girls had been on pilgrimage. The reason why he had come to England. Had he told her why he had left his homeland before? Musing, he rolled onto his belly. Sunniva was sweet-natured. She would hear him repeat things and not scold or scowl. He in turn would gladly listen to her: she could talk nonsense for him. He would ask her more about her childhood, her mother, her likes, her dreams.

He so wanted to spoil her.

She sighed a second time and shifted, facing him. A

tiny sleep crease ran down her flawless cheek. Her hair, even by the low fire, was the brightest thing in the hall.

How had he ever considered, even for a moment, anything a fellow like Edgar had told him, even a dying Edgar? He had known the man was rotten with envy. But he would make it up to Sunniva. They would marry, soon, and be a family. The girls would be as delirious with happiness as he was.

Planning their future, the wider world seemed far away, yet he could not linger abed forever. There were the horses to tend and breakfast to prepare. He would bring Sunniva a cup of ale and some cold roast pork in their bed; something for the girls, too, if they were awake when he returned from the stable block.

Whistling, Marc forced himself to slide away and skulk about for his clothes, stubbing his toes on the table as he searched for his leggings. He cursed, rubbing his foot, then grinned. It did not matter. Nothing did, this morning. Nothing would dent his truly excellent mood.

Returning later from the stable, he noticed a wisp of dust blowing in from the south. Straining his eyes in the bright, glowing, rain-washed morning he squinted into the sunrise. Nothing. There was nothing.

But he had to be sure. Marc cast himself to the ground, feeling with his fingers and all his body, listening through the snippets of birdsong for the one sound he did not want to hear.

And there it was. Steady. Relentless. Like rushing water on top of a storm cloud. He had heard it too often not to know what it was.

Their horses: he had to saddle them first. They could flee naked if need be, but they had to get out and away.

Someone was coming, and that someone had others with him—or her, but Marc did not think the leader would be a woman. He had counted twenty horses and more: a war band, he wagered, bearing down on this homestead at a gallop.

The mystery owner was returning, and not alone.

We have to get out before they get here.

Sunniva was dressed and boiling water in a small cauldron when Marc burst back into the hall. The girls were playing "tag" around their pallets.

Relieved they were also dressed, Marc bundled their things into a huge messy pile on a bedsheet and lifted it onto his back.

"We need to go. Now," he told a wide-eyed Alde.

"Quickly!" Sunniva ordered, while she refilled their water flasks with the cauldron water. "Grab a pork bone and then go outside with your uncle!"

She snatched up Isabella's rag doll, rammed it down the front of her own gown, and began ushering the three girls to the door, answering all their, "What is happening?" "Who is coming?" "Why do we have to leave?" with the all-embracing, "Your uncle will explain once we are on the road again."

Marc was proud of her, but there was no time to say so: they had to get out.

In the end, they made it to the stable. Marc had loaded up the mule and Sunniva had snatched up the leading reins of the ponies when they heard the ominous clattering of hooves.

Before he knew what she was about, Sunniva spurred

her own horse and rode out to meet the oncoming riders in the yard.

"My lords!" Her clear voice carried over the tumult. "We are a few, sorely tried travelers who availed ourselves of your roof space yesterday night. We came in peace and are leaving in the same blessed state. We took only what we needed and have left gifts in return."

Gifts? What was she talking about? Marc thought, sprinting through the heaving, sweating mass to shield her as the men and horses milled round.

"Who are you?" bellowed one of the newcomers. "Speak your name quickly!"

"I am Marc, master of horse—" The rest of his speech was lost as a score of male throats groaned and hissed. Sunniva had torn off her headsquare and her long loosened hair stopped every breath and tongue for an instant.

"I am Sunniva Cena-daughter, and my father and three brothers, who lately perished at the battle of the bridge of Stamford, were all loyal to King Harold, as I am still."

Suddenly there was silence. Men stared at the churned earth and would not look at each other.

"What news have we missed?" Marc asked.

"Harold is dead," said the warrior who had demanded their names. "He was killed on Senlac field, a long way to the south. Many of his men died with him." The man's wind-reddened face became still more hollow-cheeked, his faded blue eyes seeming to stare at nothing. "Our own lord is among the fallen."

"Then who," stammered Sunniva, "who is king?"

The warrior grimaced. "William of Normandy." He spat after he spoke, as if to clear his mouth. "William the Bastard!"

"The people will not bear it," murmured Sunniva, amidst a general grumbling of the men.

"They will have to!" snapped back the answer. "As we must now."

"Uncle?" Alde called across a sea of weapons, tugging on her lower lip with nervousness as she and her own pony were hemmed in by the foam-flecked horses of the men. "Isabella needs the midden."

"I will take her," Sunniva volunteered, quick as a lightning flash. "I will take all of you."

The men parted slowly—wearily though not grudgingly—as she guided her plucky bay mare through their battered, clustered ranks to reach the girls. There was silence as she shepherded them and their ponies outside the homestead's ditch and palisade: Marc could see the warriors watching and knew they were thinking of their own women folk. As for him, he was mightily relieved to see them go: this yard of armed men was no place for his girls. He only hoped and prayed that Sunniva would have sense enough to keep on riding, taking herself and his three far away from danger.

If anything happened to his girls. If anything happened to Sunniva—

"Hey, man, are you deaf? Who are you?"

The warrior who shouted was the same one who had spoken out before. He was a small, rangy kind of man, brown as a hazelnut, wiry and supple, though drooping with tiredness. His leather jerkin was thick with mud, his sword notched and slightly bent. His own face was equally battered; he had a massive purple bruise slashed across his chin and an egg-shaped bruise on his forehead where his helmet must have been knocked off.

Feeling at a distinct advantage in terms of age and experience, Marc nevertheless drew his sword. "I am Marc de Sens, from across the narrow sea. Who are you?"

"Thorkill of Abforde." The warrior fingered the egg-shaped bruise on his forehead. "But you are Norman!"

"Breton." Marc knew such a distinction would make no difference to the English, as the mood in the closed-in yard darkened with the men's scowls, but it mattered to him. "I came to serve the old king, Edward."

"Edward the Norman-lover?"

The other men were nudging their mounts forward by this time, buffeting against him. Marc kept his temper and his feet and answered steadily, "Edward, the rightful English king."

Thorkill continued to rub his bruised forehead: Marc was tempted to ask him if the action helped him to think. "What did he want with you, Norman?" he asked at length.

Another shove—it felt like the heel of a boot against his ribs—which Marc ignored. The longer he could keep his feet, the farther, pray King Christ, Sunniva and his girls would be escaping.

"To train his cavalry," he replied, when a second boot kicked into the small of his back. "And to tend his horses." Marc tossed Thorkill a piece of free information: whatever happened between them he saw no reason for the fellow's own mount to suffer. "Your charger has a bruised fetlock. It needs a compress of—"

"You need not tell me what it needs, *Master* of horse." Thorkill interrupted, with a sneer. "Aye, you were saying something of the like, and then your woman broke in. Do you always let her do that?"

Marc stiffened, heat rising in him like a flame. He

wanted to raise a few more bruises on Thorkill's face, perhaps give him a permanent injury. "You will speak no ill of my lady," he said, grinding out the words.

"Speek noo eel," mocked Thorkill, pulling a face. "Or what, Norman?"

So easy! From being hard-pressed to contain his anger, Marc could hardly believe it. What he had imagined he would really need to work for had dropped at his feet like a ripe plum.

"Or we fight," he said. "You rest a while, so all is fair, and then we fight." He smiled, relishing this next. "Unless you are afraid?"

Thorkill of Abforde lunged, leaning so far forward in the saddle that he was in danger from pitching from his lamed horse. "You dare say that to me, who has ridden from Senlac?"

"I dare," Marc answered. "And I challenge you. No one insults my lady. No one."

For a change, Thorkill scratched at his bloodstained, dun-brown moustache, and then his ear. "I meant no disrespect to your handsome wench, but I will fight you, Norman. For the pure pleasure of spilling your guts."

"No!"

Marc's heart plummeted into his guts. Sunniva had returned. True she was alone, but she had come back. He motioned to her, away! But she merely flicked the sides of her horse with her feet and surged closer.

"You must not do this!" she was saying. "You cannot! How then, am I to ride to my homeland? What of your youngsters?"

"Silence!" bawled the reddening, clearly disconcerted Thorkill. "What is said cannot be unsaid." He stabbed a bloodstained finger at Sunniva. "You, woman, if you cannot watch in quiet, then do not watch at all!"

"Do not leave the children alone, Sunniva," Marc said, knowing she would not be able to refuse his request. "Please. For their sake, if not mine."

She could not. Looking angry and afraid she yanked on her horse's rein and turned about, cantering away. To watch her go was a strange thing: he was glad, and proud of her, amused and stirred by her indignation and touched by her concern.

Most of all he wanted to tickle her till she cried mercy. Did she think he had no plan at all? Did she worry, even for a single instant, that this squirty little English knight could best him?

We will have a reckoning on this matter, Sunniva, he promised. *Later.*

It was hard for her to leave. Only the thought of Alde and Judith, alone and wondering, of Isabella, sickly with fear, made it possible for her to do so. Sunniva rode slowly, her head throbbing.

"Let me help," she wanted to plead with Marc. "Let me stay and fight beside you. You know what I can do with blades." But that was impossible. Who would care for the children, then?

"Damn you, Marc," she whispered, angry that he had inveigled her into this position, then horrified that she should be cursing him. She had only ever used her blades as part of a show. Could she truly thrust one into another human being?

"No," she whispered, waving to Alde and Isabella while Judith was already off her pony and pelting over the grass toward her.

Marc would have to do it, she thought, appalled. Fight a stranger, a man against whom he had no reason to be angry. And if he won, what then? Would the others let him go? Why had he thrown out that challenge? What did it matter what Thorkill said of her? And to offer the man advice on how to treat his horse!

"He is mad," she said.

"Men are terrible fools," she said aloud, swinging down from her horse to catch the stumbling Judith in her arms, glad of her warmth, her sweet childhood scent.

"Where is he?" Judith yelled, kicking against her shins. "He should be here!"

"He is coming, dear one." Sunniva could say nothing more, offer no more reassurance other than her own embrace. She smoothed the child's crumpled clothes and wiped her tearstreaked face. "There, now, you need not cry. Your uncle will be with us soon."

"When?" demanded Alde, who had also dismounted and was staring at the palisade with narrowed, hungry eyes.

"Soon," Sunniva repeated, ashamed of her inadequate answer.

Sitting very straight on her dappled pony, Isabella began to cry. As Sunniva reached for her, too, Judith let out an inhuman howl and Alde burst into tears.

"That is enough, girls," said a quiet voice behind them.

"You live!" Sunniva whipped round and then she was in his arms, with Judith and Alde jammed between them and Isabella half-crying, half-laughing. "How? How on earth did you—?"

She stopped, not wanting to know if he had killed anyone. It was sufficient, a miracle, that he was safe. He and Theo: the chestnut looked down his long nose at her and snorted, as if this outpouring of emotion was beneath him. Marc, however, was laughing: his face and eyes as bright as a boy's.

"I knew I had to be quick. I knew you or these three elflings would never wait as you should. Though I fear I had to leave the mule and our baggage behind."

"No matter," Sunniva said quickly, "You are here and whole."

"Should!" Alde was so scandalized that she stopped crying and began to hiccup instead. "That—*hic*—is not—*hic*—fair!"

"Did you fight them all with your sword?" Isabella asked, examining her thumb intently before putting it into her mouth to begin a furious sucking.

"No sword," Marc answered. "No blade of any kind," he went on, winking at Sunniva.

How dare he do that when we have been hanging in uncertainty? Sunniva thought, but then curiosity was too much. "So how?" she prompted.

He shrugged. "I confess I was inspired by your tricks with knives. I feinted a blow with my sword and threw a punch instead. I hit Thorkill on his bruise—"

"The egg-shaped one?" Alde asked, hiccups now under control.

"The very same, although I was aiming for his chin. His horse shifted at the last instant and I caught him on the forehead instead. Still he went down, landed on his rump with a wet snort, tried to rise and fell back."

Did anyone laugh? Sunniva mused, though she did not ask. The "fight" such as it was, sounded almost comic. She was surprised no other warrior had stepped in to continue it.

"Had his landing been softer, I think he would have snored," Marc went on, as if he had guessed part of her thoughts. "He and the others, they were all half-crippled with exhaustion. I have seen it before. Men can die on forced marches if they push themselves too hard. The men at the farmstead were like that: they have fought and lost a battle and then slogged their way home. To fight one lone warrior—even a Norman who is really a Breton—was too much. They were glad to see me walk out."

"They let you go?" Sunniva wanted to hit herself as soon as the words were out: of course they had let him go! He was here, towering above her, big as a tree and twice as safe.

"They were not eager to detain me," Marc answered, but now, for the first time, he twisted round to look back. "Even so, I think it best we move on."

"I agree," said Sunniva, because she did. She heartily agreed.

Chapter Twenty-Two

They had ridden all day, eating nothing and drinking nothing except cool boiled water. At sunset Sunniva spotted the sheep pen close to the track and they bedded down, with a wicker hurdle and the horses' saddle cloths slung over their heads. It was a damp, uncomfortable cave but they all slept quickly, huddled together for warmth.

Now she felt the loss of their possessions most keenly. With only stones to use as cooking pots, she had roasted and ground acorns for their supper and baked them on a thin slate as a kind of biscuit. It was poor stuff, famine fare, but they had little else. Isabella had cried all the while that she ate. Judith had slapped Alde and Alde had punched her. Marc put himself between them and they had both slapped him. He said nothing, except, "Finish your food."

Soon after, they stretched out by the tiny guttering fire, Marc in the midst of them as a kind of living, heated cushion and, to Sunniva's utter astonishment, they all slept. She even dreamed.

She dreamed of Cena when he was a young man, with fair curling hair, bright eyes and a sinewy frame.

They were walking together on a golden beach. He smiled and held out his hand to her.

"You have done well for yourself, daughter."

His acknowledgment of her brought tears to her eyes. "Thank you, Father," she said, the sound of the surf surging in her ears.

He did not embrace her but his fingers were warm and gentle against hers. He squinted out to the distant sea.

"The people will accept you," he said, after a time. "That is your duty. To lead them and to keep them safe."

Sunniva inclined her head, accepting her responsibilities.

"Marc is a good man. A fine, good man." Cena squeezed her hand, then released it. "But you must leave him, daughter."

"Never!" Tears spilled from her eyes as panic threatened to overwhelm her.

"You must! He is a Norman. Our land now is flea-ridden with Normans. He is one of the invaders! He is a known killer! If you stay with him, my death and the deaths of your brothers will have been for nothing."

Cena turned his back on her and began to walk away. The beat of the waves grew louder and as Sunniva drew in a breath to argue she found herself shouting, "No!" at a rotting post from the sheep pen. Thoroughly awake and disturbed, she broke down in weeping, only managing to stifle her sobs when Isabella shifted in her sleep and snuggled against her, her small rosebud mouth frowning around her thumb.

Biting her hand, Sunniva sat up. The thought of leaving Marc and the girls filled her with dread. The land about was becoming ever more familiar to her: she thought she could reach home from here without a guide. And if she traveled off the roads and at night she should be safe enough.

But to leave Marc . . .

She watched him sleep. She would not believe that he was a woman-killer: that kind of studied cruelty and cowardice was not in him. As for the rest, what did it matter if he was a Norman, or a Breton? He was hers, and she his. They loved each other. He had told her he loved her. She embraced that wondrous knowledge with a smile, longing to wake him so he would say it again. He was all to her, magnificent, manly, kind, surprising, engaging, full of stories. She loved his laughter. She loved the way he jangled as he walked.

She kissed the blue cross tattoo on his arm and he muttered and rolled toward her without crushing Judith who slept against his back.

We are a family, Sunniva thought. These are my family.

Yet Cena was also right. To her people at home Marc would be the enemy. They would never accept him.

The dream was a sign. Her people needed her. "Have I no choice?" she whispered. "Must I go? Must I give up my happiness?"

How could she leave him?

Marc, stirring when he felt her kiss, heard her anguished questions and guessed everything. He lay very still, forcing himself to be quiet. If she could leave, then how much, really, did she care?

I will not force her to stay, he promised himself. I will take her to the very door of her house, see her safe, and then leave myself.

He lay awake, dreading the dawn, his heart aching in his chest.

* * *

Sunniva moved late: the sun was high in the sky when she eventually yawned and stretched. The saddle cloth roof above her head was gone, the camp made tidy and Marc, Alde told her, had gone to find more water.

"He is fishing for us, too," the child went on. "With Isabella and Judith chattering on, I do not think he will catch anything." She reached toward Sunniva. "I have a comb. Would you like me to comb your hair?"

Sunniva was ashamed of the hero-worship in the girl's handsome, strong face. She did not deserve such a follower.

"Yes, please," she replied, and sat meekly under Alde's careful ministrations, while the youngster seemed intent on combing each hair in turn.

"Alde," she said, after a moment. "May I braid your hair, too?"

"Oh, yes! Yes, please!"

The child's unabashed pleasure made her still more ashamed. If she had to leave, she could not bear to say good-bye, yet to say nothing would be worse. She had to try. Alde would remember her words to pass on to the others, especially to Marc.

Oh Freya! Marc!

"Alde?" Her treacherous tongue felt too large in her jaw.

"Mmm?" Alde, her tongue protruding slightly between her teeth as she concentrated, looked up from the hank of hair she was tending. "Yes, Sunniva?"

"You know, you and your sisters, how much I care for you?"

Alde looked puzzled, as if unsure where this conversation was going. Then she shook her own sparse brown locks. "That is obvious," she stated.

"And Uncle Marc, too."

Alde giggled, covering her mouth with the comb. "Of course, Uncle Marc! We all can see how you gawk at him, especially when he is grooming the horses!"

Oh, dear. Sunniva colored to the very top of her scalp. She had not realized her interest was so obvious. "Yes, that is how grown-ups are," she said hastily, "But that means that you know, if I have to leave, I shall be very sorry. Very."

"Leave where? What do you mean? You are not going away?" Alde dropped the comb, her face becoming pinched. "You cannot! It is not fair!"

"No, no, dear one, you misunderstand." Sunniva swooped down to gather the comb and to sweep the stiff-limbed girl into a warm embrace. "I only meant if I had to leave. *If.*" She teased the ends of Alde's simple plait with the comb, sensing her relax. "Would you like one plait or more?"

Alde was entranced again. "More!" she crowed, her eyes glowing.

"Your wish is my command," Sunniva answered, spinning the girl round lightly, sitting her down on her cloak, settling to the task.

If only her own wish could be granted as easily . . .

She remained in a tense coil for the rest of that day. Marc returned, having astonishingly caught a large, succulent trout, which she gutted and cooked over warm stones. He praised her cooking lavishly and afterward announced that he was going back to the river to bathe.

"But our journey?" Sunniva ventured, trying and

failing to stop imagining herself being with him in the river, splashing together in the sun-warmed waters. To wash and soap that magnificent body—her mouth became parched at the thought.

But if I am supposed to leave him, what better time to slip away?

"As you say, the day is very warm, and we have made good progress," she said hastily, afraid she was actually spluttering. Marc gave her a wide smile that seemed to flip her heart over.

"I do not remember your comments on the weather, dear one."

"Dear one," echoed Alde, tugging on one of her new plaits. She and Judith glanced at each other and giggled.

"Hush!" Marc hunkered down and tweaked another of Alde's braids, ignoring her delighted squeak of protest. "But, as you say, Mistress Sunniva, the day is so fine we should not waste it." He stood up, swooping Alde up with him. "We shall all bathe."

"Yes!" yelled Isabella, tossing aside her fish bones.

Please no, thought Sunniva, but she could think of no ready excuse. Her mind was blank. How could she leave Marc? How could she bear to leave him? How could she leave the girls? They were her world.

If you do not go, you are a traitor to your English blood, Cena hissed in her head. *And what if your blessed instincts are wrong? What if he is a woman-killer?* She flinched and looked straight at Marc.

"Yours is a good idea. Let me first—" She scrambled for an occupation that would lull him into thinking she was all compliance. "Let me bury the remains of our meal and douse the fire—in case of dogs, who could alert strangers."

He grinned, swinging Alde to and fro in play. "Excellent!"

Sunniva nodded and knelt to deal with the fire, trying to ignore the excited exclamations of the girls. Her hammering heart slowed as she heard them move off, then quickened again as Marc returned and crouched beside her. She busied herself with earthing over and patting out the last embers.

"You look very appealing with your fingers smeared with cinders," he murmured, dropping a kiss onto the side of her nose. "Dirty little sunbeam."

Why did he have to call her such loving names? She had never known love-teasing until Marc and now she adored it. Unbidden, it seemed, she found her hands rising, mock-threatening.

"I can soot you up, too," she said, horrified the instant she spoke. What was she about with such taunting and play? She was leading him on, and it was not honest, or fair.

But Marc did not seem to care about that. He thrust his face closer. "Go to it, then."

She darted a finger forward, dagger-quick, but he was faster. He captured her wrist and flicked her hand into his hair.

"'Twill cover any gray hairs I have," he said, kissing her surprised mouth. "And later we shall see which of us is the cleaner."

"An inspection?" Sunniva breathed, thinking, say no more!

He raised an eyebrow. "Will you be looking closely?"

The words "Very closely" rose to her lips but she choked them off and merely nodded, feeling a hypocrite even with that small gesture.

How could she leave him? How could she stay?

She opened her mouth. "Take our youngsters to the river and I will follow on," she said, praying that she did not blush.

"Soon?" he asked.

"In a little while, Marc."

He knew. The instant she said his name, almost in valediction, he knew. Give her another chance, he thought. It may yet be nothing.

He rose to his feet and walked away in the direction of the stream and his laughing, scampering girls. Every step took him farther, yet he did not look back.

He knew.

Chapter Twenty-Three

She dared not watch him stalk away in case she broke down completely. Listening, tense and unhappy, she heard his footsteps fade into a muddled crashing of undergrowth as he and the girls wandered off to the river. She realized she had only moments but moved slowly, her limbs stiff and unyielding, her mind frozen.

Should she take her horse? Yes. Should she saddle it? Her fingers were icy, clumsy; she could not make them work for her.

Leave the saddle, she thought. In her distracted state, she was afraid she would drop it, alert the others. She patted her bay mare, longing to be comforted herself. If she left now, was she doing the right thing?

Marc was not English. Marc *might* be a woman-killer. Marc would always be a stranger to her people. She had to return to Cena's homestead: it was her duty.

Slowly, falteringly, she slipped a bridle over the mare's tossing head. "Easy there, girl," she whispered. "We need to be quiet."

She shook from head to foot as a large hand closed over the bridle.

"What do you think you are doing?"

Wordless as a bird she stared up at Marc. She had not heard him return—because she had not wanted to listen? Or because her heart was drumming so fast?

"Are you an utter fool?"

Tears flooded into her eyes at his harsh tone and question. His features seemed carved from granite, his eyes dark pools of fire: truly the face of a murderer. Moving with a jerky rigidity that showed his anger, Marc clamped an arm about her and hauled her against him.

"Do you think so little of me? I would have taken you to your wretched home and left you there—you need only have asked! If that is truly your wish. Ha, King Christ! Why do I even try to speak? You have made up your mind!"

It was like being driven against stone, all the breath was knocked from her. Her hands raised in a silent plea. He took both wrists in one hand and glowered at her.

"Why did you never tell me about Caedmon?" he demanded. "It was Edgar who told me the truth, while he was dying on the battlefield! Why did you never say that you had no betrothed? Do you trust me so little?"

"No!" Sunniva felt desperate: so Marc knew that Caedmon of Whitby was an invention! How could she justify it? How would he understand?

"Why did you not tell me? Why?"

"I do not know!" Sunniva burst out. "There was never a good time to speak of it! I am truly sorry, Marc, sorrier than words can say, but I was afraid—"

"Of me?"

"Of your reaction! Of losing your good opinion! Please—"

"Enough! I believe you." Something changed in Marc's eyes; there was a brief softening in his face, as if he understood. But her relief was short-lived: in another instant he had acknowledged her apology and then returned to the attack.

"Believe me, Sunniva, I can understand why you acted as you did: no doubt it seemed prudent to invent a male protector and then once created, Caedmon took on a life of his own. But do you know what is out there, right now? Armed men, desperate men, greedy men—and those are just the defeated English!"

Driving the mare's picket back into the earth, Marc tipped her over the horse's back. Her belly and breasts bounced painfully against the horse's flanks but as she tried to raise her head he held her in place.

"I should tie you thus; that would stop you from straying!" He slapped her bottom, once, twice, his hand stinging her fiercely. Ashamed, she began to weep, her tears glistening against the horse's rough pelt.

"Enough!" Marc dragged her off the horse and back into his arms again, forcing her head up so she had to look at him.

"We shall speak no more of this for now," he growled. "But later, Mistress—"

It was both promise and threat.

Now they rode on—the bathing idea had been a ploy, Sunniva realized, a test to see where her loyalties lay that she had dismally failed. Now Marc ensured that she did not attempt to "stray" as he put it, by the simple expedient of suggesting that Alde rode with her on her bay mare. Alde gave a whoop of joy at the prospect and talked at Sunniva's back for the rest of the afternoon.

Light-headed with anxiety, her stomach coiling about itself, Sunniva rode where Marc directed, oblivious to the track they were on or the countryside about them. Her bottom stung where he had smacked her, fading quickly to a low level throb of heat that was unnerving in another way, because it put her in mind of love-making. Her loins burned and itched with desire, even as her mind despaired. He despised her now.

And there was still the night and "later" to come . . .

As evening fell they came to a tiny wayside church and a smaller priest's house. Marc spoke to the priest. Sunniva did not hear what he said: the two men stood with their backs to her, mumbling together. She saw a flash of metal, silver coin, pass from Marc's hand to the priest's. Then Alde, Judith and Isabella were escorted by the priest into his home, to be welcomed and fussed over by a sparrow-boned old woman whom Sunniva guessed was the priest's mother.

She remained where she was, on horseback, while Marc approached, leading his charger and the girls' ponies.

"If you make me chase you, you will regret it," was all he said, grabbing her horse's reins. "We are bedding down in the barn."

Panic reared in her. "The girls?" she gasped, knowing that she was clutching at straws.

"Tonight they are sleeping under cover, in a good bed, with the mother of the priest. She will feed them, too. It is arranged."

Sunniva managed to wet her wind-flayed lips with her tongue. "You trust them?"

"As much as I do you," came back the stinging response, to which she had no answer.

"Later" had arrived.

* * *

Marc groomed the horses swiftly. They were skittish, nervous, sensing his anger, and he dealt with them as carefully as he knew how.

The "barn" he had paid for was in reality a low-roofed lean-to, but it was dry, with just sufficient space for their mounts and the priest's elderly dappled nag, and with a goodly quantity of straw and feed. Best of all, there was a narrow platform, used by the priest as a sleeping space whenever he or his mother had guests. The platform was where he had ordered Sunniva to stay, and for good measure he had ensured her compliance by taking her shoes and by another trick—one he was not exactly proud of, but it would serve. Angry as he was, he reckoned she was still safer with him than adrift on the roads.

Thinking of her made his head ache. Her foolish lies over Caedmon of Whitby he could accept—Sunniva had been put in a hard place by Cena: doubtless she had felt ashamed of being unwed at twenty and so she had made herself a pretend suitor. He had forgiven her for that before they had made love and her recent stammered explanations had more than satisfied any lingering hurt of his. But her action today seared him. She had been prepared to slink away, without saying a word to him. The injustice of her action seared his heart, as if she ripped it from his chest and cooked it on a griddle. Did she think so badly of him? Trust him so little? He had been willing to go with her right to her home, deliver her safely. Saying good-bye would have been almost impossible, but he would have done it. For her. How had she not known this?

And the potential danger to which she could have

exposed herself, mile by mile and hour by hour: the thought of that sickened him.

It was easier to be angry.

"I have done here," he called up to the small, prone figure lying on the sleeping platform, bundled in fresh straw and the priest's old, patched blankets.

Straw rustled and a pale face looked down at him. He almost added that the priest had given him a flask of warming blackberry tisane and a freshly baked flat bread, studded with exotic raisins: an unexpected bounty of hospitality in this isolated place. Instead he said nothing, choosing to be annoyed because she did not speak, merely nodded. Was that any kind of answer?

He lunged up the ladder, as fast as if he were scaling enemy battlements. His prize was here: he warned himself to be cold, stern as a king, but his heart fluttered like a moth. He was a moth and Sunniva the flame.

Crouching—the sloping roof was too low for him to do otherwise—he edged closer. He wanted to berate her for her folly. Mute, he stared at her.

"I am sorry."

Her apology gave him back his voice.

"Alde told me a strange tale this morning," he began. "She was distressed because you had spoken of leaving us. Of course, she did not know you meant it."

Sunniva said nothing.

"No excuses?" he jeered. "But you are usually so good at those. No 'You are a Breton, which is as bad as a Norman, and you are a murderer besides?' I thought you would trot those out."

Tell her the truth about the pilgrimage, his conscience ranted, but pride saddled his tongue and made him silent. He sprawled alongside her, marking how she did not draw back. Instead she raised her arms, extending her hands toward him.

Shame burned and then iced up and down his back when he saw how the rough cord he had used to bind her wrists together had chafed her delicate skin.

"It is your own fault," he almost said, but stopped himself, recognizing the self-justifying lie, the manipulation, for what it was.

It was still easier to be angry.

"Free yourself. You should have had enough practice."

She blanched, flinging herself back from him. "You are a bully," she said, in a taut, curiously deep voice, as if the words were being dragged up from the depths of her soul. "You are unfair."

As you were over Caedmon of Whitby, he almost said, but that was past now, over and done, so he said nothing.

"You are unfair," she repeated, and now he answered in heat:

"And you are so cowardly, you would not have said good-bye to me!"

"Stop it!" Tears streaming down her cheeks, she kicked at him, and when he registered no more than a grunt, she kicked him again. "If you knew how hard this has been for me, you would say nothing! Bully! How could you—"

Determined to prove her wrong, he dug his fingers into the ties around her wrists and snapped them apart. "Go, then," he snarled.

Instantly, she scrambled back from him, but not toward the edge of the platform or the ladder. Rubbing her wrists, she knelt up on her haunches and then leaned forward, closing the gap between them.

"I am no coward," she said.

"No, but you are unwise."

She tossed her head: the first time he had seen that haughty gesture from her. "I have my daggers. I can defend myself."

He did not remind her that her knives were in one of her headsquares and that he had placed them there after he had bound her wrists.

She tapped her arm. "You caught me by surprise. You could not do that again."

She was a challenging, haughty little changeling. "You think I could not catch you?" he demanded softly.

"By no means!"

Then let us see, shall we, Mistress? He said nothing but his flailing at her she read correctly as a feint and ducked forward, under his attack. She was very quick, too: squirming for the ladder before he had whipped round.

"No, you do not—"

His leg blocked her and then they were wrestling, spinning so near to the rim of the sleeping platform they were in danger of tumbling off. She snatched at a beam with one hand and dragged at his shirt with the other: there was a tearing of cloth but she had checked his momentum, stopped him falling headfirst into the stable.

For thanks he launched himself toward her feet, breaking her hold on him and seizing her ankles, straddling her so that his legs pinned her shoulders. She thrashed violently amidst the straw but could not fling him off.

"Let go!" She was shouting, loudly enough to bring the priest running.

"Hush!" He began to suck her toes and stroke a hand along her thighs and calves.

Instantly her breath stopped and then her struggles.

They lay a moment in quiet, he licking the delicate arch of her foot, allowing her to enjoy this new sensation.

"I have you now," he murmured, nuzzling his head in the pillow of her thighs, inhaling her sweet, intimate perfume.

"You have a longer reach, 'tis all," she complained, a drowsy-sounding mumble by his knees.

He turned so that they were facing each other.

Her small smile almost undid him but as he looked at her flawless face and felt her, lain against him in the warm straw, he knew he had to do something.

"Will you promise to stay with me, at least until we reach your home?" he asked, reaching down and rubbing her feet. Her toes were pink and he wanted to suck them again. He wanted to kiss all of her, all over.

He could see the agreement in her eyes, read the relaxation in her face, but her mouth said, "I cannot."

He raised himself on his elbow. "Why not?"

She shook her head. "My people . . . You are not English."

"So?" The excuse infuriated him. She would be saying he was a murderer next, and since he did not want to hear that from her lips he tried to kiss her.

She jerked her head away. "I am sorry," she said again, when he drew back.

"But we love each other!" he cried. When she remained silent, he tried another way: anything to breach this wall that he could sense was rising between them. "You want me," he said. "I know you do."

"Yes," she answered steadily, "I do. Now more than ever. But this is the last time I should admit it."

"Why, in the name of God?"

"You have your youngsters. I have my people. They will not accept you."

She was crying again, impaling herself—impaling them—on the dagger of duty.

"They may have to," he replied. He took her by the shoulders. "Think of it, Sunniva! There have been two great battles in this land. How many good men will have perished?"

"Too many, I am sure." She scrubbed at her eyes as if that would stop them weeping. "The priest knew nothing of any battle." Now she was being stubborn, he thought. More honor to her, but he continued his argument.

"What will be left will be the brutal, the ruthless, the slinking and the sly. And they will be out there now, fleeing on the tracks and paths of your English soil. You know this!"

As he spoke he wanted to shake her in his desperate frustration, make her realize somehow that everything was changed; more importantly, make her recognize that they belonged together.

"Allow me to escort you home."

She sighed, as if even agreeing to that was too much for her.

"Please." He put all his love into that one word.

Still she was silent, and as he thought of that, and thought of the creatures she could have encountered on her dangerous journey home, he began to be angry again.

"Do you want to be raped?" he demanded. "Have your own knives used against you by twenty, thirty louts?"

She shuddered. "Do not say such things," she whispered. "It is so difficult now. It would be so wonderful for us to be united, but can you not understand? I have responsibilities. I have no choice."

"No, you have not," he answered bitterly, determined at that moment to teach her a lesson in man-woman relations that she could not ignore. He would not lose her. He could not bear to lose her.

"You have not," he said again, and now, taking her head gently but firmly between his hands he began to kiss her, wildly and passionately.

Chapter Twenty-Four

His lips captured hers, fully and completely, and from that moment she was lost. Torn as she was, between her own tormented feelings and her perception of her duty, for tonight at least, differences of race and loyalty were suddenly not important. Something more fundamental than country or kindred was stirring within her. This mortal man had kidnapped her, like the elf princess in the stories that her mother used to tell, and now she was his.

He was hers, also, Sunniva thought, closing her eyes and ravishing his mouth in turn, teasing her tongue against his teeth and tongue. She exulted when he growled, almost like a bear or wolf might sound, and threaded one leg between hers, hugging her tightly.

"I have you again," he breathed against her neck, so closely that she could feel the vibration of his speech. "This is my time, a magic time, and here . . ." He dug a hand into the straw and raised his arm, allowing their "bedding" to slip through his fingers in a shower of gold. ". . . a magic place."

She smiled, delighted that he felt the same as she did, pleased that he understood.

"You shall see," he said, kissing the pulse point in her throat. "Yes."

He had bundled away his tunic and unlaced her gown—when had he done those things? Her question was obliterated in a piercing gush of pleasure as he fondled her breasts, easing her from her clothes in a series of swift, sure strokes.

Then his hand was between her thighs. "Should you not be fighting me, little English?" he asked, as she tried to kiss the whorl of hairs across his belly. "Am I to be an unchallenged Norman conqueror?"

In answer, knowing this would stop him dead, she threw off her headsquare and unpinned her hair. She heard his breath cut, felt his kneading, slippery fingers pause and, in a dizzying impulse of greater daring, kissed him, in his most intimate place, through his leggings.

He said something garbled in Breton and thrust his hips forward but she was out from beneath him.

The straw pricked at her flanks and stomach as she crawled in the semidarkness—when had the twilight outside changed to night? She did not know, any more than she knew what to do next. Her English blood demanded that she flee, her heart and even her sense told her quite another.

In the end it did not matter. A lean, wiry arm hooked around her middle. She tussled with the straw, seeking a purchase, but was bumped back across the platform.

"And if I were as evil as you seem to think me, you would be chastised for that." Marc tongued her ear and patted her rump, settling her back against himself. He was naked now—when had he stripped?

"It would be easy for me to have you now, would it

not?" He moved against her, so she could feel his arousal. "You are snagged in my arms and bared for my pleasure." He tickled her breasts and stomach. "If I were a Norman knight or an English thegn and had found you on the road, what do you think I would do next?"

"Let me go?" Her voice was scarcely a squeak.

He laughed and stretched out his foot, seeking to drag something back that she could not see in the warm cave of his embrace. He turned her to face him and kissed her and when he raised his head, clearly seeking something else, Sunniva realized that her hands were tied again.

"Oh!" She tugged at the headsquare bound about her wrists, but the knots merely tightened. "That is unfair!"

"If you were my captive, it would be kind."

She stared at him, mouthing "kind?"

"Kinder to tie a new slave-girl than to have her trying to escape and being spanked for her pains." He ran his hands slowly over her bottom, reminding her of her vulnerability. "A spanking could still be an option."

Sunniva closed her eyes a moment, appalled at her own swirl of thoughts. Part of her wanted this, she realized. It was as if Marc had unlocked a secret within her: this desire to be mastered and to submit.

But I must not! She struggled, pulling and writhing her arms. When she raised her wrists and tried to use her teeth on the stubborn cloth, he took her chin in his hand and raised her head.

"I can always tie your wrists behind you." His face glowed with victory. "But then you might bruise yourself with these futile squirmings. Since I will keep you, that would be a pity."

For an instant, Sunniva actually felt grateful that

he wanted to "keep" her, before a rush of shame overwhelmed her. Truly, I am my mother's daughter, she thought. It was on the edge of her tongue to admit the same, but then she remembered, with dismal clarity, that Marc already knew.

"Marc." She was too proud to extend her wrists to him a second time to beg for her release and too nervous of his possible reaction to struggle further. "Please."

"Are you hungry? I am." He smiled and playfully licked the tip of her nose. "And I am also hungry for food. We shall eat."

He cradled her in the crook of an arm while he drank from a flask. "Here." He proffered her the flask. "Careful. It is tasty, but hot."

She sipped. The blackberry tisane was indeed warming and pleasantly flavored, but she took no more than a mouthful. "Can I not feed myself?"

"No," he said simply. Tearing off a small piece of warm raisin bread he dangled it in front of her. She glared at him, clamping her teeth together.

"Not hungry?" He snaffled the piece himself. "Your rumbling stomach tells a different tale."

Now he relented and placed another piece in her bound hands, watching her chew with indulgent amusement. "More tisane?"

She almost knocked the flask away with her head but she really was thirsty. He held it carefully as she drank.

Soon—too soon for Sunniva—the bread was consumed between them.

"Now we should sleep," she announced, leaning back against him.

"You think I am tired because I caught you?" Marc drawled, flicking the knots on her bound wrists. "If I were another man—or a band of men—who had seized you, what do you think would happen next?"

She was glad of the dark that hid her blush and hid her face from the gleam of his eyes. "I would—" She would what?

"Seduce me?" He trailed a line of kisses down her stomach. "Or should I ravish you?"

Without waiting for an answer his lips pressed lower. With her hands tied she could not even attempt to stop him and a moment later, as his tongue encountered her soft golden curls, she was helpless to do so.

"Sweeting," he murmured. "I knew you would be sweet."

Feeling as if she were melting from the inside out and soaring with bliss, Sunniva found herself unable to speak.

She moaned so loudly in her pleasure that Marc was both surprised and pleased. Unable to hold back he entered her immediately after, coming after only a few thrusts. They lay a moment in quiet, Marc aware for the first time, in what seemed like hours, of the horses shifting below them.

Who in the end had ravished whom? he wondered, running his fingers through her spectacular hair. He lifted her hands and placed them on his chest, enjoying the contact. Her wrists were still bound. Idly, he considered untying her. When she next protested, he would do so, he told himself.

Maybe I am no better than a Norman, he thought. He was at least no hypocrite. Seeing her tied thus was arousing: he freely admitted it. He caressed her, relishing her responsiveness, wanting this night to go on and on.

He made love to her again, taking his weight on his arms and plunging deep within her, moving and loving it as she loved with him, faster and faster, harder and harder . . .

They fused in a blistering climax and fell asleep joined as one. In his final somnolent moment, Marc loosened her bonds, feeling her freed hands fall like a blessing across his body.

They slept well, at peace.

Sunniva stirred, scratching her nose and then her thigh and realizing as she did so that her cloth shackles were gone. For an instant she felt almost alarmed, as if she were bereft, before reason and its attendant shame stampeded into her mind.

How wanton she had been yesterday night! Even if Marc had not bound her she would not have resisted him. The memory of his lingering caresses and her own unabashed response burned in her. How could she have behaved as she did? The drink had not even been ale and yet she had behaved as if she was intoxicated.

Worse, she was greedy for more. Her body ached for his touch.

"St. Freya, how can I resist my own longings?" she whispered, horrified at what she had done.

She was still in his arms, and comfortable to be there. I should move, she thought, but then, almost as if he had sensed her intent, Marc opened his eyes.

He smiled and she was captured afresh, beguiled by the crease lines by his mouth and eyes. He kissed her, saying, "I have not seen you since yesterday night. Good morrow."

"Good morrow." It was so easy to be at peace with

him, in harmony. We belong together like needle and thread, Sunniva found herself thinking, and then she could not help blushing. Needles pierced and pricked and penetrated.

Quickly, she changed the subject. "I can repair your torn shirt, if you wish."

He shook his head. "That will delay us now. Perhaps later." He rolled onto his back, putting a small space between them, blocking her way to the ladder. "There has been a change of plan," he announced.

She waited, her breath shallow. Her instinct warned that she would not like this: Marc looked determined and at the same time apologetic; his jaw clenched, his eyes wide.

He rubbed at his stomach, frowning, as if his next words had gone sour in his chest.

"We shall go to meet the king," he said. "And swear fealty to him."

Chapter Twenty-Five

Nine weeks and countless miles later, after he, Sunniva and his nieces had already stayed in London for a month, Marc finally caught up with the new king. Tomorrow, he and Sunniva would travel from London to Westminster Abbey, where William was due to be crowned.

For now they remained in London, within its crumbling walls. It had been a strange period of weeks, Marc admitted to himself. London had, until recently, supported Edgar Atheling, the great-nephew of old king Edward, and the last male heir of the West Saxon royal house of Cerdic. Such partisan support had meant that Marc needed to be very careful as a foreigner in the city. And he and Sunniva were not always easy together, except for times like this, just before dawn, when the girls were sleeping and Sunniva lay in his arms, the strains and tensions of the day eased out of her through lovemaking. He knew she was torn between love and what she considered to be her duty. If he were a better man he would lie with her in chastity, but so long as she took pleasure and comfort from him, he would give her both.

I will marry her, he thought. *We are betrothed in our hearts. It is no sin.* He thought of the children they would have, the life waiting for them, and smiled. He would speak to the king, secure Sunniva's scrap of land for her and swear his allegiance to William. Leaving London, they would go to her homeland as man and wife. In the spring, if she could travel, they would go to his homeland. *My mother will love her. And Sunniva will have another woman to turn to.*

The thought pleased him, and he slept again.

Sunniva woke from a dream of Cena and Edgar, who were beating her. She stirred with a start, trembling, her limbs stiff, her head aching with tension. Marc grunted in his sleep and cuddled her, his leg heavy over hers.

As ever, his touch soothed her. She lay still while her heart steadied, inhaling Marc's musky scent, running her fingers across his shoulders and chest as if he were a talisman. Again she was glad that he had understood why she had made up Caedmon of Whitby as her betrothed: he had accepted her faltering explanation with a speed and generosity that made her truly relieved. Now, she tried to pray to St. Cuthbert and St. Freya, but her mind was languid, her thoughts shot through with memories of these past few weeks.

Marc was good. She was not. *Truly I am a daughter of Eve, wicked and teasing,* she decided, rolling onto her stomach the better to admire Marc's torso. She loved watching him when he was asleep. There were tiny curls all over his forehead. His face was youthful in slumber. She could see the fisher-boy he had described to her on their travels, telling of his boyhood antics, and of course, he still had a way of tickling trout . . .

Not only trout, her body reminded her, as she yawned and stretched. Remembered joy blotted out her headache and she licked her lips, wondering if she could wake him, and they join together, before the girls jumped off their pallets.

He had not bound her again. By day, he had kept her close with humiliating ease, merely by having one of his nieces ride with her. By night he had told her stories and shown her how to "read" the expressions and movements of their horses, and listened with Alde, Judy and Isabella as she explained how to patch clothing.

Skirting the edges of woodland and avoiding the cobbled roads Marc said were old Roman roads, they took care not to be spotted. Such men and women as they saw in the distance, working in fields, pasturing sheep, driving pigs, paid them little heed. No one, it seemed, was keen to challenge them. Armed men they hid from, melting into the tall grasses or wheat that in some areas remained uncut—it was hard to make hay or gather wheat in this land of war. Marc would have the horses lie down and he, Sunniva and Alde would settle by their mounts' heads to keep them down until the warriors had passed them by. Once a hunting dog came and sniffed at Marc, but he fed it some cooked trout he had been saving for their supper and the beast went away again. That night they went hungry, but they were alive.

The worse was when they saw distant fires burning: towns and hamlets being laid waste by William's forces. Then the smoke seemed to catch in the back of Sunniva's throat and her eyes pooled with tears. That devastation, looting and murder could be happening to her people: she had no way of knowing. Helpless, she would watch and in the night, when Marc took her in his arms, she would feel a double traitor. Each time she and Marc made love, she betrayed her people. Each time she looked at Marc and thought: *he is also an alien, a possible killer*, she betrayed her heart.

Musing on these things, it was a relief when Alde sat up in her bed and announced, "Judith has drunk all the ale."

"I have not." Judith's face was dark with anger, her blue eyes sullen. Kneeling up on her pallet, she placed her hands on her hips and let fly with, "Alde is a liar."

"I am not!"

"Are!"

"Sunniva, can we eat?" Isabella was tugging at her hair. "I am hungry."

"Soon, little one," Sunniva replied, wondering how Marc could sleep through this. Perhaps this distraction was not such a relief after all.

The girls were quarrelling again, Marc realized, as he groggily surfaced through a heavy wash of sleep. It was no wonder. For days they had been forced to stay indoors, barricaded within their room at the inn, while the London streets seethed with rumor, riot, fire and murder. Since their first days in the city he had gone down to the docks and harbor and hired a half-dozen Danes for their protection. These men he trusted, since one, Ragnar Fire-Breeches—the nickname had stuck ever since Ragnar had accidentally set his leggings on fire while tending a watch fire—had served with him in Constantinople. They were outside the door now, snoring in the corridor.

He had tried to hire a nurse for the girls, too, but

she had run off with her hire-money after one night. He did not blame her. No one knew who was friend or foe in these times. For their own protection they moved regularly from inn to inn, never staying in any one place for too long.

Scraping sleep from his eyes, he rolled over and tickled the scrapping Alde and Judith. In moments all three girls were on him, pinching and prodding. He let them rough with him far more than usual, anxious as he was that they might start having nightmares again, especially Isabella. London was a place of fire these days, with timber and thatch buildings blazing up like torches. Most were deliberately fired by mobs of angry men: sailors stuck too long in port, merchants losing their livelihoods as no one could trade, frightened townsfolk, suspicious of any strangers.

He tensed, almost flinging the girls off and going for his sword, before he realized that the slight draft across the small of his back was merely Sunniva, easing the shutters open a crack.

"Forgive me," she mouthed, while aloud she said, "The room needs an airing," and then, "I thought I heard a street trader, selling oysters."

"I love them!" crowed Isabella, bobbing her curls.

"Yuck!" Alde did not care for seafood.

"We must eat what there is, child," Sunniva said quickly, as Marc bounded from the bed to the door. If there was a seller, any seller, in the alleyway outside it was worth stopping the person. Naked, he put his head round the door and called to Ragnar, still bundled in his cloak in the corridor.

"There may be a street trader out in the alley," he told the man, speaking quietly so as not to wake the scullery lads and spit boys who also sprawled down the stairs.

They were on the first floor of the inn in the more expensive rooms—a slight illusion of safety.

"Food and news," Ragnar said at once. He was a scrawny, black-haired, black-stubbled, hook-nosed dancer of a fighter, agile as a leaping salmon and twice as quick. An old campaigner, he needed no more telling but was shaking his companions awake.

"Good!" Marc left him to it, and when he turned back into the room and closed the door, he found Sunniva dressed and combing Judith's thick brown mop, bringing some order to her hair. Judy was at the no-wash, no-comb stage of personal grooming and for Sunniva to be even touching her hair was a triumph.

"I want as many braids as Alde," Judith was saying, while Isabella was counting how many oysters she would eat.

He smiled: he could not help it. Without Sunniva this would be impossible: his girls would have been weeping by now. Was it down to her that they slept in peace still, untroubled though the world about them snorted fire? He rather thought it was.

"Ragnar has gone out to look," he told her. "And no, he will not harm the creature, whoever it be."

She looked her gratitude in a way that made him think of bed, but it was time they moved on, and to-morrow they would. They had stayed in this inn for three days: word would have seeped out that strangers, possibly foreign strangers, were at the Goldsmith's Inn on Fetter Lane.

She jerked her head slightly and he clambered over the straw mattresses to the small window. She eased the shutter for him to look down into the alley leading off the larger, usually more noisy Fetter Lane.

"The metalworkers have fallen strangely silent over

these past days," she murmured. "And not only because of the curfew. It is like a tomb here."

He nodded, aware as she was that London was unnaturally quiet. There were no carts. No markets. No hawkers. No drunks. Red kites picked at refuse and dogs roamed the alleys without hindrance. People crouched indoors. It was the silence of a city under siege, except that William and Edgar Atheling's supporters were supposed to have come to terms this month.

"It is since the king made peace with the city," he said, aware of Alde leaning against the closed shutter, trying to peer out. On the bed, Judith and Isabella had settled to a game of guessing. No one had sufficient energy to quarrel.

His stomach grumbled and he grinned, seeking to make light of it for the sake of the children. "If there is a seller of victuals out there, Ragnar will find them," he said.

Sunniva pushed the shutter further, pointing a narrow finger. "Every day that thing grows higher."

"The motte," Marc said patiently, aware that such a huge mound of earth and its purpose was unknown to her. She was right, though. Sometimes, when the wind was blowing in the east he could hear William's men working with their shovels and picks. Day by day the mound grew, massive and steep-sided, a defense against attack. Soon it would be topped by a wooden tower and Londoners would wake to find themselves over-looked by a Norman castle.

Beside him he felt Sunniva shiver. "I hate it," she growled, her sea eyes gleaming silver for an instant. Then she shook herself. "'Tis nothing," she exclaimed to the wary Alde. "A fleck of snow on my face. The days are growing cold."

That was true, Marc thought, and the worst was they could find no stalls open these days to buy more clothing. Ragnar had heaped them all with furs from his own ship, so they were warm enough, though the children were buried in the pelts, especially Isabella.

"What day is today, Sunniva?" Alde asked.

"It is the twenty-fifth of December." She smiled, and a thousand candles seem to light in their narrow, damp room. "Christmas Day."

"Christmas Day," repeated Judith. "Then why are the church bells not ringing?"

"It is early yet, and very cold," Sunniva said rapidly. "Bell ringers are usually very old or young: would you have them venture out and catch a cold? Even your uncle's leggings would sprout ice crystals in this weather, were we to go out now."

Alde giggled, diverted by the image.

Marc pulled on the offending leggings and crossed again to Sunniva. "We must leave soon," he warned, in a low voice. "Ragnar will keep the girls safe here and guard them, but we shall need time to cross the river. When I met him last night, Odo of Bayeux was adamant that we attend the coronation today."

Sunniva nodded, frowning. She waved at someone in the street, saying, "Ragnar has found us an eel and pie seller."

"Then we shall have breakfast," Marc said, to squeals of delight from Isabella.

The sun was still rising when Sunniva and Marc set out for old King Edward's new abbey church at Westminster. Sunniva was uneasy and not only at having to pass through London.

"What manner of man is this Odo of Bayeux?" she asked, whispering in case any townsfolk heard the French name. Marc had said London had now sworn allegiance to William. If they had, it was only because William's army were camped close by and he and his men had burned and devastated parts of the city and the surrounding countryside. Each time Marc had cause to slip out into the narrow, twisting streets she had been in an agony of anticipation and dread until his safe return, especially last night, when he was gone for hours. He could pass for English now but only two nights ago when—praise be to Freya!—the children had been sleeping, she had heard a dreadful hue and cry echo through the deserted streets: "A Norman! A bastard Norman!"

She had been trembling at the shouts and curses and shivering at the frantic footfalls under their window. Marc had warned her not to look out but listening to the mob and seeing the glare of torches through the chink in the shutters had been bad enough. She did not dare to think what had happened to the hapless foreigner: kicked and hacked to death most likely. They had not run him down by the Goldsmith's Inn but she had heard his desperate sprinting and once the wall had shaken as the stranger crashed against it.

Putting the stranger's ghastly fate from her by a deliberate effort of will, she said, "How do you know Odo?"

"I sold him a war horse in Brittany," came back the flat, laconic reply. "And gifted him several more."

The way he spoke, Sunniva knew that the "gift" had been delivered by some kind of force. Marc confirmed this by saying next, "Odo and his men had set up a hunting camp close to my mother's. He saw my horses and liked what he saw."

"Hence the gift," Sunniva remarked. "I suspect that he is the kind of man who does not take 'no' as an answer."

"Not when he was within reach of my mother, certainly," Marc agreed, his handsome face stripped of all expression. "Odo also took a drink from her well, in my mother's best silver cup."

"He kept the cup, too," Sunniva guessed, stepping round a pile of rotting cabbages whose unwholesome stink had briefly made her gag.

"He did indeed. Odo likes treasure."

"But he is a holy man!" Anxiously Sunniva glanced up, in case anyone was leaning out into the street and could hear this.

Marc snorted at that. "Bishop he may be, but he is William's half brother first and the same grasping blood flows in his fat, bald body." Marc glanced at the staff in his hand; he was using it to prod the ice puddles, in case any were hip-deep under the frosting. "Do you know he has a mace, studded with nails, or something like? It is said he uses it in battle to brain his enemies." Marc's eyes gleamed for an instant. "Of which there are many."

"How did you find him in this huge city?" she asked, falling into step with Marc down some stone steps showing fire-scorch marks.

Marc scowled at the fire-marks, his bright brown hair ruffled by a chill breeze as he raised his head, staring off into the distance where smoke still rose from field and woodland blazes lit by William's plundering army.

"Such men as Odo are easy to trace. In William's army camp, his was the most opulent tent. I bribed a guard and sent a copy of my seal ring ahead, in wax, as token of my good faith, and he remembered me.

He saw me yester evening and promised he would speak to the king on my behalf."

Yesterday evening Marc had been out past curfew, Sunniva remembered again, and while he was away she had tried to teach the girls to hem neatly, her fingers cold and fumbling in her terror for his safety. Now he snapped his fingers, as if this whole lethal business was easy, and smiled to assuage Sunniva's constant dread. "Odo gave me a parchment to show the guards at the coronation," he said, "so we may pass through unhindered."

If we reach Westminster safely, Sunniva thought, though she said nothing. Nearby, a group of ragged beggars lurked in the ruins of a charred house and these now shuffled forward, blinking, into the misty half-light of the morning. Seeing their wasted faces and desperate eyes, Sunniva looked about herself for coins but found none. Snug from the whipping wind in her new white furs, she felt ashamed.

"We can do nothing for them," Marc breathed, flipping the lead beggar some small coins and hurrying her on. "Come, I can smell a fuller's and I would be past that as soon as we may."

Her breath held in against the truly vile, stale smell of urine, Sunniva ducked under a low house beam jutting out into the alley and rounded the corner into another deserted street. She could see the river ahead, milky-white and glossy as a new ribbon, lined with wharves and jetties. Already the air seemed sweeter, the houses more fine. Some were still the sunken-floored huts she had hurried past in other parts of the city, but more were bigger, with many shutters and brightly painted doors.

"Where is everyone?" she mused aloud, and Marc

answered, "At Westminster, perhaps." His teeth showed very white in his lean face as he grinned at her. "Maybe even you English are learning to cheer the Normans."

"Maybe so," Sunniva replied, conscious of the man-made hill, the motte, rising at the edge of the city. "Will you cheer for William?" she asked.

"If he would confirm you in your bits of land, I would cheer for the devil."

"Oh, hush." Sunniva made the sign against the evil eye, wondering at the same time what she was going to do. If her fellow English did cheer for a Norman king, then would they not also cheer, in time, for a Breton lord? *Surely that is a good omen for Marc and me*, she thought, her pace quickening with her hope as Marc hailed one of the many small boats bobbing on the water and the ferryman began to row toward the nearest jetty to collect them.

Once they were on the river, Marc relaxed, to the extent he no longer fingered his sword hilt but turned Odo's scrap of parchment over and over in his hand. Sitting beside him in the narrow rowing boat, Sunniva turned her head this way and that, taking in everything. Her jaw dropped with astonishment at the bales of wool left on one jetty to spoil in the chill, frosty air, but Marc mentally shrugged: it was the way of war; people were splintered and forced from their normal lives. If William was a strong king there would be less suffering: kings were a necessary evil here on earth and only King Christ in heaven was truly just.

Marc remembered Edward the old king, dressed and perfumed like a Norman lord but pious as a monk. He remembered the king's quavering voice when he had been presented to Edward at his new great hall at

Westminster. His sponsor, one of Edward's Norman favorites at the court, had spoken of his skill with breeding and training war horses, and Marc recalled Edward's haughty distaste each time the word "breeding" was mentioned. Edward had never looked directly at him, a mere horse wrangler, throughout the entire interview.

William would be very different, he knew.

Briefly, he envied the ferryman pulling upstream against the current. He could do the same kind of work easily and this silent, bearded man did not have to be troubled with kings or nobles.

"Look! How wonderful!"

Sunniva's exclamation roused him from his gloom and he followed her pointing finger to the great cathedral of St. Paul's, probably the largest church she had ever seen. Its long nave and three tall towers, all of stone, soared above the city walls and houses, but Sunniva's finger traced the nave roof, of painted wood and now, clearly a recent, hasty repair, with a section of golden thatch.

"How it gleams in the winter light," she breathed.

He smiled, taking delight in her pleasure as her busy eyes scanned the church again. When she frowned he felt a pang.

"What is it?" he asked.

"Those girls collecting water from the well. They are the first women folk I have seen in this city."

"You will see more at Westminster." Marc prayed it would be so, and for selfish reasons. Sunniva glowed in her white furs. What if Odo or William took a fancy to her? What if one of Odo's close followers demanded her as a reward?

Let any man try to come between us, Marc vowed, fingering his sword again.

Closer they glided to Westminster, the ferryman sculling nimbly over a series of midstream rapids before settling back into a broad, relaxed stroke. An earthy tang rose from the river, growing stronger as the dwelling places of London petered out and marshland took over. Sunniva pointed to a wading bird, commenting on the gleam of its wings.

"And it is good eating, too," she added, and then she laughed, rather shame-facedly. "Especially roasted, with parsnips and turnips."

The ferryman caught Marc's eye and winked.

Sunniva turned on the wooden seat and looked at both of them. "Would it not be better to give me the parchment and for you to return to London to guard your youngsters? It is my land."

"Absolutely not. And they are safe with Ragnar."

They lapsed into silence again and now Marc could hear faint cheering. Their boat rounded a bend in the river and he could see people ranged along its banks: Londoners dressed in their best, come to stare at their new king.

Sunniva inhaled sharply. Looking where she did, Marc found his own breath stopped. The abbey church of Edward towered above them, gleaming white, in the form of a long cross, with a semicircular apse and a massive central tower.

"I never knew buildings could be so huge!" Sunniva breathed, and Marc said, "I have seen such a style before, in Normandy."

She flicked him a look. "Duke William will feel at home, then."

"King William," Marc reminded her.

Again, she teased him. "Not yet," she said.

* * *

Reaching a jetty, Marc hurried them off the boat and pushed a way through the thronging crowds—not quite a mob, Sunniva realized, but edgy all the same. There were guards standing all the way round the abbey church and men on horseback in armor, glowering at the people.

Marc seemed to know who to approach. In moments he had displayed the parchment with its precious seal and they were let through into the church.

Inside, the semidarkness after the bright morning made Sunniva almost lose her footing and the rich tumble of incense caught in the back of her throat. Marc, his hand clamped about her wrist, propelled her to a space in the nave, close to a massive carved stone pillar and only released his other hand off his sword when they had their backs against the pillar.

"Now what?" she whispered.

"We wait," Marc replied, swiveling his head, obviously trying to see Odo of Bayeux, or any of the lords of Brittany, or indeed anyone he recognized.

Of course he is one of the victors, Cena hissed in Sunniva's mind. She shut her father out, praying to the old King Edward, whose grave was in this holy church. *Please let Marc be safe*, she prayed. *Please let him not be a woman-killer. Please let us be together.*

So intent was she on her prayers that she paid little heed to what was happening further inside the church. Eventually, through the puffs of incense and the tense standing knots of armed, fidgeting men she noticed a muscular, clean-shaven, middle-aged man standing close to the high altar. Beside him were the bishops in their heavy, embroidered robes—she was too anxious to take notice of the needlework on their clothes. Beside them were a few monks, singing gamely into the not-quite-silence, and on either side of the nave, the Saxon lords and William's Normans.

They made a contrast, Sunniva thought. The Normans, clean-shaven and crop-haired, some sweating in chain mail. The English, long-haired, with full beards or moustaches, and short riding cloaks, many stained by travel. To a man they stared at the altar, not quite looking at the king—for that was certainly who it was.

William was speaking, repeating something, prompted by an elderly cleric.

"That is Aldred, archbishop of York," Marc said in her ear. "I have it on good authority that he has anointed William and—look!"

Sunniva swung her head and saw the lean, hawk-featured Aldred place a gold diadem upon the stocky William's balding head. The Normans, standing on the right side of the nave, began to cheer, the sound lost in the great church. A few of the English, standing on the left side of the nave, joined in, and Sunniva thought that she heard the accents of her own homeland, coming from the lips of a tall, elderly Englishman who reminded her of someone . . . She felt homesick for an instant, missing her mother, and then the moment was gone.

Now the archbishop of York stood back and asked the English if William was acceptable as king. A French bishop, whom Marc did not recognize, asked the same question to the French-speaking Normans.

Both sides agreed and their acclamations grew louder, each side seeming determined to outdo the other. With every shout, those waiting outside the abbey joined in until suddenly one of the guards burst back into the church, yelling something in French that spurred the whole company, Normans and English, into an unseemly stampede for the door.

Frozen into a shocked stillness as the ominous smell of burning gushed into the church and she heard screaming outside, she was conscious of being roughly bundled behind Marc. "Keep your back always to the pillar!" he hissed, tugging a monk behind him and drawing his sword to defend them all.

Outside the tumult increased. Sickened to hear the running panic, Sunniva realized that most of the congregation had fled, including the tall, bearded stranger who had put her in mind of her homeland. Like scurrying ants in a broken anthill, the clergy were hastening to complete the consecration of the king. William, paler than spun flax, seemed to be trembling. All this—on Christmas Day!

Sunniva closed her eyes and prayed for safety.

Chapter Twenty-Six

Odo of Bayeux cracked a louse between this thumb-nails and scratched at his crotch. He enjoyed relieving the massive itch—he was proud to be a man of prodigious appetites—and he enjoyed watching the people waiting in line to see the king (his brother William) as they schooled their revolted expressions into a fast, dumb docility.

All except the girl waiting with the tall, strapping knight, who hovered as close to her as a pander to his money. Standing at the back of the snaking line of folk in this bare great hall, shuffling forward a few steps every few moments as the king, his brother William, saw off another English groveler, Master Hovering Knight was aware of no one but the girl. And she was aware of nothing but him and . . . what?

Odo pushed his bulk away from the wooden pillar and snatched a torch from the nearest wall sconce, all the better to see. Hefting the torch aloft, he grinned as several of the nearest English fell back from him as if he would burn them, but the charmed pair, as he expected, did not notice the new play of shadows and light over their tryst. Master Hovering Knight was clutching his sword hilt and—

"God's bones, it is Marc de Sens," Odo muttered. He had never seen the man with such a clear, open look before. How had he not recognized him earlier? Of course, it was the girl Marc was with, she was enough to cloud any man's wits, even his own, and he was a cleric.

She was playing with something, catching something on her wrists and fingers, like knucklebones but bigger. Twigs, Odo thought, peering through the smoke. She had picked up twigs from one of the faggots ranged at the north end of the great hall and she was playing with them.

Odo strode toward the couple. The wench became better-looking with each step and not only because he had sunk a half barrel of wine at supper that evening. He sucked in his gut, realized what he was doing, and chuckled. This was one English worth speaking to.

Glancing over his shoulder, Odo saw the king leaning across the table, in supposedly kingly fashion, although Odo thought he looked as brown and nondescript as the clerk scratching on parchment alongside him. The crown of England was on the narrow strip of carpet on the table, along with the silver salt cellar, and William touched the crown as he spoke. He looked harassed and out of temper, a vein punching on his broad forehead and his dogs cringing out of range of his feet. The clerk was trying to translate his rapid French into English and no one round that table and dais looked happy, least of all the stripling petitioner from London, who could have started shaving only in this past week.

Leaving them to it, Odo progressed farther down the hall, swinging his trusty club on his belt and wondering what hour it was. Close to midnight, he wagered, midnight on Christmas Day and a stream of mewling English to see before he and William could claim their beds.

Odo thought with satisfaction of his bed. He had turned a Jewish family out in London, so he was well housed in a fireproof stone house. No woman yet to warm his feet but perhaps this pretty wench with Marc de Sens would do. Although maybe not: he might need de Sens another time, since the Breton bred excellent horses.

"It is harder to practice with twigs," the English girl was saying, "knives are easier."

Caring little for that cryptic statement, Odo approached, dropped his club and dragged the girl's headsquare off her forehead.

De Sens seized his arm and bent it back, painfully, plainly not caring who he was dealing with. "My lord, this lady is with me," he ground out through a clenched jaw.

"Naturally, de Sens." Choosing to be amused, Odo took a step back, relaxing further when the younger man released him. With a flick of a finger, he dismissed a guard who had started forward: if he wanted, he could always have the Breton flung in jail. For the moment, he had got what he wanted: a proper look at the wench. She was a beautiful little thing; bright gold hair, bright eyes, white skin pink with alarm. A complete waste in England, really: she deserved to be mewed up in a Norman castle, visited and serviced at her lord's fancy.

Odo smiled, pleased at the image, and switched to English. "Who is this lady?"

"She is the one I spoke of," Marc de Sens answered,

frowning as the girl sank into a curtsey: he was a most jealous guardian.

"What is your name, child?" Odo asked, pleased to stir the Breton's twanging temper further by speaking directly to her.

"I am Sunniva Cena-daughter, my lord. I am honored to meet you. Thank you for seeing us." Still on her knees, she glanced at his fingers, clearly looking for a bishop's ring to kiss.

He was not wearing his rings today, but Odo put her out of her pretty confusion by planting his hand on her head and intoning a blessing in Latin, amused as he sensed de Sens seething alongside. Now he snapped his fingers and tossed the torch to the hurrying guard, smirking as the guard almost dropped the flame into the rushes on the floor.

"You were practicing," Odo said.

"Yes, my lord."

Odo waited, but she said nothing more. He fingered a link on his chain mail as he paused, wondering if she might have been more forthcoming had he worn his bishop's robes. But then William had wanted him armed and ready to fight in case one of these frightened-faced English turned out to be the leader of a war band.

"I saw you at my brother's coronation," he probed. "You did not flee with the others."

She blushed but still said nothing. Beside her, Marc de Sens growled, "My lord, we have been waiting many hours and my lady is weary."

"Truly?" Odo turned a wide-lipped smile on the taller man. "She seems as fresh as a new oyster to me," he added in French, reverting at once to the girl's native tongue. "My brother the king admires courage," he went on, "and he does not like turncoats."

Still kneeling, she bowed her head. "We are all in the king's hands," she said steadily, her voice as mellow as a flute, "and in the care of the holy church."

"Do you come today seeking a favor?"

Her head came up at the direct question.

"I come today to offer my allegiance to my anointed king."

Cleverly done, Odo approved, warming more and more to the girl. He offered her his hand to help her rise, saying, "Come with me."

He took her, and the frowning de Sens to the head of the motley queue. The king saw him approach and waved aside his latest petitioner.

"Yes, brother?" William demanded in French, "Who do we have here?"

"My friend, the horse master Marc de Sens, and this—"

"De Sens?" William interrupted before Odo could complete the introduction: his brother always interrupted. "Where has he been?"

Odo stood to one side to allow Marc de Sens to answer that risky question. William might be his brother but when his eyebrows met in the middle of his forehead like that and his bald patch glowed it meant he was irritated. Reluctant to be savaged himself, Odo glanced at the tall Breton, who to his credit, replied swiftly.

"I have been trapped in London this past month, my lord, with the Atheling's supporters busy in the streets. Before that I was on pilgrimage in the north, traveling with my nieces . . ."

"You ignored my call to arms," William persisted. His blunt features burned with resentment.

De Sens did not kneel and neither did he flinch. "I

did not know of any summons, my liege, because I was away on pilgrimage."

"I have also heard a rumor that you have lived here in England." William sat forward on his chair, planting his elbows on the carpet on the table. "Is this true?"

"It is." Marc de Sens did not elaborate on this laconic statement and met William's glower with a frank and steady stare.

"Humph!" William broke their glance first, sweeping a hand across the nap of the carpet to finger his crown again. "You have been on pilgrimage before, as I recall, and it has given you small favor with the almighty."

What did he mean by that, Odo wondered.

"You live in this land like an Englishman, you did not fight at Senlac yet you come here, expecting my favor—"

"No, my lord." To Odo's astonishment, Marc de Sens interrupted William. "I came as protector to this lady, and protector to my kindred."

"Family first, eh?" William rasped, looking straight at Odo. Breathing more easily—when his brother spoke of family he was usually in a good mood and he was, above all, a family man himself—Odo risked winking at him.

William did not smile but he straightened in his seat and looked for the first time at the pretty Englishwoman standing quietly beside de Sens, waiting with prudent patience for the conversation to revert to a tongue she understood.

The king looked—and carried on looking. Head to toe, he scanned the young woman, then pushed back his chair and hurried round the table to greet her. "My lady—"

Odo swiftly supplied her name, amused when

William tried to embrace Lady Sunniva and she deftly evaded him by sinking to her knees.

"Welcome, my lady Sunniva!" William put out both hands to raise her, his grin now wide and genuine. He snapped at his clerk, "Translate!" and repeated himself.

"Welcome, my lady Sunniva!" Odo called out in English, pleased to be in the thick of things and to remind his brother the king that he knew more of this tricky native tongue than did William. He smiled at the blushing Sunniva, now with her hands trapped firmly by his brother's paws, and at de Sens, who stood looming by the king as if measuring him for a coffin. "Welcome, Sunniva Cena-daughter!"

As he spoke, a tall, richly dressed man lurched out of the snaking, shaking crowd of petitioners, took three steps toward the dais and sank to his knees.

"My lord king!" he cried, before the guards reached him, "I know this woman! She is my kin! Cena was my brother!"

Chapter Twenty-Seven

She had not seen Marc for three days, neither Marc nor his nieces for three whole days, and she was more than anxious, she felt sick and heartsick. Sleep was a stranger to her and the woman assigned to her—as friend? As maid? As guard?—fretted that she was losing weight and color.

Sunniva had no appetite. Worse, she had no answers. No one she spoke to—and she tried everyone, every stranger—could tell her anything of Marc. She feared he was not in the new king's favor. What had they spoken of, that night after the coronation, when William had questioned and Marc had answered in one or two words? She feared for him, for his stubborn pride. He would ask no favors of anyone, even of a king. It was one of the many reasons she loved him, yet in these strange, bitter times, was Marc wise? She had seen him drawn away by that fearsome fellow Odo of Bayeux, the shaven-headed bishop who wielded a club and kicked away beggars and claimed he was a man of peace. Where had they gone? Was Marc arrested? Was he imprisoned somewhere? What of his young ones? Were they safe?

She could sit still no longer. Rising from her embroidery stand, Sunniva walked past the candleholder with its fine wax candle to one of the many braziers scattered through the long narrow room and made a play of warming her hands. The walls of this windowless place were painted with scenes from scripture: Jonah being swallowed by a whale, Moses and the burning bush, Jesus casting out demons of the sick. She did not like to look too closely at the fang-toothed devils.

She and a few other noble Englishwomen had been brought here, into a secluded part of the Westminster abbey monastery. She guessed it had once been the monks' refectory, now turned into a dormitory for her and women like her: heiresses.

She was rich. Her uncle Bertolf had impressed upon her and the king that she was rich in lands. How can that be? Sunniva mused, holding her hands to the twisting flames. But Bertolf, in making himself known to her and the king, had been precise in his descriptions. He knew details of her old home, of her father and mother, of her brothers, and even more of her lands. He had brought witness to confirm his claims. Now it seemed she was the mistress of many farms and villages, places she had never heard of before. The sudden knowledge had shocked her.

It had shocked Marc, too, and she had not had a chance to speak to him in private about this matter, to explain to him that she had not known. How could she have known? Cena had never talked to her of lands, only of household duties.

Her father had rarely talked to her of his brother, either, and Sunniva thought she knew why. Pasty where Cena had been red, scrawny where Cena had been broad, loaded with jewels and fine furs and

brooches where Cena had dressed in plain stuff,
Uncle Bertolf was the consummate courtier. She remembered him as taciturn but he was not silent here.
He attached himself to the new king with a fawning
subservience that fooled no one. He fawned on her,
too, in the king's hearing but she suspected that if he
could pry her away from this strange court and get
her alone with him, it would be another matter.

My appearance must have spoilt his plans, Sunniva
thought, with a shiver. Had her uncle meant to claim
these rich lands for his own? She rather suspected he
had, in which case Marc had done her a great service
and she had not been able to thank him.

Please, St. Freya and St. Cuthbert, let Marc be safe!

"My lady?" It was the maid who made up her
bed each evening in this curious "holding place for
heiresses"—for she and the other five young women
kept in here could not leave: Sunniva had tried the door
and found it locked. "My lady, do you not wish to wear
one of your new gowns? I have another, sent by your
kinsman."

"My uncle is generous," Sunniva said quickly, as her
thoughts sped out like bees from a hive. Bertolf had
already supplied her with gowns and combs, but a
new one surely meant change was coming.

I am getting out of here, she thought, her spirits
soaring. It was as much as she could do not to snatch
the maid's hands and whirl about the room with her.

"I shall be glad to wear his gift," she said, smiling.
"Will you help me, please?" She knew the maid was a
spy for Bertolf or the king or both, but the woman—
like all Englishwomen these days—had little choice.

The maid, whose name Sunniva could not discover,
although she asked the plump, dark-haired young

woman each time she appeared, scurried to the door
and called out a phrase in French. The phrase changed
each time the maid passed in or out and now, as the
door swung inwards and the maid's round, sallow face
did not change from its habitually closed, stubborn
expression, Sunniva caught a glimpse of a guardsman
pacing outside. Beside the guard had been a tall
shadow—Marc? Or her uncle?

Soon she would know: already the maid was trip-
ping back, a new gown slung across her outstretched
arms. It was of a dark blue, shimmering material, as
light and soft as rose petals, pleated and with a sweeping bodice embroidered in gold thread. There was a
headsquare to go with the gown: a new-style headsquare, filmy and of the same stuff as the gown, to be
held in place by a silver fillet.

"How gorgeous!" another of the captives exclaimed,
leaving her game of solitary knucklebones and hurrying across the room. Two more young women also left
their books and embroidery to touch and wonder,
though the final young woman, a tall, pale girl with unbound, unveiled silver-blonde hair, watched carefully
from her pallet and would not be drawn close.

When Sunniva exclaimed in turn at the gown's
beauty, the woman who seemed to have been assigned
to her as her maid merely looked at her through
puddle-gray, flat eyes, her round shoulders sagging.

"If you say so, my lady," she remarked in a hope-
less way.

"Would you like this gown?" Sunniva asked, tugging
at her own robe. It was not much to give, but she had
nothing else, no ready money, and at the very least
the maid would be able to sell it on for food or cash.

The maid shook her head. "My lord clothes me well enough."

She said nothing more, shaking her head each time Sunniva asked a question as to where she was from, or who her lord was, or who they were going out to see. For they must be going out—why else the new gown, and such a lovely gown?

"Is this how Norman ladies dress?" one of the other girls asked, as the maid laced Sunniva into the snug bodice. It was far tighter than she normally wore her gowns and she felt self-conscious of her generous curves.

"If you say so, my lady," came back the unenthusiastic reply, and to Sunniva: "Can you sit down? I need to attach your headrail."

The maid did not cover all her hair with the filmy cloth but pinned it partway back on her head, leaving all the ends flowing so that glimpses of Sunniva's thick, glowing plait could be seen.

"I cannot go out like this!" Sunniva protested.

"Perhaps it is the style of the court," another heiress suggested, as the maid silently flitted to the door.

"Will you come, my lady?" she asked. "You may leave your embroidery."

Through her words Sunniva heard a clear command and she rose quickly. In truth she would be glad to leave, although as she whispered swift farewells to the others, she wondered what she was going to.

The maid brought her to a side entrance of Westminster Hall, spoke more French to the guard there and drew Sunniva inside. Passing a tiny alcove shrouded by a thick cloth, the maid scratched at the cloth, called out, "She is here," then turned on her heel and scooted away.

Her head held high, Sunniva did not wait for the alcove curtain to be withdrawn but lifted it aside and stood on the threshold of this private, makeshift chamber, waiting for her eyes to adjust. After the semidark of the former abbey dormitory and the vast gloom of the great banqueting hall, still full of waiting petitioners but all anxiously silent and brooding, this "room" sparkled with light.

"Ah—" Sunniva tried to count the ranks of burning candles and gave up after a score. The smell of expensive beeswax hung in the air as she rapidly took in the rest.

King William, recognizable by his ruddy complexion, square features and keen dark eyes, was standing with his back to three large candles, examining an embroidered belt, which she recognized as her own work. Beside him, lolling on a large cushion, the bald-pated Odo of Bayeux grinned at her and patted a spare cushion.

"Sit, sit, the others will be here soon," he said in his expansive way, tossing an unseen tidbit to one of the prowling wolfhounds. "Take your ease while you can. I always do." He leaned back and patted his bulging stomach. "How many water mills have you on your lands?"

Sunniva blinked at the rapid change of subject but Odo simply beamed at her and William thoughtfully rubbed her belt against his stubble.

"This good work," he grunted in English. He sounded surprised.

"How many water mills?" his half brother prompted.

"Forgive me, I do not know," Sunniva answered.

"How many fields of flax? Of wheat?" Odo persisted,

as the king fingered the belt afresh and muttered, almost to himself, "Colors good."

"My father never spoke of such matters to me," Sunniva replied crisply. This was a bizarre summons, she thought. Should she offer to make the king one of the belts?

As if he sensed her interest, William said something rapidly in French, which Odo translated.

"My brother says that his wife would value your advice on needlecraft, Lady Sunniva," he explained, drumming his fingers on his stomach as William looked at her directly for the first time.

Sunniva trained herself not to flinch from his blank, stone stare. "I am your lady's servant," she answered politely, hazarding further by adding, "And my lord Marc de Sens—"

"Best not to speak of him," said Odo, but William heard the name and scowled, firing off more French.

"My brother is disinclined for de Sens to be admitted into his court," Odo translated. "The man is notorious throughout Normandy and Brittany as a woman-killer. He has visited many shrines in both lands, seeking absolution for his sin."

"He is innocent!" The words sprang from Sunniva before she could stop them and now she did not want to: she stared at the new king of England, marking his reddening cheeks and narrowed eyes and repeated steadily, in the face of danger, "He is innocent, my lord. I know it."

William did not wait for the translation but huffed back a reply.

Odo smiled. "My brother the king says that de Sens has found no peace of mind in his pilgrimages: does that not prove his guilt?"

Before Sunniva could answer the curtain was raised again and Bertolf bowed into the room, followed by Marc. Her eyes flew to him, loving all of him and marking each small change: he had grown thinner over these past few days; he had cut his right cheek while shaving; he was wearing the tunic she had repaired for him. "Marc," she mouthed, longing to speak to him.

William, lately of Normandy, now of Normandy and England, saw the Englishwoman's anguished glance and stifled a smile. His own wife had once looked at him in the same way, adoring and hopeful, and he envied Marc de Sens. Was the Breton worthy of such devotion?

Let us see, he thought, greeting the older man, Bertolf, in halting English. He knew far more of the language than even Odo realized but for the moment it suited him to pretend that he did not.

"You see that your niece is well treated, Lord Bertolf," he went on.

"Truly, my liege," came back the smooth reply, also in English. "She blossoms in your care." Bertolf stroked his trim beard and moustache. "As do we all."

Liar! thought William. Bertolf, busy groveling, had not even looked at his kinswoman. But such men had their uses. "Better my care than that of a killer, eh?"

"I am grateful for your concern, my liege," Bertolf answered, his polished courtier's mask refusing to slip as he did not ask the obvious question.

Marc de Sens, staring at the Englishwoman as a starving man might yearn after food, showed no such restraint. "What do you mean?" he demanded, without so much as a nod for courtesy. "What is this? In what way does my lady Sunniva need your care?" The tall

Breton took a step forward, his hand going ominously to his sword hilt. "Do I have your word, William, that she is your guest, honored and treated as such?"

"Better my guest than yours," William spat back, still using English. He was unused to being questioned, and irritated by de Sens' tone.

Faster than a stooping hawk, de Sens whirled toward the woman, shielding her as he faced the other men. He had not drawn his sword but his eyes were as narrow and bright as a blade as he glared. For an instant, William felt a prickle of dread before he collected himself—he was, after all, Duke of Normandy and King of England.

"Have a care, de Sens," Odo warned, but the man would take no notice.

"Are you all right?" He spoke directly to the lady.

She blushed very prettily, to William's experienced eye. With a modern Norman gown and headrail she was most presentable, especially as the dress clung becomingly and her features were clear and fine, unmarred by pox. Her hair in particular was lush: golden enough to inspire any wandering poet. William felt impelled to touch it, but restrained himself for the moment.

Her voice was mellow and pleasing. "I am well. But Marc—"

"They have treated you honorably?"

"Yes. But Marc—"

"Woman-killer." William pushed himself away from the wall. He had faced down many men in his time and he was determined that this Breton would not intimidate him. "Why should I allow this woman here to be delivered into your dubious charge? Why not her uncle, who is her kin?"

"I am no woman-killer," de Sens ground out, "and this Englishman is unknown, untried."

"Much as yourself, de Sens!" Fired again by the Breton's non-appearance at Hastings and the battle of Senlac Field, William spoke his mind, not caring now who knew how good his English was. "You are notorious in France—'The Restless Pilgrim' you are called, restless because you are unshriven, unrepentant, guilty!"

"No!" The Englishwoman cried, hurling herself to her knees before William—between him and de Sens, the king noted. "He is innocent!"

Odo stirred on his cushion but the Englishman Bertolf was there first, gliding forward with his palms pressed together like a priest. "May I make a suggestion?"

"Speak, man." William was still out of patience and there were a hundred more English still to see: if this middling nobleman had any solutions, now was the time he should share them.

Bertolf gave a low bow. "My liege, as de Sens is a fighting man, why not a trial by battle? Let him prove himself."

"Done!" said de Sens at once.

Still on her knees, the Englishwoman with the amazing golden hair bit her lips to stifle a protest and dropped her face into her hands. William almost felt sorry for her, though not by much: de Sens should have been with him on the longboats coming to England.

"Then let the trial be the day after tomorrow, against my own champion," he said.

Tomorrow and the day after would be interesting, he thought, glancing at Odo, who gave him a knowing look.

Chapter Twenty-Eight

Horrified by this turn of events, Sunniva tried to speak to Marc but Odo hauled himself off his cushion to grab Marc's arm and her uncle was bearing down on her, a look of anticipated greed glowing on his usually pallid face.

"Come, English girl. Take a turn with me." Strong fingers snapped before her eyes and William waited till she had taken his hand before yanking her smartly to her feet and away with him. She heard Marc's cursing protest but she dare not look back, lest she provoke him to some reckless act of violence to match his earlier hot words. All she could do was as the king wanted: march with him into the main banqueting hall and then outside into an afternoon of bright snow.

"Reminds me of winters in Falaise." William pointed to a strung-out group of children on the opposite side of the river, pounding each other with snowballs. "My boy William used to love playing in snow."

Sunniva allowed the king to draw her arm through his, praying she would not slip on the sparkling cobbles and frosted, snowy grass. She was bitterly cold, without cloak or gloves, but determined not to shiver.

"Did you ever play so?" Away from the court and the press of guards, the king's command of English was almost as good as Marc's.

"Winter is a busy season where I come from," Sunniva replied. "I remember helping my mother break up well-ice, and check the cured hams, and gather firewood and—"

"Servants did not do those tasks? No matter." William shouted something in French to one of the guards by the abbey perimeter wall and turned about, staring at the great church. He seemed to be listening to a thread of song from the choristers but then grunted and moved on. "Have you children?"

Sunniva hesitated, thinking of Marc's girls. Were they safe? Was Marc with them? "In a way," she answered, her scalp tingling as she made the admission. She shivered, telling herself it was the cold.

"Walk with me to the river," William ordered. "Tell me of your uncle."

"He is an honorable man, and true to his king."

William bent his head down to hers. "You do not know him at all."

She saw the laughter-lines around his eyes and risked a smile. "Not really."

"But you know Marc de Sens?"

Was it going to be this easy? Thank you, St. Freya! She nodded, mentally taking her courage in both hands. "May I speak to you about him, sir?"

They had reached the steps leading down to the water, where a few boats sculled by. A trio of ragged figures, sweeping the steps with bits of twig instead of proper brooms, cowered away, one tumbling back into a bank of snow. A pace or two behind, Sunniva heard two of the king's bodyguards half-draw their swords. William barked an order and she heard the blades returned to their scabbards.

"Please continue." He stamped down a patch of snow with his boot.

Sunniva knew she would never have another chance. She spoke swiftly, telling of the pilgrimage: how Marc had saved her from being taken by the whoremaster, how he had stayed behind when the rest of the pilgrims had gone on, so she would not be left alone. How Marc cared for his nieces. How he had been taking her to her home. How he took care of her. How he had sought out her family after the dreadful carnage of the battle for the bridge at Stamford.

"Yet he did not complete the pilgrimage to Durham," William observed.

"Because of me. He did not want to leave me. He wanted me safe."

"You could have hurried along, caught the other pilgrims up and gone on with them."

Sunniva shrugged, not wanting to go into Marc's premonitions of disaster for Durham. Had anything indeed happened there? Marc had once told her that not all his forebodings always came to pass. She might never know the answer.

"He saw my father and brothers buried," she said, deliberately changing the subject from their uncompleted pilgrimage.

"Yes, he seems to have God's own luck at arriving just too late on a battlefield." William's mouth turned down at the corners.

"He got us away from a house filled with returning warriors," Sunniva persisted. "It would have been far easier and safer for him to ride off and leave us, but Marc would never do that. He fights for those he loves."

An idea bloomed in her mind: foolish, unusual but compelling. In her excitement she gripped William's arm, forgetting he was king, seeing only the interest in his bright, dark eyes.

"Please, my lord, I have a favor to ask. May I prove to you that Marc is innocent?" A chill breeze blew straight off the river, weaving her new gown even more tightly against her breasts, stomach and legs. Clammy with cold, she forced her teeth not to chatter. "My lord?"

"How will you do that?"

Bracing herself for his answer, Sunniva told him.

Where was she?

Marc was going mad. Odo was driving him mad. His nieces, whom Ragnar had brought upriver to Odo's "court" at the Jew's house, were nagging him, over and over, worrying at him with the same question that tormented him, waking and sleeping.

Where was Sunniva?

Odo claimed she was safe with the king, which Marc thought was slightly better than if she had been placed with her wretched, grasping kinsman. Still, it was not much better. He had seen how William had licked his lips when she came near.

Was she like him, a prisoner, but not?

He could go anywhere in the Jewish house, anywhere in London, if Odo and a score of Normans were with him. He dared not break out, not for fear of leaving his girls behind—he would never do that— but dread of what revenge William might wreak on Sunniva, once he and his girls were gone.

At least Ragnar and his men had got away from Odo, back into the greasy, brooding bowels of London.

Now he and his "friend" Odo were on the river again, being rowed to Westminster, while his girls were left behind at the Jew's house—for their own protection, claimed Odo, though Marc knew that they were hostages against his own good behavior. Sometime today he would fight the king's champion to prove his innocence. The king would choose the venue and the time.

Marc breathed slowly down his nose, closing his mind to Odo's remarks on the day and the weather. He knew William's champion: big, tough, fast. He had seen the man take blow after blow on his helmet and come back for more. He favored sweeping sword-cuts and led always with his right shoulder. He relied on his sword arm, did not move his feet much. Dangerous, but Marc knew he could best him.

And then? After he had shown the world that he was no woman-killer?

That would be a relief in itself. Pray God that today would see the end of it: peace for himself and for his girls. Isabella had suffered no more bad dreams, Alde and Judith no longer whimpered in their sleep. They had all begun to sleep more soundly once Sunniva had entered their midst.

She has been their angel, he thought, and smiled.

He rolled his shoulders and flexed his fingers, keeping his hands warm and supple. He swung his legs, drumming his feet softly against the keel of the boat. He wanted to row in place of the boat-man, more than ever today, when a thick mist rose off the milky waters and snow covered both banks. There was little to see, except the growing motte that Sunniva so detested. The mound heaved with tiny working figures, soundless in the patchy fog. Elsewhere, a few coils of smoke revealed the presence of a hut, of life, but the city remained eerily quiet. Along the riverbank, a desperate woman unlaced her gown and showed off her breasts, to leering and catcalls from the second boat, filled with Odo's guards, but they did not stop. Even paid pleasure must wait when they had been summoned by the king.

"So, you are ready." Odo waved a meaty palm in front of his eyes to ensure Marc's attention. "I am sure you will do well. Have you in mind what favor you will ask my brother the king when you win?"

"Other than sparing the life of his champion when I have him on the ground, you mean?"

"Something like, yes." Odo chuckled at his confidence, making the sign of the cross before his face: a kind of rough clerical blessing. "You did not know your pretty English maid was rich, did you?"

Accustomed to Odo's swift changes in conversation, aimed to shake and disconcert, Marc said nothing. In his concern that Sunniva was safe he had forgotten for the moment that she was rich. Why had she never told him herself? Did she not trust him? After all they had endured together, did she truly not trust him? After she had admitted to him that Caedmon of Whitby was no more than a name to her and he had forgiven her, why did she still not trust him? Was she afraid he might cast doubt upon her parentage?

"It matters not," he said, sensing Odo waiting for an answer.

He closed his eyes, pretending to pray. After today, after his trial of ordeal, Sunniva would trust him. He would prove to her once and for all that she could trust in him, and in his love.

Even so, he wished she was not rich. How could he

win her hand in marriage when she was rich and he was not?

Perhaps I should ask William for land in England when I win today, he thought, and grinned at that simple, fairy-tale solution.

The king, dressed in robes of state and wearing the golden crown of Edward, the old king, came down the jetty steps to meet them. He came alone, a thing Marc might have marveled at, had he been less concerned with where Sunniva might be.

Odo was less discreet. "By the teeth of the Almighty, do you want to be a target for every disaffected archer in London?" he roared, stumbling out of the boat, yelling to his men to cover William with their shields.

Over the general hubbub, William held out his hand to Marc.

"My champion awaits in the cloister garden," he said.

Marc gave a nod of acknowledgment, gripping William's hand briefly so the man would know he was not afraid. "I am ready," he said, passing over the fact that they would be fighting on holy ground. It was an ordeal, after all, and so God's business.

William began to stride back up the steps, Marc following a respectful step behind. Looking about, he caught no sign of Sunniva, but out of the swirling mist he heard the king say, "Whoever disarms the other will be acknowledged the winner."

"As you say." Marc was very pleased that he would not have to injure his opponent. He wanted to prove his innocence, but not at the expense of another man's life or limb.

"This is the only ordeal I will accept, de Sens."

"Of course." Marc bristled. "I have said I am ready."

William merely continued walking, reaching the top of the steps and slowing a little, to catch his breath. Marc almost collided with him but as he skewed sideways to miss the king, William added softly, for his ear alone, "It is a trial by combat, but you, Marc de Sens, are not to fight. Another has begged to do so in your place."

"No!"

"You know who it is, de Sens. They are preparing her for battle even as we speak." William stopped and faced an appalled Marc. "This is my choice, de Sens. You will accept it, or your life is forfeit now, as that of a guilty man."

"Then it is forfeit," Marc snarled. "For my lady Sunniva to fight in my place is more than an ordeal, it is a monstrous thing. I will have none of it!"

Armed men, clanking up behind them to catch up, paused on the steps and looked uncertainly at the king, then Odo. William shook his head and placed both hands out, palms down, a sign for calm.

"Your proxy will not be harmed. This I swear to you."

Marc could scarcely believe what he was hearing, "It is unfair!" he burst out. "I am the one who must prove himself, I fight my own fights!" he snarled. "I have fought my own fights since I was ten years old! You must not allow this!"

"I gave my word to the Lady Sunniva that she could be your proxy." William was relentless. "My champion will fight with one hand tied behind his back. This kind of trial, a woman fighting against a man, has happened before, in Germany."

"So are we Germans now?" At his wit's end, Marc dropped to his knees before William. "My liege, I beg you, do not allow this ordeal. Let me take my punishment."

"You are guilty, then, of woman-killing?"

Marc looked William straight in the eyes. "Yes."

William walked on, leaving Marc kneeling in the snow.

Entering the cloisters, William glanced at the central garden, open to the sky. It had been cleared of whatever herbs and snow and the earth flattened down into a hard, compacted mass, crusted with frost. On one side stood his champion, warming up with a few sword parries and thrusts. His opponent was as yet unseen, hiding behind a maze of stone pillars on the shadowy side of the cloister. William walked across the bare earth to where he thought Sunniva might be.

He spotted her in the darkest part of the cloister, knelt in prayer. He strode up and interrupted—God would forgive him, as he had important news to bring.

"Marc de Sens is coming, under my brother's care and that of my guards."

Sunniva opened her eyes and allowed her hands to fall by her sides. "He has not hurt them? Fought them? Injured them?"

"No." William coughed, a rare sign of embarrassment. "I told my brother to tell him that if he made one move toward you or my champion or any one of the court, then my archers would mow both him and you down."

"That would be only the threat that would stop Marc from fighting to protect me." She sounded proud, William thought. He was confounded for an instant by her calm, but then realized that she had expected no more and no less from de Sens: a point to the Breton. Indeed, de Sens' overriding concern for this young

woman was a thing William understood—he loved his
own wife dearly.

"Does your champion know I am the proxy?" she
went on. "I want no unfair advantage."

William glanced up and down the cloister, checking
for listening ears. A monk wandered nearby on the
south side of the cloister, his sandaled feet muffled in
the mist, but his cowl was pulled up, shutting out the
secular world. The members of the court and de Sens
were yet to arrive.

"My champion knows nothing." Except that he
would fight with one hand tied behind his back and
that if he killed or injured his enemy then he would
also quickly die. As an heiress, this girl was too valuable to lose—better she kept her lands and married
where he, William, allowed, than that they fell into
kinsman Bertolf's greedy maw. Bertolf, who had already sent word that he was suddenly too ill today to
attend this ordeal . . .

Sunniva nodded. "He should think me a youth."

William took in her loose man's tunic and leggings.
She had refused the offer of chain mail, but she had
done what she could to disguise her femininity, hiding
her hair completely under a close-fitting cap and even
dusting her face with dirt, an attempt at producing
male stubble. She looked wiry and trim and nothing
like a lad.

"Of course," William agreed, lying through his teeth.
Then he noticed the knives at her belt: long and doubtless sharp out of their serviceable, battered leather
sheaths.

"Do you know how to use those?" he asked, doubt
clouding his head for an instant. Perhaps he had been
unwise, indulging the girl in her unusual request, but

he liked to see her smile. He fully expected her to lose, and quickly. Then de Sens would be banished, Sunniva grateful he had escaped with his life and ready to obey her king when he produced another candidate for her hand in marriage.

Sunniva flicked her wrist and a tiny dagger that must have been hidden in her sleeve flew and pinned a dead leaf at William's feet. It had landed between the cracks in the stone floor—a lucky chance.

"Well done," William said approvingly, hiding his inner glee. In a few moments it would be done. Sunniva disarmed, de Sens at his mercy, the absent Bertolf confounded and then, very soon, Sunniva eager and happy to slide into his bed. She would make a spectacular mistress and later, after he had enjoyed all of her gratitude at his sparing of de Sens, he would marry her off.

He would choose well for her: he liked the girl.

Smiling at the thought of his magnanimity, William bade her farewell and crossed to the south side of the cloisters, where the monk had sped away, his own chair and banner had been brought out and Odo and his party were now arriving.

Show no fear, Sunniva chanted in her head. *God is with you. St. Freya and St. Cuthbert fight with you. We all fight for Marc, who is innocent.*

Even so, she quailed twice in the cloister grounds where her ordeal would take place. Once when she saw the champion, big and threatening as William's new caste mound, test the sharpness of his sword, and once when Marc strode toward her across the bare, cleared garden. He was blocked by a score of guards before he had reached halfway but she saw his tensed shoulders and stiff, unyielding expression and a wave of anguish scorched through her. Was he angry with her? Did he consider himself unmanned, having a proxy—and a woman at that—to fight for him?

What else could I have done? I wanted to save him. I acted without thinking, I asked the king without thinking of Marc's feelings. My one thought was to save him.

Her thoughts and her shame seared her like nettle stings but she did not look away. Whatever his opinion, she would do this for him. She knew she could settle this ordeal quickly, without bloodshed.

He smiled at her then, straight over the heads of the guards, a kind, reassuring smile. Her spirits soared like a rising lark. Buoyed up, she grinned back, smiling more widely as the king's champion planted his standard, on a broad wooden pole, before William's chair, and tugged his surcoat over his chain mail.

This was going to be easy.

Marc raised a hand. Ignoring Odo of Bayeux, who had joined him in the middle of the cloister garden and was tugging urgently on his arm, he said clearly, "God be with you."

She bowed, deliberately mute so that William's champion would not guess her sex. She saw Marc take another step toward her, dragging the burly bishop of Bayeux after him like a piece of thread, then heard the creak of a bending bow and saw Marc stiffen, his eyes widening in disgust and horror.

Already knowing what she would find, she turned and nodded to the archer positioned directly behind her, ready to shoot her in the back.

Marc swung about, his blazing eyes seeking the king's. While their gazes locked and wrestled, Sunniva checked herself over. Osric the tumbler had taught her to do this and she found it cleared her mind. Her daggers were at her belt or ready to hand. Her clothes were comfortable. Her hair was covered. Her hands were warm and steady. She pulled off her shoes, feeling the raw harsh ice on the bare earth; a not unpleasant sensation, nicely tingling.

"I am ready," she called.

Odo the bishop, still holding Marc's arm, began a rapid invocation in a language she did not understand—Latin or French or a mixture of both, she was not sure. As the guards fell back from the ground, buffeting Marc with them, she focused on her breathing and on the thick, raised seams of the champion's surcoat.

Around her the puffs of mist brightened and the abbey cloister and the people within it seemed at one and the same time to be more distant but clearer. She picked out details: the glint of sun on William's crown. The way the king was sitting on his chair, clutching the chair arms as if he was not entirely sure how this ordeal would go. Dear Marc's lips moving silently as he prayed. He was knocking his fists together again and again, a repetitive, nervous act that she guessed he was unaware of doing, such was his concern for her.

For an instant that love almost undid her, almost caused her to lose her own concentration, but then she remembered: this was his fight, not hers; she must do her best for his sake and put her own feelings aside. She let her eyes be drawn to the knot of courtiers standing behind William's chair. Amongst the disbelieving faces she saw no one she recognized.

Odo was still intoning. A monk hurried into the open space and sprinkled her and then the king's champion with holy water. The champion was standing very straight and proud as his squire bound his left arm behind his back.

She lowered her head and prayed to the Virgin, the mother of the king of heaven, and thought of her standing by the cross as her son died. She must now suffer in silence as Marc began his own trial of waiting.

In English, she heard Odo say, "This is an ordeal by combat. Whoever disarms the other will be said to have won. Whoever cuts the other, however slightly, will be said to have won. Begin."

Sunniva sprinted forward to a roar from Marc and an answering roar in her own head. She knew she had this one chance and she had to be quick.

Remembering all Osric had taught her she lifted her daggers. Spinning through the mist and sun, three streaked toward the champion, pinning him, through the thick shoulder-folds of his surcoat, to the back of his own standard pole. The man yanked and tore, slashing at the daggers with his mailed hand, but Sunniva had already launched her fourth, sharpest blade, aiming low. It sped at the man's groin and he yelled, flinching even though his mail deflected it, but his hesitation gave her the key.

She closed on him, slashing out with another small dagger, upwards at his chest and eyes, and as he feinted, trying to unsheathe his sword, charged him, knocking into his midriff, stabbing down with her final blade.

The champion shouted, a genuine yelp of pain, and stumbled back, trying to free the small dagger from between the armor on his calves and his knee. Sunniva followed, charging with all her might, knocking him off-balance.

"Hey!" Marc was yelling.

"God's teeth!" Odo was yelling.

"Enough!" William was on his feet, glaring at his stricken champion.

The man was sitting on the ground, clutching his leg below the knee. A small knife flexed like a bee sting in the top of his calf. He cursed and struck it away and a small trickle of blood came with it.

William switched his stare to Sunniva. He opened and closed his mouth twice: finally words emerged. "The ordeal is over. You have won."

Sunniva sank onto the ground and began to cry in relief.

Chapter Twenty-Nine

Later that day, close to sunset, after kicking his heels outside in the raw cold of the palace courtyard, Marc was finally admitted into the presence of the king.

He had been kept out for hours, not by the score of guards—he would have taken those on—but by William's very specific threat against Sunniva. From the moment that he entered the great hall he looked for her, frowning when he did not see her. Impatient and anxious—where was she? How was she?—he found himself standing beside the dais while the king, his brother Odo and several court favorites feasted on venison.

There was only one table set out in the hall. The English lords, Earl Morcar and the rest, were conspicuous by their absence.

"Sit, sit!" William waved Marc farther along the single table. "Hey, Etienne, make room up there!" he yelled in French. "Take a glass of wine, de Sens. Relax! You are an innocent man, proved as such for all the world to witness."

At that, the king's champion rose from the table and stamped out of the hall, limping slightly on his right side as he passed the main fire. Defeat hung

around his huge shoulders like a black cloak and the
other men were careful not to catch his eye as he left.

Marc pitied the man, though not much.

"Where is my lady?" he asked. Sunniva had been
surrounded by guards the instant that William had
declared the result of the ordeal: he had not been
able to speak to her or see her for hours.

"Resting, for the moment." William gnawed on a
deer bone and then pointed the bone at Marc. "Would
you have ripped my head off if I had shot her?"

"Yes." Marc was still enraged by the idea: if William
had done it, no one would have stopped him from
slaughtering the man.

"Honest," William grunted in return, "and entirely
what I expected you to say. Which is why I would never
have done it."

Marc shrugged. "I could not be sure."

"Of course, that is the skill of kings," said Odo, leaning across the table to snatch some of the fine white
bread set before his brother and put it in place of his
own coarse barley-bread trencher. "Now you must sit
down, Marc." He scanned Marc's face by the torchlight. "Is it my fancy, or are you still angry?"

Before Marc could answer, a herald ran into the hall.

"The Lady Sunniva is outside, my liege," he panted,
dropping on one knee before William. "She begs your
leave to enter."

William looked up and down the table. Silently,
clearly working to some prearranged plan, Odo and
the other courtiers pushed themselves to their feet
and walked to the center of the hall, where a great
midwinter fire cracked and burned. All the men had
taken their weapons. Odo had collected his cup, too,

and his fine bread trencher and was standing with the others, picking at venison.

"Sit," William ordered Marc again. "Bring a bench and put it across from me. You and she can sit together and take supper; there is plenty left."

His head ablaze with gladness that he would soon be seeing her for himself, Marc sped into the darkness of the hall. Hope and anticipation granting him speed, he effortlessly retrieved a bench from one of the piles stacked against the walls and carried it back to the dais. He set it down quickly, opposite William, and then stalked past the fire to meet Sunniva as she entered.

She walked rapidly, a powdering of light snow falling from her cloak. He moved to meet her. She faltered. Her face was uncertain, her hands clutching the edges of her cloak.

Marc stopped himself, feeling as if he had just swallowed a sword of ice. He had expected her to be nervous but not this fear—never fear.

"Sweetheart," he murmured in English, and he opened his arms.

She hung back for an instant and then she flew into his embrace. "I could see no other way," she was saying against his chest, gripping him so tightly that he feared her arms would be wrenched from their sockets. "I knew you were innocent, but I could see no other way to prove it, not without murder."

His heart raced to see her. It was a wonder to hold her again, to hear her, to truly know she was safe. She was dressed in that amazing Norman gown with that silly little veil: he dragged down her hood and reveled in the scent of her hair.

"Thank King Christ you are unhurt." He wrapped her more tightly in his arms. When he considered how close she might have come to being spitted he was torn between hugging her all night long and scolding her till her ears were singed.

"I am still angry at you," he growled against her cheek, kissing the top of her head.

"I know. I am sorry."

He put a warning finger to her lips. Now that he was quite certain that she was entirely without injury he found his sense of aggravation increasing.

"Do you think me useless?"

"I am sorry, Marc. Truly. I did not mean—"

He silenced her prattle with a long, fierce kiss, demanding submission. He ignored his own feelings of gratitude: his male pride demanded capitulation.

Not only pride. There was also fear, and shame. What if she thought less of him?

"You"—he shook her, seeing nothing but love in her yearning face. Still he longed for more assurance. "What were you about, eh?"

Her eyes pooled with tears. "Please do not be angry. I made a mistake, perhaps, because I was so concerned for you, because, too, my own pride in my own skill prompted me to act as I did. I did all I did without true thought or wisdom and I will willingly pay for it, but do not be angry, Marc."

"Later," he promised, making the word a threat, as he had once before. He knew he was being unjust, but still his anger boiled in his veins. "We shall discuss this later."

She bowed her head. "Whatever you wish."

There was a movement behind them, a scrape of a chair leg. Then: "We await your pleasure, de Sens."

William's interruption reminded Marc that they were not alone. Regretfully, resentfully, he pulled himself away to face the king. "My liege."

* * *

William noted the formal address and de Sens' resentment. Deciding that this dangerous emotion was not directed at him, he glanced at his brother, who was watching the pair with undisguised interest.

"A useful man," Odo had called de Sens and now William recalled the superb horses Odo had already had from the Breton. He himself had a favorite stud mare that was sickening with something which de Sens might very well know how to treat. He would give the man another chance.

"Come sit beside me, Lady Sunniva," he called in English. "De Sens—here." He pointed to the bench at the other side of the table.

There was a scurry of servants clearing the place beside him and setting out fresh cups and trenchers, and then the couple were sitting with him, Sunniva casting a longing glance at de Sens, the Breton not quite meeting her eye.

William chose to be blunt. "God's bones, man, you should not bear any grudge against your proxy! If she fought in your place and won, you should be glad!"

"I am glad," came back the flat response, while Sunniva coiled herself ever tighter upon her bench. William was tempted to knock their heads together, but he used words instead.

"I think you owe something to your proxy, de Sens."

Clearly startled, the man looked up from his untouched trencher of venison and, seizing the moment, William went on, "I think you owe us both an explanation." He lowered his head and dropped his voice so that no others could hear. "How is it you were ever called a woman-killer?"

* * *

This was the moment, Marc knew. There were no words to be uttered now but the true ones. He looked across at Sunniva: her warm green-blue eyes steadied him down, gave him the faith to confess.

He spoke to her, wanting her above all to understand. "Two years ago, I publicly quarreled with my widowed cousin, Agnes of Mellé. A matter of land rights and the selling of horses: we both thought we were right, but it was a shabby business. Agnes stormed off—she always did have a powerful temper—but then she was found later, before the end of that same evening, dead in her own castle. She had fallen headlong down a staircase and broken her neck."

"But you did not push her," Sunniva said at once.

Her certainty gave Marc the spur to go on.

"Aye, you are right," he said. "But, as you have guessed, that was the rumor soon enough. Many had seen us quarrel: we had fought since childhood." He felt himself blushing deeply in guilty embarrassment: even his chest hairs tingled. "As a boy I once knocked her through a window—a ground floor window, but still . . ."

His hands had found a meat bone to grind into the table: he did not know what he was doing until he saw the king glaring.

"What had Agnes done to you first?" Sunniva asked, leaning forward, elbows splayed on the table as if she were a boy.

Marc stared at the table, shame-faced. "Agnes had tripped me. I fell into the midden."

William smirked but stopped shy of outright laughter. "This is hardly to the purpose," he remarked, when he did speak.

"Not so, my lord. It shows a pattern, as in a tapestry," Sunniva replied quickly. "In this case, a pattern of trouble between Marc and his cousin. A pattern others would know and believe in. So the rumor would grow that Marc had indeed pushed his cousin again, as he did before."

"Something like," Marc admitted, while William yawned and said, "I would have done more than push."

"Quite, my lord king," Sunniva said smoothly. "Your pattern is to be relentless."

Ruthless, Marc supplied in his own head. But he was not as pretty as Sunniva, he could not risk saying it.

William yawned again. "If you did not push this Agnes of Mellé down the stairs, then who did?" he asked, confirming Sunniva's reading of his character.

"No one," Marc said quickly. "It was an accident."

He thought he had kept his face still but Sunniva leaned farther across the table and touched his hand. "Come, Marc, you have kept this hidden too long."

"What, in the name of God?" William began, but Marc, finally released by Sunniva's utter faith in him, was already talking, the words spilling from him in a great flood.

"It was just after the fire, the blaze that had killed my brother and his wife. My nieces were staying with me at Agnes' and they were crying, shrieking with nightmares every night. For days they would not play. They wanted no nurse, no one but me or my mother: their last surviving family. And then, at Agnes', Alde and Judith took a ball and kicked it about the stairs, and Isabella—

"I told Isabella she was too small for such rough play, that she must be still. Isabella brought cups and spoons to the top of the stairs leading to the castle garderobe: I saw her there and I was glad to see her so intent. She told me that she and her dolly were having a feast. Later, she remembered to take her doll with her to bed but forgot the cups."

He sighed, shamed afresh at the bitter, guilty memory. "I forgot them too, and my mother was busy in the great hall of Agnes' castle; she never knew of my nieces' play.

"It was twilight and Agnes did not see the cups at the top of the stairs. I found two by her twisted, broken body. She had stepped on them in the semidarkness, after storming away in rage from our quarrel, and lost her footing."

"But why not say?" William asked, and now Sunniva answered: just as her touch had freed his tongue, she had listened and grasped everything at once.

"You did not want the girls questioned. They had suffered enough."

Marc sighed. "I did not want to remind any of them, especially Isabella, of a childish mishap gone terribly wrong.

"What age was the girl?" William demanded.

"Isabella was five at the time of the fire that killed her parents."

"She had bad dreams after?"

"For a long time. All of my nieces dreamed of fire and death for a long time." He had done so, too, but only to Sunniva would he admit it.

Still, now that he was talking, Marc found it a blessed relief to speak, especially as Sunniva kept clasping his fingers, giving him silent support.

"I know about bad dreams as a child," William said. For an instant, a frightened boy looked out of the face of a man. "It is hell."

Marc cleared his throat and resumed his story. "In the end, I brought them away from France. I stayed at the home of a kinsman who had settled in England as part of old King Edward's entourage, brought over from Normandy to create a cavalry. I worked with him and his horses, and hoped a new life in England would help my nieces."

"Did it?" William was interested: he had stopped yawning and was picking his teeth, motioning with his free hand for Marc to continue.

"It helped a little."

"Were your earlier pilgrimages in France an attempt to comfort and settle the girls?" Sunniva asked, going, as she always did, to the heart of the matter.

Marc nodded, recalling the shrines he had visited, remembering the desperate prayers he had offered up to King Christ and his saints.

"Nothing stopped the bad dreams for Isabella. I could not have her questioned: I dared not."

"You did not want to subject her to more pain," said Sunniva.

"That too."

"And the rumors of your own guilt grew," she added. Marc nodded a second time.

"I am surprised the shrines in France failed you," William said.

"So was my mother," Marc agreed, surprising himself by that confession. Once said, seeing Sunniva's sympathetic curiosity and William's raised, questioning eyebrows, it was easier to go on.

"Later, it was my mother's suggestion that I take the girls to Durham, to the shrine of the foremost saint in England. She sent word through a messenger that she had dreamed that the journey to Durham, the pilgrimage, would help us in a way that nothing else had. I knew it would be a risky journey so we traveled in high summer, when I hoped the roads would be easy and the northerners too busy with their harvests to be any trouble to us. On the way we encountered the pilgrim party that included Lady Sunniva and her kinsmen and I offered myself as an extra warrior to protect the pilgrims. My girls met Sunniva and finally settled and . . ."

He shrugged, sensing William's waning interest. "Since the girls are happy now, I have prayed to St. Cuthbert to release me for the moment from my pilgrim vow. I shall return to the north in time, and complete my pilgrimage to Durham, perhaps next year, or when the girls are older. I shall pray then, at the shrine of the mighty saint, for Cuthbert to intercede with God for Isabella, so she will not suffer anything in mind or soul . . . The rest you know."

"Indeed," muttered the king, glancing at Sunniva. "I have eyes."

"Yes," whispered Sunniva, answering Marc, her heart going out to him as she saw the weariness and mingled grief and relief in his eyes.

Finally she knew it all. Finally she understood. Marc's every action had been inspired by love. Like herself, when he had been faced with a hard choice, he had been able to do no other than he did.

Longing to comfort him, Sunniva smiled.

William saw her smile and knew what it meant. After a moment's silence, he looked at their untouched platters. "I shall have your maid brought to you, Lady Sunniva. You can take some food with you when you return to your quarters in the abbey. De Sens, I think my brother has some questions for you regarding horses. Then you should return to your nieces."

Dismissing the pair, William rose to his feet and called for a guard.

Chapter Thirty

In any court, there is always someone who knows what is going on and that someone will sell the information. Bertolf's informer was the English maid who waited on his niece. Today, the maid walked with him beside the river while the ferryman waited to row her back to Westminster Palace.

"The king is beginning to favor Marc de Sens, my lord. The Breton has cured his favorite horse of a sickness that had kept the beast off its feed and unable to walk. The mare is now racing round the paddock at the palace and King William is gracious with de Sens. The Breton has asked for your niece's hand in marriage and William looks ready to grant his request."

This was bad, but Bertolf gave no outward sign of alarm. "Has my niece met this Breton alone, at any time?"

"No, my lord. The king keeps them apart."

"My niece knows nothing of this planned betrothal?"

"I do not think so, my lord. But she does not confide in me. She works on her tapestry and waits for a summons to the king. She prays daily, too, in the abbey church."

In hopes of meeting de Sens there, Bertolf thought sourly, as he paid the woman a silver penny and sent her off.

This was news indeed. Since Sunniva and the Breton had appeared at court, his own plans had been in flux. Her survival had been an unexpected complication. Now, though, he saw his chance.

Bertolf had heard—who could not have heard?—of his niece's bizarre intervention at de Sens' trial. He had decided to stay away and feign illness on the day of the Breton's ordeal, so the rumor of what she had done reached Bertolf too late for him to take issue with her or the king, but in the end it had not mattered. He knew that even though Sunniva had "won" the ordeal by combat, the Breton was angered by her behavior, as any normal man would be. Whatever his niece and the Breton meant to each other, they were across with each other now. Their estrangement would make his final plan that much easier.

Cena should have beaten her more, he thought, walking smartly back from the river to his London house. *When she is in my hands I will see to it.*

That afternoon, Bertolf put the first part of his plan into action. He had to begin today, before the Breton saw his niece alone and they could talk together, before the king announced their betrothal. He and his sons must be at Westminster Palace when Sunniva's "disappearance" was discovered.

And so it fell out, exactly as he had planned. He and his two sons were in the presence of the king when the hue and cry came that the Lady Sunniva was gone, kidnapped by unknown forces from the abbey church itself—an unheard-of sacrilege. All that remained were her knives, laid in a spiral on the floor of the church, beside the high altar.

Bertolf watched with barely contained glee as Marc de Sens crashed around the church and then the palace, questioning, threatening and shouting until even William had bawled "Stop!" He himself had played the part of indignant uncle to perfection, demanding assurances that she would be safe, questioning the arrangements by which she and the other heiresses had been held. Finally he had withdrawn, in icy disapproval, to his London house, to await developments there.

He would wait a week, Bertolf thought, prodding the ferryman to urge him to more speed, and then announce his departure to his own lands. William and the Breton might suspect him, but they would have no proof.

No proof at all that Sunniva would be waiting there ahead of him, secure in his family's fastness in the marshes close to the Isle of Ely, marshes no stranger had ever penetrated.

He had planned well. The marsh folk would not fail him: they knew many cunning traps and ruses and they were loyal to him. He had let them live in their own way, keeping to their old pagan ways without being troubled by priests. In return, they would do this thing for him gladly.

Sunniva and her rich lands were now his.

Chapter Thirty-One

The last clear memory Sunniva had for many days after was of walking, with a guard, into the abbey church. It had been her custom to pray within the church in the afternoon. She had hoped that Marc would hear of what she did and would come to the church to seek her out. Instead, an unknown enemy had found her.

A slender, fine-boned monk had approached her, within the sanctuary. He wore his cowl up to hide his face. His hands were hidden in his cassock. Something in the way he moved, bearing down on her guard, had alerted her that he was false. She had shouted a warning and tried to draw her best knife. The false monk, as small and lean as she was, had whipped about, faster than leaping fire, and blown something into her face.

She could remember the taste of whatever it was he had spat at her: bitter, tinged with a rotting savor.

She recalled nothing more for stretches of time, only glimpses of awareness, before another blurred figure hung over her, forcing a sickly sweet drink down her throat. She tried not to breathe or swallow but then a face livid with colors, swirling patterns of blacks and reds, a devil's face, had swooped closer while harsh hands gouged and pinched or, worse, caressed.

Part of her knew she was stunned, carried off. She could not see because she was blindfolded, she could not fight because her wrists and ankles were bound together. She lay in a bow of pain, in the bottom of a boat, she thought, her muscles cramping as she was sprawled across the boat ribs. If she tried to speak she was drugged or gagged.

Then came a long drink, forced into her, and nothing more except the sounds of galloping and high wind.

Slowly, Sunniva stretched, enduring the shrieking pain in her limbs as she realized she was no longer hog-tied and could move. Exhausted by that simple act, she lay still a moment, registering that she was naked and in a bed. Below her, she heard distant sounds of chopping and sawing. She could smell bread being baked. She listened to the rustle of thatch above her head, familiar to her since childhood. She was in an English home, in the country.

So who had brought her here? Her mind flashed to a long, lean face, staring, intent eyes, black and red swirls tattooed onto his cheeks and forehead. She shivered and opened her eyes.

"You are back with us again, Sunniva."

Her uncle sat on the bed beside her, smiling, putting aside the fishing net he was mending. He nodded. "Yes, I do mend nets: I find it relaxing. How are you now? You have had a high fever, these past days."

Sunniva swallowed. Her throat was painfully dry but she was shy of asking for a drink when she was naked.

She lay with the covers up to her ears and whispered, "There was a man, with tattoos all over his face, in great swirling patterns. He kidnapped me. Did Marc save me from him? Is Marc here now?"

"Here? Why should Marc de Sens be here?" Bertolf rose from the bed and opened a chest, drawing forth a flagon and cups. "There is no tattooed man, there never was: that is your fever speaking. Do you not remember what happened at the palace? Has your fever affected your memory?"

Sunniva frowned, her frown increasing as Bertolf poured a drink into a cup and held it out to her. By sitting up on one elbow and pinning the covers to herself she revealed only her shoulder and arm as she accepted the wooden goblet of blackberry tisane, but she did not like it.

"What do you mean?" She sensed that whatever her uncle was planning to tell her might be a lie, but even so, his next words were a shock.

"Marc de Sens has repudiated you, my dear. He could not accept the humiliation that you heaped upon him by going behind his back to the king and asking to fight in his place. He is a proud man, Sunniva. He could not forgive you."

"Forgive me?" Sunniva felt light-headed again, her world crashing away. The goblet slipped from her clammy fingers, spilling into her bed. "He forgive me? After what I did for him?"

"I am not saying he was right, Sunniva." Bertolf backed away to the door of the chamber. "I shall send women to you now, to cleanse you. Clearly, you are still weak."

"But—" Suddenly she did not want him to leave. "Where is he, then?"

"De Sens? I neither know nor care. I believe he has returned to France. You are well rid of him, niece."

She rose before her uncle's women could find her naked in a damp bed. Her clothes had been left on top of a chest and she smelled them before she put them on. They had been washed: no scent of fever remained in her underclothes or gown. Spotting no comb in the small chamber, she drew her fingers through her hair. Her hair felt glossy and soft.

Sunniva sat back down on the bed, which she had stripped of its sodden sheets, drew on her shoes and considered afresh what her uncle had told her.

That she had been sick with fever.

That Marc had repudiated her.

That Marc had returned to Normandy.

How would her uncle know that last thing? And if she had been sick, why did her hair feel as it always did?

Although she had taken only a sip of the blackberry tisane before she had spilled it, she was not unduly thirsty, as she would have been with fever. And she had looked herself over while she dressed. Her body and breasts were unmarked; there were no fever blemishes. She had a small bruise on her left wrist and a tiny scab on her left heel. Marks from being tied?

If I was taken by force, where am I?

Unbidden, unwanted, her uncle's most damning words swung back into her mind. She had tried to block the thought by being busy, but this thought was too strong.

What if Marc has rejected me?

She tried to argue against it, but she knew very well what he had said to her, the last time they had met.

"Later. We shall discuss this later." She remembered his narrowed eyes, his lean face blazing with suppressed anger.

What does it matter that Marc is not a woman-killer, that he has told me the truth behind all he did, if he has cast me off? she thought, and then was appalled at her own question.

Struggling to contain her despair, she felt a draught strike against her face as the door to her small chamber opened and two middle-aged women stepped inside. Taller than most men, tanned and sinewy, they nodded to her and, without asking, began to comb and dress her hair.

She smiled at them, asked the pair their names and thanked them for tending her. She apologized for the spillage on the sheets and offered to wash them herself.

The women said nothing and gave no sign of hearing her. Their allegiance to her uncle could not have been clearer. Taking all the bedding, they backed out of the room leaving the door fully open, hanging on its hinges.

Not caring what might be beyond the chamber, Sunniva followed.

Slipping across the threshold, she found herself in an upper-floor gallery, overlooking a hall filled with people and milling dogs. The hall was divided into two by a series of wicker hurdles: on one side folk crowded around the fire, sitting on benches, on the other were pens of sheep.

Sunniva let out a long breath in surprise. This long, wooden, thatched, windowless house was not as splendid as she had expected from her uncle, a man of the court. There was no dais here, she realized, nor any chairs. Bertolf showed his status by sitting alone on a bench closest to the fire, out of the possible back-draught from the smoke hole in the roof. He peered at her through the smoke, and beckoned.

Sunniva hung back a moment. Among the clothes left for her, there had been no covering for her head, nor any cloak. She felt exposed in her tight Norman gown, showing her braided hair. She could not even return to where she had slept, in order to retrieve a sheet she might use as a shawl: the women had taken every single blanket.

"Come, niece," Bertolf called to her.

She wanted nothing more than to hurtle back into her own room and cry on the bed, to weep for Marc and his nieces and all she had lost. But what if her uncle was lying? What if Marc was seeking her, wherever she was?

Think of a tapestry, she told herself. *The threads wind together to make a pattern all can see. If you hide away, you make Bertolf's task easier for him. Better to go out, be seen; let word travel in the district that I am here. Then Marc will surely find me. Or I can find a means to flee and escape, as I planned to before when on pilgrimage.*

Slowly, Sunniva went downstairs.

The next few days crawled along. She was not allowed to help the other women in the running of Bertolf's household, but she was expected to remain with him and his two sons. Nor was she allowed to ride, or, at first, to walk outside. Inside, there seemed to be no mending to be done and when she mentioned her embroidery, Bertolf shook his head. The excuse was always that her fever had weakened her and that she must rest.

The pretence was that she was an honored guest, but Sunniva knew what was happening. She was being kept prisoner but no one would admit it. She dared not admit it herself, least of all to her "family." Bertolf's sons in particular made her wary. They were big, coltish lads of her own age, fair-haired and skinned and with wispy beards. They reminded her too much of her own brothers, especially the twins, Ketil and Told. Her brothers were now all dead and buried and she could not grieve for them without shame. In Bertolf's sons they seemed reborn: even in the way they followed her and spied on her. Their names were Hrothgar and Wybert and she disliked them intensely.

Bertolf for his part was forever devising ways that she would be together with the pair. They must eat together, "as a family," Bertolf said. They must show her round the house. They must take her into the marshes on a hunting trip.

This last Sunniva had firmly declined, using her "fever" as an excuse. She did not trust Bertolf, or his sons, and would not willingly go alone with any of them into the marshes. Walking with Bertolf's sons around the palisade that bordered his homestead and looking out across the earth and timber ramparts she had seen these marshes. She did not trust them, either.

No one spoke to her directly except for her uncle and his sons but, from snippets of overheard conversation that she could understand, she realized that Bertolf had brought her to a place called Eldyke, or eel-dyke, close to the Isle of Ely.

The Isle of Ely was exactly that—a distant rise of land surrounded by streams, marshes and wetlands, smothered with reeds, scrub and alders, embroidered with ducks and other wading birds. It was a good place for eels—indeed, Sunniva learned that its name meant "Isle of Eels" and there was an old monastery, rumored to be rich in relics and treasure, dominating the skyline of the island.

Eldyke was another island rising from the marshes, smaller than the Isle of Ely and more remote, surrounded by marshland and patches of sedge grass. There were wooden trackways through the marshes but Sunniva frowned when she saw them. If she used them as a means of escape she would be quickly spotted in this flat landscape and even more swiftly hunted down along the trackways.

Besides, what was the point of fleeing if Marc had turned from her?

She walked out, though, as often as she could. Hrothgar and Wybert accompanied her travels, pointing to the fine wooden gates and timber fencing that bordered their father's home, bragging of how they used nets to catch birds and bring down slaves who tried to flee, describing in detail how they would hunt the wild boar at shallow water holes and bloodily dispatch them with their spears. Neither spoke of her father, or her cousins. Neither offered her any kind of consolation or sympathy for her loss. Sunniva wondered if they even knew that Cena and her brothers were dead. They never asked her anything, except when prompted by their father.

Bertolf was another matter. She feared her uncle. As the days went on, his questions concerning her "inheritance" became more pointed. He was impatient when she did not know how many fields Cena plowed for wheat, how many cattle he had, how many slaves. His question of slaves brought Sunniva out into a cold sweat but luckily her uncle did not notice: he said that, once she was fit enough to travel, they would visit her lands and he would see for himself.

"And order them accordingly," he went on. He patted her hand. "Do not trouble yourself, my dear. These matters are for men. Now, which of my boys do you like best, Hrothgar or Wybert?"

Sitting outside with Bertolf on a rare day of sunshine, Sunniva felt as if a black cloud had engulfed her. Fear crawled over her scalp and she was acutely aware of details. The feel of the bench against her legs and back. The sound of a woman milling grain by hand. The shadow of the palisade, shutting her inside this yard of beaten earth and dung. The smell of fire and drying fish turned her faintly sick as she struggled to find an answer without committing herself.

"I could not say in fairness that I could choose one above the other," she answered, with a steadiness she did not feel. "They are both fine young men, with many worthy qualities. I like them both."

She closed her eyes, overcome by unwelcome memories. The elder son Hrothgar, who smelt of rancid milk, constantly flicked twigs or pieces of food at her—any missile at all, if she was within a sword's length of him. That, she assumed, was his way of wooing her. The younger son, Wybert, had pressed himself against her only that morning, while she had been watching the sheep in the pens within the homestead. Under the pretence of pointing out the cracked horn of one of the rams, he stepped right behind her, thrusting her against the wicker hurdles as he leaned over her right shoulder, trying to peer down the bodice of her gown. She felt him hard against her and tried to move away, but his weight imprisoned her.

"You shall be my favorite tupping ewe," he hissed against her back, rubbing himself against her lewdly.

"I am in mourning for my father and brothers!" she whispered in return, sensing how fatal it might be if she refused him outright. "Such matters must wait. And are we not, as cousins, too close kin to marry? Your priest will say we cannot, and he will be right."

"We pay little need to priests in the eel-lands," Wybert replied, brushing aside the church and its teaching. "Whatever that fat old man says, we shall please ourselves. So soon, little ewe . . ." He gave her left buttock a painful squeeze and then stepped back, departing from the homestead with his hunting net, his steps sure and jaunty.

And that had been his wooing of her.

Bertolf cracked his finger bones one by one and smoothed his beard. "They are, as you say, young."

"Yes, my lord." In a show of humility, Sunniva lowered her head, sensing her uncle staring at her profile. Bertolf was a widower: was he interested in her for himself? If he was, it was utterly against the laws of the church, totally disgusting to her, but perhaps—just perhaps—this was also a chance for her. It would mean he would allow her to delay any choice between his sons at least for a few more days, until he began to "court" her himself.

Sunniva closed her eyes briefly. *Where are you, Marc?* she cried out inside her head. *What should I do if you do not come?*

The next day, so far as Sunniva could sense, Bertolf began his own seduction. He invited her on a boating trip to see the bones of a fantastic creature—"A dragon at the very least," he said, with genuinely glowing eyes. For an instant, catching a glimpse of the curious young boy beneath the courtier, Sunniva was touched, and agreed to go with him.

An hour later, out in a shallow, dug out longboat with her uncle, her two silent, strapping "maids" and a leather-skinned boatman, she was mentally cursing her own folly. Bertolf made no move toward her, did not touch her except for handing her into the boat, but he positioned himself alongside the oarsman so that he was facing her, and he took an oar—to show off his strength, Sunniva assumed. As she sat between the brooding maids, Bertolf talked throughout their journey.

"Have you had word from your own people in your lands?" he asked, rowing with a small, jerky stroke that made the oarsman beside him clench his jaw in frustration. Sunniva longed for Marc to be in his place, imagined Marc sculling the light dug out forward, skimming it across the sunlit, gleaming waters as a boy might throw a pebble. She thought of his long, bronzed arms and powerful, hairy chest, both moving forward and back, lilting toward her, then away, in a tease of activity. She thought of his long, powerful legs, braced against the bottom of the boat, and, most of all, of his smile and his bright eyes.

"No word at all, then?" Bertolf's question returned her to the present. The pain of her separation from Marc, of his possible abandonment of her, struck her deep in her chest and belly, but she smiled for her uncle and shook her head.

"I shall look into that for you," Bertolf said.

"Thank you, uncle."

His smile faltered a little at that reminder of their being close-kindred, and then reappeared. "This is a beautiful country, is it not?"

"It is indeed." It was today, Sunniva thought, with the sun bright and glowing, an orange ball high over cool blue and gray waters, with ducks and geese swirling about on the little rivers and across the huge, open skies like brightly painted leaves. "Very lovely."

"Nothing so lovely as the jewel that is in this vessel with me. Look at all this!" Bertolf released one hand from his oar to sweep it across the waters and the boat slewed into an underwater bank and stuck there.

Sunniva kept a straight face and stared off into the sedge grass as the boatman sweated to release them from the sucking mud and Bertolf gave orders and suggestions. Eventually they were on their way again, working up a narrow stream partly choked with water weed and enclosed by huge bulrushes and reed mace, their tips white and sparkling with frost.

The "dragon" bones were a disappointment to Sunniva, although she was careful not so show it. She and the maids remained in the boat while Bertolf splashed through the mud to another earth-bank where the bones were lying.

"Look at these teeth!" he was saying, running his hands over the long, curved items. Privately, Sunniva thought the "teeth" matched the description Marc had given her of elephant's tusks, but she agreed with her uncle that they were very fine.

On the return trip, Bertolf sat beside her in the boat and allowed the oarsman to do the work of rowing them back.

"You do know that the king cannot allow a woman alone to hold lands?" he said, the instant they were on their way.

"Naturally," Sunniva agreed pleasantly, more aware of Bertolf's thigh pressing against hers than of any words he was saying. "Thank you for showing me the dragon, uncle."

He stroked his beard and moustache. "I shall show you more, soon."

There was no mistaking the desire in his voice. Sunniva turned her head to watch a flight of geese, thinking of the dug out they were in and the bewildering array of water channels to become lost in. At least on the water she would be hard to track, she decided, folding her borrowed cloak in bunches across her knees.

First, though, she would have to steal a boat.

"How long must this mourning for her family go on?" Wybert demanded that evening. "I want to get her bedded and pregnant before the spring. She chattered some nonsense about our being cousins and too close kin, but our priest will not care, will he, Father?"

Bertolf grunted and did not check his stride. He and his two sons were out walking on the trackway. He was meeting someone in the marshes and had brought his boys with him to learn from the encounter. Now he was regretting his decision.

"What makes you think she will choose you?" jeered Hrothgar, between sucking the last bits of meat from a mutton bone that he had been gnawing on since supper. "She smiles at me. She likes me best."

"You think every woman fancies you!"

"Boys, boys," Bertolf said without heat, thinking them both deluded. Sunniva clearly admired older men. Even the Breton was older than her, if only by a few years.

He pursed his narrow lips, putting aside the delightful prospect of having a willing, amiable Sunniva in his bed as he considered Marc de Sens. Wybert was right about the priest falling in with their plans, but de Sens was going to be a nuisance. His niece had not mentioned the foreigner for days but he had no illusions. She would be thinking of him. She had not asked to see a priest or go to church yet, but he had no doubt that she would. She would want to pray for him. And it would be far better if she did her praying believing that de Sens was dead.

Chapter Thirty-Two

The day after her outing with Bertolf, Sunniva was
roused early, while it was still dark. The maid who shook
her awake said nothing but indicated by gestures that
she should rise and dress. She did so as swiftly as she
could in the gray and black murk, her usually strong
and steady fingers fumbling with the drawstrings of
her gown. The two maids, her "guards," brushed and
plaited her hair with no great gentleness, smothered
her in a huge fur cloak and walked her between them
out of the door.

Bertolf was waiting for her by the smoldering, low
fire, his long face grave and draped in shadows. "You
must prepare yourself, my dear," he whispered, offering
her his arm for support.

Wordlessly, Sunniva walked with him past the sleepers in the homestead. Whatever news Bertolf had
learned this early, before the rest of the household
were awake, must be evil. She dared not ask her great-
est horror, her dread that something terrible might
have happened to Marc, in case her voicing of that fear
made it real.

From the very rim of her sight she caught movement

off to her left and realized Bertolf's two sons were
following. Her hope plummeted further. Forgetting
for an instant that she no longer had her knives, she
touched her waistband, feeling foolish and helpless as
her groping hand found nothing. Even the comfort of
habit was no comfort now.

She and Bertolf had reached the outer door and
she hesitated on the threshold.

"You must come, my dear." Her uncle prodded her
firmly in her flank and she urged her limbs forward,
keen not to have to endure his touch again. Clearly,
whatever was out there he would force her to witness it.

*Please let it not be Marc, nor anything to do with Marc.
Please, Freya, let it not be his nieces. I could not bear that.
Let no harm have come to them. Please. Please.*

She was still praying when she felt the cold damp
air smack against her face and opened her eyes to
stare down at whatever she must face.

There was a circle of men in the yard, their features
indistinguishable in the low light and cloud of fog.
Mist was rising everywhere, blurring the tops of the
palisade, muffling the restive bleatings of the sheep
still housed within the homestead. The men parted to
let her and Bertolf into their midst.

Her fingers automatically flew to her waistband,
then to her mouth as she gasped at the sight before
her. She was glad of the mist, before she realized that
she must look closer: she would have to know if this
still, stiff figure was anyone she knew.

It was a man, stretched out on his side as if in sleep,
but his wounds meant that he would never wake. In the
dim light and fog, the blood on his tunic front and leggings looked black. Half his face was missing, gouged
away by some kind of weapon—Sunniva feared that it

might have been a spade. His hair was cropped in the Norman style. His cloak was foreign: the embroidery along its neckband was English but the weave of the cloth she did not recognize.

"This poor creature is a stranger to our district," Bertolf murmured, his voice oozing fake concern. "We must know for our own peace if he is Norman or not: our new king will fine us heavily unless we can prove that he is English. I fear, my dear, that he is your man, Marc de Sens."

"Roll him onto his back," Sunniva heard herself say.

The circle about the corpse glanced as one man at Bertolf, who nodded. The murdered man was turned over, his ruined head leaking blood and other matter. Sunniva raked her fists into her fur cloak, gripping tightly as she struggled not to be sick. The stranger was tall, with brown hair, and well made, with strongly muscled thighs and arms.

"He has no sword," she whispered. "Where was he found?"

Bertolf jutted his chin at the nearest in the small crowd, a wiry, bald marsh man with a ragged patch over his left eye and carrying a staff on his shoulder. He replied in the local dialect, pointing into the fog.

"On the trackway, about half a mile from here," Bertolf translated.

"He was alone? No horse? No dogs? No pack?"

More murmurings between her uncle and the crowd, then Bertolf said, "They have carried him here even as you see. There was nothing more with him, neither man nor beast."

"Where did he come from? How? By boat? Did anyone see him approach? When was he found?"

"Early this morning." Bertolf shook his head at her

other questions and did not even attempt to ask his people. "No one knows more."

Forcing her stiffened body to obey her, Sunniva knelt beside the figure. She could not look for long at the mutilated head, so tried to focus on the body and on what she knew: the clothes. She touched his long cloak and his tunic. The wool cloth felt less fine than she would have expected from English wool. Through the drawstrings of his tunic she saw a long cut running raggedly across his chest: the mark of a blade where someone had tried to slash his throat? She swallowed a mouthful of bitter bile and leaned closer, drawing his cloak off his shoulders by her fingertips.

Then she saw it, a tattoo. A blue tattoo on the man's arm. Shocked, she sat down in the dirt and began to cry.

"Call her women to come and fetch her," Bertolf ordered. "She has seen enough."

That lunchtime Bertolf allowed Sunniva to remain in her room and have a maid bring food to her. She ate a little, wept again, and lay down on her bed. The maid covered her with her fur cloak and a few rough blankets and left her to sleep away her grief.

Snug under the cloak and blankets, Sunniva did not move. She allowed the maid to leave and heard the door open and sensed her uncle enter. Again she did not stir, not even when she realized that Bertolf was not alone.

"Why do you not take her now and be done with it?" a strange male voice demanded.

"It will be better this way," said Bertolf. "A willing bed partner is easier."

"What of this Norman king? This Christian king?"

"I will keep her here. William will not know she is alive."

"And her estates will pass to you?"

Nothing more was said but Sunniva sensed that Bertolf and his companion were convinced of the outcome. Listening to these unpleasant revelations, she felt no surprise: it merely hardened her determination. When the chance came, she would need to be ready.

As the day slipped away toward evening, she stirred and tottered down into the homestead to go to the midden. The maids went with her. She motioned to her stomach and scowled and they nodded and stood guard while she braved the slops and dung of the midden. Again and again she did this: retiring to her room, lying down, sitting up and staggering downstairs clutching her belly, the maids hovering behind, trying not to smile as she groaned on her way to the privy. As twilight fell and torches were being lit in the homestead, the knowing smirks of the maids had changed into looks of sullen boredom. Finally, when Sunniva did not even attempt the stairs after one of her interminable trips outside but turned instead to return to the midden, the two maids busied themselves looking for something on the rush-strewn floor—perhaps a missing armlet, or a string of beads—and left her to it.

Sunniva hauled herself to the midden and then kept going, edging her way along the palisade, walking far more slowly than she could. If anyone challenged her, she would claim she was disoriented, lost, but no one noticed. As she had hoped it might be, the fog was her ally.

She had taken the precaution in her last but one trip to the midden of hiding a drab blanket there and retrieving it on her final visit. The dark cloth hid her completely and made her look like one of the marsh women—an old, bent marsh woman, wheezing her way to the water side, to check on her fish traps. She passed through the main gate, grunting a greeting that she had often heard in these parts to the guard. He let her through with a dreary wave of his spear, staring at her as something to watch as she plodded along the trackway; a small figure buried in an old blanket and surrounded by rising river mist.

Sunniva waited until the track twisted into a bank of tall reeds and then she began to run.

She soon found a boat, an old, warped hollowed-out log of a boat that had been abandoned in a reed bed close to the trackway. Blessing her luck and using an alder branch as a pole, she floated herself out into the endless rivers and streams of the fens. She listened constantly for any hue and cry but there was nothing: as she had hoped, the fog still worked in her favor and no one was abroad. If her luck held, her maids might even assume that she had crawled back from the midden to her chamber. She had left the blankets there in a coiled, hunched shape suggestive of a body: her maids might suspect nothing until morning.

She meanwhile traveled all night, drifting and using her alder pole to stop the listing boat from running aground. Now, looking for somewhere to hide out during the day, she admitted that she had no idea where she was.

Strangely, she did not feel disturbed by this at first. Instead, she found that her mood veered wildly from jubilation to despair. She was glad, so very glad, that she had escaped from Eldyke, away from her uncle. But always on the heels of that giddy rush of pleasure were her dark, dragging feelings surrounding Marc, who was lost to her.

I must not think of that now, she told herself, but her mind would not obey her wish: it dwelt, too, on the body that she had been forced to look at during that brutal display. The image of the murdered man played on the insides of her eyelids as she squirmed in the bottom of the log boat, trying and failing to sleep. After only a short time she gave up altogether and moved on, relishing the simple action of poling the boat onward, deeper into a small stream bordered by reeds.

She was now permanently damp, the wetness of the marsh felting stickily against her head and hands, any part of her that was not covered. As day broke she realized that the fog was not going to lift today. It had a way of seeping across everything, cloudy and muffling, smothering the outlines of the reed beds and the water until she longed for a sight of clear lines and a glimpse of the sun. She missed trees in this low landscape of bulrushes, bare-stemmed reeds and grasses, and she missed land she could be sure of—whenever she used the pole to test for solid ground, she found it sinking into foul-smelling mud.

Panic boiled in the bottom of her mind but she refused to admit to it. She was free of Bertolf and his sons, that was enough. These marshes would not continue forever. She would find a way out of them.

Unless I am going round in circles . . .

Hours or minutes later—she had no way of gauging time in this place—Sunniva stopped poling for a moment and allowed the boat to drift. Panting, she rubbed her aching arms and then her stomach, wishing now that she had eaten more of the last meal provided for her by her uncle. But her eating sparingly then, and her pretend stomach illness, had been part of a larger ploy to throw Bertolf and his people off guard so she could escape more easily. It had worked, but she was very hungry.

Worse than hunger, though, was shame. After seeing that dead body, she understood now why Marc had been so devastated by her offer to fight in his place. She was no warrior, and all the pretty knife-throwing skills she had would not make her one. Battle was ugly and trial by battle just as ugly and unpredictable as any other kind of murder. Marc had been right to be angry and alarmed with her.

Again, the ghastly picture of the murdered man rippled on the waters as Sunniva tried to fight off tears. Trembling, she rubbed a hand across her hot eyes and then froze, shocked into stillness by a new sound.

"Hey! Hey!" A man's voice calling across the marshes.

"Hey! Hey!" His cry was answered by another voice.

"Hey! Hey!" And now a third.

Sunniva flung herself into the bottom of the boat, desperately trying to pinpoint where the voices were coming from. She thought the second was closest to her but she was not sure. She was not sure of distance, either: were the men near or far? Were they seeking her?

Who else would they be looking for?

"St. Freya, help me!" she whispered, paralyzed by indecision. She had not expected Bertolf or his followers to come so far so quickly. Should she move? If she did, would they hear her?

There was a dull splash somewhere in the main flow

of water and a few moments later, the same yipping cries: "Hey! Hey!"

A dog barked, once. A duck broke cover so close to her that Sunniva almost screamed. She flinched, the boat rocking beneath her, water spilling into it and threatening to sink the ungainly vessel. Using her hands she bailed, expecting at any instant that her own soft splashing would be discovered and targeted.

Her boat was moving, deeper into the choking mass of grasses, then bursting through and out into another channel, this one with faster flowing water. Afraid to stir in case she gave her position away, Sunniva dared not bail any more. Ignoring the water lapping against her flanks, she sank deeper into the boat, and allowed it to bear her off.

Faster and faster the boat sped, the fog enveloping its wake. Sunniva gave herself over to the motion and the water nibbling at her sides no longer seemed cold now, but warm. Comforted, exhausted, she sank into sleep.

A ruddy glow burned against her eyelids. Her whole body was tingling painfully, smarting as if she had been whipped with thistles. Strong hands were kneading her flesh, rubbing her back and belly. She opened her eyes and mouth to protest.

"Hush!" said Marc, massaging her calves and thighs with a sheepskin cloak. "We are hidden for the moment, but not if you shout."

He blew warmly in both her ears and drew her into a sitting position, bracing her back against his knee. "Drink this."

Sunniva sipped at a steaming cup of a fishy broth and almost choked.

"Drink it all," Marc warned. "We need to get you warm."

Obediently Sunniva drank.

"Now sleep," Marc ordered. "I will tend the fire and keep us safe."

"Are you a dream?" she asked. "My uncle told me you were dead."

"And you believed him?"

"I believed the tattoo I saw on a dead man," Sunniva answered, with a yawn. Her body felt to be blazing with heat now, but she was still tired. So very tired . . .

Chapter Thirty-Three

Marc added more dried pine cones from his pack to the small fire, glancing around the nest of dried reeds that he had gathered together on this island of thickly growing reeds, sedge grass and bulrush. Recalling the "dens" he had made in the Breton marshes when he was a boy, he was glad to have remembered how to do it, especially here, in these chill, fog-bound fens, where even the reeds were brown and leafless, barren except for their fluffy seed heads.

The mist was both enemy and friend. It was a shield at present, saving Sunniva and himself from unwanted attention. But it could so easily have been deadly. He and Sunniva might have passed a thousand times within a boat's length of each other and never known it.

When he considered how lucky, how fortunate he had been to spot Sunniva toiling in these marsh waters, he was caught somewhere in a state between gratitude and terror. As he lay down beside her sleeping form and took her little body in his arms to comfort and warm her further, he was mortified to find that he was shaking.

No fear this, or cold, but relief. The good of all those

pilgrimages that he had made had come together today. Only the guidance of King Christ and all his saints could have made his finding of Sunniva possible.

Still he shook like a skittish horse, his teeth grinding together as he fought the weakness in his body. He felt tears run down the sides of his nose and into his ears but made no move to wipe them off: it would have meant releasing Sunniva.

I will never let her go, he vowed. *I have no true life without her. We must be together.*

Being without her had been a hell on earth. When he had left the court in pursuit of her—even William had sense enough not to try to stop him—he had gathered up Ragnar Fire-Breeches and his men and stormed Bertolf's London house. A terrified servant there had quickly told him that Bertolf had another house, far from the city amidst the fen lands. Marc had guessed at once that Bertolf would have arranged for Sunniva be taken there. Begging Ragnar to remain in London with his nieces, and sending word across the sea for his mother to come with an escort to the city and join them—for he wanted his women folk all together— Marc set out alone to track Sunniva down.

He had been eleven days seeking her, three on horseback and the rest by boat. He had been sorry to sell his horse—not his war charger Theo—for a rowing boat but it had been necessary: threading through these fens was quicker by boat than on foot, whether two feet or four.

Sunniva's knives left in church had been a sign from those who had kidnapped her on behalf of her grasping uncle. In his own homelands he had seen such spiral patterns on ancient standing stones, some still worshipped by the marsh folk of his lands. He knew them to be a pagan people, far from the ways of the church. The thought of Sunniva in their hands had been a terrible spur, but, because of his knowledge of the Breton marsh folk, he had known where to look in the fens. He knew the signs such pagans left each other, and he knew where to look for them: scratched onto elder trees or tall boulders, or feathers tied onto reeds where the water lily flowered in summer, or spirals of grass hanging from posts set in the midst of brooks where three streams met. He sought such signs and they told him the story: a golden woman—symbolized by a golden feather— taken to the fastness of the lord, in a place called—

That was where his reading of the signs had failed Marc. He had understood the golden feather, the crescent moon and antler scratches on wood for the lord, but the strange, flowing symbol for the place had eluded him. Reduced to seeking out every scrap of rising land in case Bertolf's homestead was on one of the many islands in these marshes, he had hunted for days and nights. He did not sleep for three days—he did not want to stop. He grudged every moment he was not looking for Sunniva. He ate stale bread on the move and drank water straight from the streams. Tonight was the first night he had made a fire, indeed the first night he had stopped.

And he had almost missed her. Only the shouts of her pursuers had alerted him that Sunniva was close. His first sight of her, through the fog and reeds, had been like the blessing of God, lifting his heart sky high and shattering his weariness. Thinking of the moment when he had slid beneath the waters to grab Sunniva's ponderous log boat and guide her to safety, he remembered how fiercely his heart had been beating, how much he had longed to shout to her, tell her he was there. But he dared not—not with Bertolf's men so close.

Those bastards were still close, but they would not catch Sunniva. He was determined that no one would touch her again, unless it were by her will.

She had been so cold when he had made himself known to her, as pale as a primrose frosted with ice. It had taken a good deal to warm her and he prayed she had taken no lasting hurt from her long exposure.

Please, King Christ, visit your wrath on me. She does not deserve such punishment.

He rocked her, brushing a streamer of hair from her flushed face. Tomorrow, if the fog persisted, he would cook fish for her: she needed feeding. There would be crayfish here, and eels, of course. This was where she had been taken, to an eel island.

Marc smiled grimly, staring into the mist.

He must have slept, for his next sight was of a golden feather, tickling across his chin. He sighed and raised a hand to scratch his face and Sunniva drew back.

"Hello, little one, you need not stop for me." He smiled and kissed the hanging lock of gold hair dangling above him. "Why the frown, sweeting?"

"You are so thin," she breathed. "I can feel your ribs."

"Searching for you has made me starve," Marc answered, instantly regretting his teasing as her face crumpled altogether. "No, I did not mean—"

He folded her against him as she wept, cursing his own insensitivity and wishing he had never spoken. "I am sorry," he said. "Can we not begin again?"

Can we? Her eyes asked. Even in the fog her face was bright with feeling and memory. He, too, remembered:

his foolish pride and anger at her selfless courage, his filthy threats of "later." He had made her endure "later" before, so was it any wonder she was nervous?

Or was it worse? Had she changed toward him?

As if she had seen and understood his fearful doubt, Sunniva laid a hand upon his chest. "I am so glad you came for me," she whispered.

"I have missed you so much." They spoke their thought together and then smiled at each other, the moment as delicate and magical as a spider's web. Neither wanted to break the mood as they gazed into each other's eyes.

"You have a lighter-colored cross in your left eye," Sunniva observed at length. She was lying on top of him like a golden shadow, her unbound hair covering and warming them both. "It is like a mirror image of the tattoo on your arm," she went on, resting her chin on top of her hands, on top of his chest, "except that it is light."

"Your eyes sparkle with flecks of green and blue," Marc answered, reveling in her close notice, and even in the feel of her sharp knuckles against his ribs. "They are true sea-eyes, my mermaid."

Sunniva kissed his arm several times, her lips tracing the blue cross of his tattoo. "I am glad you had this put on you," she said. "It saved me a deal of grief and pain."

Curiosity and desire warred in Marc, but the thought of his sunlight in any grief was too much for him: curiosity won. "What mean you?"

She told him then, of Bertolf's terrible tableau, where she was forced to confront the corpse of a murder victim. "The clothes were Norman and foreign-made," she went on, in a flat, tense voice. "His head and face were unrecognizable. I thought the worst."

That bastard Bertolf had put her through this. Fighting

down his fury, Marc was staggered by how ruthless her uncle had been. "You think he dressed one of his own dead folk in Norman clothes?"

She nodded. Her hands touched her own throat and she swallowed. "Then I saw the man's tattoo, upon his arm. A blue tattoo. A spiral tattoo."

"And knew at once it was not me. King Christ, what a blessing you have quick wits!" He stroked her back, longing to obliterate that foul memory altogether, loathing the fact she had suffered. "I wished I had found you sooner, before then. No woman should have to go through such a sight."

"No man, either," Sunniva said quietly.

"Bertolf treated you well, otherwise?"

"Yes," she whispered, but her sea eyes were stormy and now she rolled off him, covering her naked breasts with her hands.

In another moment she would be asking him if her clothes were dry and their intimacy would be gone. Marc sat up quickly. "Wait, you have cut yourself on your back," he lied—in truth he would have said anything to keep her close. "Let me see if it still bleeds."

She twisted herself into a spiral trying to look. "I cannot see!"

"It is the fog," Marc said, straight-faced. "We will not be able to move yet, not until the mist breaks a little." Bertolf and his men would not be moving, either, and a day's forced stillness would do him and Sunniva good— or so he fervently hoped. Cautiously, he stretched a hand to her. "May I?"

She turned at once, presenting her smooth back to him. Lust parched his throat at the sight of her trim legs and firm buttocks and he swayed a little, feeling as if he had drunk a bellyful of mead.

"No, the cut is clean enough," he said, unable to prevent his fingers from tracing the lines of her shoulderblades. How could Bertolf and his sons have lived so near to this delectable woman without attempting to touch her? His imagination raged with violent images of revenge as he curbed his voice. "It is healing well."

If she had been touched against her will then it was his duty to help her, not impose himself upon her. If she wished to speak of it, then he must hear her. If she did not want to talk of her captivity then he must respect her silence. He felt her tremble and his guts clenched in frustration. How could he help her? How?

"It is a little stiff, though," he heard Sunniva say. "The cut on my back."

"I can make you a salve," he said at once.

She half-turned. "You are certain we are safe here?"

"Very sure. Even without the fog." He had chosen the island of low, dense scrub and reeds with great care and disguised the log boat.

"Your youngsters are safe?"

Marc smiled at Sunniva's habitual inquiry.

"Very safe. For sure I would not leave them otherwise."

"For sure you would not," she nodded, her eyes brightening. "Good! How did you find me?" she asked after a moment.

"I heard your pursuers and knew you would keep away from them." For the first and only time, Marc felt a certain gratitude to Bertolf for giving some sign, even if it were a negative sign, of Sunniva's whereabouts. "I knew you would keep to the smallest water channels that you could, not for speed but to hide."

"I could not risk a chase on open water," Sunniva agreed.

A silence fell between them, pierced only by the soft lapping of water as a water rat splashed somewhere out in the streams. Sunniva hesitated and licked her lips. "A salve would be good."

He could see she was blushing and knew at once that she had guessed his lie and yet was still playing along with it. Hope charged afresh in him, making his heart race.

"Rest." He touched her arm gently, guiding her back to their bed of rushes and furs. "Let me make up the fire and then make your salve."

Her golden eyebrows drew together. "What do I do?"

"What every lady does," Marc answered, his intuition sweeping him along in a happy blaze of confidence. "You comment on my efforts and tell me where I am going amiss."

She smiled at his jest, but frowned as quickly. "Marc, I am no lady," she said in a rush. "I know you were angry with me because I did not tell you I was an heiress, but I swear by St. Freya that I did not know! And even if these lands exist, how can I claim them? In truth, I do not know what I am. I cannot even be sure that Cena was my father. What if Ketil and Told were right?"

"I do not believe them," Marc answered, giving her a light push to sit her down on his furs. He had forgotten the twins and it was no pleasure to remember them. "Your brothers had dirty mouths."

"And the priest? The priest in my own homeland?"

"Forget this for the moment," Marc said, exasperated that she should be worrying at the matter now, when they were finally reunited and he was trying to make her happy. "I care not what status or kin you have, only that you are Sunniva."

"I care, though, and I cannot dismiss it."

He wanted to yell at her that he loved her, and he almost did, but the campaigner in him knew that such a shout would bring Bertolf down on them for sure. "Give me some peace, woman," he growled. "Let me feed the fire before it burns out."

She glowered at him and he was glad to see her flare of spirit after what she had been through. Trying not to smile as she flounced about on her bottom on the furs, drawing sheepskins around her narrow shoulders, he tended the small blaze and then left her to find the herbs he needed and the fish he wanted.

He was back quite soon—this was a tiny island, and he knew there were enemy forces abroad, becalmed by the mist as he and Sunniva were but alert and eager to make trouble.

The fire, he noticed, still burned clearly, without that black smoke that could give away their position. Sunniva was a small, unmoving lump in the furs, rather too still for sleep.

"I could not find my clothes," she murmured from beneath the sheepskin.

"They are still drying on a bush," Marc answered, glad he had stuffed them under his cloak when he left her alone. He knew it was a shabby trick but he felt no guilt. "They will be dry when we have eaten."

He saw the tip of her nose emerge at the mention of food and had to fight down his desire to kiss it. Sunniva was no wild horse but she was as wary as one at present: he must go carefully.

He busied himself with preparing the crayfish and eel, talking meantime of the mist and how he had gone sprawling in the mud at one point and of the sleek, fat otter he had seen swimming past their island; tiny, everyday details that he hoped would make her feel safe. As the eel and crayfish boiled in their stone "basin"—a naturally hollowed-out stone that he could use as a cooking pot—he turned to making the salve.

This was nothing new. He had made many salves— for horses.

He was vividly aware of his shortcomings as a human healer, but he had gathered what he could by guesswork. Every woman he had ever known, including his mother and lately his nieces, loved sweet-smelling things, and to that end he had found some rose petals—incredibly he had found several fistfuls still surviving this winter on a sturdy rosebush growing in the middle of their island—some yellow-headed coltsfoot and, rarest of all, a clump of sweet fen violets, flowering very early.

The scent should please her, if nothing else, he thought, as he placed the flowers together on a flat stone. *And though I am very glad she is not truly cut, putting the stuff on her will please me.*

"How beautiful."

Even bundled tightly in sheepskin he had not heard her approach: she was so nimble and light-footed.

"I gathered them with you in mind," he replied, and on impulse, he took a few rose petals and scattered them in her hair. "Now they are beautiful."

She blushed, her cheek more glowing than the pink petals falling between them from her sunburst of hair. "Marc?"

He smiled encouragingly, about to ask her if she might prefer the violets as a posy, when she stumbled to her knees, speaking swiftly.

"I am sorry for what I did at Westminster Palace

and for sneaking behind your back to the king and taking your place. I had no right and you were right to be angry, Marc! I am sorry, really sorry, and please believe me when I say I never meant to shame you. I made a stupid mistake—"

"Enough!" Marc tried to stop this flood of words. "You did nothing wrong, woman! I was the one who was too arrogant." He tried to clasp her shoulders, to hug her, but she slipped out of the sheepskin, evading his loving capture like the mermaid she was and, to his astonishment, cast herself over his lap. "What, by King Christ, are you about?"

"Here I am, Marc," she gabbled, "I know I wronged you. Please, if you are still angry, chastise me as you see fit. Across your lap or over your knee, 'tis your choice."

"Enough," Marc said again, without heat. This was the consequence of his threat of "later!" *I must never do it to her again,* he thought, appalled at himself as he lifted her hair so he could see her screwed-up face. *I must vow to try.*

"I was also wrong, Sunniva, far too stubborn in my pride," he admitted, brushing her forehead with his thumb. "When you meet her, my mother Matilde will tell you it is my abiding sin. I would say that she is also stubborn, although my mother would not agree."

He stroked the side of her face as her pretty features relaxed, trailing his fingers down the taut tendons of her neck. "We are both still learning each other, sweeting, and I must warn you, I am no saint."

"Saints can be angry," she replied, as if not entirely convinced.

"Maybe, sweeting, but I am not. I vow I would have done exactly as you did, had I been in your place." He leaned closer to her, ignoring the dull ache in the base of his spine, and whispered in Breton, "I love you."

She understood the sentiment, if not the words, and now, as she sagged over his knee, he risked glancing over her, admiring the sweep of her flanks and her mottled, blushing skin. She was warm under his hand.

He patted her bottom and she gave a tiny sigh that reassured him more than a thousand words. Whatever Bertolf had done to her, he had not injured her in that worst way. She would not be so yielding over his lap had Bertolf forced himself upon her. "Little Sun-Maid," he murmured, feeling less and less saintly by the instant.

She sighed again, then wrinkled her nose. "What is burning?"

Marc cursed and scooped her off him onto the bed of rushes but was too late: the water in the stone cooking "pot" had boiled away and the crayfish were half-scorched.

They ate them anyway, and then the eel. Sunniva delighted in teasing Marc by telling him the story of the Saxon king Alfred, famous even in her northern homeland for burning good food. Marc grinned at the tale and she smiled, pleased to see him pleased. She had been so afraid of that stubborn pride he had admitted to, but in the end his understanding had surprised her.

I would forgive him much, she thought, as Marc disappeared into the fog to dispose of the remains of their less-than-perfect meal. *Perhaps he is the same with me.* The idea pleased her as she fed the fire again then took a drink of mead from the small leather flask that Marc had carried with him from London.

There was a crack of dry reeds behind her.

"Is there any for me?" Marc asked, reaching over her shoulder to take the flask. He had stripped off his clothes and, as he climbed into bed beside her, pulling the furs over them both, she sensed the shock of his long hard body even before they touched.

"We should rest while we can; sleep out this mist."

He kissed her lightly on the lips and sank onto his belly, his arousal obvious. He did not close his eyes but continued to look at her.

"Sleep if you wish, Sunniva. 'Tis your choice."

She smiled and reached for him.

Their first time, after so long apart, was fast, glorious and almost too noisy. Marc longed to bellow out his moment of release but dared not and Sunniva recognized the ever-present danger: she clapped her hand over his mouth as he came. Her warm, slippery fingers clasped over his lips made the moment even more intense.

Afterward, they lay sprawled like horses in a sunlit meadow, limbs akimbo, their bodies sheened with sweat and spoke loving nonsense to each other as their breathing steadied.

"We should sleep," Marc said at length. "Tomorrow, fog or no, we need to move."

Jubilation of spirit had made Sunniva wakeful. "Could we move now?" she asked, gratified when a look of disappointment crossed his face. "To sleep together is wonderful," she reassured, "but can we not steal a march?"

He smiled. "You think like a warrior: plans and campaigns. But it is too risky."

"You searched the marshes at night."

"Not in fog." Marc's bushy eyebrows locked as he

frowned. "You could not endure another session in these chill waters."

At times, Marc was overprotective, Sunniva decided, charmed nonetheless. "We can take care," she said. "It will mean we see your youngsters all the sooner."

"Humph!" Marc flicked her bottom and crawled from the furs. "You drive a hard bargain, mistress." He tossed her clothes to her from somewhere: they were dry and warm.

"I will earth over the fire and clear the camp," Sunniva replied, caught between laughter and sympathy as she saw that Marc was aroused again. She was tempted to tease, delay their departure, but the thought of Bertolf and his followers sobered her. It was hard, though, leaving their misty reed space. They could no longer be lost in each other. Her breasts and the space between her legs ached as she dressed and dismantled their bed, dragging the reeds here and there, trying to make it seem that this tiny island had been inhabited by nothing but mice.

Soon the boat was ready and they were, too. Marc had packed the boat with rushes and stowed their things. They set off into the mist-bound waterways in utter darkness, without moon or stars to guide them, but Sunniva had never felt more light.

There was one bad moment when Marc, a dark, shifting shadow in the prow of the boat, motioned with his hand for her to duck. His hand was gripping his sword as they waited, at stretch like leashed hunting dogs scenting quarry, and heard a soft splashing coming closer. Still they waited, bobbing like a leaf on the sluggish current, unable to row or pole in case that very action gave them away.

Sunniva spotted a tiny face rising out of the water by the side of their boat and bit down on a yelp of surprise, but Marc whistled softly through his teeth. "Otters are playful creatures and fearfully inquisitive," he whispered. He waited until the otter swirled and dived away and then handed Sunniva a stick of alder he had split in two. "Not much of a paddle, I know, but it will serve."

She nodded, glad to be able to help, and, both of them rowing, they sped forward once more into a larger channel, moving against the current.

She was a good traveler, Marc thought, kneeling up in the log boat to row. As the darkness faded to a dusky rose and the sun began to burn off some of the river fog, she began to ask him riddles.

"This is one way we English pass the long winter evenings, so it is a skill you need," she said.

"Ask away," Marc answered. It passed the dull time of rowing and he could still listen and keep watch. Her voice lilted to him over his shoulder, teasing and playful.

"A giant, now toppled,
hollow and dead,
still glides where it never would
when alive."

That was easy. "This boat," Marc answered.

"Here is another," Sunniva paused to wrap her own headsquare about her alder paddle to save her hands against the knobbly bark. She had offered to tear it in two for him to share but, when Marc shook his head, she cleared her throat and declared,

"This knave creeps and clings,
A friend to mischief, the enemy
of sight. The sun may drive him off—"

"You cannot claim fog is male," Marc interrupted. "It is a woman. Listen." He listened himself first, checking all about was still and reedy, no dogs or busy hunters, then spoke.

"She winds her promise of mystery about you,
Endlessly deceiving and beguiling. Softer than dew."

"Not so," Sunniva replied at once. "Listen—"

And so they went on, moving slowly but steadily through the fens until they reached a point where the mist seeped away and they found themselves on a river, rowing to a fording place.

Chapter Thirty-Four

Once away from the ford, Marc and Sunniva walked all day along paths and tracks, flattening themselves into the dead grass whenever they heard horses. Sunniva saw no one, although Marc told her a troop of armed men had passed within a bow's length of their last hiding place, beside a single lime tree. Crouched under the lime's low branches, they could see little, but Marc counted a score and two horses from the rush of galloping hooves and said it was probably a levy of the king's. Sunniva agreed, although she guessed that Marc was trying to disguise the truth from her: that the men on horseback were Bertolf's warriors, searching for her.

Toward evening the landscape became less flat and they saw the thatched nave of a tiny barn of a church rising above them on a low hill.

"Where is the village that goes with this church?" Marc hissed, scanning the horizons. He gave her a quizzical look. "Do I pass as English?"

"More and more, except for your sword," Sunniva whispered back, "But"—She stopped, not wanting to raise the specter of Bertolf having told people in this region about either of them.

He looked at her, his amber eyes clear yet warm. "We do not have many choices, and all are possibly evil ones." He inhaled deeply. "I can smell frost in the air. I do not think we should camp out again tonight."

He meant she could not stand a night of cold, Sunniva thought, ashamed of her own weakness. "If we make a good fire?" she ventured.

He smiled and took her hand in his. "Let us go carefully, and see. They may welcome us here. Wherever here is."

They made for the little church, standing in its shadow on the brow of the small hill. The roofs of a few houses appeared in a widening valley below them but Sunniva hung back. "Let us try the church first," she whispered. "If anyone is inside, surely they will be Christian."

Marc noted the "surely" but said nothing, remembering the pagan signals he had seen on the fens. He decided to go with her instincts and gently pushed open the heavy door.

"Who is that?" a voice called from within the square box of the church.

The lit stub of a candle was raised toward their faces and before the slender light was blown out Marc had a glimpse of a swarthy, bearded figure carrying both candle and walking staff.

"You are strangers," the voice continued.

"We are." Marc saw no point in denying it.

"We need your help, Father." Sunniva had more courage or faith than he did: she took a step forward, into the dark. Marc felt compelled to step with her, his fingers tight around the hilt of his sword.

"I see you need it." The voice had shifted to the left of Marc. "Come with me to my house: we can talk in comfort there."

The priest stalked past them both to the door, adding, "You are lucky I came to the high altar tonight for a candle. Most evenings I leave the church to God."

He opened the door on their astonished faces and left it ajar for them to stumble out after him.

The house of the priest was a simple thatched lean-to, built against the southern wall of the church. Inside, Sunniva saw a bed, a fire, a bubbling cauldron hanging over the fire and a row of tall pots standing at the end of the bed.

"I am brewing love philters," the priest said, catching her look. "Both men and women use them and sometimes they ask about my God. I teach them a prayer to say when they drink the philter: sometimes they remember. Sometimes they come to church at Christmas, or at Easter. They fetch me from the village if a cow is sick, or a sheep has trouble giving birth. They know they can trust me with their animals. But I am one of the Lord's warriors here. This is a Christian outpost, a small fortress in a sea of pagans. I built the church myself, from quarried Roman stones. I had a cross on the high altar, made of silver it was. The Lord inspired Bertolf Fen-lord to take it with him, the one and only time he came to worship here."

He smiled and relit the candle by the fire. "I need to measure out a final ingredient for my potions tonight and stir it in well, until the color of the philter changes. So I need candlelight."

"You cannot do this work by day?" Sunniva asked,

intrigued by how much the priest had told them, and how quickly.

"No, little maid. The pagans would not trust the potion if I made it under the sun."

"Are they all pagan here?" Marc asked.

"For the most part. Bertolf allows them to be so and sets no example for them."

"So you are Bertolf's enemy," Marc said.

"I prefer to say that he is no friend of mine." The priest nodded to his bed. "Sit down and let me work, then we can eat. I shall be glad of your company."

"What is your name, sir?" Sunniva asked.

"I am Father David," said the priest. "And you are Sunniva the Fair and Marc de Sens, or the gossip of the fens is wrong. Be at peace!" he added, smiling into Sunniva's startled eyes. "You are safe and welcome in my house."

They ate well that night: roast fowl and steaming wheat pancakes, washed down with mead. Father David blessed the food and he seemed very glad of someone to talk to. Sunniva guessed he was lonely and understood why he might be willing to shelter them, given her uncle's lack of support for his ministry. He was keen to draw them out and, when she told a little of her abduction and the "showing" of the dead fen-lander dressed in Norman clothes, he nodded vigorously.

"The tattooed men are Bertolf's most loyal followers: he allows them free rein in the marshes, to worship what idols they wish. Bertolf was evil to kill one of his own men in such a cause." He frowned, then brightened. "And you, my lady? Now that you are free, what is your will?"

"Mine?" Sunniva was startled by the question and

she automatically glanced at Marc. "To care for my people, I suppose."

She blushed, feeling that a feeble response, but the priest smiled.

"Well said!" He handed her another spit of roast fowl and pushed his stocky body off the bed, moaning a little and rubbing his knees. "This damp from the fen leaches into your bones. Now you must excuse me, both of you. I have an errand to run before we turn in for the night."

"For sure," Sunniva said quickly, wondering all the same.

Marc wondered, too, and he made no bones about following the priest outside. "Forgive me for asking, Father David, but where are you going?" he asked in a low voice.

"To fetch my little Christian flock, what else? You need witnesses if you are to marry." He thrust his bearded chin at the taller man. "You want to marry her, I take it?"

"Of course! But Sunniva has had many shocks of late: I need her to be sure it is what she wants."

The priest laughed, clapping him surprisingly hard on the back. "Believe me, man, it is! I have seen the way she looks at you, and t'other way about."

"But I have had no chance to ask her! What if she says no?"

"I asked her," Father David answered calmly.

"What!"

"When she held the candle for me over the last jarful of potion."

Marc recalled them standing close together, their heads bent low over the jars. He felt the breath stop in his throat. "What did she say?"

"Yes, you idiot! And that without any love philter! You two are one soul, right enough, and overripe for marriage."

He strode off into the dark, calling over his shoulder, "Finish your supper, and keep that lass of yours warm. We shall have a bonny wedding here, before the night is done!"

Marc returned to the lean-to in a happy daze to tell his spectacular wife-to-be the news it seemed she would already know.

It was the strangest wedding Sunniva had ever attended, and the most joyful.

She wore the Norman gown because she had no other, and kept her hair uncovered and unbound because Marc loved her hair. The service was conducted by the light of two slim candles, inside the tiny church.

Her wedding was witnessed by three old men, a young mother suckling a baby and a rounded, brown-robed matron who carried a small black and white dog with a cyst healing on its front leg. The young mother gave Marc one of her finger rings to be their wedding ring and, when Marc placed the narrow copper band on Sunniva's finger, the tiny church rang with applause, quickly stifled by the grinning priest.

Beside her, Marc looked as dazed as she felt, and his smile was the broadest she had ever seen. He kissed everyone, even, in a distracted moment, the little dog.

Father David hugged them at the door to the church, before opening the door and pushing them outside. "Go on to my house. It is yours tonight. Here is something for you." He thrust a parcel at Sunniva and shook his head at her thanks and protests. "It is a pleasure, my lady, and my Christian duty besides! Now go off, the pair of you, and do not concern yourselves with me!"

Marc did not need telling twice. He swept his bride high in his arms and carried her over the frosty ground to the little lean-to at the side of the church. Inside, a spark of fire still burned that flared into life as Marc added more wood.

"Happy Candelmas, my wife," he said, as he laid her onto the bed.

"Happy Candelmas, husband," Sunniva answered, twisting a lock of hair in her fingers. "Though, to be fair, I do not think it is quite time for Candelmas yet, unless I have missed or miscounted more days than I know."

"Contradicting me already?" he teased.

"Not for the world!" she exclaimed, then relaxed when she met his eyes. "Only when you wish me to," she added, slowly kicking off her shoes. "Or when you make a mistake. Or when I please."

She was a saucy little madam, sitting barefoot in the middle of the made-up bed, firelight sparkling in her hair and eyes.

"Is that the truth of it?" Marc murmured. He picked up the mystery parcel and rolled it along the bed to her, then grabbed her as she leaned forward to retrieve it. "You can always trick a woman with presents!" he chuckled, tickling her fiercely.

"Ah!" she cried, her face creasing, and he released her at once, at which she charged him with her shoulder and knocked him flat on the bed.

"And you can always fool a man!" she giggled.

Her laughter stopped as he ran his hands under

her gown, caressing her legs and feet. "That is not fair," she said.

She had an adorable pout, he thought, kissing her lips and drawing her down onto him. "Behave," he warned, sliding her off him and winding one leg around both of hers.

"Because it is our wedding night?" she breathed, placing one of his hands upon her breasts, a bold move that delighted him. "Or because you would tickle me some more?" Her blush was scorching as the fire.

He did tickle her then, just to hear her giggle again. She wriggled beneath him, not struggling too hard, stopping when he lifted her left hand and kissed her wedding ring finger. "I am so glad we are wed," he said.

"As am I. Shall we see what the priest has left us?"

"Little mercenary!" Marc yawned with relaxation and dragged the parcel close. They untied it together and lay the revealed objects between them.

"What are they?" Sunniva asked at length.

"Some kind of jewelry?" Marc hazarded. He picked up one of the many strings of threaded beechnuts. It felt light and smooth in his hand.

"For fruitfulness, perhaps?" Sunniva wondered in return. "Beechnuts to symbolize fertility? Perhaps the holy father does the same for the pagans in his flock, as another way of trying to win their trust."

"Think of it as his blessing," Marc said. He did not want her to consider the priest too much, not least because he did not want her to remember at this moment that they were in Father David's bed.

The father knows and approves, he told himself. *Does not the Bible say we should be fruitful and multiply?*

Sunniva lifted up one of the long strings, the dried beechnuts rustling softly between her fingers and drew it over Marc's head. "It looks well on you," she said, blushing all the more. "I feel like a little girl, playing at wearing jewels."

Perhaps that is the point, so that we play in our love, Marc thought, threading a string of beechnuts through Sunniva's hair. She in return "crowned" him with another thread, looping the ends around his ears. He obligingly wiggled his ears, causing her to collapse onto the bed in fits of laughter.

He wound another string around her middle, drawing the ends over her stomach.

She wrapped a thread about his forearm.

"I dare you to wrap a string somewhere else," he teased.

She smiled and moved in on him again.

Later, lying naked in a messy, easy heap together, crushed beechnuts spilling into their hair and over their bodies, Sunniva said, "I wonder if Father David knows anyone who can sell us horses?"

"I am sure he does." Marc kissed her. "I shall ask him tomorrow."

"I can sell my hair to pay for them."

Marc sat up with a jerk. "You will not! I still have some coins, and even if I did not, I would not have you cut your hair."

Sunniva wagged a finger at him. "Or else?"

He narrowed his eyes. "Stop trying to provoke me, wife."

She knelt up against his back, wrapping her arms around him. "Why should I stop, husband?" she whispered, skimming her hands across his chest and stomach, her fingers circling and spiraling, tracing each rib and muscle in turn.

His head tingled as every part of him became yet more alive and sensitive. He smelt her own body scent against his own skin and grew more aroused, reaching behind himself and mirroring her caresses with his own.

She cupped his balls, her slim, work-roughened hands driving him to the brink of explosive pleasure.

"Harder!" he panted, twisting about and winding his arms around her.

He entered her kneeling up and they writhed and moved together in the ancient mating dance of woman and man. Though he tried to hold back to prolong the exquisite moment for himself and her, her sweet, pliant body stormed his senses and he surrendered to her utterly, shouting as he came.

"That was so lovely." Sunniva snuggled against him and it was so tempting to drop down into the bed, into blissful sleep, but he knew her needs had not been completely met.

"Roll over," he whispered.

"It does not matter, Marc. I love it when you lose yourself in me. Truly, it does not—"

He stopped her protest with a long kiss and put her on her hands and knees, slipping one hand between her legs to finger her intimate place while he cupped and circled her buttocks with his other hand. In moments she was gasping afresh, lifting her bottom higher to meet his hands.

He smacked her round little rump, a few swift, light slaps that sounded very loud in the tiny hut, and she closed her eyes, lowering her head to the bed as her hands reflexively grasped the tumbled blankets. "Yes!" she hissed, "Yes, please!"

"Steady, my sweet," Marc murmured, and now he lifted her over his lap, spanking her and sliding his long fingers in and out of her, savoring how she groaned and squirmed over his knees, how she lifted her hips, offering her richly pinking bottom to his loving punishment. He watched her closely, careful to give pleasure, ready to stop and comfort if the warmth in her loins became sore, but she was meshed in the rhythm and spreading heat and happy yielding of the moment, gasping and moaning her pleasure.

As she raised her bottom ever higher he quickened the pace of his smacks and suddenly she stiffened and shuddered, a low, long cry issuing from her tautened throat. He switched at once to caressing her glowing haunches, feeling the gush of her pleasure as her sex opened and closed about his fingers. "Sweeting," he murmured.

She moaned anew and wriggled against his rising manhood. "Make love to me, Marc."

He entered her from behind, plunging into her. They came as one, calling each other's name, and swept into a richly dreaming sleep.

gloves and leg-irons right," I promise. But your
is right. We are surely mad for hunters."

Chapter Thirty-Five

Four days later, Marc and Sunniva returned to
London and a hectic, happy reunion with Alde, Judith
and Isabella in the Jew's house that Odo of Bayeux had
appropriated for himself. Marc's mother Matilde had
arrived from Brittany but Sunniva could not meet her
yet—Matilde was out in the city when they arrived,
down in the docks with Ragnar and his men, bargaining
for fish.

"We shall wait for her," Marc said, sitting with all three
of his nieces on his lap as Sunniva warmed her hands by
the fire. She smiled to see them together, relieved that
the girls were pink and thriving, sleeping and eating
well—she knew that because they had told her.

But her meeting with Matilde was not to be. Scarcely
had they settled, it seemed, than a herald from Odo
appeared at the house to summon Marc and Sunniva
to the new castle of London.

"Do not go!" Alde said, her face fierce in disapproval.

"We cannot ignore the wishes of Odo," Marc said,
as Judith and Isabella set up a chorus of "It is not fair!"
"You have just come!" "We want Sunniva to play with us!"

"And I will," Sunniva said, above the pouts and

glowers and leg-kickings. "I promise. But your uncle is right. We must go. It is good manners."

"Good sense, too, with Odo's spies everywhere," Marc muttered, as they tugged their steaming cloaks onto their weary shoulders.

Closing on the motte by boat, Sunniva acknowledged that she felt no better about the new castle of London. It dwarfed the nearby houses and was littered with Norman masons, cutting stone and wood, building walls and ramps and teetering pieces of scaffolding, sending dust and fire sparks everywhere. To comfort herself she touched her wedding ring, thinking how bright it looked on her hand.

Sitting beside her in the boat, Marc saw her looking and winked at her. "Not far now," he mouthed. Sunniva nodded, glancing at his strong, tanned hands and wishing it were night and they were alone. She loved discovering new ways of touching him, and adored his many ways of touching her. She imagined tormenting him with her mouth, kissing and licking him all over . . .

A shout from the riverbank interrupted her daydream and she realized that Odo of Bayeux had come to the jetty to meet them.

"Well met, de Sens!" he roared across the water, "I knew you would get her back for us!"

He added more in French that Sunniva did not understand, the ends of his long cloak trailing in the frosted mud as he whirled his arms. Sensing Marc as stiff as a blade beside her, she was not surprised when he slowly stood up in the boat, putting himself between her and the burly warrior-bishop.

"My wife and I are glad to see you again, my lord,"

he said, his deep voice carrying above the constant din of the masons' hammers.

Odo's broad smile splintered like ice on a winter pail. "Married, de Sens? Already?"

"And binding, my lord."

"I do not recall that being part of our agreement."

"The king did not forbid it. He approved the match."

"You wanted to be sure of her, did you?" Odo asked sarcastically.

"I acted as I saw fit."

Their rowing boat now bumped against the jetty but Marc made no move to leave it. He was scanning the men behind Odo—looking for archers, Sunniva realized, a hot flood of terror drenching her body. She forced herself to keep her composure: to panic would do no good.

But what exactly had Marc agreed with Odo and William? Why was Odo scowling, pulling at his fleshy lips with thumb and forefinger as if he would tear them off? "My brother the king will not like this, de Sens."

"The king knows I am his loyal and faithful man," Marc answered, in a cool, clipped manner. "This way I go to my lands with the daughter of the old lord as my wife; her people will accept me more quickly because of our marriage."

Was that why Marc had married her? The better to secure her lands?

Sunniva kept her head up but inside she felt to be burning with shame and confusion. She glowered at Marc but he would not look at her: he was intent upon Odo.

"You saw Bertolf the renegade?"

Sunniva stifled a gasp at Odo's harsh description of her uncle.

"No, my lord."

"He will be dealt with in time." Odo looked at her, his square features livid with poorly controlled anger. It was as if their previous, pleasant dealings had never happened. "No matter, you may go. Get to your lands, make yourself useful there."

Odo turned his back on both of them, stamping back to the rising castle without even a farewell.

Marc was silent on the boat-journey back to their lodgings and Sunniva was not sure what to say to him. As they disembarked, he lifted her straight into his arms, without giving her time to move herself.

"I can walk," she protested, but he took no notice, lurching from the boat and striding away from the river as if the fiends of hell were at his heels. "I know these Normans," he said once, through clenched teeth. "They promise, then withdraw. They make a pact, then change the terms. William is as bad as the rest of them."

He did not speak again, although Sunniva asked several times what he meant. When they reached the Jew's former house and Marc began bellowing orders to Ragnar and his men to pack, Sunniva said nothing. She now had another ordeal to face—that of meeting Marc's mother.

Again that meeting was not to be. Matilde, Sunniva learned, had arranged for herself and her granddaughters to stay for a month at the house of the widow of a Breton goldsmith living in the city. Matilde had returned from buying fish and immediately set out again. She and the girls were already gone.

When a red-faced Ragnar relayed this news in the stable-yard of the Jew's house, Marc's comment was sour: "Ever my mother gives trust with one hand and withdraws it with the other. She has been this way ever since the fire."

"Perhaps your mother feels she has acted prudently, to keep your youngsters in comfort and relative safety while all is so uncertain," Sunniva began, but Marc whipped around to face her.

"Not to my mind," he said, and stalked off to harangue an unlucky stable-lad who had just dropped a parcel of bedding into the dirt.

Chapter Thirty-Six

So Sunniva returned to the place where she was born, traveling almost the full length of Ermine Street from London to a small village called Hanstone. She did not know where she rode, never having been so far away from her home in her life before, but Marc had hired guides, and she trusted him.

He had also hired Ragnar Fire-Breeches and his men to ride with them, something Sunniva decided she must discuss with Marc. Her people might not view the sudden appearance of a Breton overlord and a gang of ex-Vikings with any great ease or pleasure: it would be well that Marc and Ragnar understood this, before they reached the borders of her land.

Or was it her land? Odo of Bayeux had acted as if she had no rights in the matter at all, as if the king had gifted the land directly to Marc.

If he wanted my land, Sunniva thought as she rode, *Marc need not have married me to get it*. Brought up with the concepts of responsibility, of having a duty of care for others, particularly those less fortunate than herself, this idea did not comfort her. Instead she felt superfluous, no more than a pretty piece of baggage.

And there was always the nagging question of whether or not she was Cena's kin. If not, she really was perhaps no more than baggage.

"You are my wife," Marc said, when she raised the matter with him, as if that should be enough, and he silenced her fears with kisses. But in the morning, riding again, Sunniva brooded. At one point Ragnar remarked in that clipped way of his that she lacked color and for the rest of that day she forced herself to chatter about London and the girls—although even that subject was difficult, with Marc muttering darkly about his mother's lack of trust.

That night she dreamed of her own mother. Ethelinda, more confident and glowing than she had ever been when alive, came out of Hanstone church on the arm of Father Martin the priest and with a crowd of villagers following on.

"Who are you?" she asked. She was young in the dream, as young as Sunniva, and as beautiful as Sunniva had known her.

"Mother, it has been so long," she answered, longing to embrace her, marveling to see Ethelinda smiling when she could not remember seeing her mother smile in life. "It is so good to see you here."

She took a step forward, but Ethelinda's flawless face clouded.

"I know you not," she said. "You are a stranger. You do not belong with us."

And her mother drew back into the church, leaving Sunniva facing the mob. The villagers closed quickly about her, drawing their knives . . .

Sunniva came awake suddenly and dared not sleep for the rest of the night.

Still she and Marc moved north. On their third day of traveling the countryside about them changed from being flat, with stretches of dense woodland and marshy heathland, to a more rugged aspect. The ground itself began to rise, emerging from the featureless plain in a great curved outcrop, so that the whole looked like a huge half-buried worm. A few spindly rowan trees clung to those few places where the cliffs were almost sheer; in other spots where the land rose less steeply there were patches of woodland and fields of grazing sheep.

Sunniva felt her pulse quicken at the sight, and even more at the smell—the loamy scent of the land itself, as familiar to her as her own scent. Sensing her excitement, Marc smiled at her and she took his hand as they rode side by side along the road.

"We are getting close," she said.

"I know it," he answered. "From you."

She thought of her dream again and suddenly wished their journey was a thousand miles longer. How would the people view her? Would they accept her? What would they think of Marc? He was their lord now, but would they truly accept him? She knew he would be just, but what if they rebelled because he was not English? Would he be patient with them? Would they ride into Hanstone now and be met with flowers or with stones?

"Do the folk here know that we are coming?" she asked. "Have you sent word?"

"No to that, but they will know all the same, soon enough," Marc replied, riding in that loose-limbed style he had, and turned his head this way and that, watching out for trouble.

He released her hand with a tiny pat and touched his sword. Then he pressed the blue tattoo on his arm—for luck, Sunniva assumed and a nervous gesture she had not seen from him before. Tense herself, the blood singing in her ears, the sound of her breath seemed very loud in the silence. She prayed to all the saints she could remember, begging for their peace and mercy.

Around her Ragnar's men were also muttering, some fingering charms and rune sticks. Everyone looked strained. When a bird broke cover and fluttered skywards in a blaze of wings, the entire company flinched and then laughed.

"It will be old men and lads, remember, so go easy on them," Marc said gruffly. "Keep in mind, too, that some may not know that they have lost Cena as lord."

"Or their own lords," Sunniva put in, thinking of those women whose men must have perished with Cena at the Bridge of Stamford. Feeling ashamed of her new married status, she did not meet Marc's glance but stared straight ahead, which was how she spotted a bobbing movement at the roadside and saw a small, freckled face peeping out from the ditch.

"That is Arni No-Hair!" she breathed, recognizing the shepherd boy from his domed, bald pate—he had lost his hair two winters back when she had helped his mother nurse him through a fever. He had lived, but his fine blond hair had never grown back. In a burst of fevered anticipation, delighted that here was someone she knew well, Sunniva rose up from her saddle.

"Arni, it is me! Sunniva! Arni!"

Her cries went unheeded. As fast as a stooping bird of prey, the boy dropped back into the ditch and vanished.

"Let him go," said Marc, as much to her as to his men. "I understand the nickname now: when you first mentioned him it made no sense, but now I see that the lad is as bald as an egg."

"But he knows me," Sunniva protested, her mind flayed with the injustice of Arni's lack of trust in her. "I gave him ale when he was sick, and mopped him down. Last winter I gave his mother one of my gowns and an iron cooking pot." Her brother Edgar had beaten her when he saw Arni's mother wearing the gown. "By St. Freya, he knows me! Why should Arni No-Hair think I would do him harm?"

"'Tis not you he dislikes, but us," Marc answered. "And he shall tell the others that you have returned." He motioned over her head to Ragnar. "Let us pick up the pace and, mark this well, I want no corpses at this homecoming. I am their lord now and would not start my rule with a massacre."

He spurred his horse on to lead the way, calling to Sunniva. Too anxious to be exasperated at his high-handedness, Sunniva obeyed.

They rode up the broad escarpment, through woodland and over fields, galloping for the hilltop. Now Sunniva could see the thatch of house-roofs and twists of smoke and suddenly, ahead of her, standing apart from the village and its church, there was her old home.

How mean it seems, she thought, struck by the sagging roof, the lack of windows, the broken storage barrels in front of the single door. The stables were silent and the dairy was empty. Strangely homesick all over again, realizing she had imagined a home that had never really existed, she felt ashamed of bringing Marc to such a low, neglected place.

I left it in better order than this! Where are the dogs and cats and cattle? Where is the hog? Where are the servants? Where is anyone?

"When the lady of the house is absent, chaos is king," Marc remarked, correctly interpreting her distress. "But we shall soon make this right."

Heartened by the "we" Sunniva looked about more closely, her spirits rising further as she realized the village and its lands were unscathed. In the south, King William and his men may have ransacked and burned but her in the heartland of her home, the place she knew best, all seemed unchanged.

Except for one thing. "Where are people hiding?" she asked.

"Let us attend to your hall first, my lady," Marc answered, leaping down from his horse to inspect one of the broken barrels. "They will come to us in time."

He winked at her. When she continued to frown, he stepped back and wound an arm around her middle, half-dragging her from her palfrey to give her a smacking kiss.

"Come, Sun-light, all will be very well," he murmured, waving off the inevitable ribald comments from his men. "These are your own folk and you are their lady. This is the first of your lands and we shall visit all of them in time."

When I discover where these other lands are, Sunniva thought, wishing that she felt as confident as Marc was now. His earlier nerves seemed to have deserted him, whereas she was more on edge than ever. All her previous fears had returned, with heart-stopping intensity and arrow-sharp speed.

What if the folk here did not take to Marc? What if they turned away from him, blamed her for marrying a foreigner? What if they turned away from her, for being the bastard daughter of an unfaithful slave-wife? What if Marc grew tired of her, as Cena had of her mother?

"Marc, what agreement did you make with King William?" she whispered urgently, thoroughly disconcerted when Marc whispered back, "Only that you are the prettiest wench in England."

Giving her no chance to answer, he turned his head to the black-toothed, swarthy Fire-Breeches. "English, remember, Ragnar," he called out, a reminder that they should use the native tongue. He stroked Sunniva's face, tracing her covered hairline, then he stalked off in that clashing walk of his, going straight to the door and pushing through it.

Sunniva's breath hissed in her throat as Marc disappeared into the house. In another instant she was off her horse, avoiding a startled Ragnar and sprinting for the darkened entrance.

"Do not hurt them!" she cried, desperate that Marc should make a good impression, that above all he should not be attacked, lest he strike back. "They will be nervous of strangers. Let me explain our presence."

She was pleading to Marc's broad back, but to no one else. Feeling foolish, she stopped short inside the hall, wondering again where everyone had gone. Where every *thing* had gone.

"What has happened here?" she stammered, raising her arms to the empty walls and roof beams.

"Where are the curing meats, the hangings, the tables, do you mean?" Marc countered, twisting round to her as he stood by the dead fire space, hands on hips and fingers tapping the hilt of his sword. "I think your people have decided that their lord has gone and have helped themselves to his goods."

He grinned, shedding ten years in a moment. "No more than I would have done, if I were them."

Sunniva almost sagged like the roof, such was her relief. "You are not angry?"

"What use would that be? Now, tell us what to do, my lady."

"You? You and your men?" Part of her was amazed: warriors doing housework?

"To be sure," Marc replied, and he took her hands in his. "Now I am home, I wish to spend tonight in my own bed, and in comfort."

A few moments later, black-browed Ragnar looked nonplussed at the idea of wielding a broom, but a glower from Marc had him sweeping out the floor rushes with a will. Sunniva left Marc and his men to that while she sought out cooking pots and spits. Finding only a single spit, buried under ash in the fireplace, she turned to Marc who had just come in from the stable.

"What food have we brought with us?" she asked in a low voice.

"Salted meat and fish, some wheat seed, some oats. A jar of honey. A barrel of mead." He grimaced, folding his arms across his chest. "The horses must make do with the grass. There is no hay in the stable."

"We shall do better tomorrow," Sunniva vowed, pretending a confidence she did not quite feel.

"We shall hunt tomorrow," Marc answered. "Fresh game will draw these folk out, for I intend to share it with them."

He was being cheerful, too, and she smiled at him, wondering what he really thought.

Where were her people, though?

"Perhaps I should go to Arni's house," she said to Marc later, shaking musty bedding with him out of doors while Ragnar and a guard picked their way in the twilight to fetch more water from the well, using one of their own horse pails.

Marc shook his head. "The door to the hall is open, the fire is lit, we have mead and oatcakes and honey to share," he said. "Let the villagers come to us."

But will they? Sunniva thought. *And is it Marc, the foreign lord they are rejecting, or me, their English cuckoo child?*

Evening drew on and she piled furs about the fire for them to sit in comfort while they ate. Marc took some oatcakes and left them on top of the broken barrel in front of the doorway. When a shadow later sped toward the barrel, he motioned to Sunniva to keep singing the song she had started and to his men to keep still. The oatcakes on the barrel vanished and Marc whistled in time to her song, encouraging his men to join the chorus.

"It is the same with horses," he murmured to Sunniva, as Ragnar bellowed out a tuneless version, "If you are calm and patient, they will become curious and be drawn to you. We are doing good work here, tonight."

"What if the villagers come to steal more things tonight?" Sunniva murmured, ashamed to be asking the question.

Marc smiled. "We shall keep watch all night," he replied. "But I think they will surprise you."

At daybreak the following day, Sunniva stepped out into the stockade and rubbed her eyes. She could scarcely believe what she was seeing.

"Go on," said Marc behind her, pressing his hand lightly against her back. "They are real. Touch them." He leaned down and kissed the back of her neck, making her whole body down to her toes tingle with pleasure. "Do you recognize them?"

Out in the yard, amidst a speckling of fresh snow, were two tables laden with wall hangings and cauldrons and crocks and spoons and knives and wooden cups. Feeling as if she were in a dream, Sunniva kicked her way through the snow and dirt to the nearest table and picked up a wooden goblet. It was painted around its middle in blue and gold.

"Cena drank from this on feast days," she said. Did that mean the villagers, the people, accepted her as his daughter?

Dazed, still scarcely daring to believe it was all real, she raised her head. Beyond the rough ditch and wooden hurdles enclosing the homestead she could see figures gathered on the road outside.

"They came in the middle of the night, while you were sleeping," Marc said, holding out his hand. "May I see it? 'Tis a handsome thing."

Slowly, she stretched out her arm and when he took the cup from her goblet, a ragged cheer issued from the watchers.

"I believe that counts as a Welcome Home, my heart." Speaking, Marc caught her and the goblet into his arms, lifting her high.

"See your lady returned!" he shouted in English. "Come now and give her greeting!"

Through a haze of tears, Sunniva spotted the shiny bald head of Arni No-Hair lunging toward her like a battering ram, heard the lad's pounding feet, ahead of all the other villagers, as he rushed into the yard, yelling, "Sunniva's back! She's back! I told you she would come back!"

Chapter Thirty-Seven

There were many greetings then, and reunions, some very sad as wives learned the terrible news of the battles of the Bridge of Stamford and guessed that they had probably become widows.

The simpleminded daughter of the farrier came and laid her pox-marked face against Sunniva's shoulder, then insinuated her sticky fingers into Marc's large hand. Marc kissed her palm, which sent the woman into giggles of delight. Marc was almost bowled over by the strapping figure of the farrier's daughter as she catapulted herself into his arms.

"You have made a friend for life there," Sunniva remarked.

"The best kind of friend, then," said Marc, hugging the woman and whirling her right off her feet, spinning her about as he would spin Alde or Judith or Isabella.

"More!" the woman crowed, but then Marc and Sunniva were mobbed by more villagers: old men returning a pot to Sunniva and extending a hand to Marc; children shuffling forward out of the mass from behind their mothers to stare up at Marc's height;

girls secretly comparing their loose, baggy robes to Sunniva's French gown.

It was only much later, when the villagers had helped Marc and his men drink all the mead and Marc asked for lads to help him in the hunt, that Sunniva realized she had missed one very important person.

Thoughtfully she set about her work for the day, replacing wall hangings and dragging the tables back into the hall. For the moment she avoided the tiny bedchamber at the back of the hall, with its bitter, personal memories for her of Cena and her cowering mother, and concentrated on making the communal area clean and habitable again. She labored steadily, answering Arni No-Hair's excited questions about London and the new king, promising old mother Friga that she would walk down later to Friga's hut with some venison stew. She remained very aware of busy, wiry Ragnar sharpening daggers and swords in the yard and very conscious of missing Marc, even as she reproached herself for being foolish—without Marc going hunting, there would be no fresh meat for tonight.

And still the one very important person had not been near.

She did not speak to Marc about it when he returned to the homestead in triumph, the villagers and his men proudly carrying the freshly killed deer between them. Instead she instructed the village women to help her with preparing the meat, a role familiar to her since childhood. To her relief, the women took her directions without question: surely that showed she was accepted back as one of them?

Partway through skinning the beast, she was reminded of her missing knives and wondered briefly what had happened to them.

She wondered, too, what had happened to her mourning for Cena and his sons. Now she was at home again she had expected to miss them, if only a little, but their absence remained nothing but a relief. Even the villagers did not seem to notice they were gone. Not one of them told Sunniva that they were sorry for her loss.

Is it because they truly do not care or because they know something? Sunniva fretted as she jointed the deer. *Do my people know that I am not Cena's daughter? That my mother really was unfaithful? Is that why the priest has not visited to bless this house?*

The next day, as Marc groomed the horses and explained to a gang of assorted boys that it was not a good idea to creep under the hooves of a war horse, he spoke to Ragnar.

"Send men down to London with a message and money to my mother. All is secure here, so 'tis time she and my girls came north, before the spring thaws turn the roads to mud."

"As you wish." Ragnar gave him a curt nod. Then, smoothing his long moustache with his fingers, asked, "What ails your wife? Is she in pup?"

Marc kneaded one of his charger's fetlocks, glad that Ragnar could not see his scarlet face or hear his racing heart. If Sunniva were with child that would be a gift better than all the gold and incense of Constantinople. Their child: a youngster with Sunniva's spectacular hair and his skill with horses and her skill with knives.

I must give Sunniva back her knives. I have them in my pack and she must be missing them. Tomorrow, after our visit, I shall return them to her.

"Pray King Christ she is," he grunted. "And hope that is all it is."

Greasing a saddle, Ragnar leaned over the hurdle that Marc had placed in front of the stable door to stop his horse from trampling the milling boys and answered softly in French, "Perhaps she misses your nieces."

"That too," Marc said, "Which is why I want them sent for."

Abruptly he began lifting Theo's hooves, to check his shoes. "Have you seen the priest of these parts?"

"No, but then I have not been looking closely." Ragnar cracked his knuckles together. "Do you remember that priest in the great church in Constantinople, who caught us carving our names in the marble pillars?"

Ragnar went off into happy reminiscence, sailing the seas of memory, raising his voice slightly to draw in his admiring audience of English lads. Marc grunted and nodded and left him to it: he was considering the absent village priest.

That night, snuggled against Sunniva as they bedded down with Ragnar's men in the great hall of the homestead, Marc had still not forgotten the priest but now he dreamed of his mother. In the dream, Matilde walked through the door of the house and up to his head, standing beside his long body, tapping a foot. In life she was svelte and light-boned, with curling dark brown hair that was gray at its ends and a handsome, hook-nosed face and deep brown eyes that her granddaughter Alde had inherited. In the dream she seemed as tall as Marc himself.

"It is time, my son," she said. "I would see my daughter-in-law."

"I know, Mother," Marc replied, feeling in the dream both irritated and yet happy—the way he often felt, dealing with Matilde. "I sense the moment, too, which is why I have sent for you and my brother's girls. But you will not order Sunniva."

"As I do you, sometimes? But how you would miss my advice and resent it, if I did not! Still I would not dream of it, my son. She is a woman. She has sense. This is *her* land, not mine."

She smiled at him, a less generous smile than Sunniva's but still a smile, and then she vanished.

Good-bye, Mother, Marc thought, rolling over, back into deeper sleep.

"But where are we going?" Sunniva asked, in the afternoon of the following day, feeling like Alde or Judith as she did so. She knew that Marc's mother and nieces were coming north to join them but she and Marc were not on Ermine Street, looking out for their party. On a bright, blue-skied, snow-clad day, Marc had walked with her through the village and out again. Already they had crossed two fields and passed by a small wood and her shoes were damp with soft snow.

"Just a stretch farther," Marc replied. "I was given precise directions."

To where? Sunniva wondered, as the muscles of her legs began to burn after kicking her way through drifts of snow. She knew of no dwellings here, on the downward slope of the great ridge.

"I must have missed the main path, but I was told she moved to this place in the summer, while you were away on pilgrimage," Marc said, his breath hanging in the still, cold air. "The mother of Arni No-Hair said everyone in the village helped to build it."

"She talked to you?" Sunniva felt obscurely

aggrieved: the mother of Arni No-Hair was very shy and hardly spoke to anyone.

"Aedilberg talked to me and laughed, especially after I gave her the deer offal."

They do accept him, Sunniva realized, in wonder. And part of her was glad, but a tiny, mean side of her mind whispered that it meant he did not need her at all.

"Why did you marry me in such haste?" she asked, stopping in the snow to stare into his face.

"What is this?" he huffed, smiling down at her in a tender way that made her want to burst out caroling again. "Do you regret our wedding already?"

"Never! But why did you not want to wait until we returned to London? You could have had your family about you," she added, very cunning.

He shrugged. "I took the moment King Christ offered us." He clasped her shoulder. "Come, sweetheart, your nose is turning red with cold."

Sunniva held her ground. "Marc—"

He took her hand and squeezed it. "In strict truth, sweeting, I thought it best that we were married before we saw William or his brother. To them you are a valuable property, an heiress. They would say that they gave me leave to search for you after you were kidnapped because you are an heiress. And if you had been still unwed on your return to the palace of Westminster, you would have been someone to dangle before lords as a prize."

"As Cena used to do," Sunniva murmured, feeling scarcely comforted.

"Look." Marc interrupted her by drawing back the snow-covered bough of a pine tree and pointing.

Sunniva felt her jaw sag with astonishment. The turf-roofed hut was perched on the side of the hill, low and partly dug into the hill so that it seemed part of the landscape. Only the smoke issuing from the smoke hole revealed a dwelling—and the pattern of footsteps running to and fro through the pine trees to the house.

"Who lives here?" she whispered.

Marc smiled. "Come and see. We are expected." He swept his long green cloak back from his arms, revealing the pannier of gifts he had brought with them.

A few more wading steps through powdery snow brought them to the well-trodden path, then a door, sunken it seemed into the hill. Marc tapped at the door while Sunniva shook the snow from her gown and cloak.

"Welcome! Good wassail!" called a voice within, and Marc crouched and entered, holding the door for Sunniva. She too ducked beneath the low wooden lintel, carved with many runes and crosses, and felt her face glow with heat from a great, glowing fire pit, set close to the threshold.

"Welcome, Sunniva!" said the voice. "We have much to speak of. Light the candles, will you, Marc?"

Sunniva glanced at her new husband. "You know this person?" she mouthed, embarrassed when he blew her a kiss and swung past her to light rank after rank of fine wax candles—there was so many that Sunniva felt for an instant that she was in a cathedral, bathed in light.

The light flared and grew, illuminating the seated figure at the far side of the fire pit, and a great loom, and pieces of embroidery—dozens of them, completely filling the hut. Surprised, Sunniva instinctively stepped forward to study the work, teetering for an instant at the edge of the fire pit before Marc, with a curse, caught her back.

"She was ever thus," chuckled the figure. "Eager

and quick. Her mother and all the folk hereabouts found her a delight. Only her wretched father and my miserable son thought otherwise."

Sunniva looked more closely at the figure. "I know you," she began, and then memory and recognition dawned. "Mistress Cynwise!"

"Did you think me dead?" The woman lifted a candle balanced on one of the horizontal bars of the loom and brought it close to her face.

"Of course not." Smiling at the small, plump figure opposite, Sunniva hoped that the old woman would not guess that she had not thought of her at all—not for many, many years. She felt ashamed, because an age ago, another distant time, this brown-gowned, fur-draped woman had been her mother's friend. Her thoughts flew to a scene fixed in her memory when she was quite a little child: Ethelinda and Cynwise sewing together in a small room, by daylight, while she had played with a small, rough-coated dog. She remembered her mother laughing, kissing Cynwise's round, sallow face, and wondered, with another stab of guilt, how she had ever forgotten.

"How are you?" she asked.

"Older," came back the blunt answer. "But people take care of me. Not my son, with his mind on God and higher matters, but the village folk see me right." She nodded to a bubbling pot of stew. "Serve me and your man and get some for yourself. You will be staying the night."

Sunniva glanced anxiously at Marc but that arrangement was accepted, it seemed; he had already put down his pannier of gifts and sprawled on his elbow by the fire pit, his back set against the fur-lined outer door.

"Good!" said Cynwise, stabbing her staff on the

beaten earth floor in emphasis, "I like a man who can take his ease. Unlike my boy . . . Have you met him yet, my son the priest?"

Sunniva was so astonished she almost dropped the stew bowl she was handing to Marc. "Your son? Father Martin is your son?" she stammered. "I never knew that!"

"Few did, only the old ones of the village. Your mother knew, of course, but she never spoke of it. The villagers were guided by her."

Marc spoke from behind his steaming bowl of stew. "Why was this kept secret, mistress?"

"Why do you think?" Cynwise blew on her bowlful of stew. "My son does not want it widely known! And you need not pity me, either," she added, pointing her spoon like a dagger at Sunniva. "We never got on. He was always a jealous, envious little beast." She shifted in her seat, scratching her shoulder against the loom. "He is supposed to be ill now. He will not leave his church, the misery!"

"But you do not believe it," Marc said, swatting a fire spark off the pannier.

"Not a bit . . . Any cheese in there, Marc de Sens? Yes, young lady, I know your lord's name! He visited this morning, as a lord should. Cut me logs, he did, and very neatly, too."

"Here, mistress." Marc rummaged in the pannier, rose and stretched across the fire, dropping a small linen bundle into the old woman's lap. "Why do you think your son is pretending to be ill?"

"Because the smug, self-serving fool does not want to see her, of course." She nodded to Sunniva, her wrinkled brown eyes very sharp. "He does not want to be questioned. Somewhere in that shriveled soul of his he is ashamed."

Abruptly, she twisted round on her seat to look Sunniva straight in the eyes. "You do look like your mother. I loved her so much."

"So did I," said Sunniva, too overcome for the moment to do more than whisper. Marc gently stroked her arm but Cynwise did not hear Sunniva's response; she was still speaking.

"My son made me give your mother up, give up our friendship while you were still a child. He said it was unseemly for the lady of the lord, and the daughter of the lord, to visit my house. Unseemly!" she snorted. "He was ever ashamed of me."

No, he was jealous, Sunniva thought.

"He envied your friendship," Marc remarked. "Did he have few friends himself?"

"None."

She spoke with relish, Sunniva thought, and her disquiet deepened.

"Did Cena give him small respect?" Marc persisted.

"Cena? Cena thought him a useless mouth to feed. Which he is! When old mother Friga's cat died last month, he would not give the creature a blessing! He told her it was not Christian. As if he would know!"

Sunniva glanced at Marc. The woman's bitterness filled the hut and she wondered why. A suspicion hovered in her mind but she hesitated to ask, in case she caused more pain.

"You hate your son," said Marc in his deep, calm voice. "I think at times all mothers do."

"No son can be as bad as mine," Cynwise rapped back, fast as the shuttle in her loom. "You think I cast him off? He rejected me! And after he had taken my promise. Even that was not enough for him!"

When my mother was ill, all that long winter and spring, this woman never visited, Sunniva remembered. *My memories of her are all when my mother was young and I was a child.* "I have not seen you to speak to for years," she said aloud. "Why is that?"

"My son's doing! He told me Cena did not want me to be friendly to Ethelinda, that I was coming between Ethelinda and Cena! I asked Ethelinda and she admitted that Cena was berating her after each time we were together. I asked my son to speak as priest to Cena, to ask for charity and allow two women to be friends. Do you know what my son did? He went to Ethelinda and told her she must respect her husband's wishes and obey him! Ethelinda felt she had no choice but to break with me. Then my son made me promise that I would not approach Ethelinda first. I thought that would satisfy him and Cena, but weeks turned into months and Ethelinda never came near. My son never came near me, either. It was years later before he admitted that he had told Ethelinda that I no longer wanted to see her."

The old woman's lip curled. "He waited until she was dead before he told me. Then, when it was too late, he claimed he told that lie for a higher good. Those were his words, 'higher good.' He was a meddler! He did it because he could not bear to see me happy! I moved out of the village after that. I could not bear to see his smug face."

Listening, Sunniva could only be sorry—even for Father Martin. If mother and son truly endured the relationship Cynwise had described, then no one in this sad triangle was the winner. As a son, it must be hard for Father Martin to know that his own mother despised him.

"I wanted to be your nurse, but my son stopped that," Cynwise went on. "He knew I loved you more than I loved him."

Sunniva sighed, pitying the poor priest even more.

"He is not your friend," Marc breathed warningly in her ear. "And now I hear more of Mistress Cynwise, I am not sure she is, either."

"So why are we here?" Sunniva whispered.

"To learn of your parents, I hope. Someone must know the story. I thought it might be this woman."

"Finished talking between yourselves, have you?" Mistress Cynwise asked, with a scowl.

Marc answered something that Sunniva missed; she was thinking of her mother. "Did my mother have a paramour?" she almost asked, but stopped herself in time—how would she know if the answer was true?

Poor Marc—he brought me here to try to help me and yet it seems we are on a wasted journey. Cynwise is too old, and too bitter.

She put down her stew bowl and looked about the hut, idly allowing her eyes to rest here and there. She did not know what she was seeking; inspiration of a sort, some sign.

And then she saw them. Between the newer, simpler samples of embroidery were older pieces, stretched on frames to best show off the skillful work. Sunniva rose and weaved a careful path through the frames, intent on two pieces in particular.

She picked up the nearest candle and looked closely at the pair.

"This is my mother's work," she breathed. "I remember her making this embroidery when I was younger than Isabella, although I have not seen it since."

She turned back to a startled Marc and a blushing Cynwise. "Why do you have my mother's embroidery?"

Cynwise thrust out her dimpled chin. "Do you think it would have lasted at Cena's? That man could not care for a cow, much less needlework!"

"Even so, mistress, when all is said and done they are Sunniva's," Marc remarked, stepping close himself. "Look, there you are, sweeting."

Sunniva followed his pointing finger. On the larger of the two embroideries were two figures, running into each other's arms. One was unmistakably Cena as a younger man, tall, fair-haired, with a long moustache and red leggings. The small figure was of a girl with raised arms and flying yellow hair. From the small, intricate stitches, both appeared to be smiling.

Sunniva touched the figure of Cena, running her fingers over the wool, recognizing each stitch. As she did so, memories rose from the bottom of her mind, like sweet water drawn from a deep well. Cena, teaching her to ride on her first sturdy pony. Cena ruffling her hair and embracing Ethelinda, lifting them both in his arms. Cena bringing his wife a necklace of daisies and herself a daisy bracelet.

Cena is my father, she thought. *I know it now for certain.*

"He loved you both then," Marc said, stroking Sunniva's cheek in the same way that she now remembered Cena caressing her mother's.

"Yes, he did." Sunniva felt tears running down her face but inside she felt at peace, the strain of months washed away. The foul insinuations of her dead, rapidly fading half brothers and of the priest, of Cynwise's bitter son, no longer mattered. With this love, revealed in this work, Sunniva knew that her mother would never have been unfaithful, however sad and difficult the end of her marriage had been. Here was the proof.

Blinking away more tears, she noticed that the smaller embroidery was unfinished. It showed the Virgin Mary, in her dark blue robe, with a bright gold nimbus around her head. The face was stretched in outline and one eye had been completed.

Behind her, Marc inhaled sharply. "She has your eyes."

"It was for the church." Cynwise's harsh, dry tones cut across them, reminding both of where they were.

Sunniva gave a slow, sad smile. "Then I shall finish it," she said.

Chapter Thirty-Eight

The rest of the evening was quiet. Cynwise did not talk much, except to ask for more cheese out of the pannier and to tell Sunniva to make up their beds by the fire pit. She seemed disappointed that Sunniva was not going to confront her son on the morrow, but brightened when Marc promised to stop by her hut every week, and when he offered to make her a good luck charm out of horsehair.

"That was a kind thing you did," Sunniva said to him later, when they were in bed and Mistress Cynwise was snoring at the other side of the fire pit. "The charm, I mean."

"It was little enough. I can show you how to make one, if you wish." Marc hugged her to him. "Lovely," he whispered.

"Did you marry me for my land?"

Sunniva clapped a hand to her mouth the instant she spoke, horrified by her own directness. "I mean—"

"I really should groom you sometime, like a little golden mare," Marc murmured, sweeping a hand over her stomach. "Brush you down and smooth you over, polish your nails and braid your mane."

"Marc!" The candles had been dowsed for the night but even so Sunniva was sure Marc could see her blush; his eyes had a very bright look.

"Did you?" she persisted.

"Marry you for land? Of course! And for love and companionship and pleasure and play-fights and children. And in a day or so my nieces and mother will join us, and we shall be a family at peace, in a land where together we shall build peace. I shall start tomorrow, when I visit the priest, and then we shall both go out, visit all your lands in time."

"Our lands," Sunniva reminded him.

"Yours, for you are ever my lady," Marc responded firmly. He kissed her, then, a lingering, sweet kiss that made her dizzy. "You were once my captive, Sunniva, and now I am wholly yours. Rule me and your lands as you wish, exactly as you wish."

His fingers were ruling her at the moment, making her forget everything. "I love you, Lady Sun-Light," he said. "So very much."

Sunniva trembled at the ardor in his face and voice.

"Let go," Marc whispered in her ear. "Let me love you as you deserve to be loved. Let us make a child together, sweetheart."

He swung her beneath him then, kissing and caressing, enfolding and entering, his lord to her lady, while snow fell softly outside and the world was made new with the new year and new life.